Soorun Beeraje was born in Mauritius. He is a retired University Lecturer. Initially, he trained as a nurse in the UK, then became a lecturer and went on to hold senior academic posts in health studies for 32 years. He likes sports, reading, writing, walking and travelling.

I dedicate this book to my beloved family for their continued support and encouragement.

Soorun Beeraje

The Fatal Tuesday

To Jane & George

With Warmest Wishes

Soorun Beeraje

25th December, 2016

AUSTIN MACAULEY
PUBLISHERS LTD.

Copyright © Soorun Beeraje (2016)

The right of Soorun Beeraje to be identified as author of this work has been asserted by him in accordance with section 77 and 78 of the Copyright, Designs and Patents Act 1988.

All rights reserved. No part of this publication may be reproduced, stored in a retrieval system, or transmitted in any form or by any means, electronic, mechanical, photocopying, recording, or otherwise, without the prior permission of the publishers.

Any person who commits any unauthorized act in relation to this publication may be liable to criminal prosecution and civil claims for damages.

A CIP catalogue record for this title is available from the British Library.

ISBN 9781786125750 (Paperback)
ISBN 9781786125767 (Hardback)
ISBN 9781786125774 (eBook)
www.austinmacauley.com

First Published (2016)
Austin Macauley Publishers Ltd.
25 Canada Square
Canary Wharf
London
E14 5LQ

Acknowledgments

I would like to express my gratitude to the publishers for enabling me to publish this book.

Chapter 1

An anonymous letter, received by the Vice Chancellor of Westworth University in London, threatened the reputation of the institution and could possibly have had serious consequences on its survival. The letter alleged that a senior academic was illegally charging foreign students to secure a place on the University's nursing course, and if this practice did not stop, a copy of the letter would be sent to the press.

The relatively new Vice Chancellor was shocked and horrified at the thought that a scam could possibly be in operation at the University. His immediate reaction was to treat the allegation very seriously, and that appropriate steps should be taken to get to the bottom of this.

To avoid a scandal developing, the Vice Chancellor decided to deal with this matter urgently and confidentially. He set out to take the following actions immediately; no one in the University should be aware of the threat, and he would ask Alexander DuPont known as Alex, a Private Investigator, to establish the truth and find the perpetrator.

As it happened, Alex had already arranged to meet with the Vice Chancellor to discuss the possibility of looking into another case. An unusual incident had taken place at the University where two computers (laptops) were stolen amidst the strictest of security. Following a Police investigation, the laptops were never found. Not satisfied with that outcome, the Vice Chancellor was determined to get the case resolved. On the recommendation of a friend, he had approached Alex to investigate the computer thefts.

Alex, a recently qualified lawyer turned Private Investigator with no previous experience in investigating criminal cases, agreed to consider the offer. He was in for a big surprise, as little did he know, that a more complex situation awaited him. The meeting between him and the Vice Chancellor would be held on Monday 6 June at 8.30 am.

He needed a helping hand to get up early on that Monday morning, having had a fantastic weekend with his friends and his girlfriend. Jenny, his Personal Assistant, duly obliged, ringing him at 6.30 am. On a few occasions previously, she had assumed that responsibility whenever he had a very important meeting with clients.

'Hello Jenny, thanks for the call,' Alex answered his mobile in a half-sleepy voice.

'You're welcome. Don't forget, you have to be at the University at 8.30 am. You've got less than two hours to get there.'

'I know,' Alex replied, and rang off.

Alex got out of bed quickly and went through his daily routine to get ready. Five minutes of yoga and ten minutes of exercises which included stretching, press-ups and half squats. That was followed by a quick shower and shave. Breakfast consisted of a glass of orange juice, a cup of tea and a slice of toast. He dressed smartly as usual, then picked up his briefcase, and was soon on his way to the University.

During term time, most Monday mornings at the University were quiet and uneventful.

Lecturers and students would walk in through the reception area, looking glum. They would have preferred their enjoyable weekend to have lasted longer, but unfortunately they had to return to their daily grind of lectures. The only interruption to the peaceful environment enjoyed by the receptionists would be, when some students would ring, to find out which room their lectures would be held in, because they hadn't bothered to check their weekly timetable.

Occasionally, a member of staff would ring in to report sick or to say they would be in later.

But on this particular Monday morning, the receptionist received a phone call from a totally different channel which she described as 'intriguing' as it was from the Vice Chancellor.

He phoned the reception desk early in the morning to inform them that he was expecting an important visitor by the name of Alexander DuPont, and to let him know when his guest arrived.

Both receptionists were on duty as their day started at 8 am. They were rather surprised to receive a call from the Vice Chancellor (VC). Julie took the call.

'What's the matter? You looked stunned,' Mary, her colleague, asked.

'I've every reason to. That was the VC informing me about a guest coming in, this morning. I've never had a call from him before.'

'I haven't either. Special guest, I suppose.'

'Can't wait to see this guy.'

It was an unusual call, not so much the time he phoned, as he normally worked from 7 am till late in the evening, but because he had never contacted the reception desk before. It was the responsibility of his Personal Assistant, Gill, to make these arrangements, but her shift started at 9 am. It must have been a very important matter for the VC to get involved.

Both receptionists had been working at the reception desk for nearly five years. They had only exchanged greetings or the occasional brief, courteous chat with the VC and other senior members of staff in the University. It was an informal environment and everyone was on first name terms.

At 8.30 am sharp, a smart looking man, dressed in a navy blue pinstriped suit, white shirt and a fuchsia floral tie approached the reception desk, stating that he had an appointment to see the VC. He was tall, slim, good-looking with black wavy hair and in his mid-twenties. Julie greeted him with a warm smile. Actually, she moved Mary aside gently, to attend to the guest and said, 'Your name, Sir.'

'Alexander DuPont. I've an appointment to see the Vice Chancellor,' he replied.

After pretending to check the appointment book, Julie smiled and said, 'We're expecting you, Mr DuPont, just a moment, Sir.'

She phoned the VC and informed him accordingly.

Dr. Peter Graves, the Vice Chancellor, came down in the lift from his twelfth floor office to meet his guest. The VC shook hands with his guest and said, 'Welcome to Westworth University Mr DuPont, I'm Peter Graves, the Vice Chancellor. But please, call me Peter.' He was dressed in a grey suit, pale blue shirt with a pink tie. His guest returned the compliment by introducing himself and also said, 'Please call me Alex.'

The receptionists kept their eyes on the job but their ears were picking up every word.

Putting it mildly, they were a bit nosy. Anyway they couldn't miss hearing as the whole conversation was taking place right in front of the reception desk. After the exchange of greetings, both men took the lift to the VC's office, to talk in private.

Mary, a married woman in her forties, was also taken by the stunning looks of Mr DuPont and couldn't help observing the flirtatious approach of her much younger colleague towards the guest. 'My God, you really were all over him, weren't you? You couldn't take your eyes off him.'

'You can't blame me for that. He is tall and very handsome with wavy hair. Judging by his surname, he could be French.'

'He speaks like an Englishman. Anyway, I wonder what your boyfriend would say.'

'Don't worry about him, he isn't here.'

Once in his office, Peter made coffee. Alex sat on the sofa and cast his eyes across the place.

The office consisted of a large meeting area with a rectangle table and eight chairs, a separate desk with an armchair, bookcase, storage cupboards, two sofas, a wardrobe and en suite facilities. It was a very impressive office.

At first sight, anyone would be taken by the sheer comfort of the place. While drinking coffee, Alex remarked, 'You've a very nice office. I've been told you're someone of good taste.'

That compliment was music to his ears; he enjoyed people praising his little enclave where he spent most of his time. It had even been rumoured that he had stayed overnight a few times.

'Thank you. It's not too bad. I like it here. Since I took up the post of VC last year in September 2004, life has been hectic and I've enjoyed every moment of it,' the VC replied.

For different reasons, both men were anxious to start. Alex was dying to find out why he was there, and what exactly he had to do. He hadn't been given much information, only that he would be expected to look into computer thefts that had occurred recently at the University. Peter, on the other hand, couldn't wait to brief Alex of what was expected of him, so that he would be able to keep his meeting with the Chairman of the Board to discuss the coming budget proposal.

'You've been highly recommended by my dear old friend, Robert. We met at Oxford as undergraduates, and have remained the best of friends ever since. He was Best Man at my wedding. I've a lot of respect and admiration for him,' the VC said.

'Robert spoke very highly of you as well.'

'That's nice of him. Well, Robert informed me that you are the right person to assist me in solving my problem. You're a Private Investigator, and have been doing the job for over a year with resounding success, I believe. In fact, you own the Mayfair Investigative Agency and prefer to call it simply the Agency. Am I correct?'

'Yes, I've been fortunate with my business. The Agency has two other members of staff; my experienced Personal Assistant, Jenny and my Associate, a very versatile support called Scott. We work very well as a team.'

'You're also a lawyer. A few years ago, you completed your training as a solicitor under the supervision of Robert.'

'That's right. Robert was superb as a mentor. I owe him a lot.'

'I also understand that your Agency only deals with issues relating to wealthy individuals and corporate organisations.'

'That's correct,' Alex said, and thought that the VC had been very well briefed by his old boss.

'I would like you to look into the computer thefts for me.'

'Could you tell me about it first?'

'OK. Let's get down to business. The reason you're here is to find out why we are losing expensive University equipment. We've lost two computers (laptops) within two weeks. There is only one entrance to the building on this site which is also the only exit. There are two emergency exit doors, and the key to these is secured in a glass container attached to the wall. And yet, someone still managed to steal the computers, and walk away through the door which has a security guard standing there at all times. It's quite baffling how this happened.'

The description was made with the emphasis on the words security, disappointment and frustration. It was the first time in the history of the institution that a theft had taken place. The VC was at pains to make that point. He stressed, 'One doesn't associate stealing with a University. People come here to learn and they should feel safe to do so in this environment.'

Alex listened attentively whilst nodding in agreement.

The VC continued, 'We had to call in the Police. Not nice, a bit scary. We had to reassure the students and staff that the Police were only doing their job. They shouldn't worry about anything.'

'When were the laptops stolen?'

'The first one went missing during the first week of May, and the second one, the following week. The most worrying aspect of the thefts is that the missing laptops contain sensitive data about the students.'

'What type of sensitive data?' Alex asked.

'This data includes students' personal details – names, addresses, mobile phone numbers, sickness, absence, assessment results and progress reports,' the VC explained.

'Was this data stored on encrypted files?'

'Yes. The files were password protected. Only the Principal Lecturers and the senior staff were given the password.'

'How far did the Police get with their investigation?'

The VC's face looked a bit glum and he expressed his dissatisfaction with their work.

'They did their best, given their shortage of manpower, but to no avail. I fear they had more important and bigger cases to solve. After a fortnight, they stopped their investigation due to no apparent evidence or witnesses. That's why I've decided to get someone like your good self to look into this. I cannot stress highly enough that it's essential to find the laptops and the culprit,' the VC said.

Alex didn't take his eyes off the VC's facial expression which suggested to him that the VC was about to provide more information. The VC moved to the edge of his very comfortable chair near his desk and said, 'Sorry to tell you, I've also come across another more pressing matter. Last Friday, I received a very disturbing letter.'

He removed an envelope from the inside pocket of his jacket and handed it to Alex.

'Have a look at this. Over the weekend, I've been at my wits end to know what to do with it.'

It was a typed, anonymous letter sent to the VC, requesting him to investigate and take appropriate action to stop foreign students being charged money by a senior academic to obtain a place on the nursing course, if not, a copy of the letter would be sent to the press.

'This is unbelievable,' Alex said. He looked puzzled.

'My sentiments exactly. But I have to do something to sort this out and I don't know where to start. You're the only person to know about this, please keep it strictly to yourself. I haven't mentioned it to any other member of staff yet.'

'Of course. You've my word. How can I help?' Alex said, instinctively.

'I hope I'm not putting you under undue pressure, if I ask you to take on the case about the letter as well. I'll fully understand if you can't.'

After a very brief pause, Alex replied, 'I'll have to give your proposal some careful thought before committing myself.'

'That's to be expected. Just to let you know, I've discussed the letter with the Chairman of the Board of Governors who is appalled. He wants this to be resolved as quickly as possible, in order to protect the good name of the University. I've informed him of your Investigative Agency and the reason why you would be here. Both of us would like you to look into the case of the anonymous letter in addition to the stolen laptops. In fact, the letter should take priority over the computer thefts.'

Suddenly, the letter became more important than the two stolen laptops. Alex was in a quandary. He was expected to investigate the case about the stolen laptops, and then found himself being burdened with a more complicated task. His eyes were wandering around looking for a credible answer to give, the tip of his tongue was licking his upper lip and his throat movement confirmed the swallowing of saliva. He was tense.

'The leak of this letter would cause immeasurable damage to the reputation of the University and it would take a very long time to recover from the bad publicity. Student recruitment would be badly affected. We could lose excellent lecturers to other reputable Universities for their own career development. The economic impact on the institution would be unbearable. Could you investigate the issue regarding the "letter" whilst looking into the computer thefts?' the VC said.

'It will be very difficult,' Alex replied.

'Please keep this confidential. I would like you to find out who is responsible for these fraudulent activities and report direct to me. I've no idea at all who that person might be. No one should know about this particular "letter" and the investigation. It is crucial that everyone is aware you are only investigating the computer thefts, but secretly you would be addressing matters relating to the anonymous "letter" at the same time.'

Alex was silent and looked worried.

'What do you think? Would you take the job? I'll be very grateful if you do, you'll be very well rewarded. I've got to say, you're my only hope right now,' the VC said.

'It's getting more intriguing. Initially, it was the computer thefts and now this very important matter of extortion as well,' Alex replied.

'I'm sorry about that,' the VC said. He was sympathetic but needed to get the jobs done.

Alex was thinking. It would be a big challenge and could provide him with an ideal opportunity to develop his expertise in criminal cases. He had nothing to lose.

'I am interested, but first I would like to check on our workload with my personal assistant.'

The VC nodded. He was very persuasive. In his role, he was used to getting people to do a job for him, and he was using those skills pretty effectively. He could sense Alex's enthusiasm to have a crack at the investigations.

'That's perfectly understandable,' the VC replied.

Both men stood up, with their eyes fixed on one another, contemplating the outcome of their conversation. The VC preferred to get the whole process started immediately whilst Alex wanted to tread carefully at the prospect of dealing with this daunting challenge.

The VC broke the tense atmosphere that was developing. 'I must call the Chairman of the Board.'

That gave Alex the opportunity to contact his personal assistant to touch base, and said, 'I'll be outside.' He closed the door. There was no one in the corridor and he took out his mobile.

'Hi Jenny, only a quick call and listen carefully please.' He filled her in with the details of the computer theft case but did not mention anything about the letter.

'Are you taking up this assignment?' Jenny asked.

'Yes. Well, we'll discuss this later as I have to let the VC know my decision in the next few minutes.'

'Don't forget, we have already got plenty to do.'

'I know. I'll see you soon,' Alex replied.

After taking a deep breath and exhaling whilst lowering his shoulders, clearly Alex was leaning towards a positive decision about taking the job on offer. The big and rather complex challenge of the cases appealed to him, and he felt he could handle these successfully. He hadn't experienced failure in his new career yet, and that optimistic feeling was based on this record and his intuition to do well. Once the VC finished his call, Alex reappeared in his office.

Alex happily informed the VC. 'Having had a chat with my personal assistant, I've decided to take on the job. In addition to the current work of the Agency, I will spend as much time as possible carrying out the two investigations. Is this agreeable to you?'

'That's wonderful news. I'm really delighted with your decision,' the VC said, and shook hands with him to seal the agreement.

'To do the job properly, I'll need to talk to some of your staff and students, and have access to relevant documentation. I'll also require your permission to move freely in the building.'

'Of course, I fully understand the importance of your requests. I'll be sending an email informing the staff about you and your responsibilities, and that they are to assist you as required. You'll be provided with a small office on the eleventh floor and given a visitor's pass. Any problems, just let me know.'

'Good. When would you like me to start?'

'Straightaway!'

'That's suits me fine. I need to be away tomorrow for a scheduled surveillance duty with Scott, my Associate. I'll be here on Wednesday.'

'I do understand you have other engagements and Wednesday will be ok.'

It was 10.15 am and the VC said, 'Let me take you on a tour now to show you where most of the staff are based. Hopefully, you might meet some of them.'

Alex welcomed the opportunity and replied, 'I'm looking forward to it.'

Chapter 2

Having walked down two flights of stairs, the VC opened the door to the tenth floor and led the way. At that very moment, a beautiful young girl was about to come through. She was in her late teens. Alex held the door to allow her to pass. He couldn't help noticing the troubled face of the girl. She appeared to be in a hurry. Perhaps, it was her coffee break and she was rushing to get back to her class. Although she had a faint smile, she looked pre-occupied, edgy and unhappy. Alex quickly noticed the name on her ID badge, as Margaret Johnson.

She almost dropped one of her books, looked at Alex and said, 'Thank you.'

Alex replied, 'You're welcome.'

Time was of the essence. The briefing for Alex continued as the VC decided to take him round the floor, and introduced him to as many staff as possible. He met a few lecturers, only shaking hands with them, as they seemed to be rushing around. The VC had planned a very quick introduction so that Alex's presence on the premises would be noted, and possibly explained in part to his staff, the reason why he was there. Alex was impressed by the reception he received from the teaching staff and was quick to express his appreciation, and said, 'Warm welcome, indeed.' The VC smiled and nodded in agreement.

The VC was very keen to get the computer theft case resolved rather quickly - wishful thinking.

If the Police hadn't succeeded, what chance would an up and coming Private Investigator have? He would require the support of the staff and students, plus plenty of luck to succeed.

The VC recognised that and said, 'It's a tough assignment, but as you're a resourceful professional, I believe you will no doubt figure out how to solve this, preferably, very soon.'

'My team and I will work very hard to resolve these issues for you,' Alex replied.

A big row was taking place between two lecturers in Jack Dempsey's office. Alex couldn't see their faces as the office door was closed. Almost every word could be heard by anyone outside the office. They were shouting at each other loud enough to be heard, and making threatening remarks. Expressions such as 'the poor results are your fault' were made, to which 'your curriculum is causing the problem' was shot back. The first speaker described the other as 'a creep and carrying tales' whilst the other shouted back, 'you are a weakling and a doormat'.

Naturally, fellow lecturers were curious to find out what was going on. Some of them were just looking in amazement. Others were preparing themselves to go to the classrooms, assembling their teaching notes or photocopying materials for their lectures. Teaching sessions would resume soon, following the coffee break.

In fact, they were in the thick of their exchange when the VC knocked on the office door and walked in. He asked them to keep their voices down. Both lecturers were surprised to see the VC. The effect of the VC's intervention was quite dramatic. The place returned to a resemblance of normality.

However, it was also an ideal opportunity for the VC to introduce Alex to the two Principal Lecturers with the condescending voices towards each other. Seeing the VC accompanied by a stranger entering the office, both stood up immediately. Touching Alex's right shoulder gently with his left hand, whilst fixing his eyes on the lecturers, the VC smiled and said, 'Please meet Alexander DuPont, a Private Investigator, who will be looking into the computer thefts for the University. Alex has kindly agreed to start the investigation immediately. Undoubtedly, he'll be meeting you both and other relevant members of staff in due course.'

Alex offered his right hand to them, which was warmly received. The tall chap with blonde hair said, 'I'm John Fairbanks, Principal Lecturer in Adult Nursing. I hope you've more luck than the Police in solving the computer thefts. I'll be happy to help, anytime.'

He was followed by the other guy who was of medium height with black hair said, 'I'm Jack Dempsey, also a Principal Lecturer in Adult Nursing, pleased to meet you. See you around.'

The VC then said, 'We had better leave you two to get on with your work.'

After stepping into the corridor, the VC reassured Alex, 'I don't usually go round these floors, only on certain occasions when special dignitaries such as politicians or business people are visiting the premises. At least, you've been able to meet John and Jack.'

Alex was very interested to find out the nature of their disagreement, but that would keep for another day. He had to follow the VC, and listen carefully to what he had to say, as every bit of information was going to be useful to his investigations.

Having passed John's office, the VC knocked on the door of Gail Weston, the Deputy Dean.

'Come in,' Gail called out.

'Hello Gail, meet Alexander DuPont,' the VC said.

Alex and Gail shook hands gently, smiling at each other politely. The VC explained to her why Alex was there.

'Let's hope you find the culprit very soon,' Gail remarked.

With a slight bow of his head, Alex replied, 'I'll do my very best.'

The VC was very proud to show Alex around. He was also quick to emphasise that the University offered well equipped offices and excellent teaching and learning resources. 'Every effort will be made to increase and improve the facilities all round the University to keep up with course implementation, development and progress. The latest investment I have in mind, is to install a full information technology system for the benefit of both lecturers and students. The support staff will also be given the opportunity to utilise the new resource. But first, I have to convince the Board of Governors of the value of the new technology scheme so that the members will agree to commit funds.'

Alex was taking it all in with a deep pensive look.

As computers were tools of information technology, it was conceivable that the loss of the two items could have a bearing on the overall strategy of the VC. That notion hadn't escaped Alex's chain of thought. Was that the underlying reason for his service? He chose not to be presumptuous and preferred to wait for the rationale. As luck would have it or it could be seen as a shrewd tactic by the VC, his doubt regarding the motive for his initial appointment was about to be clarified.

'A huge policy issue is on the agenda. I have to persuade the Board of Governors that the increased funding for the information technology scheme is fully justified, and will be beneficial to the institution. It's also my first major project since my appointment as VC and I can't afford to fail in securing funding.'

'You shouldn't have any problem with that surely.'

'I'm afraid I do have one. I've been told that the Board is not pleased with the loss of the two laptops, as it doesn't enhance our reputation. The Chairman has told me to get to the bottom of it quickly. In other words, find the thief, preferably before I submit a paper to the Board to request funding. That's where you come in.'

The VC further emphasised, 'Once you've found out who's done it, then, I'll be able to take action accordingly. That will demonstrate my determination to deal with this matter emphatically, and I'll be able to further tighten up the security and monitoring of equipment. Consequently, that will strengthen my request for more funding. It is crucial that we have an efficient information technology system in position before the next academic year starts in September, as this will impact on the delivery of the curriculum. We have to be highly competitive in the field of higher education. Another point worth noting, is the more I think about it, the more I'm convinced that this is an inside job. It infuriates me that one of our employees has stolen from us and is likely to get away with it. Or, if students have done it, they will still be able to graduate. Either way, the thought sickens me.'

'I can understand your reason to get this resolved.' Alex felt the VC had approached his mentor Robert because he wanted to get someone on the job that he could trust.

The VC gave him a map of the building which showed the twelve floors which were utilised by both staff and students, and explained, 'Ground floor consists of a reception area, mini shop, kitchen and dining room, and the utility room. The entrance to the building and the exit are through the only door on this floor. There are two emergency exit doors; one is found at the back and the other on the side of the building. The keys for these doors are kept in a sealed glass unit fixed on the wall close by. The first floor is for support staff including the recruitment office, administration office and allocation of student clinical experience. Assessment office, administration offices, photocopiers and storage cupboards are on the second floor. A large Library occupies the third floor. More reading areas are available on the fourth floor, and the audio visual aids section is sited on the same floor. The University counselling service is also based there. The teaching accommodation is based on the fifth to the ninth floor. Lecturers' offices are on the tenth and eleventh floors. The VC's office, Boardroom, staff common room, meeting rooms and a few lecturers' offices are on the twelfth floor.'

Having gone over the plan with his guest, the VC said, 'I need to go to a meeting in a few minutes. I think it'll be helpful for you to meet Tom Evans, the Audio Visual Aids (AVA) technician who is responsible for the overall running of that department which includes the management, storage and use of the teaching and learning equipment.'

'Thank you. The sooner I start the better.'

'That's the spirit. By the way, I hope you have found the tour interesting and informative.'

'Definitely, nice to meet some of your staff.'

'OK, let's take the lift to the fourth floor. May I suggest you try and find out as much as you can from Tom; I've got a feeling that the Police didn't interrogate him enough.'

'I will do,' Alex replied.

They were about to leave for the fourth floor and were waiting for the lift to arrive when a tall man in his forties with grey hair and sleeves rolled up, walked in through the door.

He looked worried. He raised his head, spotted the VC and said, 'Good morning, Peter.'

The VC replied, 'Ah, Matt, good morning to you as well. Where are you heading to?'

'I'm on my way to see John about recruitment,' Matt replied and stopped.

Then, the VC made the introduction. Turning to Alex, he said, 'Matt Hughes is the Recruitment Officer for students and has been with us for about 18 months.'

Alex shook hands with Matt and said, 'Pleased to meet you.'

The VC explained to Matt the reason why Alex was there.

'If you need any help, just let me know. I'm on the first floor,' Matt said.

'Thank you,' Alex replied.

They headed to the fourth floor to meet Tom Evans, the Audio Visual Aids (AVA) technician.

The VC made the introduction. Tom shook hands with Alex and said, 'Nice to meet you.' Tom was kind of expecting them. The VC asked him if Alex could have a chat with him.

'I'm very busy right now. I'll have more time on Wednesday at 10 am, shall we meet then?' Tom said.

'That's ok. See you on Wednesday,' Alex replied.

Both the VC and Alex left Tom's office.

'Well Alex, keep me informed and good luck. I must leave you now.'

'Thank you.'

Alex left the University for the Agency and the VC headed for his meeting.

***

The Mayfair Investigative Agency was based on the first floor of a town house in Mayfair. The offices were very comfortable and well equipped. Jenny's office was at the front so that she could welcome any visitors and clients, and attend to their queries before getting Alex involved. It was a practical and good working area. The usual office equipment such as a desk, chairs, phone, stationery, computer, printer, filing cabinet and a cupboard were present in Jenny's office.

There was also a decent sized kitchen to make coffee and have lunch. It had a sink, kettle, a supply of crockery, microwave, a fridge and a small table with six chairs. It had en suite facilities and a sitting room with a three-piece suite and a television.

Scott's office was rather small but very comfortable and met the basic requirement for him to do his job. He also had a nice armchair to relax in. Anyway, most of his time was spent in the field, gathering information and evidence.

The nicest office belonged to Alex as he had to meet affluent clients. It contained all the high quality office furniture and equipment with the required comfort for a Private Investigator to impress his clients.

Being the owner of the Agency, he ensured that the accommodation had sufficient resources for his staff to do their job. With the hard work and commitment of his staff, his Agency had developed into a productive, successful and financially viable business. The progress had been made at a rapid pace due to a number of wealthy clients. Through his connections, Alex was able to get a lucrative business stream, and he wanted that trend to continue for a very long time.

Jenny and Scott couldn't wait to hear what Alex had to say. After a blow by blow account of his visit to the University, to which his team had listened attentively taking it all in, Jenny was the first to ask. 'How did you find them?'

'They were pleasant and nice,' Alex said.

'I guess they probably didn't have much choice but to be nice. Those academics always give me goose pimples. In fact, I'm wary of their attitude of being superior and knowing it all, when more likely than not, they haven't got a clue about most of the stuff that they're supposed to teach.'

'They aren't like that at all.'

'Well I don't care. I'll keep away from them.'

A quick evaluation of the time he spent at the University that morning was that he would have to tread carefully during his investigation. Alex added, 'A few senior people appeared to be stressed out. Even a student I came across at the entrance to the tenth floor looked unhappy. But the receptionist was cute and helpful.'

'I'm not surprised; women always do things for you. Just because a receptionist is pretty, it doesn't mean that she is nice. Anyway, you shouldn't mix business with pleasure,' Jenny warned.

Alex detected a tinge of envy in the views expressed by Jenny. It could be because she didn't get the chance to go to University. Anyway, her negative feelings should not be allowed to influence his determination to solve the computer theft case. He had promised his old boss that he would do everything to assist his friend at the University. He was also fully aware, that he would require the assistance of both Jenny and Scott to be successful with his new case, so their co-operation was going to be essential.

It was Scott's turn to quiz Alex next. 'What exactly are we taking on here?'

'As I said, we need to find out about the two missing laptops.'

'You mean, who has stolen these?'

'That's right. And we need to do that pretty quickly.'

Jenny chipped in. 'What about the other cases?'

'We have to continue working on them as well. As you both know, our client list consists of wealthy individuals and large corporations; they deserve our best attention,' Alex pointed out.

'Those clients will expect results as well,' Jenny reminded him.

'I know.'

Scott remarked, 'It would have been nice if we were consulted before you agreed to accept the job.'

Alex decided to provide them with more details. 'I understand. I spoke to Jenny about it and expected her to let you know. The Vice Chancellor (VC) appeared desperate and he is a close friend of my old boss. As you can see, it would have been difficult for me to turn it down. In any case, the sooner I get on with it the better.'

'Jenny did tell me. Is it worth spending a lot of our valuable time on this, seemingly small, and not that important matter? Considering the type of clients on our books, this case is very ordinary. The chance of finding these laptops is very low or nil. Can't they just tighten up their security?' Scott said.

Jenny nodded in agreement with Scott. 'Do we have to take this job?'

'We do,' Alex said. He also emphasized the point. 'The stolen laptops contain sensitive data as regards to the students. If this falls into the wrong hands, it can cause enormous problems for the students and the University.'

Alex felt he had to stamp his authority as he owned the agency. Jenny and Scott were his only employees since setting up the business. Jenny used to work for his uncle as a PA and had been with the Agency, literally, from day one. She was in her early forties, attractive, single, intelligent, medium height, slim, well dressed and very good at her job. Scott, was a recently retired Detective Sergeant, married with two grown up children; intelligent, competent, reliable, he had joined the Agency 9 months ago. All three complemented each other well with their range of different skills to solve their clients' cases. They had established a very good working relationship and did not want to jeopardise it through a minor disagreement. 'Listen, both of you. We've plenty to do. I've given my word on this one, and I intend to keep it.'

His message was getting through as his voice suddenly began to sound more serious and determined. Jenny and Scott realised that their boss meant business and they had no choice but to go along with him. Both Jenny and Scott didn't pursue with their inquisition any further, and decided to get on with their work.

'When do you want us to start, then?' Jenny asked.

'Well, in fact, I've already done so this morning. Tomorrow, Scott and I are on surveillance duty. The work at the University will start properly on Wednesday when I meet with Tom Evans, the Audio Visual Aids technician.'

'What does that mean?' Jenny asked.

'I understand Tom is responsible for all the teaching and learning equipment used by the lecturers and students. He should be able to shed some light on the stolen laptops.'

'Going by what you said about the place, it is possible this guy Tom could have done it himself,' Scott pointed out.

'Funny you should say that, the VC also kind of suspects him as well. I want to give him the benefit of the doubt, and hear his version of events first, before making up my mind about him.'

Chapter 3

The next day, Alex and Scott had to follow up some leads in one of his cases regarding a client who wanted his wife's every step watched. They had a successful stakeout and collected some useful information for their client.

On Wednesday, Alex arrived by car at the University at 9 am and was looking for a space to park. Ahmed, one of the security officers was quick to spot him and direct him to an empty space, reserved for senior officers. Alex was pleasantly surprised. It was the first time in his life he had been treated with such great respect and personal attention. After parking his car, he entered the building through the revolving door. He checked the security officer's name badge and said, 'Thank you, Ahmed. It's much appreciated.'

Ahmed replied, 'You're welcome Mr DuPont. Here is your visitor's pass which you should hang around your neck when you're on site, now let me take you to your office on the eleventh floor.'

Alex was very impressed. 'Everything has been organised very quickly for me, thank you and please call me Alex.'

The office was somewhat small and definitely not as luxurious as that of the VC. There was one decent sized table with two locked drawers, a phone, appropriate stationery, a table lamp and a chair. A locker with a key to keep his personal items and two additional, comfortable chairs were cleverly positioned to make maximum use of the available space.

Alex was pleased with the accommodation.

'Well this is very nice, Ahmed. I like it.'

'Glad you like it,' Ahmed said, and wished him well. 'I hope you'll enjoy your short stay with us. Here is your office door key. If you need anything at all, please let me know.'

While taking the key, Alex said, 'Thank you again, Ahmed.'

He sat in his comfortable chair with his elbows leaning on the table and considered that he was very fortunate to be treated so well. For the VC to provide him with an office on site, demonstrated his determination to get the computer theft case and, the issue of the anonymous 'letter', resolved quickly. For his part, he would have to work hard to meet the VC's expectations.

Suddenly, he remembered he had a meeting with Tom Evans, so he rushed down to the fourth floor.

Once he got there, Tom invited Alex to sit on the chair next to his, which was only a couple of feet away.

'Thank you for seeing me, Tom,' Alex said.

'No problem, delighted to help.'

'So, this is your department.'

'Yes, this is my little patch. Let me show you around.'

Tom walked him around his department which was really a very large room. It had to be; the teaching and learning resources were stored there. The room was packed with all sorts of equipment such as overhead projectors, slide projectors, video cameras, CD players, flip chart stands and screens. Two large cupboards stood against the wall which were full of writing materials, empty charts, CDs, tapes, acetates, and stacks of photocopy paper. A large industrial Xerox copier was situated by the wall as well. There was a separate desk and chair for his deputy, Rose, who was multi-skilled. Her job was to provide a secretarial service but mostly to help Tom provide AVA equipment to teaching staff and students and, she deputised for Tom when required.

Tom was about fifty, of short build and slightly plump. He was wearing jeans and an open necked shirt, appropriately dressed to move equipment around the building. As he had already set up the teaching aids in the classrooms according to the lecturers' requests, he now had some free time to spare for his guest.

'Thank you for the tour.'

'Tell me what you would like to know and I'll be pleased to provide you with the relevant information.'

'Well, if you could start with the moment you noticed the laptops were missing.'

'Right. Every teaching room has got a computer installed which is fixed to the table for security reasons. The lecturers each have a desk computer in their office as well. In addition, there are ten laptops in the department available for lecturers' use just in case any computer isn't functioning well in the classroom. At the time of the thefts, we were experiencing some problems with some of the computers on the seventh floor, so the lecturers had to make use of the laptops. It was decided to utilise these in the classrooms whilst the repair of the fixed computers was taking place. In addition, lecturers were allowed to take a laptop home after signing for it and then later return it to the AVA's office. Alas, we lost two laptops and this took place about four weeks ago.'

'How long were these laptops used in the classrooms?'

'At least two weeks, before the first laptop went missing.'

Alex gave a puzzled look. 'Why did it take so long for the repair to be carried out?'

'Unfortunately that's how the system works. We were waiting for the engineers to sort out the problems. The maintenance for computers is contracted out to the suppliers. They were waiting for some parts to arrive.'

'Have the computers been repaired now?'

'Oh, yes.'

'Do you keep a record as to who was borrowing the laptops and responsible for their return?'

'There is an equipment borrowing book, which is kept in the department. Any borrowed laptop and its return is entered, dated and signed by the lecturers. At the time of the thefts, this had not been carried out efficiently.'

'Why?'

'Unfortunately, my deputy was off sick. I was on my own. The actual monitoring hadn't taken place and that gave the thief an ideal opportunity to steal the laptops. Actually, when we lost the first laptop from Jack's office, I informed the Dean, David Mallory. He told me not to worry too much about the laptop, as it would soon turn up.'

'When did the Police get involved?'

'A week later, when I discovered a second laptop was missing from John's office, I informed David immediately. He discussed the matter with the VC who contacted the Police.'

'Why do you think the Police was called in, then?'

'Because the two missing laptops contain sensitive data about the students.'

'Did all ten laptops contain this data?'

'Yes.'

The phone rang. Tom answered it and passed it over to Alex. The VC was on the line and requested that Alex join him straightaway as an emergency had arisen.

'Tom, thank you for your time and I fully appreciate your detailed explanation of the computer thefts. I need to leave you now as I have to be somewhere else. I'll see you again. Bye.'

Within a few minutes, Alex was with the VC.

'Come on in Alex,' he said.

There was a feeling that something bad, if not very bad, had occurred. Everyone looked serious with their eyes wandering from one to another and yet, not a word was uttered. Their faces were pale, with deep pensive expressions. Everyone was standing still with their arms hanging by their sides. The VC stood up from behind his desk, then walked to his office window and just stared into space for a few seconds and then said, 'How could this have happened?'

The atmosphere in the office was one of incredulity and desperation. Judging by the restlessness of the VC and his own immediate assessment of the facial expressions of those present, Alex sensed that he was about to discover the worst of news and his fears were realised.

Looking at Alex, the VC said, 'One of our students has been found dead in her flat. This is really terrible and appalling news. She came from South Africa to study and become a qualified nurse, and we've not been able to look after her. She's only been here since last September. Very sad.'

At a time like this, people often could not find the right words to express their feelings of outrage, anger and revulsion. Alex managed only to say. 'I'm very sorry to hear this.'

'Thank you, Alex.'

'How did it happen?'

'We don't know the details. It appears she died during the night. The Police suspect she was murdered. They informed us this morning.'

The other two people in the room had their eyes fixed on Alex, probably wondering about his presence. Why was he called to join them? One of them was Gail whom he met last Monday and they exchanged a nod and grin. It was the first time he had seen the other guy.

'Is there anything I can do to help?'

Alex offered his assistance to the VC.

'Thank you. We'll discuss how you can help us, later.'

Then, he introduced Alex to the Dean, David Mallory and informed him of Alex's presence and role in the Faculty. Clearly, he didn't know that Alex had been employed by the VC to undertake an investigation into the computer thefts; he had been away for a few days. As far as the Dean was concerned, the Police couldn't solve the case, and that matter was closed. He was very surprised that another investigation had been lodged. Initially David was speechless, then quickly regained his composure, and welcomed Alex by offering his hand with a faint and disconcerting smile.

Everyone remained on their feet. The VC said, 'We are waiting for Detective Sergeant (Sgt) Cooper from the Criminal Investigation Department to arrive, and then we'll begin.' They started to mumble. David moved closer to Alex and said, 'If you want to see me, I'm always at your disposal and if there is anything you need, just let me know.'

Alex acknowledged the help with a nod and said, 'Thank you.'

He noticed the Dean was in his fifties, rather short in stature, middle aged, plump, smartly dressed, blue eyes, craggy face, grey hair and had a limp on his right leg. His assessment was interrupted by a knock on the door.

The VC opened the door and said, 'Come on in Detective Sgt Melanie Cooper.'

'Good morning,' Detective Sgt Cooper replied and walked into the office.

'It's very good of you to come here to tell us about this awful state of affairs,' the VC said.

She was in her black trouser suit and white shirt. She looked young, slim with shoulder length blonde hair and of medium height. She smiled and nodded gently through the introduction.

Everyone sat down at the table. The VC asked the Sergeant to start the briefing.

Detective Sgt Cooper flicked through her notes, her blue eyes were directed towards everyone and said, 'It's a tragic loss of a young life. I feel for all of you.'

That sentiment was very much appreciated. Everyone stiffened their lips whilst keeping their mouths closed and their wide opened eyes focused on her, waiting to hear the briefing.

'It would appear that Margaret Johnson, a student nurse, was assaulted in her flat last night, Tuesday 7 June and died immediately. She was found by a cleaner. Apparently, the cleaner knocked on Margaret's door at 7.30 this morning. When there was no reply, she inserted her key in the door and noticed it was unlocked. This sounded an alarm to her that something was wrong because the door was usually locked. If Margaret was inside and didn't want to be disturbed, she would hang the 'DON'T DISTURB' label on the outside door handle. She turned the handle down and eased open the door slowly. She couldn't hear any sound and thinking the flat was empty, she proceeded inside to start the cleaning. It was then she saw Margaret lying on the floor in her tracksuit. She called out her name. No reply. She approached Margaret to establish what was wrong. There was blood under her head and she wasn't breathing. The cleaner realised something very bad and serious had happened to Margaret. Quickly, she went to get help from one of her colleagues who was cleaning in the next flat. The supervisor was on the same floor. They were all very frightened and the supervisor called 999. The Paramedics and the Police arrived at the flat within minutes as they didn't have far to travel. I am leading the investigation. The crime investigation team has carried out a search of the property. No weapon was found. The Coroner checked the body and pronounced her dead. His initial assessment suggested that she was hit on the back of her head with a blunt and heavy object, became unstable and fell to the floor. She probably died straightaway. She sustained a wound to the back of her head. There was blood under her head on the floor where she was found. The time of her death is thought to be between 8pm and 10pm. The Police are treating this as a murder. Margaret's body has been removed from her flat and taken away for a post-mortem to establish the cause of death. It is suspected that she could have been involved in a fracas with someone. There were books on the floor and a chair had toppled over,' Sgt Cooper said.

After a brief pause, she then continued, 'During the fight, she could have been hit very hard by the same person and then, fell to the floor and died instantly. The scene of crime has been cordoned off. The forensic team is continuing with their work. My team has already started looking for the killer, and any evidence connected with the incident. Now, what is most urgent is to inform the next of kin.'

A short period of silence followed. Everyone was looking at each other, searching for comfort. Detective Sgt

Cooper courteously remained quiet, thus allowing time and space for those present to grapple with the outrageous act.

Having listened to the report from the Sergeant, everyone looked rather shaken with the sordid details of the way the crime had been committed on one of their own students. Their faces were drawn in, sucking the inside of their cheeks, swallowing the saliva they could muster as their mouths were getting dry. Gail was blinking nervously. Probably, it was the first time they had encountered such a ghastly situation.

'This is unbelievable, sad and very distressing. Surely, one of the residents must have heard some noise or seen someone entering or leaving the residence as her flat was on the ground floor next to the entrance door? Every effort must be made to find the maniac who has murdered this promising student,' David said angrily.

'Actually the initial enquiry indicates that other residents who were in, had not heard any untoward noises, or noticed any strangers coming into or leaving the building,' Sgt Cooper confirmed.

Alex recognised Margaret's name instantly and asked the VC. 'Is she the same Margaret Johnson, with a distressed look, that we met at the door on the tenth floor last Monday?'

'I'm afraid so,' the VC replied.

'My God,' Alex replied in total disbelief. 'She was such a pretty and innocent looking girl.'

'I agree,' the VC said, and then turned to the Sergeant. 'Thank you, Sgt Cooper. The next of kin is Margaret's uncle who lives not far from the campus.'

The VC agreed to make available the uncle's address and phone number to the Sergeant.

'After you make contact with him as part of your investigation and inform him of the very sad news regarding Margaret, I'll ring him to express our deepest condolences.'

'I'm very sorry to give you the details of this horrific news. It can't have been easy for you to listen to this. If you want me to come and talk to your colleagues and students, I'll be available. Just let me know,' Sgt Cooper said.

'Thank you for your compassion and kind offer. There is a counselling service on this site. We'll inform everyone in the Faculty of Margaret's tragic death, and arrange for counselling sessions for those who require support. We'll also fully co-operate with the Police. The staff and students will be available to assist you with the investigation.'

Sgt Cooper nodded in appreciation and promised, 'We'll get the person who has done this.'

The Dean and the deputy Dean left. The VC explained Alex's presence at the University to Sgt Cooper, and that Alex owned the very successful Mayfair Investigative Agency. Then he turned to Alex and added, 'The Sergeant was the officer in charge of the computer theft case.'

Both the Sergeant and Alex smiled at each other.

The VC said to Alex. 'You have just arrived to look into the computer thefts, now we've got another more serious case on our hands. Finding Margaret's killer should be given top priority.'

Alex felt the VC would like him to be involved in solving the murder case as well. He was deeply moved by the briefing, and didn't hesitate in offering his help. He was very impressed by his quick encounter with Margaret, and saddened by her death. Nothing would be more satisfying to him than to bring her killer to justice. He said to the VC. 'If it is alright with you, I would like to work closely with the Sergeant to find the killer. That, also depends on how the Sergeant feels about it.'

The VC was rather pleased to hear Alex's offer and said, 'To be honest, I feel very reassured to hear that. What do you think Sgt Cooper, is this a workable option?'

Sgt Cooper quickly replied, 'Thank you for your assistance, Mr DuPont. This is something new to me and the department. I do not recall receiving help from someone who is not a Police Officer in this manner. I'll need to contact my boss, the Inspector at the department and discuss this with him first, and then I'll let you know.' Sgt Cooper left the office to phone her boss.

In the meantime, the VC decided to share some confidential information with Alex.

'I'm sorry to increase your workload. Events are overtaking us rapidly. I had to inform the Chairman about Margaret's untimely death. He was shocked and saddened to hear it, and wanted me to put in every effort to find the killer. He asked me to employ your Agency outright to take charge of this case. I had to explain to him about the willingness of Sgt Cooper to commit Police resources to get results quickly. Then, the Chairman suggested that you represent the University and assist Sgt Cooper. I'm delighted you've already agreed to do so.'

'I'm pleased to help in any way I can,' Alex said.

'Thank you,' the VC acknowledged his assistance.

Alex's head was buzzing with the unexpected events evolving throughout the day, and at a tremendous speed at that. What had started as getting himself settled into his new office, to meeting with Tom, and then had ended up with the unfortunate issue relating to the murder of a student. All of a sudden, a deep thought struck him and he began to visualize a possible scenario. Only last Monday, the VC informed him of the anonymous letter regarding the illegal charging of foreign students to obtain University places on the nursing course, and then the next day, a foreign student on that course was murdered. Was there a connection between the two incidents?

Chapter 4

Whilst mulling over the offer of help, Sgt Cooper stepped outside the office and contacted her boss at the Police department to discuss it. A few interesting thoughts were buzzing through her pretty head. She was conscious of the fact that she and her colleagues could not find the person who stole the two laptops. It was embarrassing for her department but they had bigger fish to fry at that time. A few weeks later, she finds herself back at the University to solve a murder case.

Her new challenge was to find the killer of a student nurse. Everything should be done to get results and she couldn't possibly let the department down again. The burden of that enormous responsibility rested on her shoulders. She had to deliver on this one.

Whilst briefing the senior staff of the University, she noticed their eyes were totally focused on her and they were taking in every detail of the case. She wondered whether they had any confidence in her to be a success second time round. Undoubtedly, she was slightly nervous. To make matters more intriguing, a Private Investigator, whom she had never met before, was present. By all accounts, he could be very much on the ball or not at all. She didn't know much about him. To be fair, she thought Alex acted in a very professional manner.

Working with a Private Investigator hadn't crossed her mind prior to coming to the University. It would mean being dependent on and sharing information with someone from outside the department. A question of trust was bound to arise. Establishing a trusting relationship with Alex could take some time. But time was precious and in short supply. Other on-going cases in the department would still require her full attention. Given a choice, she would prefer to work solely with her own team.

In the circumstances, it would be tactful and diplomatic on her part to appreciate the help she had been offered. How much she would utilise that support would depend on the pace at which the investigation evolved? It would be churlish to turn down Alex's help. Therefore, she had to put a positive spin on her request to her boss so that he would agree to Alex coming on board.

'Hello Sir, I'm still at the University. I have just finished briefing the VC and his senior staff. They were shocked to learn how the student nurse could have been murdered, but they were grateful to me for informing them. To be honest, it was a difficult task to perform,' Sgt Cooper reported to her boss, Richard Jenkins. Then, she discussed Alex DuPont's offer of help.

'What do you think of him? Do you believe he could help?' Richard asked.

'He is a Private Investigator who has been hired by the VC to investigate the computer theft case which we couldn't resolve, if you recall. He is very young, confident, articulate, smart and willing to assist. I don't know anything about his background. It sounded like a genuine offer of help. The VC has faith in him,' Sgt Cooper explained.

'Well, we do have a couple of staff on sick leave. Getting some assistance on this case from a sort of professional could prove beneficial. You need to keep a very close eye on him though. We do not want anything to go wrong with this investigation and we certainly don't want this Alex guy to mess things up for us. Don't forget this is Police business and we are fully in charge of the case. Alright, you have my permission to work with him on this murder case.' Richard was very adamant and direct with his consent and agreement for her to work with Alex.

'OK Sir. That's fine with me.'

'I guess if we co-operate with the VC on this one, it would be better for the relationship between the Police and the University. After all, we did our very best to solve the computer theft case but we failed. Make sure you find the killer. Good luck with this case and your new found so called partner.'

'Thank you, Sir.'

On her return, she was sporting a faint smile and looking at the VC, she said, 'I'd welcome any assistance I can get; we're experiencing problems with staff shortages in the department at the moment. We'll need to work closely together and please remember the crime investigation department is in charge. I recognise Alex is currently working on the computer theft case for the University, but as far as the murder case is concerned, he will be expected to report to me.'

Detective Sgt Cooper confirmed the decision of her department.

'I'm fine with that arrangement. I'll also be expecting full co-operation with the Sgt and her colleagues. Then together, we'll find the killer,' Alex replied.

Watching these two good-looking, intelligent, smart and highly motivated individuals who had just met and yet agreed to co-operate for a good cause, could only warm the VC's heart, he welcomed the forming of the partnership and cupped his hands. 'That's absolutely fantastic. I'm sure you two will get along very well together and do everything possible to solve this case. Thank you both.'

'That's settled then,' Detective Sgt Cooper said.

'Would it be possible for me to visit the scene of the crime sometime?' Alex asked, as he wanted to start immediately.

'Of course, I'll inform the Officer to expect you and take you round the scene of the crime,' Detective Sgt Cooper confirmed.

Both Alex and Detective Sgt Cooper exchanged mobile numbers and agreed to meet the following day at one o'clock for lunch in the Red Lion pub, which was not far from the Faculty, to develop a strategy to deal with the murder case.

Detective Sgt Cooper agreed to bring him up to date with any new developments. She looked at her mobile as there was an incoming text message. That prompted her to be on her way. 'I've got to get back quickly. I'll keep in touch. See you tomorrow, Mr DuPont.' Then she left.

Alex had to pinch himself to make sure that he wasn't dreaming. His involvement was getting more challenging as he spent more time at the University. Doing his old boss a favour by agreeing to help the VC had turned into three cases rather than one with phenomenal speed. Initially, he thought the job of dealing with the computer thefts would only take a few hours or at most a few days out of his normal schedule. Increasingly, it appeared that a lot more resources would have to be applied to deal with the three cases in a pragmatic way.

Suddenly, it began to impact on Alex, the extent of the commitment that was required on his part. He pondered on the success or failure of the tasks. It would certainly test and stretch his ability as a competent investigator. The contribution of his team would be vital. Success would, no doubt, enhance the image of his agency and add a new dimension to attract new business.

Conversely, failure would not really affect his type of service because his clients thus far had largely been wealthy individuals and large corporations. He had nothing to lose and plenty to gain.

The VC was pleased that Alex and Detective Sgt Cooper had agreed to work together and he could sense a genuine respect between them. That could generate a tremendous understanding, relationship and determination in finding the killer. He was optimistic that their partnership would be productive. He interrupted Alex's chain of thought. 'What are you thinking?'

'Just about the tasks in hand, really.'

'I'm sure you'll cope very well. I do apologise for burdening you like this. Robert told you to come and see me about the computer theft case and you have ended up with another two cases.'

'Thank you for acknowledging the predicament that I find myself in. I guess that's how things work out sometimes. But these things aren't insurmountable.'

'Glad to hear your positive attitude.'

'I have to be.'

'I'm pleased you'll be working closely with Sgt Cooper. It'll help to catch the killer.'

'In the circumstances, I welcome the opportunity,' Alex replied with a smile.

The VC reassured him. 'We'll discuss the terms of our agreement for the three assignments shortly and please keep me in the loop. I would like the computer theft case and the murder case to be resolved quickly, if possible, and please don't forget about the letter.'

Alex replied, 'I'll do everything I can to resolve all three cases.'

'Thank you,' the VC said. He also confirmed, 'Both the Dean and deputy Dean have been told to provide you with any relevant information that you require for your investigations.'

'Thanks. I'm looking forward to working with them,' Alex replied.

He would obviously need their assistance in solving these challenging cases.

'How do you find your office?' the VC asked.

'It's very nice. Thank you for providing me with the office, visitor's pass and a parking space.'

'You're very welcome,' the VC was clearly happy to help. He left Alex to get on with his work.

He needed to get acquainted with the relevant people and familiarise himself with the environment of the computer theft case in the first instance. Would he be treated nicely by the academics, especially when he started to dig into their responsibility with regard to using and safeguarding the laptops?

He was familiar with the culture in higher education institutions. From his own experience as a university student at Oxford, most academics were a law unto themselves. They did not suffer fools gladly. Never keen to account for their time and performance, they resented the notion of being challenged on any issue. Most of them could be breathtakingly arrogant to their own junior colleagues and students or even ignorant to outsiders.

On his way back from his car to the building, he met Matt Hughes. They exchanged greetings. Alex had to start his investigation rather quickly and decided it was an opportune moment to meet with Matt; the sooner he started seeing senior people the better. Matt was one of them. Alex asked to see him for a few minutes about the computer thefts, thinking that he would then be able to eliminate him as a witness from his list.

'Of course, let's go to my office. We can get some privacy there,' Matt said.

Matt closed his office door. 'Really sad to hear about the student's death.'

'It's very sad indeed. What a loss?' Alex added.

Then both sat down. Alex asked, 'How often do you use the laptops?'

'I'm not fond of computers, myself. Pam, my Personal Assistant tends to use it extensively. Call me old fashioned, I prefer the traditional way of writing things down.'

'Could you shed any light on the two stolen laptops?'

'To be honest, I've no idea at all. Only that they have been stolen. The Police were involved and they couldn't find them nor the identity of who had stolen them. Anything else?'

'No. Not at the moment. I understand you are interviewing candidates for the next intake in September?'

Matt was relieved Alex had changed the subject. As it was his turf, he was keen to explain. 'The Faculty is holding one of its regular recruitment days when selected candidates are invited to attend for interviews. Every day of the week is used for this purpose for a number of weeks each year to ensure that the two intakes per year will have adequate students to commence the three-year nursing course. The Faculty takes these days very seriously. The recruitment procedure needs to be put into operation a few months in advance to meet the quota of students required for each academic year. Securing the established number of students is a target set by the Faculty, and will provide the finance for the healthy running of the Faculty. Undoubtedly, a lot rests on successful recruitment to ensure suitable students will be on the course for the whole three years. Dropouts will be minimal, if any. All students will complete the course and become competent qualified nurses.'

As the Recruitment Officer, Matt Hughes, was responsible for these events. 'From the receipt of applications to the offer of places on the course, I am responsible for making sure the whole process runs smoothly. All the lecturers are expected to be involved in this activity. Due to teaching commitments and clinical visits to their allocated wards, it isn't possible for many lecturers to be available to conduct the interviews. A list of dates is sent to lecturers well in advance to enter their names for the interviews. In the end, only a handful of teaching staff are available to contribute to this task.'

'You've a key post in the organisation; the right calibre of students has to be recruited and the target recruitment numbers have to be met. Otherwise, the Faculty would be in trouble, financially. I guess you need to have a very good strategy for recruiting,' Alex remarked.

Matt was humbled by his comments. 'I'm only the Recruitment Officer doing the administration work, processing the applications and scheduling the recruitment days. Lecturers do the selecting.'

'Still, it's a crucial role to perform. How long have you been doing this job?' Alex asked.

'Just about 18 months,' Matt replied.

Alex was trying to find out whether there was any connection between the recruitment officer and the anonymous letter. 'I guess the selection of these candidates is carried out objectively to ensure the recruitment of high calibre students.'

'Of course, the University policy is followed correctly.'

'So there is no possibility of any sub-standard candidate getting through?'

'No, none at all.'

'If any lecturer were to ask you for a favour, to consider an acquaintance of his possibly enrolling on the nursing course, would you do your best to accommodate his request?'

'I'm afraid not. Every potential candidate must submit a completed application form which would go through the required checking process. Applications are not treated leniently or subjectively. High standards of selection and interviewing must be adhered to by everyone.'

'Can you tell me if the Dean is involved in recruitment at any stage?'

'No he isn't. He's far too busy to take part in recruitment activities at this level.'

Alex thought that if Matt had refused to do a favour for a colleague, then he could not be involved in the extortion case. Clearly, Matt was sticking rigidly to the agreed recruitment procedures for candidates. Therefore, he would eliminate Matt from his list of suspects, for now.

Although Matt had organised the activities of the recruitment day, he said, 'John was due to be present at the interviews to provide support and advice to the interviewers, if required. There would be three or four panels to do the interviews. Each panel would consist of a Senior Lecturer/Lecturer and a clinical nurse manager.'

At that very moment, John knocked on the door, not expecting Matt to have a visitor.

He usually met up with his friend, Matt, in the recruitment office before heading to the interviewing rooms.

'Come on in, John. Have you met Alex?' Matt said.

John replied, 'Yes, I met Alex on Monday. Hello Alex, how are you?'

'I'm fine, thank you. By the way, how soon can we meet?'

'How about tomorrow morning at 10 am in my office?'

'I'll see you then.'

Matt noticed that John was a bit jumpy. 'Are you alright, John?'

'Why?'

'You looked pre-occupied, serious, worried.'

John replied, 'This business of Margaret's death is tragic. I'm devastated. Why and how did it happen to an innocent young girl? What a waste of a life. She had her whole life ahead of her and a wonderful career to look forward to. To die at such a young age is a tremendous loss. She was a remarkable student; bright, friendly, caring and helpful. We are going to miss her terribly. I hope her killer is found very soon. The police need to catch that despicable person and give him life imprisonment, but first I would like to get my hands on him.' He was expressing his disappointment, sadness and anger in a personal way.

'It's very sad indeed,' Alex said. 'No stone will be left unturned in pursuit of her killer. Everything possible will be done by everyone. It is the very least Margaret would have expected from the University where she had tried to seek a future for herself. The VC has already set the process of achieving that in motion.'

John added, 'I was her personal tutor, so I knew her very well.' He then turned towards Matt and asked, 'Anyway, how many do we have today?'

'25 candidates,' Matt replied.

'By the way, don't forget the list. Are you working from the "list" I gave you?' John asked.

'Everything is fine, no problem,' Matt replied, and winked at him.

They were discussing recruitment affairs and Alex thought it was the best time for him to take his leave. He said, 'See you later.' He went straight from the University to check on the crime scene.

Matt had been surprised at John's sharp tone of voice.

'Are you ok?'

'Why?'

'You sound angry.'

'I'm sorry for my manners. You don't deserve to be spoken to like that.'

'Has someone been upsetting you?'

'Yes.'

As it happened, word had travelled very fast from the tenth floor to the first. The argument-cum-discussion between John and the other principal lecturer had been reported to him by another lecturer.

'I heard you'd had a ding dong with someone,' Matt asked diplomatically.

'It was Jack. He thinks he knows it all,' John said angrily.

'You shouldn't get involved with him. He's not worth it.'

John sat on the chair and placed his elbow on the table. He was starting to cool down and acting normally. 'You won't believe what he said.'

'I'm listening,' Matt replied.

'He called me a creep and accused me of carrying tales to the Dean.'

'That's totally out of order. You can take a grievance order against him or send in a written complaint to the

Human Resources Department. He can't say things like that to you.'

'I know.'

'How did it all start?'

'Well I went to Jack's office and asked for a copy of the minutes from last week's course management team meeting. He went berserk; shouting at me for not attending the meeting. He had to do all the work whilst I was gallivanting. In fact, I had been to the clinical area to sort out a problem concerning a student's non-attendance.'

'Did you say that to him?'

'You know what he's like - too serious. He thought I made up the incident relating to the student.'

'That's amazing. Who does he think he is?'

'He chairs the course management team meetings, so he thinks he's in charge of everyone in the Faculty.'

'I still think you can't let him get away with it. If you do, he would feel he's got one over you. The chair of the course management team meetings needs to get on with the members not antagonise them.'

John thought about what was said for a few seconds, and then replied, 'I'll deal with it in my own way, at the right time. I need to get on with the interviews. It's nearly 2pm.'

'I've already left the candidates' file with Jane Fergusson, Senior Lecturer who is overseeing the organising of the panels to conducting the interviews. Each panel consisting of a lecturer and a clinical nurse manager are currently familiarising themselves with the candidates' files prior to interviewing.'

'That's great. Let's hope we recruit a good number of suitable candidates to complete the group for the September intake.'

Chapter 5

The next morning, Alex decided the time was right to bring both Jenny and Scott up to date with the developments at the University and his plan to deal with these. They all arrived early at 8 am. Although he knew that they were not that keen on him taking the computer theft case, simply because it didn't fall within the type of cases they had been accustomed to, yet he wanted to forge ahead.

He informed them of his encounter with Tom Evans and about Margaret's murder. They both looked horrified when they heard about a student being murdered. It was pretty much unheard of.

'That's shocking. How did it happen?' Jenny asked.

'She was murdered on Tuesday 7 June between 8pm and 10 pm in her flat. It's tragic. A young South African student nurse who was very beautiful, intelligent and caring: she didn't even get the chance to complete her course and have a career in the nursing profession.'

'That's a crying shame. So sorry to hear that,' Scott added.

'What is happening about catching the killer?' Jenny asked angrily.

'As I said, the criminal investigation team is on the case to do just that. Incidentally, I've offered to help them as much as I can,' Alex said, and informed the pair of his stance.

Both of them looked at him with amazement and remained quiet. They frowned and had their eyes fixed on Alex, as if waiting to hear more.

'I know we are very busy but I want to see the killer brought to justice. I just can't forget the face of Margaret when I opened the door for her to pass through; innocent, beautiful, worried with a wonderful smile,' Alex expressed his view strongly. 'I'll be working closely with the Police to find the killer. Both of you will be required to help as well. Together, we'll have to find the killer'

'Anytime, we'll be ready to assist,' Scott said. Jenny nodded in agreement.

Alex continued with his feedback. 'Tom Evans, the AVA technician, gave me a detailed account of his work and responsibilities. He provides the AVA services to the lecturers and students. He appeared genuinely surprised at the missing laptops, this had never happened before. There is a monitoring system to keep check on the use of resources. Whilst his deputy was away on sick leave, the two laptops went missing. It is reasonable to conclude that too much trust is placed in the lecturers to return the laptops to his department and rigid bureaucratic procedures to get the equipment repaired.'

'Did you get the feeling that Tom did it?' Scott asked.

'That's hard to tell right now. Of course he had every opportunity to remove the laptops one by one in an appropriate manner so as not to raise any suspicion. In any case, the security staff were hardly going to stop the AVA technician to check his bags. He would be the last person you would suspect of committing such a crime. Usually, the AVA technician does not steal from his own department that would be too obvious.'

'There could have been an accomplice to assist him, though,' Jenny said.

'I've thought about that. Again we have to wait and see, who that person might be, if any?' Alex explained. 'You see there is only one door, at the front of the building, through which everyone gets in and out. There is a door at the back and one on the side of the building both of which can only be used for emergency purposes. These two doors are kept locked twenty-four seven and the key is secured in a glass box which is fixed to the wall.'

'So anyone could have stolen the laptops and walked out unchallenged by the security officer?' Scott asked.

'That's right. Everything is done on trust. As you are aware, in an educational organisation, no one is expected to be involved in any criminal act. Hundreds of people enter and leave the building every day. You couldn't possibly carry out a search on all of them,' Alex stressed.

'And it has been over four weeks since the thefts occurred. The computers are long gone and probably never to be found,' Jenny said.

'Yes. The Police investigated the thefts and couldn't find the thief or how these were carried out. They decided to close the case within two weeks,' Alex said.

'And now you've been called in to re-open the case?' Jenny checked.

Alex nodded in agreement.

Since listening to the VC's account of events and his plan for the information technology scheme to be implemented, Alex had a feeling that he could solve the case.

'Here is what we should do. Scott, I want you to check with the computer shops in the surrounding areas, see if they have bought any laptops during the last few weeks.'

'Will do. I'll start straightaway,' Scott replied.

'Thank you, Scott,' Alex acknowledged.

'How about me, do you want me to do anything?' Jenny asked.

'You can find out about John Fairbanks on the internet, that would help,' Alex said.

'Why John and who is he?' Jenny asked curiously. 'John is a Principal Lecturer. I've this gut feeling that he was up to something but can't put my finger on it. I don't know enough about him, in fact very little. A bit cocky and rather tricky with shifty eyes,' Alex said.

'OK. Are you going back to the University?' Jenny asked.

'Yes I am. I'm going to meet the principal lecturer, John Fairbanks, this morning. Then at 1pm, I'm having lunch with Detective Sgt Melanie Cooper in the Red Lion pub to discuss the murder case,' Alex replied quickly.

'It's alright for some. Is she pretty?' Jenny was being nosy.

'Since you ask, she is actually but very professional too so don't get any ideas,' Alex said with a smile.

'That's why you're looking your very best today,' Jenny observed.

'I dress in the same manner every day. Suit and tie. You know very well that I'm going to the University to carry on with the investigations. I never mix business with pleasure,' Alex explained. 'See you both later.'

***

After reporting back to his team in the early part of the morning, he was a bit concerned about the amount of time it would take to get to the University as he had an important meeting with John to discuss the two stolen laptops.

Once he arrived at the University, Alex left his briefcase in his office and went straight to meet John. He was on time for their meeting. John was at his desk working whilst waiting for Alex to arrive. John offered Alex a chair. 'Please have a seat and make yourself comfortable.'

'Thank you,' Alex replied, and sat directly facing John to maintain eye contact.

'What do you want to ask me?' John enquired.

'First of all, can I say how sorry I am about Margaret's death.'

'Thanks. I can't believe it at all.'

'The whole place must be badly affected by this loss, especially Margaret's friends.'

'Of course. Everyone seems to be in a daze and wondering how this could have happened to their friend and peer.'

'I can understand that.'

'I hope the Police find the killer very soon. If only I could get my hands on whoever did that to Margaret.'

'Let's hope they find the killer.'

'Have the Police asked around thoroughly in order to get this guy?'

'I believe they have already started interviewing the residents, asking the neighbours if they had heard any noise, seen anyone entering or leaving the residence. That would help their enquiry.'

'And have they got anywhere yet?'

'Not to my knowledge.'

'Has anyone been interviewed at the University? What about Jack?' John raised his voice.

'Why Jack in particular?'

John was slightly taken aback by Alex's remark.

'Simply because he read the riot act to Margaret last week and apparently threatened her position on the course because she didn't do well in her assignment, and I suspect a few people must have heard their exchange.'

'That doesn't mean Jack should be a suspect. We don't know what was said exactly. I'm sure these incidents are common occurrences in this place. Certainly, I agree with you that proper enquiries should be carried out in the University as well. Anything that would assist our search to find the killer should be fully explored,' Alex said, and was ready to explain and reassure him. 'I fully understand how you are feeling at the moment; we all have to be patient and thorough in our attempt to solve Margaret's murder. I'll be seeing Margaret's classmates tomorrow morning to see if they can help in any way.'

Alex felt he needed to let John know that he had agreed to assist the Police with their investigation into Margaret's death.

'The VC wanted to make use of my services as I'll be on site investigating the computer theft case. Sgt Cooper and her team are totally responsible for Margaret's murder case. It was agreed that I should work closely with the Police in the pursuit of Margaret's killer,' Alex pointed out.

'Ah, that's reassuring to know,' John said.

Surprisingly, John looked a bit unsettled. His mannerism changed rather quickly from raising his voice and gesticulating to expressing his anger in a quieter tone, he looked pensive and was speaking rather slowly. Then he changed the subject.

'OK. What is it you want to ask me? I don't really have a lot of time to spare. I'm sure you'll understand.'

'I promise I won't take too much of your valuable time. Well, it's to do with the stolen laptops really. I understand one of the laptops was stolen from your office. If you could tell me what you know about them.'

'OK. I can only repeat what I told the police a few weeks ago. For practical reasons, I had to use the laptop for my teaching. On a few occasions, I have taken one laptop home after informing Tom and then returned it the following morning. On this occasion, I was going to return the borrowed laptop to Tom in the morning but I was teaching at 9 am. When I came back to my office at coffee time, I noticed the laptop had gone and I informed Tom immediately. How we lost the two laptops, I have no idea.'

'Was it the second laptop to go missing?'

'That's right. The first one disappeared from Jack's office or so he claimed!'

Then he suggested, 'Maybe you should ask Jack, who is very keen on information technology and forever fiddling with computers.'

'Thank you for that. Is there anything else you could tell me that would help my investigation?'

'Apparently, the Police carried out a thorough investigation and could not find the laptops or the thief. I really don't understand why the VC has asked you to look into this again.' John had an intriguing look on his face

'Well, the VC wants to get to the bottom of it and he's very worried about the students' personal data on these laptops,' Alex said with an assured and confident voice.

That seemed to unsettle John a bit. His eyes began to wander and he kept looking somewhere else whilst talking to Alex.

He noticed John was in his early forties, 5ft 10, blonde, smartly dressed, articulate and intelligent and kept running his fingers through his hair - a sign of nervousness, maybe.

'I've nothing more to add,' John said.

He was anxious to tell Alex about the big row he was having with Jack last Monday.

'Incidentally, the other day when you and the VC walked into Jack's office and we were arguing with each other, I do apologise for our shouting match.'

'Think nothing of it, that sort of thing sometimes happens between colleagues.'

John knew that Alex would be talking to Jack as well in due course and wanted to get his side of the story in first. 'The reason I was angry with Jack that day was because of his attitude towards me, he has always been derogatory. He accused me of carrying tales to the Dean, which is without foundation. No evidence from him has been produced to substantiate his accusations. Just because he is the chairman of the course management team meetings, he thinks he's superior and knows it all. He is very friendly with and too lenient towards the foreign students and tends to ignore their shortcomings. He can't see that. Everyone thinks Jack is weak and struggling to do his job well.'

Alex had quickly figured out the game John was playing and had no intention of supporting his stance. He said, 'Oh, right. I hope you'll settle your differences soon and I'm sure the institution would benefit from both your contributions.'

Alex remembered John was in a hurry and, not to get involved in the internal personnel affairs, he swiftly changed the subject and brought his enquiry with him to a close. 'Thank you for your time, John. I better go now. We'll probably bump into each other again. Please don't forget I would appreciate any help you can give me on both the computer theft case and Margaret's death.'

'I would be glad to assist anytime,' John said with a smile. Then Alex left.

A relatively productive interview for Alex as John was very experienced and smart, only willing to give little away. Judging by John's interactions, it seemed as if John was conducting the interview and not Alex. That led Alex to form the opinion that John could have enlarged a bit more on the computer theft case which he had tried to avoid but was keen to put the blame on Jack, not directly though. It was evidently clear that John disliked Jack, not only on a professional level but also on a personal one. One thing was in John's favour; he was still in a state of shock regarding Margaret's death which was understandable.

Chapter 6

Alex rushed to the Red Lion. As the pub was only a short walk from the University, Alex had decided to leg it. The weather on that June afternoon was dry and warm which spurred Alex to get into his stride rather quickly. There was an additional motivation for his desire to get to his destination; her name was Melanie and she was a real beauty.

It was the first time in his new career that Alex was meeting with a Detective Sergeant to discuss the circumstances surrounding a murder case. He was apprehensive but somewhat confident to play his part as an investigator. As it was his first venture into a murder case, the truth was that he had to learn as much as possible from his guest.

True to form, Alex arrived bang on time. He had never been late for an appointment and prided himself in keeping to the time agreed. Whilst approaching the bar he spotted the Sergeant, sitting at a table in the corner at the back of this very grand pub. She recognised him and caught his eye. She signalled to him, with a side nod of the head, to join her. He was already on his way.

'Hello Detective Sgt Cooper, nice to see you again. Have you been waiting long?' Alex asked with a wide smile and offered his hand which was met by the warm hand of his guest.

'Nice to see you too. I've just arrived myself. Please drop the Detective Sgt lark, just called me Melanie,' she replied.

Alex sat opposite her. 'That's fine and please call me Alex. Can I get you a drink?'

'No thanks, I'm fine for the moment.'

She already had a large glass filled with a diet coke, ice and a slice of lemon. Alex ordered a diet coke with ice as well. They smiled at each other shyly, as if they were on a date. She was dressed in her navy blue trouser suit and pale blue shirt, looking beautiful as Alex expected her to be.

'I hear from the Officer that you went to the crime scene yesterday.'

'Yes I did. Thank you for arranging the visit.'

'Did you notice anything untoward?'

'Oh no. I went into the flat of the victim, walked around and had a good look. As expected all the evidence has been taken away.'

'At least you've seen the crime scene and now it is easy for you to make the connection.'

Alex decided to change the focus of their conversation. 'That's right. Shall we order our lunch?'

'Of course. We don't have a lot of time.'

The atmosphere in the pub was nice and pleasant. It was a bit noisy and half full. Most people were having lunch with their drinks. Both Melanie and Alex were about to do the same.

Both agreed on a ham sandwich.

The meeting was partly to get to know each other as they were going to work together and to exchange notes on the murder case. Melanie started.

'I met with Margaret's uncle yesterday and gave him the sad news. He was devastated. He mumbled to himself and kept calling her name. He could not believe that his beautiful niece was not here anymore. I reassured him that we would do everything we could to catch her killer. This morning I was with him when he identified the body. He will be informing Margaret's parents back in South Africa immediately, and once the body is released, he will organise the funeral.'

'It couldn't have been easy for you to do that,' Alex said sympathetically.

'Thank you. It's part of the job and has to be done. It is tough. By the way, after the autopsy tomorrow, I'll probably get more information from the Coroner,' Melanie replied.

'At least contact has been made with Margaret's family, and steps will be taken to have her funeral as soon as the post-mortem is carried out and the cause of death is confirmed. I don't have anything new to share with you. I'll be seeing Margaret's classmates tomorrow morning at 9 am. Maybe someone will come forward with helpful information,' Alex said.

'Do you want me to come with you to see the students?'

'Yes, if you could spare the time.'

'I'll see you in the reception area of the University building at 8.45 am then.'

'Good. That's settled. If I can change the subject, why did you become a policewoman? It is rather surprising, given that you are so confident, very intelligent with excellent communication and interpersonal skills. You were superb the other day when you briefed us about Margaret's death and displayed sensitivity, sympathy and empathy of the highest order. We were all very impressed by you.' Alex was in his element and wanted to know the real Melanie.

'Thank you. That was quite a speech. I am impressed. I studied Law at Oxford, your old stomping ground. After graduation, I had to decide between joining the police force or studying at the College of Law to become a lawyer. The catching of criminals and bringing them to justice appealed to me more. So here I am. Naturally, there is an element of danger in my job and this comes with the territory. So far, I have enjoyed the work. If, in the future, I get tired of police work and do not enjoy it as much, then I'll re-evaluate my position. Maybe, I'll choose to join the other side of law and become a lawyer. I do see myself staying in my chosen field.'

'That's very interesting and a pragmatic way to look at one's life. In my opinion, for what it's worth, you're doing a great job as a Detective Sergeant and long may it continue. I'm sure your Inspector would vouch for this. Your current profession can't afford to lose you.'

'I don't know about that. I'm sure the profession will manage perfectly well without me.'

Melanie was feeling rather uncomfortable by Alex's compliments. She looked at Alex, shook her head from side to side, wide-eyed and with a faint smile.

'My honest opinion.'

'Anyway, that's enough about me, what about you?'

'What do you want to know about me?'

'Your career, I guess.'

'Not much to tell, really. I get the impression you already know a lot about me.'

Quick as a flash, Melanie said, 'Not a great deal.'

They finished their lunch and had another diet coke each whilst chatting away.

'OK. I'll tell you what I know about you, to dispel your curiosity. You went to Oxford and the College of Law.

You became a lawyer first, then decided to open an investigative agency. Now we are both involved in the same ventures, although from different perspectives.'

Melanie explained eloquently and gave Alex something to think about.

'That's fair enough. You're correct. When I left Oxford, I went to the College of Law and subsequently joined a law firm, qualified as a solicitor and practiced for two years, very interesting work indeed. Had to put in long hours almost every day. I came across an elegant and wealthy client who needed to get some information about her husband's personal activities and asked me if I could help. She told me that I would make a large amount of money easily in the process. I had to decline because the firm didn't provide that type of service. She was surprised to learn that the firm didn't have a facility for these lucrative ventures. She went on to say that wealthy people and corporate organisations were ready to pay very handsomely for such investigative services. She suggested that I should consider a change of career and would double my salary with less hours of work. It, kind of, appealed to me. I always wanted to own a business enterprise and work for myself.'

'That's quite a narrative. I must say,' Melanie said, and was very impressed.

'It was a hard decision to take; stay at the firm or be adventurous and open an agency to cater for this challenging, exciting and seemingly lucrative market. After some sleepless nights and careful consideration, I decided to embark on my new career. And here I am.'

Alex gave an open and honest account of the crucial decision he had to take.

'My family, friends, colleagues and senior people at the firm tried to persuade me not to go ahead with it. I thought it was the right time to branch out. I was young, motivated and ambitious and if I did not succeed, I could always go back to practising law. My parents are very annoyed about my decision.'

'I must say, I would have found it very hard to give up the work and lifestyle of a lawyer in the city to settle for owning and running an investigative agency. You're certainly a brave person. I wish you luck,' Melanie said.

'You see in a law firm, a lawyer only earns a salary which is not a great deal. The partners benefit immensely from the vast amount of money generated by the long hours of work put in by lawyers like me.'

'So you're after making loads of money?'

'Nothing like that. By setting up a business, of course I hope to make money. That wasn't the only motivating factor. The opportunity of being independent and choosing what type of work to take on, developing strategies on how to solve problems and putting into practice skills that I have acquired. That's what drives me.'

Having listened attentively to Alex's account of part of his life, Melanie was fascinated by his charm, honesty, easy going manner and self-assurance. She had to pinch herself to get back to the real world, more importantly she was on duty and had to remind herself that she already had a boyfriend. She realised they had been talking for a while and had to get back to work.

'Well, I wish you all the best,' Melanie said. 'See you in the morning.'

'Yes, of course,' Alex replied. They got up, headed to the door, said their goodbyes and then left the pub. Alex walked back to the University to pick up his briefcase and Melanie drove back to the Police station.

***

Jack Dempsey, Principal Lecturer, had heard through the grapevine that Alex had been interviewing John that morning. Given his dislike and contempt for John, and because of his lack of respect for him, Jack became even more keen to have a meeting of his own with Alex. From his recollection of past incidences, John would have painted a really black picture of him. Jack was under no illusion that John disliked him and would engage in any scheme to undermine him. He was relieved to come across Alex in the reception area and stopped him. 'Hello Alex. How are you?' Jack asked.

'I'm fine, thank you,' Alex replied.

He noticed Jack was looking at him and waiting to say something but could not bring himself up, to do so. He saved Jack the embarrassment.

'If you are free, Jack, I would like to have a chat with you about the computer thefts.'

'Sure we can go to your office.'

They took the lift to the eleventh floor.

'First of all, Jack, I would like to offer my condolences to you regarding Margaret's death, a tragic event.'

'Thank you. It's very sad. Everyone is affected by her death. Everybody appears lost at the moment.'

'Natural reaction, I suppose,' Alex said, and reassured him. 'Incidentally, just to let you know, I am helping the police to investigate Margaret's death as well.'

'I'm pleased to learn that. Your involvement in the investigation of the murder case would be most welcome.'

'I hope you don't mind me asking about the incident when you raised your voice with Margaret, last week.'

'I can explain that. I saw her about her module assignment which she had failed for the second time. I run the module. I impressed on her that failure on her third attempt would result in her being thrown off the course. She needed to pull her finger out and pass the assignment or else. That's all I said to her.'

'Thank you,' Alex said with his eyes fixed on Jack.

'Am I a suspect?'

Alex put him at ease. 'Not really. We have to explore every possible avenue. How do you get on with students and colleagues?'

'I get on well with most of them but I think John is beyond the pale. I tend to make the foreign students feel more welcome and help them, as much as I can, to settle into their new environment.'

'Assisting these students to settle on the course is very noble of you.'

'What would you like to ask me about the computer thefts?'

'Basically, what has been your involvement with the two stolen laptops?'

'I'm not aware how the laptops were stolen but I have used one as part of my teaching aids. Whenever I had the need to take a laptop home to prepare my lessons, I've done so with the permission of Tom. I've also returned the laptop the following morning. You could check it with him. Unfortunately on this particular day, I left a borrowed laptop on my desk with the intention of returning it to Tom at coffee time. Following a team meeting, when I got back to my office just after 10 am, I noticed the laptop was not there and I informed Tom straightaway.'

'That was the first laptop that went missing.'

'Yes it was the first one and it is very worrying that someone could get hold of the students' personal data stored on these laptops.'

'Absolutely correct. The sooner the laptops are found the better,' Alex concurred, and pressed him further. 'Can you tell me more about these computers and their use?'

'It's no secret that I am very keen on information technology and as chair of the course management team, have spent a fair amount of time persuading my colleagues to use it on the nursing courses. I know the VC would like to implement it on a wider scale in the University. That's progress. However, a few influential members of staff are against its use.'

'I'm rather surprised at lecturers not willing to embrace IT.'

'Among the principal lecturers, John is not keen but then again he is only interested in himself. He is arrogant and ignorant in equal measure. By the way, I do apologise for my behaviour when the VC and your good self popped into my office and caught John and me arguing.'

'Think nothing of it. Things like that happen between colleagues.'

'My major issue with John is that he doesn't care much about maintaining high standards which a professional nursing course requires. With the assistance of Matt Hughes, Recruitment Officer, John has been recruiting average students onto the course, in some cases, even below average students as well. According to the VC and the Dean, John was doing a great job with recruitment. It puts bums on seats. If students failed their assignments for the third time, he would find excuses to give them an extension to keep them on the course. The longer these students stay on the course, the VC and the Dean are delighted because John's action will save the Faculty thousands of pounds each year. No wonder they are fond of him. The Faculty is paid several thousand pounds a year by the NHS Trusts for each student on the course. Therefore, the more students remain on the course ensures the Faculty would be guaranteed an agreed sum annually. As a principal lecturer, John should attend all or most of the course management team meetings, but he rarely does. That's why we were shouting at each other in my office.'

Jack expressed himself with a certain degree of disapproval about the lowering of standards in the Faculty.

'Right. I can see your concerns clearly.'

'We are preparing these students to become qualified nurses so that they can give the highest standard of care to patients, which they so richly deserve. By maintaining a high standard of teaching, learning and assessment throughout the course, we can ensure that we produce competent trained nurses for the future. That's the goal of the Faculty of Health Studies which most of my colleagues and I work very hard to achieve.'

'I wonder if I could ask you about the recruitment of students. You seem unhappy about the way it is carried out.'

'Yes, go ahead.'

'Do you think that someone is tinkering with the selection process and hence average or substandard students are recruited?'

'Who knows? You'll have to ask John about that as he is more involved in the process. I only participate in the interviewing of candidates. Everyone is expected to implement the procedure for recruitment according to the Faculty recruitment policy.'

'Thank you.'

Jack stood up, signalling that he was ready to leave which suited Alex as well because he wanted to go home as he was meeting his girlfriend that evening. Alex also stood up.

'It's been very nice talking to you, Jack. Thank you for your time and enlightening me regarding what you and your colleagues are trying to achieve. If you come across anything that would assist me with my investigation into the computer theft case and Margaret's murder case, please do let me know.'

'Will do. See you around,' Jack replied on his way out.

Alex reflected on his encounter with Jack and concluded that it was productive and informative. In many respects, Jack came across as a caring, proud professional.

He set out to give Alex a comprehensive picture of what was supposed to happen and what actually had taken place. Much to his dissatisfaction and disapproval of the compromising of standards, he found himself powerless to do anything about it.

Persuading the Dean and the VC to change their tactics with both recruitment and the creative method of keeping failed students on the course would be a step too far for Jack. These two senior people were interested in ensuring that the Faculty operated satisfactorily and there were adequate funds to maintain all educational and managerial activities.

Consequently, the full complement of students should be recruited and retained, which would in turn generate funds to meet the requirements of the Faculty. Both were pursuing different routes to achieve the same aim, to keep the Faculty thriving.

Following Jack's passionate explanation of how to do things properly, Alex was able to have an insight into some functions of the Faculty. He had no doubt that Jack was an educationalist of high principles, one who perhaps did not like John but had the interest of the students at heart. It would appear that Jack was not connected with the anonymous letter because he came across as a decent guy.

Chapter 7

Bright and early, Alex went straight from his flat to his adopted office at the University. At 8.45, he went downstairs to meet Melanie in the reception area. They were very pleased to see each other; both were grinning and shook hands.

Alex was in his navy blue suit, pale blue shirt and a purple coloured tie with small faint black dots. Melanie wasn't to be outdone in the outfit department, she wore a light grey jacket and skirt and a pink blouse. She looked radiant with her shoulder length blonde hair.

'Good to see you again, Melanie,' Alex said in admiration. So he should. The glamorous Sergeant provided him with a mouth-watering sight to behold, looking very beautiful.

'Nice to see you too, Alex,' Melanie replied with her wide eyes focused on his, and her head slightly bent displaying a certain degree of shyness in a young girl.

'Shall we make our way to meet the students in classroom A,' Alex suggested.

'By all means, please lead on and I'll follow you,' Melanie concurred quickly.

Classroom A was on the fifth floor. They used the lift which was full of students, heading to Classroom A as well. There were twenty-nine students in total in the classroom.

Only five male student nurses, the rest were female. The age possibly ranged from eighteen to thirty. There was a pensive and serious look on the students' faces. It was a natural reaction as they had been affected by their loss. It was a very difficult time for them. At 9 am, Karen Fletcher, Lecturer, introduced both Detective Sgt Cooper and Alex to the students and explained the purpose of their visit.

Both guests said, 'Thank you' to Karen, then moved forward and said, 'Good morning' practically together and the students responded warmly. 'Good morning.'

Alex took the floor first as he had requested to see the students. His voice was soft and relatively sad, demonstrating concern, and his facial expression was serious. He showed both sympathy and empathy in his address to the students.

'First of all, let me convey our condolences to you all for losing your classmate and friend in such tragic circumstances. It must be very hard for you to come to terms with Margaret's death and also understand the reason for it. Detective Sgt Cooper is leading the investigation. As I'm here looking into the computer thefts as a Private Investigator, which no doubt you have heard of, I've offered to assist Detective Sgt Cooper and her team to find Margaret's killer.'

The atmosphere in the classroom was sombre. The students looked sad and somewhat lost, as if a blanket of intense grief had spread over them. But they were alert and wanting to hear of any possible solution to the pain that they were going through. All of them sat up in their chairs with elbows leaning on their desks and eyes fixed on the speakers, ready to receive clarification, explanation and reassurance.

Alex paused for a couple of seconds to give the students time to digest his starting brief and observed they were very attentive and keen to listen to him. Detective Sgt Cooper decided to chip in.

'Hello, I fully endorse what Alex has just said, my condolences to you all, as well. I would like to inform you that the Coroner is currently conducting the autopsy. Following that, Margaret's body will be released and then her funeral can take place. I would like to reassure you that we are doing everything possible to find the killer. My team is working continuously in that pursuit. I promise you we'll leave no stone unturned in our endeavour. If any of you has any information that will help us, please do not hesitate to come forward and let us know. Alex is on site most of the time, you can contact him easily. Again, I'm very sorry about your loss.'

Detective Sgt Cooper was to the point, as expected from a Policewoman. But she was sympathetic, sensitive and caring which the students appeared to appreciate.

Alex took over and said, 'My office is on the eleventh floor. Any of you who wish to talk to me regarding Margaret's death, you'll be very welcome and I'll see you at your convenience. It is very important to have as much detailed information as possible which may be relevant to the case. So please, do not hesitate to come forward and discuss anything with me in confidence, especially the way Margaret has led her life, her interests, friends and contacts. We need your help to solve Margaret's murder and find her killer. Thank you for your time and for listening to us.'

Suddenly, one of the students stood up and said in a crackling voice. 'You will find the person who killed our dear friend, Margaret, won't you?' She was blonde, slim and tall.

'We promise you we will do exactly that,' Alex reassured her.

Both Alex and Detective Sgt Cooper were conscious not to take any more of the students' valuable time from their lesson. They thanked Karen who had stayed throughout their talk to the students and left the classroom together.

Talking to a group of bereaved students was no easy task for either of them. They handled the situation very well and even gained the respect and appreciation of these students. For their part, the students appeared as if they knew now that someone was taking the whole matter seriously. Detective Sgt Cooper had plenty of experience in dealing with relatives and friends in such cases, but it was the first time she had gone to talk to a group of student nurses about their murdered friend. As for Alex, it was a brand new experience altogether. Even when practising as a lawyer, he hadn't performed a duty of this magnitude and sadness.

Melanie praised Alex for his efforts.

'You did well there, Alex. The students appeared to be taking in every word you said. That's a very good sign. Positive. And you looked like a natural performer.'

'That's very kind and generous of you. I only mentioned what has to be said. You were very good and I could see the students were hanging on to every word you said.'

'Thank you.'

'What do you think of the students' reaction to us?'

'I think they are suffering, some more than others.'

Maybe because of her experience in dealing with such cases, she was able to spot that particular aspect a bit more quickly than Alex.

'I agree. I also thought they were very appreciative of our efforts to meet and sympathise with them, as we expressed our determination to find the killer and seek their help.'

'That's absolutely right.'

They were both moved by the students' calm, accepting and hopeful manner under the circumstances. It was clear that both were determined to get the job done and were prepared to give their very best to achieve it. There was a lot of professional respect between them. They began to feel comfortable in each other's company which would contribute to establishing an effective working relationship. But, they also had to get back to their individual agenda for the day.

Melanie said, 'It was a productive meeting. Thank you for inviting me to join you in your talk to the students. It was a brilliant idea. I'll have to get back to the department. Keep in touch.'

'Thank you for coming with me to the classroom. You gave me tremendous help and support. I have to see some more people here. See you soon,' Alex replied.

***

The investigation into the computer theft case was gathering momentum. Alex was fully engrossed in it and was driving it with vigour. His next move was to meet up with a large group of lecturers to discuss their involvement in the use of laptops. The meeting was held in a classroom and approximately forty teaching staff including senior lecturers and lecturers attended.

'Good morning to you all. Thank you for making the effort to meet with me. I wish to express my condolences to you on the death of Margaret; a tragic and unnecessary death,' Alex said in a humble voice. The lecturers were taken by Alex's remark and acknowledged his sentiment by nodding.

'I've agreed to assist the Police with their investigation into Margaret's murder. If you have any piece of information in connection with her murder, please contact me immediately. I'm currently using an office on the eleventh floor. Any help will be greatly appreciated,' Alex said, and continued. 'Now I would like to move on to another pressing matter, the two stolen laptops. Could you tell me about the policy for using this equipment?'

One of the senior lecturers was quick to let Alex know of her amazement at his appointment in the first instance.

'I'm very surprised that the VC has decided to bring you in to investigate further the computer thefts. Not that I'm complaining,' Jane said. She expressed her opinion strongly.

'You are?' Alex asked politely.

'Jane Fergusson, Senior lecturer,' Jane replied.

'Thank you, Jane. Well, I'm here to find the laptops or the person who stole them.' He deliberately steered away from discussing the VC's decision.

'I understand lecturers made use of the equipment for their teaching sessions in the classroom where the computers are secured to the desk under lock and key. The procedure of using the laptop was fully adhered to. These laptops should not be removed from the AVA department and the premises without the permission of the AVA technician.'

Jane articulated her strong feelings about the responsibility of her colleagues clearly. 'I believe I can safely say that every lecturer is mindful of the policy on how to use the laptops. We recognise these laptops are a valuable tool for our teaching and treat them with a great deal of care.'

'Thank you. I also believe you do just that,' Alex said, and nodded in agreement with her statement. 'In addition to the classrooms, where else are the laptops used?'

'Well, occasionally, the lecturers take the laptops with them to the clinical areas to teach student nurses and these are returned to the AVA department on the same day or the following day at the latest,' Jane explained, and continued. 'We are expected to enter the date, time, name of equipment and sign the equipment borrowing book before removing the equipment from the AVA department and then follow the same procedure on its return. Since the thefts, before removing a laptop from the building, the lecturer must obtain a signed authorisation note from the AVA department to be shown to the security officer. The AVA technician monitors these activities very closely.'

'So nobody can remove any equipment or teaching aids from the AVA department without the permission of Tom Evans.' Alex wanted to make sure he got the correct facts.

'Absolutely,' Jane replied emphatically.

'Have any of you ever seen any laptop lying loose in an empty classroom?'

Alex was going through a list of questions and hoped to obtain the relevant information that he was seeking.

'No,' another senior lecturer said. She decided to chip in and support Jane. 'By the way, I'm Ann Maynard, Senior Lecturer.'

'Thank you, Ann,' Alex said politely and decided to persist with his line of questioning.

'Have you, at any time, noticed anyone leaving the building with a laptop in his/her hand?'

All were shaking their heads from side to side, indicating that they had not. Alex was aware that lecturers or indeed any other member of staff could not be expected to check on everyone leaving the building. In any case, what would they be looking for?

'As no theft has occurred in the Faculty before, there was no need to suspect anyone at any time. Since the thefts had taken place, undoubtedly we've all become more vigilant,' Ann commented.

'No one would be able to tell if someone was hiding a laptop in a bag whilst walking out of the building, especially if in a group of people,' Jane added.

'I guess the security officer would be able to check,' Alex asked.

'I suppose so. Given that only one security officer is on duty most of the time, it's very difficult to conduct a thorough check on everyone who leaves the building. Also a large volume of students are going home at the same time,' Ann replied, and shed more light on the complex challenge of implementing the policy of stop and search.

Alex was aware of these potential problems but it was refreshing to hear the lecturers were on the same wavelength as him. The frankness and willingness with which the lecturers conducted themselves left Alex in no doubt that they treated the laptops seriously because they were dependent on these to perform their job of teaching. It appeared they fully understood the importance of this equipment as part of the delivery of their teaching sessions. At least, the views and passion, which he just heard expressed by the lecturers meant the laptop thief would probably come from elsewhere.

'May I thank you very much for your time and contribution. You've been very helpful. If you do remember anything at all, that you believe I could use in my investigations, you know how to get in touch with me,' Alex said. The meeting ended, Alex left the room for his next appointment.

Chapter 8

Jenny had arranged an appointment for Alex to meet the Dean of the Faculty that morning.

In addition to getting the Dean's view on the computer thefts, Alex expected to explore the issue regarding the letter as much as possible. In a subtle way, he had to find out whether the Dean was involved.

When Alex arrived at the Dean's office, he had to sit and wait in the Dean's Personal Assistant, Vicky's office, as the Dean's meeting with Jack had overrun. 'Can I get you a cup of coffee while you are waiting, Mr DuPont?' Vicky asked politely.

'No thank you, I'm fine,' Alex replied.

Again he had to listen to an angry exchange between two senior people. It would appear that Jack had raised the issue of the lowering of standards with regard to dealing with stragglers in the Faculty. The Dean was adamant in his reply which Alex heard clearly, 'Jack, for the umpteenth time, nobody is doing anything to compromise the standards, whether in recruitment, retaining, teaching, assessing or supporting of student nurses. As far as I'm concerned, all my staff are giving their very best to maintain the standards. I can assure you everything is fine.'

Jack was no pushover and he gave as much as he got. 'I'm afraid I don't share your optimism. Since you aren't prepared to look into this situation at all, I don't think there is any point in continuing with this conversation, but I do expect you to make a note of my complaint.'

Alex was shuffling through his papers, keeping his ears open on the conversation next door.

The door was slightly ajar. Luckily, Vicky had just stepped out of the office. Alex couldn't see the Dean and Jack, but heard every word they said. Alex wondered whether the Dean had deliberately left the door in that position so that he could hear everything - a ploy perhaps.

The Dean replied, 'Well, I fully understand your concern, but your complaint is baseless. There is no credible evidence to support it.' Then, in a conciliatory tone, he added, 'You worry too much Jack. Relax, we're all doing our best to meet the needs of the students.'

Jack left. Vicky returned and noticed Alex was still waiting to see the Dean. After a few seconds, she knocked on the Dean's door that was already open and asked Alex to go through to the Dean's office. The Dean stood up and said, 'Nice to see you again, Alex. Sorry to keep you waiting.'

They shook hands and sat down. The Dean was dressed in a black suit, white shirt and red tie.

'No problem, David. I've just arrived anyway.'

'What can I do for you?'

'First of all, let me say, how sad I am about the tragic incident of Margaret's death.'

'Thank you. As a father of two young adults, my heart goes out to her parents. I understand you are helping the Police to find the killer.'

'I am indeed. '

'That's good. Are we any closer to catching the killer?'

'Not really.'

Alex cleared his throat and said, 'I wonder if I can ask you about the two stolen laptops.'

'Yes, of course.'

Alex informed him that he had already met with Tom Evans, the two Principal Lecturers and a group of lecturers regarding the subject. That was to put the Dean in the loop and to avoid any embarrassment in his reply with regard to the stolen laptops.

'You've been very busy, Alex.'

'The VC wants this matter resolved quickly.'

It was the second time that the Dean had met Alex since his appointment. He did not think highly of the VC's decision to re-open the case and, least of all, to employ a Private Investigator who hardly had any experience in criminal cases. He was fully aware that Alex had been a successful lawyer and had been running a lucrative investigative agency. Nevertheless, he thought Alex lacked the right experience for the job.

'It's a shameful state of affairs, these computer thefts The Police with all their know-how couldn't solve this case. I've been quite puzzled as to how your good self, on your own, can find the laptops and the thief.'

The Dean expressed his concern very poignantly.

Fortunately, Alex wasn't a member of his staff and so chose to ignore the unkind dig at his appointment. He did not want to play the Dean's game by getting involved in either defending or promoting himself. He was interested in finding out what had happened and how to deal with it. Alex recognised the Dean was a very experienced senior academic, shrewd and astute in dealing with people.

'Is there anything you could tell me about the two stolen laptops?' Alex got to the point.

'Well, you probably heard it all before you got here. However, when the second laptop went missing, we had no choice, especially the issue as regard to the sensitive data about the students on these laptops, but to call in the Police. They investigated for a fortnight and decided to close the case on the grounds of insufficient evidence claiming anyone could have stolen the laptops. It would be difficult, if not impossible, to find the thief. The actual value of the laptops didn't warrant any further use of their resources. That has led me to believe that your chances of succeeding where the Police have failed, is not very good. We'll co-operate with you. To be honest, I'm not hopeful about your investigation,' the Dean said with a degree of arrogance.

'I wonder why you feel like that. After all, I've only just started.'

Alex felt the need to counter the Dean's position.

'No offence intended. It's logical that one person is unlikely to succeed where many could not.'

'None taken. Well, I understand the Police had too much on their plate at the time. Staff shortages and pressure of work resulted in a rather short and sharp investigation. Important evidence could easily have been overlooked. Not intentionally, of course. I do have the time to spare and would like to be thorough in finding the thief and the laptops.'

'I understand your Agency has been in operation for over a year. How much experience do you have in dealing with criminal cases?'

Alex did not like that line of questioning. He felt the Dean was challenging his integrity and professionalism.

'You're correct in that the Agency was established just over a year ago. It has been a highly successful time for us and we have covered a whole range of investigative work. As for my experience in criminal cases, it really depends on how one defines criminal cases. Crime is committed on various scales in all sorts of shapes and sizes. During my training as a solicitor in a very large city firm, I had a six-month seat in the criminal department and found the experience invaluable; it has equipped me well to cope with the current situation.'

Alex spoke like a lawyer with authority, confidence and clarity. His eyes were fixed on the Dean and didn't even blink during his discourse. He had the opportunity to put the Dean in his place and did so very well, like throwing the dart to score a bullseye. His reply took the Dean by surprise because he didn't expect Alex to be so sharp and to the point.

'I hope you'll understand that I was being merely curious about your background and experience to solve the two cases, nothing personal.'

'I don't mind discussing matters regarding my suitability to do the job, but that has already been addressed by the VC when he appointed me. I'm more interested in getting the computer thefts resolved quickly and helping the Police to find Margaret's killer.'

Alex decided to press home the upper hand he'd seemingly established with the Dean.

'I believe we're all keen to do just that,' the Dean said with a subdued grin.

'I was hoping to work closely with you on this matter as you're in charge of the Faculty.'

'As I said, I'll be only too happy to help you, anytime.'

The Dean was rather conciliatory in his expression.

Alex was feeling uncomfortable and getting somewhat angry with the Dean's overall attitude. He needed to ask the Dean questions because he was the head of the Faculty and was expected to know almost everything that happened on his patch. Furthermore, he thought it was courteous to speak to the Dean as his Faculty was being investigated. Despite the Dean's condescending behaviour towards him, Alex decided to continue. 'Thank you. Anything else I need to know?'

It was quite apparent that the Dean couldn't get control over Alex. He wasn't used to being treated like that, especially by a young man. Alex kept to his agenda in a professional manner and refused to get personal.

'Not really. I'm sure you have been told about the procedure for the use of laptops in the Faculty.'

'Oh, yes. I'm aware of the procedure. Well, thank you again for your time. We'll catch up with each other later.'

Then, Alex decided to use the opportunity to address his other investigation regarding the letter as he believed there could be a link between the anonymous letter and Margaret's death.

'Can I ask you about the deceased student?' Alex said.

'Yes, go ahead,' the Dean replied.

'Did you know her?'

'No. Not personally. I don't deal with students directly. My staff take care of that sort of thing.'

'Have you ever met her, at all?'

'I don't think so.'

The Dean appeared as if he was telling the truth about not knowing Margaret. After all, it was unlikely for the Dean to be involved in operational matters and dealing with individual students.

'Thank you. Well, I have to go now.'

'Good. See you.'

Alex stood up and left.

***

Whilst still recovering from his conversation with the Dean, Alex went to his office and phoned Jenny. 'Hi there. Any news about the laptops?'

'Scott has come across a particular shop which has recently bought a laptop. It probably has nothing to do with your case. People often sell laptops for a variety of reasons,' Jenny replied.

'Thanks. I'll talk to Scott later.'

'How did your chat with the University people go?'

'As far as the students and the lecturers go, it went alright. The one with the students was rather difficult as they had just lost their friend, Margaret. I believe Sgt Cooper and I handled that sensitively. The second one, with the lecturers, was productive. I saw them on my own. I got to learn how the lecturers implement the procedure for using the laptops.'

'I didn't know that woman was going to be with you.' Jenny was not holding back.

'By the way, her name is Melanie Cooper and she's very nice and helpful.'

'I bet she is. You watch her. You can't trust the Police.'

'Don't get paranoid now. I have to work with her.'

'What about your chat with the Dean?'

'It was a weird one.'

'Why?'

'The Dean was full of himself and condescending in his remarks towards me. He gave me the impression that he wasn't pleased that the computer theft case had been re-opened. As far as he was concerned, it was all a waste of time.'

'I could have told you that. In fact I did tell you,' Jenny was stirring it.

'Alright. But not with the same motivation. You see, the VC is keen to find the thief and the Dean couldn't care less about it. I don't understand.'

Alex continued, 'He even challenged the integrity and achievements of the Agency. I felt he was really having a pop at me.'

'What? He'd the cheek to do that. You should have punched him on the nose. I hope you didn't let him get away with it.'

'You know me better than that. I dealt with him sharply and he climbed down a bit.'

'Good for you.'

'There is some conflict that currently exists among the senior staff. Whilst waiting to see the Dean, I overheard him being very strict and firm with Jack Dempsey, Principal Lecturer. It is certainly not a happy ship.'

'Don't forget you're hired to sort out the computer thefts and not to deal with their personnel problems.'

'I know. But it's interesting to observe the dynamics of those who could potentially be involved in the computer thefts. I want to focus on my remit which also includes finding the killer of the student nurse.'

'That poor student. Finding her killer, I believe, would be most welcome by everyone.'

'Anyway, I'll be going home from here as I have to go out tonight. It's getting late for a Friday anyway. You had better go home as well.'

'Who are you going out with tonight?'

'Don't you worry about me, I'm a big boy.'

'Your uncle has asked me to keep an eye on you.'

'I must leave you now. You have a very nice weekend. See you on Monday, Bye.'

'And you.'

Alex rang off.

Before going home, Alex rang Scott on his mobile. 'Hi Scott, how is it going?'

'Not bad at all. I made some progress with the Montgomery case and have got a lot of important information as to his daily routine now and the kind of people he has been interacting with. I'm sure his wife will be well satisfied with our work.'

'Well done, Scott. Do you think we could wrap that particular case up soon?'

'Pretty much, I'd say.'

'By the way, Jenny told me that you've come across a computer shop which has bought a laptop recently. Do you think it is related to the computer theft case at the University?'

'I don't believe it is. I went back to check again with the shop assistant who told me it was an old lady who brought her laptop in. It was not an expensive and sophisticated one like you have in a University.'

'OK Scott. Thanks. It's getting late. You had better go home now. Have an enjoyable weekend and I'll see you on Monday.'

'Will do. Thanks, Alex. You have a lovely weekend too.'

Chapter 9

The second week started with more exploring and acquiring information about the environment and the people who worked in the institution. Up until then, everyone had been welcoming, supporting and encouraging with the exception of the Dean who was sceptical of the new investigation. In fact, John was also somewhat dubious about Alex's presence on the premises and his task of solving the computer thefts. Nonetheless, they had all offered their assistance if required. It was evidently clear that no one was expecting him to succeed. The only person who was hoping he would come up trumps was the VC.

Unknown to the members of the Faculty staff, he was also conducting his parallel investigation into the anonymous letter alleging that extortion was being carried out by a senior academic. He was keen on finding out more about the senior staff, to pick up potential clues regarding this particular crime. The next person on his list to meet was the Deputy Dean whom he hoped might shed some light on both his investigations. His unpleasant meeting with the Dean had led him to assume that the Deputy would be more approachable. No real reason for it to happen but he was hoping to have an easier ride. That notion was based on the assumption that the Dean and the Deputy could not both be obnoxious and arrogant in the same organisation.

As the Dean was unbearable, the Deputy would be the opposite, he hoped.

Alex went to see the Deputy Dean, Gail Weston, whose office was next to John's. As far as he was concerned, she was the last senior academic to be interviewed. It was coffee time. She heard a knock on her office door. Getting up from her desk, she walked to the door and opened it and said, 'Hello Alex. Good to see you again. Do come in and have a seat.' She had been expecting him.

'Good morning. Nice to see you as well. Thank you,' Alex said whilst making himself comfortable.

The Deputy Dean was quick to make the first move to break the ice and establish a relaxed atmosphere for their chat.

'To make things easy, please call me Gail. Would you like to have a cup of coffee as I'm going to have one myself?' Gail asked.

'Please. That would be very nice,' Alex replied.

That suited Alex down to the ground as he preferred an informal setting to allow him to relax and get his host to provide him with responses relevant to his search for the truth. He was very impressed by her approach. Gail was in her forties, relatively tall, slim, shoulder length red hair and was dressed in a beautiful and elegant navy blue dress. She spoke assuredly and gently with a smile and moved smoothly. Suddenly, he realised he was facing an astute, elegant and sophisticated senior academic.

'Do you take milk and sugar or....'

'Milk and one sugar please.'

'Now how can I help you?'

'First of all, can I say how sorry I am about the death of Margaret. It's a very sad loss.'

'Thank you. It's very sad, indeed. We welcome your meeting with the students who seemed to appreciate your efforts and so do we. I hope you and the Police will catch the killer very soon.'

'I hope so too. We will do everything possible to find the person responsible.'

Both were keen to get back to the main reason for their meeting, to discuss the issue of the computer thefts. Gail was aware of Alex's encounters with various members of staff, the Dean and the students during the last few days he had been on the job.

'I guess you would like to talk about the computer thefts.' Gail changed the gist of their conversation.

Alex sensed by Gail's quick change of tack that she couldn't wait to tell him something else as well.

'That's right. In addition, you will probably be aware that I have met a group of teaching staff, Matt, John, Jack and the Dean,' Alex put her in the picture but she already knew that.

'That's correct. How did you get on with them?'

'They were very informative. I have been able to piece together the storage and use of the computers,' Alex said. 'Could you tell me your involvement in the computer theft case?'

'Well, I personally did not handle the sordid business, the VC was responsible for calling in the Police. I was only informed of what was happening in a meeting at which the VC was present. People were quite tense in the Faculty while the Police carried out their investigations which lasted for a couple of weeks. Both the Dean and John were very tetchy and snappy at the time. Tom Evans was very worried. The VC was angry and he made it known to everyone in the staff meeting. It was a difficult case to solve as the thief was long gone. With the relaxed atmosphere and an open environment, anyone could have stolen the laptops and walked out of the building without being noticed,' Gail explained.

'Thank you. You mentioned the behaviour of the Dean and of John being somewhat erratic. Any particular reason?'

'From what I could gather, they possibly felt the pressure more than anyone else. It would appear that the Dean was in close contact with John about the case.'

'Why would that be?' Alex pressed her further.

'It's no secret that both the Dean and John get on very well with each other. There is an obvious chemistry between them. Naturally, in times of tension and stress, they feel comfortable working together,' Gail said, as diplomatically as possible.

'Is John the blue-eyed boy of the Dean?' Alex wanted to find out more.

'In confidence, you could say that. The Dean thinks very highly of John and has been very fond and protective of him.'

Alex felt that she did not like the arrangement between the Dean and John. 'Do you believe their working relationship is productive for the Faculty?'

'I'm sure in many instances they have contributed immensely to the good of the institution,' Gail said, and shed more light on their involvement.

'Forgive me for saying this. I get the feeling that you do not approve of the Dean and John working together so closely.' Alex was fishing.

'The effects they have on others are my concern,' Gail pointed out.'

'What would that concern be?'

'To tell you the truth, the Dean seems to confide more in John than in me as his Deputy. That's very annoying. I'm in my fifties with no attachment. My husband passed away two years ago and my two grown up children are married and settled. I don't need to carry on working. I can take early retirement at any time, especially as the University is offering a package for voluntary redundancy. I don't like people being treated unfairly.'

Gail was practically expressing her deep personal dissatisfaction.

'Sorry to hear about your loss. Gosh I thought you're in your forties.'

'That's very kind of you. I wish I was,' Gail said with a lovely smile and then continued.

'The Dean was overlooked for the job of VC last summer. He doesn't like the current VC because he is young and full of good ideas to move the whole University forward, whilst he is old, not progressive and basically jealous. John is full of himself and doesn't miss the opportunity to let everyone know it. For the last two years he has been instrumental in extending the unsuccessful students continuance on the course by giving them an extension on compassionate grounds, so that they could re-submit their assignment. Instead of these students being dismissed, they stayed on the course thus saving the Faculty several thousands of pounds each year. Overnight, John became a hero in the eyes of the Dean. The effects of the decision of allowing poor calibre students to continue with their studies on the standards of nurse education, was never considered,' Gail outlined the rationale for their arrogance with great aplomb.

'I guess that's why John and Jack were having a massive argument about high standards last Monday in Jack's office,' Alex said.

'Of course you know about that because you and the VC walked in on them. He is not in the same league as Jack who is a bright, knowledgeable, professional, caring, well respected colleague and a real gentleman. John is envious of Jack and always tries to undermine him,' Gail said, and was very explicit with her disgust.

'Jack has planned the current nursing curriculum which was approved by both the University and the national regulatory body for nursing and nurse education. It was generally recognised by everyone that he did an excellent job and made a significant contribution to the high standing of the Faculty in the field of nurse education. He has continued in the same vein as the chairman of the course management team; John won't be able to hold a candle to him.'

Alex chanced his arm by prodding a bit further, after all, the more he knew about the senior staff the better for his investigation into the extortion case. 'That's bad. Does the VC know about the Dean's attitude towards him and the lowering of the standards of nurse education in the Faculty?'

'No idea. I'm sure he's focused on his own agenda of managing the whole institution instead of bothering himself about the Dean.'

'If you don't mind me asking, should you decide to retire, there will be a vacancy. Who do you think could get your job?'

'Personally, I would like to see Jack get it because he fully deserves it and will do a great job. It would be a great career move for him. But, I rather suspect that with the help of the Dean, John would be promoted to the Deputy Dean's post in the Faculty.'

'Quite a story. Thank you. I appreciate it.'

Gail realised she had probably told Alex a lot more than she should. It was an opportunity to vent her pent up feelings about her position and status to Alex whom she felt she could trust.

Knowing that Alex was a lawyer, she felt she could probably confide in him, similar to a client outpouring feelings to a therapist. Consequently, it became a cathartic experience for her.

Suddenly, she was more relaxed and took the initiative to refocus on their original conversation about the computer thefts.

'Any closer to solving the computer theft case?' Gail asked with a smile, whilst knowing very well that he was not.

'Not quite, but we're working on it. No doubt this is a rather complex case. As you rightly pointed out earlier on, anyone could have done it and it will be very difficult to solve. However, we've come across a few crucial leads that we intend to pursue and so hope for the best,' Alex replied with a confident tone.

'I'm also worried about the students' personal data on these laptops and the possible consequences,' Gail expressed her concern.

'I fully understand,' Alex said sympathetically.

'And I wouldn't discount the possibility of an insider job, myself,' Gail was keen to make her contribution.

'Anything you would like to share with me?'

'Not really. Just call it a woman's intuition, I guess.'

'Thank you very much for your time and for sharing that useful information with me.'

'Pleasure to talk to you, Alex. If there is anything I can do to help, please do not hesitate to contact me.' Gail stood up and offered her hand.

Alex got up, shook her hand and left.

After leaving the Deputy Dean's office, he walked to his car and allowed himself time to reflect on a very productive meeting. Clearly, he felt that the Deputy Dean was being badly treated by the Dean. She was hurting but was powerless to do anything about it. The positions of both the Dean and John were strong and domineering.

That was some interview for Alex to ponder on carefully. He had obtained more organisational and personal information than he had expected. How much of what he had heard could be relevant to both investigations, remained to be seen? Fortunately, the Deputy Dean was a willing talker and prepared to place her trust in him. She also came across as an honest professional who cared passionately about her job and her working environment. What a lady! Alex admired her frankness.

Chapter 10

As far as the investigation into the computer theft case was concerned, Alex was due for a welcome break. After lunch whilst re-entering the building, he saw the security officer who smiled at him and he nodded and smiled back. He headed to the reception desk to check for any messages and meet one of his newly found friends, Julie.

That usually pleased Julie no end, because she got her chance to see and talk to her favourite man. The reception area was quiet and Julie was on her own at the desk.

'Good afternoon, Julie. How are you today?' Alex said, looking at her.

'Good afternoon, Mr DuPont. I'm very well and how are you?'

'I'm fine, thank you.'

'That's good. What can I do for you?' Julie asked with a cheeky smile.

Alex thought that it would be an understatement to say that Julie was enjoying herself.

'Any messages for me?' Alex asked smiling with his eyes fixed on Julie's eyes which were warm and inviting.

Julie replied, 'Yes, two messages. Can you contact Detective Sgt Cooper and Scott, your Associate?'

'Thank you, Julie,' Alex said with a gentle nod without taking his eyes off her beautiful, flushed face.

He walked to the lifts and waited for one to arrive. He heard a voice calling his name and it was the same security officer. 'Mr DuPont,' the security officer said in a rushed voice. 'Can I see you for a moment?'

'Of course. What is it?' Alex was quick to reply. He moved towards the security officer who signalled to him with his head to go into a waiting room nearby.

Alex was taken aback by the invitation and did not know what to expect. He had seen the security officer around but had never engaged in any conversation with him before. They both headed to the waiting room which was quite small. It was used by visitors to wait for their appointments with the Faculty staff. The room was well lit, warm and comfortable with a few armchairs spread around. Both sat down facing each other.

'What can I do for you?' Alex asked.

'Well it's more what can I do for you, Mr DuPont,' the security officer replied confidently. 'I have some information which I don't know if you could use in your investigation. I understand from my boss, Ed, that you asked him whether he or his security staff had noticed anything unusual happen during the time when the laptops went missing.'

'Oh yes. I remember asking him,' Alex replied with an air of expectation in his voice.

'I believe I came across an incident which could be described as unusual,' Wayne said.

'Good. First of all, call me Alex. It's less formal that way.'

Alex could sense something important was about to unfold and tried to put his informant at ease.

'In that case, please call me Wayne,' the security officer replied.

Both men smiled at each other and were ready to talk serious business. As the place was quiet, Wayne had been given permission by his boss to meet with Alex for a few minutes, and he wanted to get on with it. He was shuffling in his seat, indicating he was in a hurry as he did not have much time to spare.

'I hear you're investigating the stolen laptops and you're asking around for information to assist you,' Wayne said, and got to the point quickly.

'Yes, I am. What information would you like to share with me?'

'It has, you see, always bothered me why a particular senior member of staff was carrying a large black holdall, bulging at the seams, to his car,' Wayne said with a deep frown on his face.

'OK. Can you tell me more? For example, when did that happen and who is the senior member of staff?'

'To be honest, I don't like that man. He's rude, arrogant and talks down to students and teaching staff.'

'Has he treated you in that manner?' Alex asked, trying to get him to talk freely.

'He wouldn't dare talk to me rudely,' Wayne retorted. Alex could see why. Wayne was from the West Indies, well built, tall and in his fifties. He could look after himself easily and, by his sheer physique, would put the fear of god in most people.

'What is his name?' Alex was getting restless.

'Mr Fairbanks. John Fairbanks. He's a Principal Lecturer,' Wayne said emphatically.

'Alright. What else can you tell me?' Alex was leading Wayne to disclose more.

'Well one evening, it was around seven o'clock, Mr Fairbanks was heading out of the building with his brief case in one hand and a very heavy black holdall in the other hand. I asked him if he wanted me to help him carry the black holdall. He thanked me and told me he could manage. I was going off duty at the time. Both of us were walking side by side to the Faculty car park at the back of the building. He even asked me what I was doing that evening. I told him it was my daughter's birthday and I had to get home quickly. I remarked his black holdall looked heavy, to which he replied jokingly that he was overloaded with scripts to mark which had to be returned to the assessment office within two days. He was asked to do some emergency marking as one of the lecturers had gone sick. I remember the incident well because it was 12 May, my daughter's birthday,' Wayne went to great lengths to recount all this.

'Great, I'm glad you remember the incident,' Alex said, and acknowledged his effort and was keen to keep him talking. 'What made you think there was something wrong with him taking work home? Lecturers often take scripts home to mark.'

'True. Lecturers do just that on a regular basis. On that evening it looked a bit strange to me. You see, lecturers carry the scripts home in a medium size brown satchel issued by the assessment office, but Mr Fairbanks had a large black holdall with him with thick and hard objects inside. I don't believe the bag contained scripts for marking,' Wayne said, and crystallized his observation.

As a security officer for five years, he had come across a lot of people carrying all sorts of bags with them to work and on their way home. Alex realised and appreciated the acute observation skills of Wayne as a security officer who was obviously very good at his job. It would appear that not much would go unnoticed by him.

'Have you ever told anyone including the Police what you have just told me?' Alex checked in case someone else knew about it.

'No. I haven't told anyone because I hadn't appreciated the importance of the whole affair until last night.'

'Why have you decided to talk now?'

'Honestly, there is no particular reason. As I said before, I don't like Mr Fairbanks' attitude when he behaves stupidly towards others, but, I haven't got anything personal against him. It's something that's been bugging me. And probably there is a simple and legitimate explanation for him to take that large holdall home with him at a time when the Faculty has lost two laptops,' Wayne said, and shrugged his shoulders.

Then he continued, 'I heard the VC has hired you to look into the stolen laptops. I also understand you approached my boss asking him whether any member of his staff had noticed any one carrying anything unusual with them. As it happens, I was talking to my wife last night about the beautiful presents my daughter received on her recent birthday. That triggered my memory about my encounter with Mr Fairbanks on the way to the car park and, that he had a bulging black holdall with him. Alarm bells rang. So I decided to tell you what I know as soon as I could. I suspect he did not have a bundle of students' assignments for marking that evening. On the other hand, I'm not saying that he stole the laptops and smuggled them in a black holdall. But it's up to you to decide what to do with the information I just provided to you.'

'Thank you very much for telling me about your recollection of Mr Fairbanks' action that special evening, Wayne.'

'I need to go back to work. If I can be of any further help, you know where to find me.' Wayne got up and was heading for the door.

Alex also stood up and shook Wayne's hand and said, 'Thank you again.'

That could be a real breakthrough for Alex. A lead he felt was well worth pursuing as it might be valuable to his investigation. So far, through his persistent questioning of a whole range of people at the University, he had drawn a blank. No clear lead to follow as such until he fortuitously came across Wayne. He was somewhat persuaded by Wayne's account of his encounter with John on the evening of 12 May. Wayne appeared quite certain of his story. He wanted to reserve his judgement until he had explored the lead thoroughly.

***

Armed with the information from Wayne, Alex took the next obvious step which was to drop in on the assessment office to establish whether John had agreed to mark scripts around the 12 May.

As he was already on the premises, it was the logical approach to take.

The assessment office was on the second floor. Alex decided it would be quicker to walk up the stairs. It was a busy place. Students were standing in a long queue to see one of the assessment staff, notably about their assignments. He walked through, passing the students, he spotted the office of the Assessment Officer and knocked gently on the door which was half open.

'Come in,' someone shouted. Alex presumed it was the Assessment Officer and walked in slowly.

'Good afternoon. Can I see the Assessment Officer, please?' Alex said in a mumbling voice.

'Yes, I'm the Assessment Officer.'

'Pleased to meet you. I am Alex DuPont and am investigating the computer thefts.' Alex offered his hand. The Assessment Officer looked pleasantly surprised and shook Alex's hand.

'Nice to meet you. I've heard a lot about you and have seen you around on a couple of occasions but did not get the chance to introduce myself, I'm Phil Brown. Please have a seat.'

'Thank you. I do appreciate it,' Alex replied.

'Please call me Phil. I understand you are investigating the computer thefts and helping the Police with Margaret's murder case as well. You're going to be very busy, indeed.'

'That's correct. Please call me Alex. I would like to offer my condolences to and your staff about the tragic death of Margaret and we'll do everything to find her killer very soon,' Alex said humbly and reassuringly.

'Thank you, Alex. We are in a state of shock. A tragic loss. The sooner you find the killer the better,' Phil said, and expressed his sadness.

'We'll do our utmost, I promise you,' Alex replied.

'What can I do for you?'

'Well, can you tell me anything you possibly know about the two stolen laptops?'

'Nothing really. There was a Police investigation in which I wasn't involved. The laptops weren't found and the thief hasn't been caught. That's about it.'

'Thank you for that. Tell me, do you keep records of the scripts that lecturers are expected to mark?' Alex decided to get to the point.

'Of course. The record includes the number, group, name of module, date taken, name of the teaching staff and the due return date. The scripts are placed in a brown satchel which the marker collects from this office and returns to this office,' Phil said. He also showed an empty brown satchel to Alex.

'Thank you. Will you be able to tell me whether you or your staff asked John Fairbanks to mark some scripts as an emergency around 12 May,' Alex asked with a serious look.

Phil got up and went to a set of shelves where a set of records for script marking was kept. He checked and said,

'There is no record of that here. I do know for a fact that we haven't experienced any emergency marking for over a year. For certain, all the marking for that period was undertaken on time and completed accordingly. There was no outstanding marking to be done urgently. If there is any emergency marking to be done, I am responsible for approaching the marker to do us a favour. As there was no need for such action, I can vouch that John was never asked to mark any scripts.'

'That's very clear, indeed,' Alex said whilst nodding in appreciation.

'What has this got to do with your investigations?' Phil became curious.

'Probably nothing. Please can I ask you to keep our conversation confidential?'

Alex tried to secure Phil's support.

'Yes I will,' Phil promised sincerely.

'You've been of great help to me. Thank you for your time. I must leave now.' Alex got up and shook Phil's hand with gusto.

Chapter 11

It would appear that Alex had managed to see all the key people at the University as far as the computer theft case was concerned. Even a reliable lead had fallen into his lap which could yet prove significant for his investigation. By all accounts, he was determined to follow the lead with the assistance of his Associate.

But first Alex had to talk to Melanie who had been trying to get hold of him. He phoned her from his office. 'Hi Melanie, how are you keeping? I've got your message to ring you. Sorry I'm a bit late....'

Melanie interrupted him. 'Oh don't worry about phoning now and not earlier. I've been very busy as well.'

'Are you well?' Alex demonstrated his caring side. Deep down, he really cared about her.

'I'm fine, thank you. How are you?' It was Melanie's turn to be caring.

'Good, thank you,' Alex replied. 'Anything I need to know.'

'Well yes. You probably remember last Friday the Coroner was conducting the autopsy,' Melanie said.

'Of course I do,' Alex replied.

'The Coroner informed me today that the outcome of the autopsy confirmed his initial assessment; Margaret was hit by a blunt and heavy object to the back of her head, then became unstable, fell to the floor and died instantly. The time of death was between 8 pm and 10 pm,' Melanie explained.

'That's confirmed it as a murder case as was initially suspected.'

'A definite murder case which we intend to solve as soon as possible, and bring the killer to justice.'

'What will happen next?'

'Margaret's body will be released tomorrow and her uncle will fly with the body to South Africa where the funeral will take place.'

'I guess it is the wish of her parents.'

'Yes. I've just informed the VC who is meeting with Margaret's uncle later today. He will then let the students and staff know the outcome of the autopsy and the arrangement for Margaret's funeral.'

'Thank you for telling me. It's very sad indeed.'

Clearly, the conversation was affecting both of them. Alex decided to change the direction of the interchange on the phone by probing into the task of her team.

'How is your investigation progressing?' Alex asked.

'I believe my team is working very hard. Two of them have had to interview all the residents, domestic staff, porters, residence manager and those living close to the residence building since last Wednesday. As you know, Margaret's flat was on the ground floor, the first one next to the entrance. Unfortunately, no one heard or saw anything on that Tuesday evening,' Melanie explained

'What about the security for the building?' Alex asked.

'The residence manager works and lives on site. No security staff, only a night security officer from another residence which is the main and largest building who would call hourly to check whether the front door is locked from midnight onwards,' Melanie said.

'How is the front door kept locked?' Alex asked.

'The door is self-locking. Every resident and those working there have the code for the digital lock to open the door and then they push it to lock after entry or exit. Apparently, it had been impressed on every one through a circular that the front door should be kept locked at all times. The back door on the ground floor and three more floors are fire escape doors whose keys are kept in a glass container secured to a nearby wall,' Melanie explained.

'So there are no witnesses, no evidence of finger prints on objects found in her flat?' Alex asked.

'That's the situation. Undoubtedly, we'll continue to investigate,' Melanie said. 'Have you come across anything during your travels and inquisition that could help this investigation?'

'Funny you ask. The right answer is no. But I have a feeling about a couple of people... only a feeling, nothing concrete.'

'Would you like to share it with me?'

'I am not sure right now. Let me work on it and gather more information and then I'll tell you. I promise,' Alex reassured her.

'How is your computer case going?' Melanie changed the subject or was she just curious because she was unable to solve that case herself.

'Not bad at all,' Alex sounded a bit cagey.

'Have you cracked it yet?' Melanie was teasing.

'Do me a favour. You must be joking. Progress is hard to come by but I believe, I could have come across a break which I'll have to check on first.'

'You don't give a lot away, do you Alex?'

'It's not that. I just like to be sure of the facts first.'

'I guess it's your legal experience coming to the fore, but I agree with your stance.'

'Thank you. I'm glad you understand. Rest assured, as soon as I'm satisfied with what I've got, I'll be pleased to tell you.'

'Fair enough. As they say, once a lawyer always a lawyer,' Melanie replied. 'You have obviously made some inroads towards solving the case.'

'I suppose you could say that. Don't get carried away. It's only a hopeful start, that's all.'

Alex was trying to play it down, in case he didn't succeed.

'That's a lot more than I achieved. I hope someone does a bit of talking to help you. We drew a complete blank. No one was willing to co-operate, considering they knew the laptops contain students' personal data. Anyone could have stolen those laptops. It was surprising that security was not tighter in a place with so much expensive equipment. The VC is a good man and wanted the case solved quickly, but unfortunately, we couldn't deliver. It wasn't for lack of trying, I can assure you. I sincerely hope you have more luck, Alex,' Melanie said, and was very honest with her comments.

'I'm grateful to you for enlightening me of your efforts to find the stolen laptops and the thief. I'm sorry that you didn't succeed. I would welcome any help you could give to me as far as this case is concerned.'

'OK. I understand. Can we meet tomorrow afternoon in your office at the University?' Melanie asked.

'Of course, it will be nice to see you again,' Alex was delighted at her suggestion. 'By the way, the other day in the pub, you mentioned that you knew I graduated from Oxford. How did you know that?'

'Someone told me,' Melanie said coyly.

'Can I ask who exactly?' Alex was more determined to find out.

'Don't worry, I'll tell you tomorrow.'

'I'll hold you to that. Shall we meet at 2pm?' Alex suggested.

'That will be fine. See you tomorrow,' Melanie confirmed and rang off.

Ever since Alex had met Melanie in the pub, one comment had been bugging him; he felt he was at a disadvantage before he met her because she already knew a lot about him. The crucial question was 'how'. Alex was certain they had never met before and did not remember seeing her during his time at Oxford either. The worst part was that he did not mention his concern to her at their meeting in the pub. Maybe he was overwhelmed by her beauty.

***

Following his constructive and fruitful chat on the phone with Melanie, he felt good within himself. Talking to Melanie seemed to propel him into a happy mood. Then who wouldn't be, judging by her nice, pleasant and beautiful disposition. Anyway he needed to move on. The next step was to contact Scott. Before he could do that he had to answer a knock on the office door. It was now 4pm.

'Come in, the door is open,' Alex called out.

The tall, slim, beautiful blonde girl he had met in classroom A walked in. Head slightly bent with her blue eyes fixed on Alex, she moved in gently. Alex stood up and said, 'Please have a seat.'

She sat down on the chair next to his desk and began to wonder why she was there. Feeling somewhat embarrassed, she quickly decided to leave. 'I apologise for disturbing you and I shouldn't be here. I must go now.'

She stood up and was heading for the door.

'Hold on a minute. You came to see me about something. Why don't you tell what's on your mind?' Alex suggested.

She stopped, paused for a couple of seconds and then walked back to her seat. She was very quiet and continued to look at Alex.

'We met in the classroom the other day. You asked me to find Margaret's killer,' Alex tried to break the ice and make her feel a bit more comfortable.

She nodded in agreement.

'What's your name?' Alex asked.

'Alison. My full name is Alison Stewart.' She perked up a bit.

'Alright Alison, why do you want to see me?' Alex asked.

'It's about Margaret. I'm not sure if I'm right to say anything.' She stood up. So did Alex.

'Wait a minute, please just sit down. You know you can trust me and whatever you tell me will be kept confidential,' Alex reassured her. She sat down, looking serious and worried.

'I know how hard it has been for you and your friends since losing Margaret. How are you coping?' Alex asked sympathetically.

'I'm alright and my friends seem ok as well, but we are all feeling very sad at the moment,' Alison explained.

'I understand. Have you or any of your friends been to see your lecturer or the counselling service for counselling and support?' Alex asked.

'In our group we're providing comfort and support to each other,' Alison replied.

'That's good to know, but if you or your friends require further support, please do not hesitate to contact your lecturer, the counselling service office or me,' Alex reassured her. Then she settled down, managed a smile and looked a bit more relaxed. He tried to get her to talk.

'You are Margaret's friend and I believe she would have been very proud of you coming forward to try to help find her killer,' Alex told her. She was quiet for a few seconds.

'You wanted to know about Margaret's lifestyle and interests,' Alison said.

'That's right,' Alex replied and waited in anticipation to hear about Margaret's personal life.

Alison said, 'As you know Margaret was a student on a bursary, like all of us, which wasn't much to live on, especially the type of lifestyle she liked and enjoyed. She loved clubbing, wearing expensive clothes, shoes and jewellery. She was nice, beautiful, elegant, intelligent, hardworking, self-confident and had the taste for the good life. We had been very good friends from day one on the course.'

'Thank you for telling me about Margaret's personality and personal tastes. How did she get to fund the expensive lifestyle that you have just described?' Alex probed.

Alison looked at him with wandering eyes whilst thinking whether she should disclose further information about her best friend's personal life.

Alex encouraged her to continue. 'I understand how you feel at the moment, but, any information could be extremely helpful to the investigation.'

'She had a shady side to her life,' Alison said softly.

'If I heard you right, you said something about 'shady'. Can you say more about it?'

'She was working as an escort, at night only. She felt no one would be able to see her at that time.'

'I see. There is nothing wrong in what she was doing to earn some extra cash.'

Alison was surprised at Alex's understanding and accepting attitude. She was expecting him to be annoyed with her.

'Do you think her escort duty could have contributed to her death?' Alison asked succinctly.

'Hard to say at this stage. It could, on the other hand, perhaps not. We'll certainly investigate that aspect of her life,' Alex reassured her.

'Thank you for not being judgmental about her life,' Alison said with a smile.

'That's ok. Very useful information indeed. Well, I'll have to share this information with Detective Sgt Cooper to establish whether there is a possible connection between Margaret's escort work and her death.'

'I understand,' Alison replied.

'Thank you for the information. I do appreciate it. If you can remember anything else that would be helpful, please do not hesitate to contact me.'

'I'll have to go now. Thank you for seeing me,' Alison replied, and stood up.

Alex nodded with a smile and opened the door for Alison. 'Bye for now.'

The meeting with the students seemed to have paid off. Alex was delighted with the way Alison had decided to come forward with such very useful information. He felt Alison was very brave to take the initiative to contact him. However, he also believed that Alison had not told him everything, yet, possibly because he had not asked her the right questions, choosing to use a measured approach in the first instance. Pressurising an informant too much initially could be counter-productive. A softly-softly strategy could eventually provide the desired result.

Time to talk to Scott. Alex phoned and found him at the Agency. 'Hi Scott, how are you? I've got your message. I hear you're looking for me,' Alex asked.

'Yes, I believe I may have spotted the computer shop which bought one of the stolen laptops,' Scott pointed out.

'That's great news. Where?' Alex asked.

'As it happens, I had to go to Hammersmith town centre this morning to do an errand for the wife. There are a couple of computer shops on the high street. After my shopping, I decided to call into these shops to make tentative enquiries.' Scott stopped to gush out some air from his mouth. He couldn't contain his excitement.

'And then. Don't stop, go on,' Alex was keen to know more.

'The first shop confirmed that they had not bought any laptops for over two months, at least.'

Scott said quickly because he knew Alex was getting restless as he could hear his heavy sighs continuously. 'Fortunately, one of the assistants in the second shop told me that he remembered buying a laptop around the middle of May from a tall guy who was well dressed. Do you think that's our man?'

'I must say Scott, sometimes getting information from you is like pulling teeth. You do take a long time to get to the point. All the same, good work.'

'What do we do next?' Scott was keen to move on.

'I think the best thing to do is for us to go and see that shop assistant again tomorrow at 10 am. I'll see you at the office in the morning,' Alex said.

'Great. See you tomorrow then,' Scott replied.

Needless to say Alex was over the moon. First it was Wayne and Phil, then Alison and now Scott with a possible break. He sensed the tide had begun to turn in his favour and reminded himself to calm down and not to count his chickens yet. It was time for him to go home.

Chapter 12

It was an opportunity for the three of them to have an impromptu meeting to touch base about the progress made for their existing clients. During the last week, Alex had been pre-occupied with the University business, leaving Jenny to help with the research, manning the office and dealing with enquiries. Scott had been pursuing his own research on clients and surveillance duties.

'Let me start with the Montgomery case, Scott has practically finalised the collecting of evidence, I'll see Mrs Montgomery as soon as she can make it and bring the whole case to a successful end. Well done to both of you. Three weeks of hard work will be lucratively rewarded.' Alex was very pleased with his team and the continued progress.

Both Scott and Jenny allowed themselves a wide smile and a chuckle. They were fully aware of what success meant to them and the Agency. Hence, they were committed and put in consistently high performances to achieve their overall goals. More importantly, they were enjoying every aspect of the venture. In addition, they knew Alex valued their contribution immensely.

'What about the other three cases?' Jenny asked.

'As you know, the policy is to have four clients at any given time; this is manageable without putting too much pressure on us. We'll use a similar strategy to provide our clients with the information they have requested. Again an element of research and surveillance will be required. Luckily for us, life moves fast in the city. We have to keep up with it or be ahead of it, if possible, and obtain the right results to solve our clients' problems. We'll continue in the same vein. My involvement will be less for obvious reasons. I'll help as much as I can,' Alex outlined the way forward.

'Mr Faulkner has rung again and wants to know what progress has been made in his case as he paying the Agency by the hour,' Jenny said whilst looking straight at Alex.

'I know he's been restless for results from the beginning. We've made a lot of progress in his case. Once we find the last missing piece, that will be it,' Alex said.

'That's right. I'll probably wrap that one up by tomorrow and I am very close to settling the other two cases as well,' Scott reassured them.

Alex brought them up to date with his involvement at the University. 'Just to let both of you know, we possibly have two lucky breaks. The first one is to do with the computer case. One of the security officers told me that on 12 May he saw John Fairbanks taking a heavy black holdall home with him. John told him that he was taking scripts to mark. The security officer did not believe him. Due to the bulging shape of the holdall, he suspected that there were laptops in it. I also checked with Phil Brown, the Assessment Officer, who confirmed that he didn't give John any scripts to mark on that date.'

'And the second break?' Jenny couldn't wait to hear it.

'The second one is concerning Margaret's murder case. One of her closest friends told me that she was doing escort work to supplement her bursary. It's possible that it has a connection with her death. I'll be discussing this with Detective Sgt Cooper this afternoon,' Alex informed them of the progress of the two cases.

'That's very promising news. At least your efforts are yielding positive and encouraging results,' Scott remarked with a cheery smile. Jenny nodded in agreement.

Although business was booming for the Agency, no one was getting complacent. The continued success of the Agency depended on having a regular number of cases on the books. As the Montgomery case was almost resolved, Jenny drew Alex's attention to their workload.

'We need to get more work,' Jenny warned.

'Don't worry. I've got a few things lined up that will keep us very busy for a while,' Alex said, and kept his troop's hopes high. 'Now, Scott, are you ready to go to Hammersmith?'

'Yes I am,' Scott replied.

Hammersmith wasn't far from their office, only seven stops on the underground. Within 40 minutes they were in the computer shop. Scott went straight to the shop assistant who confirmed he had bought a laptop.

'Hello Adrian. Remember me. I came yesterday and we were talking about your purchase of a laptop,' Scott tried to re-connect with his contact.

'Yes. Of course I do. You work for some private investigative agency,' Adrian confirmed.

'Good. Let me introduce my boss, who owns the Agency, his name is Alex,' Scott informed Adrian.

Adrian offered his right hand to Alex. 'Pleased to meet you Alex.'

'Alex shook his hand. 'Nice to meet you too, Adrian. We are very grateful for your help. Do you mind going over what you told Scott about the laptop you purchased?'

'Sure. According to our records, the purchase of the laptop took place on 13 May for the sum of £200. I remember the transaction vividly because it was Friday the 13th.'

'Before you tell me anything else, I would like to inform you that we're currently investigating a computer theft case and that's why we would like to ask you some questions,' Alex put Adrian in the picture.

'OK, that's fine. We've nothing to hide. What do you want to know?' Adrian asked.

'Tell us about the guy,' Alex said.

'The guy who brought in the laptop was in his forties, tall, blonde hair, charming and articulate and he wanted a quick sale. He said he was in a hurry. The laptop was in pristine condition and relatively new. It was a good business deal for us.'

'How long did the transaction take?'

'Not very long, maybe half an hour.'

'Did he show any proof of purchase for the laptop?'

'He said he had lost his receipt of purchase which isn't unusual in such circumstances.'

'Anything else you could tell us about him?' Alex continued, in order to find out more.

'He was a smart and pleasant guy. I noticed he kept running the fingers of his right hand through his hair pretty often, and he smiled nervously.'

'Did he give any reason for selling his laptop?' Alex kept the pressure on.

'He said he needed the money to buy a new Apple computer,' Adrian said, and then turned to Scott and pointed out. 'Your boss is very thorough with his line of questioning.'

'This is a low-key approach, I can assure you. You should watch him when he is operating on full throttle,' Scott explained to Adrian.

'You could have fooled me,' Adrian replied and waited to be quizzed further. Unfortunately for him, there was no sign of any customers to save him from additional questioning. Alex was contemplating his next move.

'Were all the data deleted on the files of the laptop? Alex asked.

'Oh yes. There was nothing left.'

'Is it possible for you to give us the serial number of the laptop?'

'This is confidential. Will this get me into trouble?' Adrian was being cautious.

'Not at all. You're cooperating with us in an attempt to solve a criminal case,' Alex reassured him.

Then the penny dropped for Adrian. 'What do you mean by a criminal case?'

'As I mentioned earlier, we're working on a case regarding a computer theft which makes this a criminal case. And, it is possible that the laptop we've been discussing was stolen and did not belong to that guy. We need to establish the facts regarding this laptop. You don't have to worry about anything at all. In your shop you buy and sell laptops. You've already helped us a great deal for which I'm very grateful. It would help us more if you could give us the serial number of the laptop,' Alex explained clearly to eliminate any doubts.

'Alright. I'll show you the serial number. I will leave it on the counter and walk away for a couple of minutes. It's up to you to write down the serial number,' Adrian tried to co-operate.

Alex wrote the serial number down correctly. He smiled and said, 'Thank you very much, Adrian.'

They shook hands with Adrian and then headed for their office in Mayfair.

'Do you recognise the guy he was taking about?' Scott asked.

'I think it's John Fairbanks, he has the habit of running his fingers through his hair.'

'Your computer case is solved then,' Scott said with a big grin.

'Not so fast. We need Adrian to identify him first, before accusing him of any criminal act. Also the serial number of the laptop must be checked with the University's records as well. Admittedly, if these turn out to be positive, we may have a case against him,' Alex reminded him of the due process of the law. 'We still have to prove how he did it?'

'What's your next move?' Scott asked.

'I don't know yet, I'll have to think about it,' Alex said with a puzzled look. Both of them hopped on the underground and went back to the Agency.

***

On their arrival Jenny asked them, 'Would you like to have some sandwiches?'

Alex replied, 'Yes please.'

Scott informed them that he had brought his own.

Jenny brought Alex a selection of sandwiches and a cup of tea. He grabbed a chicken salad sandwich and gorged it as quick as possible. Jenny remarked, 'Why don't you sit down and eat properly?'

'I'm in a hurry Jenny,' Alex said whilst collecting his papers to take to the University.

Alex had to rush to the University as he had an appointment with his sexy looking girl at 2pm. As usual, he arrived on time for his appointment. He was always conscious of being punctual. There was a knock on his office door.

'Come in,' Alex called out.

In walked Melanie who had really dressed to attract Alex's full attention. 'Good afternoon, Alex,' Melanie said with a wide smile.

'Good afternoon to you as well. Have a seat. You look very smart,' Alex remarked.

He really would have liked to say she looked very beautiful but unfortunately, had to maintain a professional approach. Melanie was wearing a pale blue blouse with her knee length blue skirt and matching jacket. As it was a small office, she sat on the chair which was relatively close to that of Alex. She had crossed her legs and was sitting upright with her long and beautiful neck straight. Her attire and appearance would knock anybody off his perch effortlessly.

'And you,' Melanie returned the compliment, always with impeccable manners.

'Shall we start with Margaret's murder case first or your knowledge of my background?' Alex asked, trying to establish what their strategy was going to be?

'I think the murder case first,' Melanie replied.

'Absolutely. Any developments?'

'Well, the team is still going through the interviewing process. No witnesses and no evidence have been secured yet.'

'Having no witnesses and no evidence makes the task harder.'

'I agree. But our work will continue to find her killer.'

'In fact, that leads me nicely to a possible break in the investigation.'

'Right. Tell me about it,' Melanie said, and became impatient.

'A friend of Margaret called Alison Stewart, came to see me yesterday. If you remember when we went to meet the students last week, a blonde girl asked us to catch Margaret's killer soon,' Alex said.

'I remember her,' Melanie confirmed.

'Well she told me that Margaret was doing escort work to get extra money to fund her exciting lifestyle. She enjoyed having expensive clothes, shoes, handbags and jewellery. She also liked going to clubs, theatres and cinemas. Do you think aspects of her lifestyle could have contributed to her death?'

'You mean an infatuated client who became jealous and possessive and wanted her for himself. When she did not respond to his wishes, matters got out of hand. They fought and the client killed her,' Melanie presented a possible scenario.

'That's exactly what I was thinking.'

'Our investigation has shown that she didn't take anyone to her flat in the residence on that Tuesday night. My team will make enquiries with the escort agencies in the area.'

'That's a good idea. Never know what we might find?'

'How are you getting on with your computer case?' Melanie changed the subject.

'As I mentioned yesterday, I have received some information which I've been following up.'

'Any progress made so far?'

Alex was not too sure about telling her the details of his investigation. As they had been working together on Margaret's murder case, they had developed an element of trust. Melanie had also given him an account of the Police involvement in the computer theft case and the reason the Police could not resolve it. He felt that her honesty deserved to be treated with respect and the truth. So, he told her of his conversation with Wayne, the security officer, Phil, the assessment officer and Adrian, the shop assistant.

'You have been working hard, Alex. In fact, you're almost there,' Melanie expressed her genuine appreciation to him.

'We're not quite there yet. I believe John Fairbanks is the main suspect. But we need concrete evidence of how the thefts were carried out?'

'I must say, I'm surprised that you suspect John Fairbanks. He has always struck me as a pleasant, helpful, intelligent, articulate, popular and professional man. He would have been the last man I would have suspected. I still don't believe he's your man,' Melanie expressed her doubts strongly.

'I have a different view of him. He's too clever by half. I wouldn't trust him easily,' Alex replied emphatically.

'Anyway, do tread carefully.'

'I'm working on getting the evidence.'

Although both of them had different views on John Fairbanks regarding the computer thefts, their relationship was not affected. The respect they had for each other remained undiminished.

'It's time we talked about how you came to know so much about me?' Alex said, more in hope than expectation.

'You're right, I did know a fair amount about you before we met in the pub,' Melanie admitted.

'Well, are you going to tell me?'

'Do you remember someone by the name of Martin?'

'I know a few people called Martin,' Alex replied quickly.

'This one was with you at Oxford.'

Alex looked down with his eyes wandering around for a few seconds, searching his memory as to who might that be? Melanie was staring at him, waiting for a reply and knew Alex would get there eventually.

'Do you mean Martin Blackshaw?' Alex suddenly remembered.

'That's right,' Melanie replied with a cheeky smile.

'Oh my god!' Alex said exasperated and with a deep sigh.

'Why?' Melanie was curious. She thought Alex would be pleased.

'What did he tell you about me?'

'Martin only told me that he knew you as you were at University together and nothing else, I promise.'

'Although we were in the same college, we weren't close friends.'

'I believe he thinks the same as you.'

'How do you know that?' It was Alex's turn to be curious.

'Because Martin and I are very good friends,' Melanie said.

Alex sensed that their conversation was getting rather personal and he was not prepared to venture in that direction, however much he fancied her or was infatuated by her.

'Oh.' Alex decided not to pursue it further.

'Don't you want to know the nature of our friendship?' Melanie asked.

'Well, not really. Unless you want to tell me.' Alex was being as careful as he could.

'We've been going out together for a while,' Melanie explained.

Alex was stunned by her statement which rendered him speechless. Not what he was expecting at all. He allowed himself a quiet chuckle. For some unknown reason, she felt she could relax with Alex and could speak freely. Could it be his sharp legal skills were getting the better of her or was she infatuated with him?

'What's funny?' Melanie asked shyly.

'Nothing is funny. Nice to hear that. I'm pleased for you both,' Alex said tongue in cheek.

'So now you know. I only know a little bit about you,' Melanie reassured him.

'Thank you for telling me about it. Anyway, may I suggest we get back to our day job.'

Alex tried to change the subject rather politely as he did not want to know the details of her personal life.

'Of course. I'll have to get back to my office,' Melanie said and got up to leave.

'Again, thank you for coming to discuss and share information on both cases with me,' Alex expressed his appreciation. Melanie nodded and then left.

Chapter 13

From Alex's perspective, the investigation into Margaret's murder had, at last, got off the ground with the information he had received from the student. Melanie promised to allocate her own Police resources to establish if there was any connection between Margaret's escort work and her death.

Alex had a feeling that somebody would know more about her and her lifestyle and hoped they would contact him or the Police. But he was still of the firm opinion that there was a link between the letter' and Margaret's death.

As far as Alex was concerned, he was not ruling anything in or out. He kept an open mind.

In the dark hours of the night, Alex often wondered about the massive responsibility he had committed himself to regarding the three cases. He intended to deliver. It was not unthinkable to a Private Investigator with a legal background that the three cases could relate to one main source.

A daunting task lay ahead of him to locate this source. It was only a passing thought. Then, his luck changed.

The murder was given a fresh impetus. It was the turn of one of the lecturers to approach Alex regarding Margaret's murder. Karen Fletcher went to see Alex in his office.

'Nice to see you again, Karen. Do sit down,' Alex welcomed her and offered her a chair.

Karen sat in the chair facing Alex and looked pensive. 'Thank you.'

'What can I do for you?' Alex asked.

'I should have come to see you earlier, but I didn't think it was important,' Karen said.

Alex looked puzzled. 'About what?'

'Margaret's murder.'

'OK. Why don't you tell me what you have on your mind?' Alex encouraged her to keep talking.

'Well, the day before she was murdered, I overheard John Fairbanks and Margaret having a vigorous argument in John's office. John told her if she didn't listen to him, she would be discontinued from the course and deported to South Africa. Margaret rebutted by making a counter threat that she would report him to the VC about his money-making activities,' Karen said.

Alex was intrigued by her statement. 'What time did this take place?'

'Around 10 am,' Karen responded emphatically.

Suddenly it clicked. It was after that argument with John that Margaret was leaving the tenth floor in a rush looking very upset. The VC was taking Alex to the tenth floor that Monday morning when Alex had held the door open for Margaret. Karen's description of the incident coincided with the time Margaret was leaving the tenth floor.

'Did you raise this issue with John?'

'No I didn't. Actually, I didn't tell anyone else either. It's only this morning that I decided to tell you. I'm not sure whether it will have a bearing on the murder case.'

'Alright. I'll discuss your statement with Detective Sgt Cooper. You met her when we came to address the students the other day.'

'Yes.'

'Is there any more information you wish to give me.'

'No, that's all I know. To be honest, I had to wrestle with my conscience since her brutal death. I'm a member of John's team of lecturers. He has been my manager and mentor for a couple of years. I must say it has been an enjoyable learning experience for me. John has taught me a lot, generous with his time and advice whenever I needed it. Occasionally, he would take us all out for a drink in a local pub. In fact, every lecturer in our team speaks highly of him,' Karen expressed her dilemma.

'I fully understand how you feel.'

'This isn't easy at all. I am the module leader for Margaret's group and I feel I owe it to her to assist in the investigation. The thought of not doing anything to help catch Margaret's killer has been playing on my mind. Although I like and respect John, I also believe that this is the right thing to do. I sincerely hope that the disagreement between John and Margaret is not connected to her death.' Karen stopped and wiped the tears. 'I wish to remain anonymous and expect you to respect the confidential nature of my involvement.'

'Absolutely. The contents of our meeting will only be shared with Detective Sgt Cooper and no one else. You've my word on this,' Alex reassured her.

'Thank you for being so understanding,' Karen said.

'Well Karen, I appreciate your courage to come forward with information which could prove useful to our investigation. Please keep this to yourself and thank you again,' Alex said. Then Karen left.

***

Immediately, Alex contacted Melanie on his mobile and informed her of the content of his conversation with Karen. He put her in the picture with regard to the position of Karen in her role as a lecturer and a member of John's team.

'Do you think she's genuine and telling the truth?' Melanie was checking the validity of Karen as a reliable witness.

'I believe she is. It couldn't have been easy for her to come forward and potentially get her boss into serious trouble. She revered John as her team leader. It's clear she heard John and Margaret arguing and the threat of deportation John made against Margaret and apparently, Margaret also making a counter threat that she would report John to the VC about his money-making activities. This could be a motive for her murder but, of course, we'll have to prove it,' Alex expressed it in a legal context. 'In fact, the VC and I saw Margaret leaving the tenth floor just after 10 am on that Monday. She looked upset and was in a hurry to leave. I held the door open for her. This tends to support Karen's statement.'

'What will happen if she changes her mind and withdraws her verbal statement?' Melanie was considering every eventuality.

'I don't believe that will happen. She was very serious and wanted to remain anonymous for obvious reasons.'

'I see. What do you suggest we do?'

'Do you want to interview Karen?'

'That won't be necessary as you've already met her.'

'Would it be better to pay John a visit and establish what he said to Margaret? A useful lead to follow.'

'I must admit John strikes me as a nice guy. I don't think any good will come out of us questioning him but I'm open to persuasion.'

Alex raised the tempo. 'This is the second time you have described John in a complimentary manner, first in the computer theft case and now in the murder case. Being pleasant to people, doesn't act as an automatic bar to criminal activities.'

Melanie was quick to respond. 'Oh, don't get me wrong, it's perfectly possible that John had made the threat.'

'I believe we need to see him soon to seek clarification about the threat he made to Margaret the day before her death. No harm in trying.'

'OK. We'll do that.'

'You're leading the investigation and I'm only assisting you. It would be better if you could set up a meeting with him as soon as possible and let me know.'

'Right. I'll get back to you,' Melanie said.

Alex strongly believed that coming across Margaret on that Monday at the University might have been a coincidence but it had also proved to have a profound effect on him in wanting to find her killer. At least, Alex had been able to get things moving on another case. While he listened to what Karen said about Margaret's response to John's threat, his mind was drawn to the issue of the letter. The words used by Margaret were money-making activities. Was there a link between the two?

Alex was aware that money-making could relate to a whole range of enterprises. It could be an outside interest entirely, for example, consultancy work, conducting workshops and seminars, or speaking at conferences. Incidentally, John had the experience and was fully capable of performing efficiently at these. The only reason the VC would be concerned was if John was engaged in the above activities during University time and without permission. Hence, it did not appear that Margaret's threat was worth pursuing at that time. That approach was put on the back burner.

***

Alex and Melanie went to see John together. Melanie had arranged a meeting at 2pm in his office to discuss an issue raised about Margaret's death.

Usually John was friendly and charming but on that day, he was serious and looked worried. Possibly because it's not often someone receives a visit from the Police regarding a murder.

'Please come on in and have a seat,' John said. He sat in his chair at his desk. 'What do you want to see me about?'

'We're here to check something with you, about what you said to Margaret the day before she was killed,' Melanie informed John.

Melanie was leading the interrogation, and Alex was just in attendance on that occasion, but reserved the right to ask questions, if appropriate.

'What was I supposed to have said to her?' John asked angrily.

'First of all, do you remember seeing Margaret around 10 o'clock on that Monday morning?'

Melanie tried to establish the sequence of events.

He paused for a few seconds.

'Of course I remember. I'm her personal tutor and I saw her around 10 am on that Monday regarding her lack of progress on the course,' John explained.

'Do you remember what you said to her?' Melanie asked.

'She needed to work hard to complete the course successfully, otherwise she would be discontinued from the course,' John said.

'Did you threaten her in any way?' Melanie asked.

'No I didn't,' John replied.

Melanie looked at Alex for vibes to either stop the questioning or carry on. Alex adopted a straight face and stared at her, suggesting she should probe further.

'Are you sure? We have heard from a reliable source that you told her that she would be discontinued from the course and threatened her with deportation to her home country,' Melanie said.

'Who told you that?' John asked.

'I'm not at liberty to disclose that person's name. You seem to concede that you did make that threat. Is that correct, John?' Melanie said.

'I'm not conceding to anything. It goes without saying that if she were to be discontinued from the course, the Home Office would withdraw her visa and she would be sent back home,' John explained succinctly.

'But making that statement in a temperate voice could be construed as a threat,' Melanie kept on pressing.

'I may have used the word deported instead of sent back home. There is nothing sinister about that. I was only telling her the truth,' John said.

Having thought beforehand to leave out the counter threat Margaret made against John, about reporting his money-making activities to the VC, Alex felt it was an opportune moment to test the water. His mind was in overdrive.

'Did Margaret threaten to report you to the VC?' Alex asked.

'I don't remember her making any threat to me, you've been misinformed,' John defended his position. 'What was she supposed to have said to me?'

John was just as cunning and was fishing for more information from Alex.

'Only about reporting you to the VC for your money-making activities,' Alex added.

John shook his head from side to side in disbelief. 'Again, I'm sorry I don't remember Margaret making any kind of threat to me at all,' John was adamant.

'Are you involved in any such activities?'

It was the right opportunity for Alex to explore any connection with the claim of the anonymous letter.

'Let me say categorically that in my own time as a senior academic, the only activities I have undertaken are addressing conferences and undertaking consultancy work in curriculum matters. This is a normal practice in the world of academia. Of course, the financial rewards are very good,' John enlightened them about one of his roles.

Alex fixed his eyes on John whilst listening to him attentively and then turned to Melanie, indicating with a nod that she could take over.

'Did anything else happen between you and Margaret on that morning?' Melanie asked.

'No,' John replied emphatically. Then he went on the attack. 'Am I a suspect in Margaret's murder?'

Both Melanie and Alex were quiet. Melanie raised her eyebrows to Alex. Then Alex chose to butt in.

'John, you aren't a suspect. I'm sure you'll agree and to be fair to Margaret's murder case, we have to follow any lead we encounter.' A brief pause followed.

John agreed with Alex. 'Yes, I do understand.'

'Could you tell us where you were on Tuesday night between 8 pm and 10 pm?' Melanie asked.

'Why?' John asked intriguingly.

'Just a routine check,' Melanie said firmly.

'I was with my girlfriend,' John replied.

'What is her name and how can we get hold of her?' Melanie asked.

John stared at her and Alex. 'Her name is Jane Fergusson, Senior lecturer in our Faculty and her office is on this floor.'

'We'll check with her,' Melanie said.

'I'm sure she'll say we were together that Tuesday night,' John replied.

Melanie felt she had exhausted her line of questioning and said, 'Thank you, John.'

Both Alex and Melanie left John's office.

Given the fact that Melanie had been impressed by John's attitude towards her in the past, she conducted the enquiry with the utmost professionalism. Then again, Alex was not expecting anything less. Alex acknowledged her performance. 'You did well. You were incisive and business-like.'

'Thank you. That's very kind of you,' Melanie replied.

'I must say John conducted himself confidently,' Alex remarked.

Both Melanie and Alex were in deep thought. They had not achieved a great deal by quizzing John. Melanie asked, 'Do you think he told us the truth?'

'I don't think so. He's crafty and he knows how to manipulate situations to his advantage. The only thing I noticed was that he looked unsettled and defensive. Our meeting has undoubtedly shaken him... devious enough to cover his tracks.'

'I'm inclined to agree with you,' Melanie said. 'What do we do now?'

'I believe we have to keep an eye on him. Until we've more substantive evidence against him, there is nothing we can do right now. He's as guilty as sin, though,' Alex replied.

'We've to tread carefully with him, otherwise if he lodges a complaint against us, we'll be in trouble,' Melanie warned. Then she left and Alex went to see Tom.

***

It was time to check the serial number of the stolen laptop with Tom Evans. As Alex had not seen Tom for a few days, he wanted to touch base with him again. On the last occasion they had met, he had had to leave their meeting quickly to go to the VC's office.

Tom could have more information to share with him.

'Hello Tom, have you got time to spare?' Alex asked.

'Nice to see you again Alex. Come on in and have a seat,' Tom was rather pleased to have a chat with him.

'Good to see you too,' Alex replied, and sat down.

'How is the investigation going?' Tom was curious to find out. After all, as the AVA technician, he had a vested interest in the computer theft case.

'Actually not too bad. We've made some progress.'

'Well, have you found the stolen laptops and caught the thief yet?'

'Not quite. But we're getting there.'

'What can I do for you?'

'In fact, I very much hope you will be able help. Would it be possible for you to give me the serial numbers of the two stolen laptops?' Alex requested.

Tom went quiet for a few seconds. 'What do you need the serial numbers for?'

'Just to do some checking around,' Alex explained. 'I understand that there is a purchasing file for equipment in which detailed records regarding the purchase of computers are kept.'

'That's right. I'll need to obtain permission from the Dean to let you have a look at the purchasing file because confidential matters are recorded, such as financial details.' Tom was getting officious. Alex could understand the reason.

'How long will it take to obtain the authorisation?'

'I can't say but I'll contact him later today.'

'As soon as you receive the authorisation, would you be kind enough to contact me.'

'I'll certainly do that,' Tom confirmed.

If he could not have access to the purchasing file for equipment in the AVA office, he would have no choice but to contact the VC. The checking and confirmation of the serial numbers would confirm the identity of the computer thief.

Chapter 14

Although staff in the Faculty had been affected by Margaret's murder, the place had been running as usual. Everyday normal activities had been maintained. The work of the recruitment department was no exception. Matt ensured that suitable candidates were invited for interviews and a programme for interviewing was in operation.

The recruitment of students had gone very well and the Faculty was on its way to achieving the quota of students required for the next intake in September. Naturally, Matt was delighted with his efforts and his colleagues' contribution to the scheduled interviews of candidates. It was his second year of students' recruitment and he had managed to have a full complement of students for each intake. He had a good record which rightly, had invited praise from the Faculty and the VC.

Full support was given to him throughout his campaign of recruitment by John. It had not gone unnoticed by almost everyone that these two had been responsible in making the recruiting of students so successful, especially when it had been reported that, nationally, other higher education institutions had been experiencing great difficulties in meeting their student targets. Both Matt and John had done a sterling job in keeping the Faculty viable financially. However, some undercurrents had begun to surface regarding the interview process.

Matt was not happy with the way events had turned out. Since Margaret's death he had developed doubts about his interactions with John concerning recruitment. Matt decided to pay him a visit. John was in a jolly mood and very talkative. During their conversation, John made an announcement that, initially, shocked his friend.

'Relax Matt, we've done very well with regard to recruiting new students, although admittedly there are still a few more interviews to do. Then those recruited, will be put on the waiting list, anyway. We've almost got our quota for the next intake. The Dean and the VC are well satisfied with the recruitment..'

'I'm worried. In fact, I'm very worried,' Matt said.

'Don't be daft. What are you worried about?'

'I don't know how to say this,' Matt was cautious. He didn't want to upset his old friend.

'Anyway, I've a piece of good news to share with you,' John said.

'OK. What is it?' Matt asked.

John could sense that Matt had something on his mind and wanted to discuss it with him because he looked serious, pensive and a bit frightened. Matt had not smiled at John since he entered his office. He was also aware that in the past, Matt would get very concerned and worried about any inconsequential incident. 'I have run into some money and I am going to buy a sports car and go on an exotic holiday,' John said.

Matt was gobsmacked. 'You've always complained you don't have enough money to last the month. Where did you get such an obscene amount of money from?'

'I've done some outside work which has paid well,' John explained.

Matt found it hard to believe him. 'It would take an awful lot of time and consultancy work to get that amount of money, for you to be able to buy a car and go on holiday.'

'Believe me, I've done a great deal of outside work actually. Anyway, what do you want to talk to me about?'

'It's about Margaret's murder.'

'What about it? It's very sad but we've got to move on. We can't do anything to help. Leave it to the professionals to find the killer. Detective Sgt Cooper and Alex are working hard to solve the case.'

'Well, I've been looking at the "lists" of candidates' names you gave me to help them get onto the course,' Matt said reluctantly.

'And,' John replied calmly.

'Margaret's name is on one of them,' Matt said.

'So what. Only you and I know about this. No one else does,' John reassured him.

'What will happen if the Police find out?' Matt asked.

'Nothing. Don't forget you've been helping these poor students to get on the course and make a future for themselves. In addition, on completion of their course, they will go back to their original country and help their own people. Your contribution to and participation in this fantastic venture is truly remarkable and is much appreciated,' John said.

'I recognise that.'

'Margaret's name being on the "list" isn't the reason why she was killed.'

Matt remained unconvinced by John's explanation.

'The Police might take a different view. The South African Embassy could contact the Police to find out how she was killed. Through their enquiries, if the Police talk to those people at the Embassy you have been liaising with, about helping these students to get on the course, we could become suspects.'

'You're letting your imagination run away with you. Trust me, everything is fine,' John tried to reassure him.

'I must say, John, I'm worried.'

'What do you suggest we do?'

'I don't know. I haven't been sleeping well lately. I want to tell the VC about these students and my involvement. I don't want to lose my job.'

'What on earth do you want to do that for?'

'Hopefully, he'll be lenient towards me for being honest and won't take any action against me.'

'That's nonsense, and don't you ever forget who got you this job in the first place? You owe me a great deal.'

John raised his voice to remind Matt of his obligations.

'Believe me, I'm very grateful to you for that.'

'I believe you should keep quiet and hold your nerve. Just imagine if you go and tell the VC about our little plan to assist these foreign students, what do you think he'll do.'

John raised his voice again. Matt shook his head in amazement.

'The VC will have to discipline us for not implementing the recruitment policy to the full and for devising our own strategy to get these students onto the course. We could be sacked. Do you want that to happen?'

'No. I don't want us to lose our jobs,' Matt replied.

'Forget about this matter. Go about your work and life as normal. You'll soon get over it.'

'I hear what you are saying. But...' Matt said sheepishly.

'Matt, remember you owe me big time and I mean real big time. Don't say a word to anyone.'

John was of the opinion that Matt had not been persuaded by his argument. It would be better to leave things as they were because he could not change Matt's mind.

Matt left John's office totally dismayed. Without the bending of the rules, Margaret would not have been on the course and would still be alive today. His concern was becoming more acute, regardless of how much John had tried to dismiss the significance of it. Inexplicably, Matt had become pre-occupied with the notion that Margaret's murder might end up having a connection to the 'list'. Through their investigation, the Police might make the link between the murder and John's contact at the Embassy. Ultimately, it would lead to the 'list'. As a result, he would be implicated and seen as an accomplice to the murder.

***

There was a copy of the Faculty magazine in Alex's in-tray, he picked it up. The magazine was produced monthly. He noticed a picture of John on the cover and he took a long hard look at it. It prompted him to think that John's picture could be used to enhance the investigation in his computer theft case. He tore off the cover from the magazine and put it in his inside jacket pocket.

As he had planned to go to Hammersmith town centre that morning, he decided to call into the computer shop to have another chat with Adrian.

'Good morning, Alex. Nice to see you again,' Adrian welcomed him warmly and offered his hand which Alex shook.

'Thank you and good morning,' Alex replied.

'What can I do for you?' Adrian asked whilst tidying his counter.

'I hope you'll be able to help,' Alex said.

'That depends,' Adrian replied.

'I know you come across many customers and it'll be unfair to expect you to remember the details of our conversation the other day,' Alex was trying to set the scene when Adrian interrupted him.

'I'll never forget you, Alex. You and your companion, Scott, were asking me searching questions about a laptop sold to us on 13 May. Am I right?'

'That's correct. You're very good,' Alex used the opportunity to praise him, to make him feel very important.

'Thank you,' Adrian replied with a wide grin.

Alex got to the point by removing the cover of the Faculty magazine from his jacket pocket and showing it to Adrian.

'Can you have a good look at this picture and tell me what you can see, Adrian?'

'This is the guy who sold the laptop to us,' Adrian exclaimed instantly.

'Are you sure that you bought a laptop from this man on 13 May?' Alex checked again with Adrian.

'I'm absolutely sure,' Adrian replied emphatically.

'Thank you very much for identifying the guy and for your time. I do appreciate it,' Alex said while shaking Adrian's hand. He headed back to the Agency to share the good news with his team.

***

It was lunch time when Alex arrived at the Agency. Luckily for him, Jenny had already got him some ham sandwiches and a yoghurt which he devoured within minutes. He had to rush as he was expecting to see a potential client for his Agency's business.

Alex had already received a phone call from this client who spelt out to him what she needed to be done. In his office, he spent over an hour with the client, listening to her demands, discussing details of her requirements and agreeing the terms of arrangement including his fees.

Alex always drove a hard bargain and his service was not cheap because he always delivered on what he had promised.

Once the client had left, Alex briefed his team about where he was at with the three cases. Scott was shocked to hear about the third case Alex had agreed to take. 'Alex, have you gone completely mad?' Scott asked.

'Why didn't you tell us about it before? Jenny added.

'This isn't our area of work. It's very difficult to find out anything about an anonymous letter. It could take a lot of our valuable time and yet, not resolve anything. Time which could be spent on cases which would pay well,' Scott pointed out.

Alex was trying to chip in but both of them were so annoyed that they could not control their disapproval.

'This is becoming a habit. First it was the computer theft case, then the murder case and now the letter, what next?' Jenny asked.

'Let me explain,' Alex said.

'We're supposed to be a team, and yet we weren't consulted on taking up any of these three cases. That's not fair,' Scott stated his opinion firmly, and made his feelings plain.

'Have you two finished now?' Alex asked in a stern voice.

'No. Would these three cases bring in the same amount of revenue as our normal business streams?' Jenny got to the point somewhat ruthlessly.

Alex did not know what had hit him and was speechless for a few seconds. He knew Jenny and Scott had every reason to question him over their workload. If the roles were reversed, he most probably would have felt the same way, ignored and taken for granted. Now, he had to tread carefully. 'Actually no. Let me explain my rationale for accepting the case regarding the anonymous letter. I've already given you my reasons for the computer theft case and the murder case.'

Alex raised his eyebrows whilst looking at them.

Both nodded in agreement. Alex noticed a sign of reconciliation in their faces. Obviously both of them had reacted strongly to Alex, on hearing about the third case. They had got their anger off their chest and were ready now to hear what Alex had to say.

'The VC received this anonymous letter about a senior academic charging students to get a place on the nursing course. I'm sure you'll agree that this is a very sensitive issue to be handled with great care. Otherwise, the reputation of the University will be badly affected and this could have untold consequences. From day one, the VC asked me not to tell anyone, and I haven't, until now. I feel both of you need to know because you are involved in one form or another. Admittedly, I'm doing all the legwork on the three cases. That's all really,' Alex was at pains to explain.

'Sorry, I lost my cool,' Jenny was quick to apologise.

'I'm sorry as well,' Scott said.

'There is a very slight possibility that there is a link amongst the three cases,' Alex threw that hot potato in for their reaction.

Both appeared stunned at that disclosure. 'Do you have any evidence to that effect?' Scott was quick to ask.

'Not yet. As I just said, it's only a gut feeling,' Alex replied.

'You've solved cases before on your gut feelings,' Jenny reminded him. 'I didn't know you had so much on your plate. Again, I'm sorry about my outburst earlier.'

'That's ok, I understand. Let's move on. I went to see Adrian this morning and after looking at this picture, he confirmed it was the same guy who sold him the laptop.' Alex showed them the cover page of the Faculty magazine.

'Who is he?' Jenny asked.

'His name is John Fairbanks, Principal Lecturer at the University,' Alex explained.

'Do you think he stole the laptop from the University?' Scott asked.

'We'll find out shortly. I'm yet to check on the serial number,' Alex said.

'Do you think he is responsible for the three crimes?' Scott pressed him further.

'I don't know. All the signs have started to point in his direction. Nothing may result from our efforts, but he's worth pursuing at the moment,' Alex explained.

At that stage, Alex informed them of Alison and Karen dropping in on him and providing him with useful information. He also explained that Melanie was pursuing the issue of the escort agency and she would be checking on John's alibi as well.

'It looks like these so called witnesses prefer to talk to you rather than the Police,' Jenny observed.

'I guess I'm on site, so they can contact me easily and discreetly,' Alex explained.

'What do you want us to do?' Scott asked.

'By the way, I contacted our usual sources and couldn't find anything sinister about John Fairbanks. He's clean,' Jenny butted in quickly.

'Thanks Jenny,' Alex said. 'Can you check on how many escort agencies there are in the vicinity and let Scott have their addresses and contact numbers?'

'Will do,' Jenny replied.

'Scott, can you check with these escort agencies about clients who used the services of Margaret regularly. Then contact these clients to check their whereabouts on the night of Margaret's murder. By the way, the Police are doing the same thing as you. Be discreet.' Alex felt that by finding the jealous or irate client, the murder case could be solved pretty quickly.

There were smiles all round. Normal business was resumed. Personal differences were forgotten. Everyone was behaving as if nothing untoward had happened amongst them and just got on with their jobs - a happy family once again.

Chapter 15

Matt was still pondering over the announcement of John's extravagance. He was suspicious of John's claim as to how he had obtained this large sum of money. Since their teachers' training course days, John had pleaded about his shortage of cash. He never had enough money. Suddenly, he was boasting about buying a sports car and taking an exotic holiday which really caught Matt's attention in a big way. What was troubling him was where did John really get the money from?

From the beginning, he was dubious of John's motivation for helping the South African students. Matt believed that John had not been telling him the truth but he could not figure it out.

He doubted John's altruistic venture to help his diplomatic friend, by offering places to these students on the nursing course.

He felt obliged to go along with his plan because John had got him the job as recruitment officer. Initially, John asked whether he could do him a favour of accepting 2 students, then 15 and then another 25. Gradually, the numbers seemed to be increasing. John had another 25 on his 'list' for the next intake in September. He could not carry on with it. John had made it clear that he should not tell the VC because both of them would be in trouble. From a cathartic standpoint, Matt felt he had to talk to someone and chose to speak to Alex, probably because Alex was an outsider.

Matt spoke to Alex on the phone. 'Alex, can I see you sometime?'

'Hello Matt. Of course you can see me. When do you want to meet?' Alex replied.

'How about tomorrow afternoon at 5.30pm after I finish work?' Matt suggested.

'That's fine. I'll come to your office.'

'No, I'd rather meet you in your Agency office, if that's alright with you.'

Alex was puzzled as to why Matt wanted to see him so far away when he could pop up a few floors and do just that.

'Of course we can meet at the Agency. Do you know how to get there?'

'Oh yes, I have the address and will be able to find you.'

'Is there anything I need to do or prepare for our meeting?'

Alex was fishing for the reason for this request.

'You don't have to do anything, Alex.'

'OK. Can you give me an idea why you wish to see me? I'll understand if you prefer not to do so at the moment.'

After a brief pause Matt said, 'Actually, I want to talk to you about the matter of a "list", I'll explain in detail tomorrow.'

'OK. I'll see you in my office at 5.30 pm.'

He would have preferred to find out more but Matt rang off. Alex was a very shrewd man anyway; coupled with his legal experience he would instinctively examine every detail of an incident and every word of a conversation. Matt used the word 'list' which set his brain waves in action. He remembered that he first heard that word when he met Matt and John in Matt's office. John had said to Matt 'Don't forget the list' and that statement had stuck in his mind. It could be, Matt believed, that the 'list' had a great significance to his investigations. Hence the reason, Matt had decided to meet with him secretly away from the University.

***

Brian Simpson, Chairman of the Board of Governors, usually held meetings at the University on Thursdays. He asked the VC to request that Alex meet them in the VC's office at 9 am.

Alex accepted the invitation with great interest as it would be nice to meet up with the two men who were responsible for using the services of his Agency.

'Good morning Alex, do come in,' the VC said.

Once he was in the office, the VC introduced him to the Chairman. 'Meet Brian Simpson, the Chairman of the Board of Governors for the University.'

'Nice to meet you, Sir,' Alex said humbly.

'And it's very nice to meet you as well, Alex. Through Peter I've heard a great deal about you, your credentials and the work you've undertaken for us. Please call me Brian,' he said. 'As you are dealing with these high profile cases on our behalf, I thought it's time we met face to face and get to know each other. You've kept Peter informed of your actions and he, in turn, me. I do apologise for not meeting with you earlier but I've been exceptionally busy with University matters.'

All three men sat down and had coffee while talking about Premier League Football. Then the direction of their conversation changed. 'We're all busy people, so let's get down to business. The Board meeting will start in an hour's time. The reason I asked for this meeting Alex is, firstly to meet you and secondly, to discuss my concerns with you. Is that ok?' Brian set the scene for their meeting.

'I fully understand.'

'Peter had discussed with me at great length, the urgent matter of the computer thefts and that of the letter before he met you. Peter and I decided to ask you to look into both these cases for reasons, I'm sure, he has explained. The resolution of the computer thefts would, no doubt, assist Peter in his pursuit of securing funding for his IT project. More importantly, the resolution of the issue regarding the letter would protect the reputation of the whole University,' Brian said. A brief pause followed.

Then he continued, 'Crucially, we also have a murder case on our hands and the Police will do their best to catch the killer. This isn't only about my business interests in South Africa and my admiration for their people, but it is also to do with students feeling free and comfortable to come and study at our University. There is a lot riding on finding the killer which will reassure existing and future students and staff that it is safe for them to be here.'

Brian was keen to explain to Alex the rationale for his employment and the potential consequences of the three cases.

'I do share your sentiments and my team and I will do everything we possibly can to resolve these cases,' Alex replied.

'How are the investigations progressing?'

Alex looked straight at him and said, 'We've made a lot of progress on all three fronts. If I can take them one at a time. On the computer thefts, I've found the shop where the laptop was sold. More checks have to be carried before I can confirm the alleged thief.'

Peter interrupted him. 'That's excellent news.'

'On the matter of the letter, progress has been slow. I can confirm to you that I'm seeing a potential witness tomorrow who could shed more light on this matter and also the murder case.'

Now it was the turn of Brian to get excited. 'I must say that sounds very optimistic.'

'On Margaret's murder case, two witnesses have come forward to see me and I've passed on the information to Detective Sgt Cooper. We have already seen John Fairbanks and clarified with him one of the witnesses' statements. I must say at this stage, John isn't a suspect. I hasten to add Sgt Cooper had informed both the Dean and the VC of our intention to interview John Fairbanks. The Police are continuing with their enquiries. These developments have taken place during the last few days.'

Alex stopped for any comments. Both men nodded and looked pleased. Evidently they were very impressed.

'You seem to be on top of it all, Alex,' Brian acknowledged his hard work.

'The first week you familiarised yourself with the place and the people and the second week you've begun to make some serious inroads into these cases,' Peter added.

'Detective Sgt Cooper and her team, my own team and I are all fully committed to finding the killer of Margaret and the signs indicate that we will do so in due course. The Police are not involved in the other two cases which are my responsibility. Again, the same commitment is in operation to solve these. We may have to tread on some toes to get results,' Alex said.

'Don't let that deter you from your investigations. You do what you need to do. You have our full support,' Brian reassured him.

Initially the atmosphere at the meeting was quite tense, especially for Alex, but towards the end he had them practically eating out of his hands. His legal skills were put to excellent use and his employers were mesmerised by his performance. In fact, Brian and Peter were not expecting the progress that had already been achieved by Alex.

'It's been a real pleasure to meet you and good luck,' Brian said warmly.

'Thank you for giving me the opportunity to meet with you,' Alex returned the compliment.

'See you Alex,' Peter said with a satisfied smile.

'And you,' Alex nodded, also with a smile. Smiles were on show all around.

It was time for both Brian and Peter to leave for their Board meeting.

***

Alison contacted the Agency to make an appointment to see Alex. Jenny arranged for Alex to see her at the University. Alison went to his office on site.

'Hello Alison, nice to see you,' Alex said and offered her a chair.

'I hope you don't mind seeing me,' Alison asked.

'Not at all. How are you?'

'I'm ok, thank you. I do miss my friend.'

'I understand. I do share your grief. Time is the healer. Anything I can do to help, please ask.'

'Thank you.'

Then she took her time to utter the words that she wanted to say. She sat on the edge of the chair, wringing her hands and looking at him with her head slightly tilted. Alex made an attempt to calm her down, as she probably had some information to give him about the murder.

'Take your time. No need to worry about anything. No one can hear what you say as the office next door is empty. People hardly come on this floor. You are safe to speak. Anyway, you've been here before. Thank you again for telling me about Margaret's escort activities, the Police and my team are investigating these,' Alex reassured her.

She felt a bit more relaxed and ready to talk. She lowered her shoulders and managed a faint smile.

'It's about Margaret. I remembered something she said during one of our social gatherings in the Residence,' Alison explained.

'What did she say to you?'

'I don't know how important what I'm going to say will be?'

'It may have a big influence on our investigation, you know. Don't worry about anything. Even a small amount of information could make a significant contribution.'

'She said that a senior academic had asked her for money.'

Upon hearing Alison's disclosure, Alex sat upright, straightening his backbone and, moving his head slightly forward, he asked, 'Money for what?'

'For her to stay on the course.'

'How does that work? She was already on the course.'

'Apparently that's how she got on to the course, by paying for a place.'

'I don't understand. You mean she paid to get onto the course.'

Alex was astonished to hear it.

'That's right.'

That statement stunned Alex and he could not contain his disgust. 'It's unbelievable.'

'Actually, the way it worked was that Margaret had paid a senior academic through a third party, attended for interview and was then given a place on the nursing course.'

'Did that apply to all students?'

'No. Only some of the foreign students paid.'

'What's the name of the senior academic?'

'She didn't tell me.'

'Who is the third party?'

'I don't know. Again she didn't say.'

'Anything else you would like to share with me?'

'Well, Margaret told me that this person wanted her to give him an extra £500.'

'Why?'

'The senior academic obviously noticed her lifestyle and believed that she had plenty of money and could afford to pay more money to stay on the course. Margaret was a strong-willed person and could stand up for herself very well. When she refused to accede to his outrageous demand, she duly reminded that person that she had already paid a large sum of money to get a place on the course. The senior academic threatened to get her deported back to her home country.'

Alex's antennae were on full alert. Karen Fletcher had informed him of a similar threat made to Margaret. He kept his composure and continued to encourage Alison to express herself.

'How was that going to happen?'

'To be honest, Margaret wasn't serious enough with her studies. She used to enjoy her social life a bit too much. As a result, she didn't do well in her written assignments. The senior academic was aware of her progress or lack of it and that was what he used to threaten her. She was told she would be discontinued, her visa would be withdrawn and she would be deported.'

'What else did Margaret tell you?'

'Well Margaret told him she would report him to the VC for his money-making activities.'

Alex noticed that there was a strong similarity between Alison's statement and that of Karen Fletcher. Now it was the turn of Alison to ask a searching question. 'Do you think that senior academic could have killed Margaret?'

'Truly, I don't know. I can't answer that question.'

'That's ok.'

'I want you to know that you've been very brave in coming forward with this important information which will, no doubt, help the investigation.'

'I hope it will help to catch Margaret's killer.'

'So do I. I'll have to share this information with Detective Sgt Cooper who is leading the investigation into Margaret's murder.' Alex was keeping everything above board.

'I understand,' Alison replied, and left.

Listening to Alison talking about a senior academic asking for money from a student, the small matter of the letter just flashed in front of Alex's eyes. The same student had had to pay a large sum of money to obtain a place on the nursing course. Supposedly, this payment for a place linked across to the allegation made in the letter regarding charging of students. Had he, unexpectedly, come across a crucial break. More information and proof would be required to get to the bottom of it.

Chapter 16

Recently, there had been some fast moving developments in Margaret's murder case. Alex needed to get hold of Melanie and let her know of the latest information he had received, which could prove crucial to the case. He made contact with her from his mobile phone.

'Hi, how are you?' Alex asked.

'I'm fine, thank you. Good to hear from you. How are you keeping?' Melanie replied.

'Have you got a couple of minutes to talk?'

'Yes I have, but I can do better than that. I'm quite close to your Agency office so I could call in to see you.' Melanie was curious to see where he was based.

'That would be great. I'll see you in a few minutes.'

Alex could not believe his luck; he wanted her to visit him at the Agency and see his place of work at first hand.

'Jenny, could you tidy up the place as I'm expecting a very special visitor? Thank you,' Alex asked nicely.

'The place is always tidy. Who is this so called special visitor?' Jenny was curious.

Alex had to be very careful in his reply to Jenny who kept a sharp eye on him. Ever since his uncle had asked her to ensure Alex was alright, she had taken that task very seriously. She had tended to overprotect him at times. She would, no doubt, size up the visitor and make her assessment clearly known to him.

'It's Detective Sgt Melanie Cooper. She is coming to discuss the murder case.'

'Oh, I see.'

The front door bell rang via the intercom. Jenny answered and pressed the button for the door to open. 'Come through Detective Sgt Cooper.'

The front door opened and Melanie entered the Agency office.

Jenny was waiting to welcome her. 'Nice to meet you, Detective Sgt Cooper. Let me take you to Alex's office, he's expecting you.'

'Very nice to meet you too. Thank you,' Melanie said with a smile and followed Jenny.

By that time Alex had opened his office door. 'Hello Melanie, come on right in and have a seat. Thank you, Jenny.'

'Would you both like a cup of tea?' Jenny asked.

'Yes please, milk and no sugar. Thank you that's very kind,' Melanie said.

'My usual, please Jenny,' Alex added.

He could not believe how nice Jenny was towards Melanie. Previously, Jenny had always warned Alex to be careful and not to trust Detective Sgt Cooper. As usual, he was bowled over by the sheer beauty of his guest who was dressed in a grey striped skirt suit and a bright pink blouse which had the top two buttons open. Her shiny blonde hair made her look really glamorous.

'You've a very impressive office. It's very nice and plush.'

'That's very generous of you, thank you. We like it.'

'Well, you wanted to see me, Alex.'

Melanie wanted to get on with it.

'Oh. You make it sound like an invitation.'

'Now, now. Let's keep it strictly business.'

'Of course. I will. It's to do with the murder case.'

He described in detail to her what Alison had told him. To keep her own records up to date, Melanie took copious notes as Alex gave a detailed account of Alison's statement.

By that time, Jenny had knocked and entered with a tray containing two cups of tea and few chocolate biscuits on a small plate. 'Enjoy your tea,' Jenny said with a wide smile.

'Thank you, Jenny,' Alex replied. He was very impressed by Jenny's gesture.

'I love chocolate biscuits,' Melanie said.

'So do I. Please help yourself.' Alex offered her the plate of biscuits and she took one.

'OK, shall we resume now,' Melanie said.

'Yes, of course. What do you think of Alison's statement?' Alex asked.

'We need to follow it and investigate accordingly.' Melanie put her point across.

'Would you like to meet up with Alison and discuss this further?'

'Not at present. She seems to trust you and feels comfortable providing you with useful information. If I get involved, she might withdraw and become reluctant to come forward. Not everyone trusts the Police as you know very well. Do you believe she's got more information to share with you?' Melanie was reacting cautiously.

'Hard to be precise. I've got this gut feeling that Alison might disclose more crucial information soon. As she was the closest to Margaret, it's possible she could be our best hope yet of catching the killer.'

'In that case, let's wait for further disclosures from her before we take positive action.'

'I would like to address the current information hypothetically, if I may,' Alex said, and wanted to provide an analysis of the information received.

'Please go ahead,' Melanie was very interested to hear him.

'I believe there is something very pertinent to the case. If you remember in the statement of Karen, the Lecturer, about the threat John was alleged to have made against Margaret. We saw John about it and he denied making such a threat,' Alex said.

'I do remember it very well. Incidentally, we checked and John was with Jane Fergusson, his girlfriend, on the night Margaret was murdered. Apparently, he was with her from 7 pm. I did leave you a message on your mobile,' Melanie confirmed John's alibi.

'Yes I did get your message. There is strong similarity between Alison's statement of a senior academic's threat towards Margaret and Karen's statement of John's threat to Margaret that took place on the same day. What do you think?'

'I'm inclined to agree with you,' Melanie said, and briefly drifted in a pensive mood.

'John has already denied any threat against Margaret but there is also a strong similarity between Alison's statement of how the threat was made regarding Margaret's deportation, and John's explanation to us of the way he used the word deportation to Margaret,' Alex impressed on Melanie the link between the two statements.

'Are you saying that the senior academic is John Fairbanks?' Melanie asked intriguingly.

'That's exactly what I'm saying,' Alex replied.

'Did Alison mention John as the senior academic?'.

'No. She didn't know who the senior academic was?'

'To be honest, I do find it hard to believe that it's John.

As I've said to you before, John strikes me as a real gentleman and a top professional,' Melanie said.

'Appearances can be deceptive as well. Depending on the circumstances, a criminal act can be caused by anyone at any time without prejudice. I do believe that the evidence, thus far, points tangibly in John's direction,' Alex was at his legal best.

'But why would he do such a thing, if indeed he has?' Melanie stated, and still not fully convinced.

'Difficult to put my finger on it exactly. I'm only dealing with the facts. A possible scenario could be as follows. He probably got into or found himself in a desperate position, couldn't control his emotion and, unintentionally, ended up committing a criminal act.'

'I can see your point of view. How do we proceed in the absence of clear evidence?' Melanie asked.

'We can't say for sure it was John who committed the crime. Karen said she heard John make a threat to deport Margaret, but not to kill her. Motive, Means and Opportunity have to be proven conclusively. We are quite a distance away from providing the proof. First of all, concrete evidence placing him at the crime scene is needed.'

Alex focused on what needed to be done.

'OK. It's only conjecture right now. On my return to the department I'll discuss the issue of academic staff charging students for a place at the University. I'll let you know if we find anything from our archives,' Melanie said purposefully.

Alex was in a dilemma. Should he tell Melanie about the case of the letter now or should he wait a little longer, when he would be in possession of all the facts? What would happen if Melanie's team started to question people about the issue of students being charged? Everything would become public and it would affect the reputation of the University. It would appear that he had no choice but to disclose the case of the letter. Given the rapport he had established with Melanie, it would be very difficult not to tell her the truth which, until now, he had hidden from her. However, the time had come for him to bite the bullet and let her know.

'Melanie, I've a confession to make,' Alex said quietly.

'What do you mean?' Melanie was puzzled.

'I'll come straight to the point.'

'I think that will help me understand what you're talking about.'

'Well, when I first met the VC to discuss the computer thefts, he told me he had a more pressing problem for me to solve. To cut a long story short, he'd received an anonymous letter stating that a senior academic had been charging foreign students money in exchange for a place on the nursing course and, if this wasn't stopped immediately, a copy of the letter would be sent to the press.'

Alex paused.

'What does the anonymous letter have to do with our investigation?' Melanie could not see the connection.

'The VC asked me not to tell anyone about the letter. He asked me to investigate the allegation made in the letter discreetly, whilst investigating the computer theft case. He and the Chairman of the Board believe the leaking of this letter will have a catastrophic impact on the reputation of the University. Recruitment and retention of both students and staff would be severely affected.'

Alex gave the rationale for the secrecy.

'I still don't understand the connection,' Melanie said. Then the penny dropped. 'Why didn't you tell me about it at the beginning?'

'I made a promise to the VC. That's why?' Alex replied.

'Alex, we're supposed to be working together and trust each other.'

Melanie was disappointed but had to maintain a professional outlook.

'Look, I couldn't let you and your team investigate the issue of illegally charging students for a place at the University. It would spread like wildfire and the whole country would know. It would have a negative effect on the reputation of the University. That's why it's better I tell you now before you ask your team to look into the matter,' Alex explained his position.

'What do you want me to do then?' Melanie was steaming with anger.

'May I suggest that you keep this information secret for the time being and not to start your investigation yet; as this will prevent potential damage to the University. Let me handle it first. I believe I'm quite close to cracking the case.'

Alex waited patiently for her reply.

Following a big sigh, Melanie warned, 'Alright. I'll wait, but not for long.'

'Thank you, I do appreciate it,' Alex replied.

Melanie was obviously not pleased that she was being kept in the dark regarding the investigation into the letter case which Alex had been conducting. Being an astute professional, she could also recognise that Alex had been employed by the University and, therefore, he had to be loyal to his employers. After all, he was only assisting her in the investigation to find Margaret's killer. Technically speaking, the computer theft case and the letter case were solely Alex's responsibilities. Getting mad with Alex should not be an option for her to contemplate. Instead, she should focus on the murder case and work alongside him.

'So, you've been handling three investigations at the same time. If you hadn't told me I wouldn't have known. I must say, you're very resourceful,' Melanie said, and managed to maintain her composure.

'It was a coincidence really. Events occurred at such a great pace when I first met the VC. Initially, it was the computer theft case which was then coupled by issue of the letter. As soon as I started conducting the investigations, Margaret was killed. And you know the rest.'

'I understand you've a job to do and by what I've seen, you're very good at it.'

Melanie complimented him on his work ethic.

Their discussion was coming to an end. Melanie stood up. Alex went close to her, offering an olive branch and asked, 'Can I take you to dinner tonight?'

Melanie moved her pouting lips up and down and looking up said, 'Why do you want to take me to dinner all of a sudden?'

'I thought it'll make up for our difference of opinion on the subject of the letter, you looked a bit unsettled,' Alex explained.

'I see. There is no need, honest,' Melanie replied. Secretly, she was delighted he had asked but did not want to show it.

'I would like to, unless you…'

'Unless what?' Melanie was getting curious.

'Maybe you've a date with Blackshaw or you would prefer not to have dinner with me. Either way, I won't be offended.'

'Oh dear. Let me make it clear, for a start, Blackshaw is abroad on business and I don't have any objection to having dinner with you,' Melanie was quick to rebut.

'In that case, would you do me the honour of having dinner with me tonight?'

'You don't give up easily, do you? Of course, I accept,' Melanie acquiesced.

'Shall we go to the Excelsior restaurant in Mayfair? We'll meet in the bar at 7.30 pm,' Alex suggested.

'That's suits me fine.'

'Do you know where the Excelsior is?'

'I've been to the Excelsior before. I'll see you there at 7.30 pm but won't be able to stay late as I've got an early start tomorrow morning,' Melanie was happy to confirm.

'Yes, of course,' Alex replied.

'Thank you for the tea, Jenny. Bye,' Melanie said while passing her office and Alex walked her to the door.

'Bye,' Jenny replied. By the time she had stopped typing and came out of her office, Melanie had left.

'She's gone,' Alex informed her.

'Oh. She's very nice, isn't she?' Jenny said.

'Yes, she is,' Alex replied.

'She's too nice and beautiful to be a Policewoman.' Jenny was never slow on expressing her opinion strongly.

'If you say so, Jenny.'

'Why don't you ask her for a date?'

'I thought you didn't like the Police in general.'

'Melanie is an exception. I think you should ask her for a date.'

'You used to refer to her as 'that woman' and said I should be careful with her. Don't trust her and all that. Now you seem to have changed your mind all of a sudden.'

Alex again reminded her of her prejudice.

'That was in the past. You've to admit, she is gorgeous and very well mannered.'

Jenny was getting very persuasive.

Alex was pleased to hear that Jenny liked Melanie but he did not want to give any indication that he also liked Melanie, but in a totally different way.

'By the way, Melanie and I are meeting for dinner tonight,' Alex informed his pushy PA.

'That's wonderful. I'm sure you will both enjoy yourselves,' Jenny gave her blessing.

'Thank you, Jenny,' Alex responded.

Chapter 17

Before leaving his office, Alex decided to check with Scott about the cases he was working on including the escort agencies.

'Hi Alex. I'm making progress on the Faulkner case,' Scott said.

'That's great. Any luck on the escort agencies?'

'I have actually. I followed up on the addresses Jenny gave me. There are only three locally, so I paid them a visit. Margaret was on the books of one of them for the last six months or so. She had a few outings with four different clients. I quickly set out to check on them. On the night of Margaret's murder, two of them were abroad, one was out with another escort lady and the fourth one was with a friend who confirmed his story.'

'Was she registered with any escort agency in the Central London area?'

'Both Jenny and I have phoned every escort agency in that area, and she hadn't registered with any.'

'Did you find these agencies helpful?'

'After I explained the reason for my enquiry, all the agencies were helpful. I was also told the Police had contacted them as well.'

'Good work. Would you say then, we can rule out the theory that Margaret could have been murdered by a jealous client?'

'Through my enquiries with the escort agencies, I can confirm that theory is a non-starter.'

'I agree.'

'Do you think more witnesses will come forward?'

'I hope so.'

Scott changed the subject. 'By the way, have you been able to check the serial number of the laptop with Tom, the AVA technician.'

'I went to see him about it. He had to check with the Dean before allowing me access to the purchasing file for equipment,' Alex replied. 'I'm waiting to hear from him.'

That prompted him to be pro-active and contact Tom to find out whether he had received permission from the Dean, yet. 'OK Scott, must go, and talk to you later.'

***

Alex knew that Tom Evans usually worked till six o'clock on most days. There was still some time left before Tom left. Alex rang Tom to find out about his request to check the serial numbers of the stolen laptops. 'Hello Tom, it's Alex here. How are you?' Alex said.

'I'm fine, thank you. I guess you're ringing me to check whether the Dean has given the authorisation.'

'I am actually.'

'I've got the go-ahead from the Dean and you're welcome to do the checking at a convenient time for both of us.'

'As it's late Thursday afternoon now, can I come to see you tomorrow morning?'

'I'm afraid I'm very busy tomorrow morning. May I suggest on Monday at 1pm.'

'Monday afternoon will be fine. See you then.'

There was high expectation on Alex's part, that evening. Having dinner with a beautiful woman was always exciting and if it happened to be Melanie, it would add a special ingredient to spice up the atmosphere. Melanie was also harbouring pleasant thoughts of her own about Alex as she had enjoyed his company every time they had met.

Alex was at the Excelsior restaurant early to welcome his guest. He was in the bar and chose a small table not far from the entrance so that he could have clear sight of Melanie when she arrived. As soon as Alex spotted Melanie coming through the door, he left his seat and went to meet her.

'Hi Melanie, good of you to come. We're sitting over here.' Alex extended his right hand which was warmly received by Melanie's soft hand.

'Glad to be here, wouldn't miss it for the world,' Melanie replied whilst taking her seat.

'What would you like to drink?' Alex asked.

'May I have a glass of red wine, please,' Melanie replied.

'Certainly.' Alex called the waiter to place his order. The waiter arrived and was holding his silver tray. 'Drinks, Sir.'

'Yes please. A glass of red wine and a pint of your best bitter,' Alex said.

The waiter took the order and disappeared, returning in a few minutes with the drinks.

True to form, Melanie did not disappoint in her outfit. It was quite warm that evening. She wore an above knee pink dress with a peach coloured cardigan. He was in his blue suit, white shirt and a purple tie. Both of them looked stunning together.

'You do look beautiful this evening. I like your dress,' Alex complimented her.

'You're looking very smart and I like your tie,' Melanie returned the compliment.

The drinks arrived. They toasted each other with a simple 'Cheers' by clinking their glasses together.

'The table is booked for eight o'clock. It won't be long before we move to the restaurant,' Alex informed his guest.

'That's fine,' Melanie replied with a smile.

'Did you have far to travel to get here?' Alex asked.

'Not really. I've a flat in Westminster,' Melanie replied.

'Have you told Blackshaw about our dinner tonight?' Alex was on a fishing trip.

'I've hardly had any time to contact him since your invitation arrived late in the afternoon. He is in the far east right now, time difference and all that,' Melanie replied. 'By the way, his name is Martin.'

'Of course it is. Forgive me for addressing him as Blackshaw, it's a habit from our days at University. I was only wondering if he would have objected to you coming,' Alex explained.

'What for? I'm in an intimate relationship with him but that doesn't mean I can't do what I want.'

Their table for two by the window was ready and they made their way to the restaurant holding their drinks in their hand. Interestingly, Melanie ordered vegetable soup, sirloin steak, French fries, onion rings, salad and tartar sauce and Alex had the same with mustard instead of the tartar sauce. They had similar taste. Alex ordered a bottle of red Mouton-Cadet of which Melanie approved.

'Your choice of wine is excellent,' Melanie remarked.

'I like drinking French wines,' Alex replied.

'To be honest, I'm not an expert in choosing wine at all. I just enjoy drinking red wine,' Melanie said.

'That's alright, as long as you enjoy it,' Alex tried to make her feel comfortable.

'Excuse me for being personal, but are you French?' Melanie asked.

'No I'm English, born and brought up in Surrey. My surname is DuPont because my father is French. Following his studies at University, he settled in England. Later he married my mother who is English,' Alex was delighted to explain his background.

'Very interesting,' Melanie said.

They were enjoying the atmosphere which was buzzing with happy people chatting away; some were joking and laughing, waiters were rushing around and soft music played in the background.

'You know I am in a relationship with Martin, can I ask whether you're in a relationship right now?' Melanie asked.

'Sure you can ask and I'm happy to say that I am,' Alex put her at ease.

'I'm delighted for you,' Melanie gave a lukewarm answer.

'We've only known each other for a short time,' Alex shed more light on his relationship which appeared to change Melanie's mood positively.

Then she switched to a more general topic. 'Do you come here often?' Melanie asked, because she noticed the waiters recognised him and were exchanging greetings.

'Been here a few times. And you?'

'Only once, last year.'

'It's a very nice and friendly place which serves excellent food.'

'I agree with your superb choice.'

First course was over and the second course was served. They were eating and drinking with ease.

'Your PA, Jenny, was very welcoming towards me. She's nice,' Melanie remarked.

'Jenny is alright. She's been with me since I started. She is nice, kind, caring, astute, hard-working and reliable.'

'She's very fond of you and you of her.'

'You're very observant.'

'Couldn't miss noticing the interaction between you two. You displayed warmth towards each other.'

'That's about right. It isn't always a cosy relationship, you know. She can be sharp in expressing her views and I've to act like a boss sometimes. But, we've mutual respect and care for each other. She used to work for my uncle who retired and went to live abroad. Jenny helped me to set up the Agency.'

'Very nice. I'm glad it's working for you both.'

'Do you mind if I change the subject and talk shop?' Alex asked.

'Of course you can,' Melanie replied while thinking once a lawyer, always a lawyer.

'I want to talk about the murder case.'

'As long as no one hears us. You're still a typical lawyer, aren't you?' Melanie set the tone.

'I can hardly hear you, let alone anyone else,' Alex replied.

Then she said, 'First of all let me give you a report on the issue of the escort agencies. My officers have searched the whole of London for escort agencies. They confirmed that Margaret was not registered with them, with the exception being one agency in Hammersmith. This agency confirmed that four clients had used the services of Margaret. Following further enquiries, it was established that all four were not at Margaret's flat or in the vicinity on that fatal Tuesday night between 8pm and 10pm. Therefore, we've concluded that Margaret couldn't have been murdered by a jealous client.' Melanie practically wrapped up that particular notion.

'Your account of the investigation corresponds with the one I heard from Scott.'

'You mean to say that you knew all along about the escort agencies. I don't believe it.'

'I planned to inform you about it tomorrow. I didn't want anything to interfere with our meal this evening. Given your close relationship with Martin, I may never get this chance again. I hope you understand,' Alex said with his eyes fixed on hers.

Melanie appeared to be unfazed by Alex's concern. 'Don't bring Martin into this and tell me, when did you find out about the escort agencies?'

'I talked to Scott before leaving for home this evening. He told me, more or less what your guys reported to you. I asked both Jenny and Scott to contact all the escort agencies in the area about Margaret and her clients. Scott did the leg work, Jenny used the phone and they carried out the enquiry efficiently. I had to satisfy my own curiosity by undertaking this approach.'

Alex explained and expected her to be annoyed. That would have spoilt their meal. Much to his surprise, she was not affected by his actions.

'Acting like a true private investigator, finding out for yourself. Well, you've a job to do and you take your responsibilities seriously,' Melanie remarked while thinking Alex was a very competent and resourceful guy.

Alex was relieved to hear her being so understanding and went back to their conversation about John. 'If I could go back to the issue of John. What do you think of him now?'

'As I've said to you before, he is a charming and professional man.'

'Do you think he's involved in the murder case?'

'I understand where you're coming from, but I'm not convinced that he is. In fact, the witnesses' narratives are, I'm sure, genuine but it's very difficult to pin these on John.'

'I've a gut feeling that he's involved in all three cases: computer thefts, murder and extortion.'

'Really! How can you say that?' Melanie looked very surprised at Alex's announcement.

'Every path I've explored, since I accepted the job at the University, seems to lead to him,' Alex explained. 'Don't get me wrong, I also believe John is a good professional but the way he approaches his work appears to be different from other Principal Lecturers.'

Melanie was pondering on Alex's statement while indulging in her well-done sirloin.

Alex's brain cells were also fully stretched and he was deep in thought.

'I can see your point of view but have you got the hard evidence that is needed?'

'Not yet, I'm working on it,' Alex said whilst knowing that she was right.

'How do you get on with the people at the University?' Melanie asked.

'Well, on the whole, I've experienced a mixed reception. I do get the odd look, now and again, from some senior members of staff, indicating their disapproval of my presence. Others such as the students, lecturers and the support staff do not really care. I'm not obsessed with John but he clearly does not want me there and the Dean, David Mallory, believes that I'm wasting my time.' A brief pause followed whilst Alex enjoyed his sirloin.

'Both Gail Weston and Jack Dempsey are alright. I'm very grateful to Wayne, Phil, Alison and Karen for their inputs which have helped to move the three investigations on in a constructive and positive way,' Alex explained, and then paused briefly and got back to his sirloin and a large swig of wine.

'When we were investigating the computer thefts, I couldn't get any help from any of them. They gave me the impression that I was intruding in their protected environment. Some of them have taken to you. Maybe your charm works well and produces results,' Melanie said with a smile.

'I don't know about charm. I think because the investigation is the VC's initiative, some feel comfortable or even obliged to assist. I also believe addressing both the students and the lecturers has paid off,' Alex said, and continued, 'The VC has provided me with everything I need to get results; I do feel pressurised to deliver.'

'From the moment the VC spoke to you after I finished my briefing on Margaret's murder case, I felt he liked you and had faith in you,' Melanie added.

Both of them finished their main course and their empty plates demonstrated they had fully enjoyed their food.

'Would you like some dessert?' Alex asked.

'No, thank you. No room for dessert I'm afraid. You can have some, if you like,' Melanie was encouraging him.

'I'm full as well.'

Melanie looked at her watch and reminded Alex. 'I need to go.'

'Already?' Alex replied. 'I remember you've to get up early.'

Alex asked for the bill. Melanie offered to pay but Alex was having none of it. 'Happy to pay the bill, it's my treat,' Alex informed her.

'Thank you,' Melanie replied with a beautiful smile.

They left for the rest room and met later in the bar.

'Would you like a drink before we leave?' Alex asked but he already knew the likely answer.

'Oh no. I've got to go. I've enjoyed the evening, the meal and the company, thank you,' Melanie replied while quickly pressing her right cheek onto Alex's right cheek.

'You're very welcome, the pleasure is entirely mine. I had a fantastic time and thank you,' Alex returned the compliment. They were standing outside the restaurant and the weather was still mild and pleasant.

'Will you be alright walking to the underground station on your own?' Alex asked.

'I'll be fine, it's only ten o'clock. Have you got far to go?' Melanie asked.

'About ten minutes' walk from here,' Alex replied.

'Thank you again. I'll contact you tomorrow,' Melanie said.

'Be careful how you go?' Alex expressed his genuine concern about her.

'Don't worry about me, I can look after myself,' Melanie reassured him.

'I do hope so. Speak to you tomorrow. Bye.' Alex realised that as a policewoman, Melanie should be alright.

They left for their respective flats. After a few steps, both turned round and waved.

It was an ideal opportunity for these two to strengthen their rapport. Signs were promising as both could not take their eyes off each other. Undoubtedly, there was a mutual appreciation of their professionalism between them.

Walking home in the warm night air, Alex thought the evening was a success. The venue was sumptuous, the company was very pleasant and the food was simply divine. What else could a man ask for?

Chapter 18

On Friday, Gail entered her office at her usual time of 7.15 am. She had left home early enough to avoid any traffic congestion from her home in Epsom to the University. It also provided her with the opportunity to do her paperwork and prepare for her endless meetings, undisturbed. But surprisingly, at 8 am, her phone rang on the outside line. The lecturers usually would get to their offices by 8.30 am. She was puzzled by the phone call, wondering who it might be. Even the clinical areas did not start ringing until after 8.30 am. Technically, she was not on duty yet. There was no need to answer the phone. It could be someone calling a wrong number or who knew that she would be in her office. On second thoughts, she picked up the phone. 'Hello Gail speaking, can I help you?'

'Hello good morning, my name is Deborah Styles, wife of Matt Hughes, Recruitment Officer. I'm phoning to report that Matt is unwell and won't be coming in to work today,' Deborah said.

'Thank you for letting me know about Matt. I hope he'll feel better soon,' Gail replied. The caller rang off.

Gail was taken by surprise. She was under the impression that Matt had been separated from his wife for a while. Maybe her understanding of his marital life was misplaced. The next thing that concerned her was what was wrong with him. It must have been serious enough for him to go off sick. Matt's sickness record had been exemplary since he had joined the University.

Unfortunately, it was recruitment day. Matt's Personal Assistant, Pam, had been working in the recruitment office for many years and was familiar with its daily activities. Nevertheless, Gail would have to give a helping hand to ensure that things ticked over until Matt's return to work. At 8.30 am, she went down to the recruitment office to inform his PA that he had gone off sick.

'Hi Pam, good morning,' Gail said.

Pam was startled by her presence. It was the first time she had seen Gail in the recruitment office so early.

'Good morning, Gail,' Pam replied, looking puzzled.

'I thought I'd better come down to tell you in person that Matt is not well and won't be in today.'

'I'm sorry to hear that. Nothing bad, I hope. He's always been in good health,' Pam expressed her surprise.

'I understand. Do you have any urgent matters that need to be addressed today, apart from the recruitment day activities?' Gail wanted to know about Matt's workload.

Pam carried out a quick mental check and then faced Gail and asked her, 'Did he say anything to you about the interview file for today's interviews?' Pam was now more concerned about her own work.

'No, I wasn't told anything about any interview file.'

'Apparently, he's taken today's interview file with him. Did he ring himself?' Pam asked.

'No. His wife rang,' Gail replied.

Now it was Pam's turn to feel confused. She also thought that Matt was separated from his wife. 'I didn't know Matt was back with his wife.'

'Anyway we live and learn all the time. I'll ring Matt to get his permission to go into his apartment to collect the interview file. Then, I'll contact Jim, caretaker of Matt's apartment block which belongs to the University, and inform him to expect Wayne, the security officer to collect the interview file for today's interviews from Matt's apartment,' Gail replied.

'Thank you. But, how would Wayne know which interview file to pick up?' Pam threw a spanner in the works.

'Are you saying that Matt takes more than one interview file with him?'

'Sure. He has to sift through the interview files for different days and there are a lot of candidates to be interviewed. Therefore, one interview file is allocated for each interview day. The system works very well. The day before the interviews, he would usually take the interview file home to carry out a final check to ensure the relevant documentation is available for the interviewers. He likes to sort these out manually and then passes them on to me. Then, I cross-check these against the information stored on the computer. Matt doesn't like using computers, prefers the old-fashioned way, but he can use the computer for searching, retrieving and storing information.'

Pam described the administration process and disclosed Matt's preference or his shortcomings, depending on one's point of view.

'Alright, as you're familiar with the interview file, you had better go with Wayne to Matt's apartment to avoid confusion and delay. I'll let Jim know you'll be accompanying Wayne and will be there within the next hour.'

Gail wanted them to get back as soon as possible.

'I'll be happy to go with Wayne,' Pam confirmed.

'Have the interviews for next week been organised, in case Matt is still sick?' Gail asked.

Pam made a quick check through the files in the top draw of Matt's desk while Gail waited. 'Matt appears to have everything under control for next week. The candidates and the interviewing panel members have confirmed they will be attending,' Pam reassured her.

'Glad to hear it. I'm sure they will be here. Would you need help to cope with today's interviews?' Gail asked.

'I don't think so. I'll be fine. I managed the business of all the recruitment activities with a supervisory input from John for over six months before Matt started working here. Anyway, John usually pops in on interview days to have a chat with Matt about some "list" and then he would lead the interviewing. I can always rely on him for ensuring today's recruitment event runs smoothly,' Pam replied.

'I forgot. Of course you did. Undoubtedly, John will be here to ensure everything goes well. In the meantime, if you require any help, please do not hesitate to contact me.'

'I'm sure things will go as planned.'

'Alright. I'll be in my office most of the day if you need me,' Gail informed her and then headed for the tenth floor.

***

Following their first encounter the week before, Gail and Alex had developed a mutual respect for each other. It would appear they were two very good professionals who enjoyed doing their job to the best of their ability. Gail's mood changed positively after setting eyes on him. She was fond of him. 'Nice to see you Alex and how are you today?' Gail enquired.

'Fine, thank you. And you?' Alex replied.

'Good. I've just been to the recruitment office to inform Pam that I received a phone call from Matt's wife, Deborah Styles early this morning to tell me that Matt has gone off sick,' Gail said.

Alex was wondering what happened to Matt. They had a meeting arranged for 5.30 pm at the Agency for that afternoon. The meeting was supposed to be confidential. Alex was not going to disclose that to Gail.

'I'm sorry to hear Matt is not well,' Alex sympathised.

They stopped in the corridor, out of the way of passers-by, chatting away.

'I haven't seen you for a few days. I'm sure you've been very busy,' Gail said.

'As you know, plenty to do and not enough time to do it. The two investigations have really kept me on my toes,' Alex replied.

'How are the investigations going?'

'If I may say so, a fair amount of progress has been made and we continue to work hard to solve both the computer theft case and the murder case,' Alex reassured her.

'Glad to hear it. You do have two big tasks on your hands. We had a positive feedback from the VC that you are really in the thick of it and making headway into both cases,' Gail said with a smile.

'Thank you. I do appreciate it,' Alex acknowledged her compliment and support.

They then both went to their respective offices. Alex felt that by virtue of her long experience in the Faculty, Gail possessed a vast amount of useful information regarding the place and the people and he hoped to tap into this shortly.

***

Having heard that Matt was off sick, Alex contacted Jenny to let her know.

'Hi Jenny, I'm phoning to say my meeting with Matt at 5.30 pm is cancelled.'

'Why?' Jenny asked.

'A few minutes ago I was told by Gail, the Deputy Dean, that he is not well and will not be coming in to work today.'

'It means you have a free afternoon,' Jenny reminded him.

'Yes, it looks like it. Still, I've got plenty to do.'

'Was the meeting with Matt about something connected to your investigations for the University?'

'I guess so. He didn't want to see me in my office over here which would have been convenient for him, but he chose to meet at the Agency.'

'Did he say why?' Jenny was persistent.

'I'm not certain, but I would hazard a guess that he didn't want anyone from the University seeing him talking to me. Clearly, he had some very important information for me.'

'Do you know what it could have been about?' Jenny continued with the interrogation.

'He mentioned something about a "list" which I've no idea what that means. I can only guess it has to do with a list of students' names,' Alex enlightened her.

'Then it's a shame Matt's gone off sick.'

'I know.'

Jenny decided to change the subject because she was dying to know about Alex's dinner date with Melanie.

'How did your evening with Melanie go?' Jenny was being nosy.

'It went very well and we had a fantastic time, if you really want to know,' Alex was rubbing it in.

'Very pleased to hear it. Are you going to see her again?' Jenny was persistent at the best of times.

'Pretty sure I will soon. We're working together to solve the murder case, remember,' Alex pointed out.

'I'm only asking.'

'Coming from you Jenny, anything is possible. In fact, Melanie is supposed to ring me today, about the murder case. I've got to go now.' Alex brought their chat to a close.

***

Alex had been looking forward to his meeting with Matt especially about the secrecy in which they were going to meet. The second variable was clearly the issue of the 'list' which Matt mentioned on the phone. He would have to wait for Matt to return from sick leave, then he could obtain a sensible response to these two components. It was possible that what Matt would tell him could in itself have a significant influence on his investigations. As a Recruitment Officer, he was in middle management and had access to crucial information which Alex could utilise to catch the potential criminal or criminals.

Back to reality, by the time Alex managed to get into his office, the phone was ringing.

Alex picked up the phone and said, 'Hi can I help you?'

'Hello Alex, I was hoping you would be there,' the VC replied. 'Would you mind coming to my office right now.'

'I'm coming up straightaway,' Alex answered. The last time he received a similar phone call from the VC, tragically it was to do with Margaret's suspicious death. He was hoping for a more pleasant announcement this time; having said that, he noticed the same sense of urgency in the VC's voice. He braced himself for the unexpected.

'Good morning, come on in and have a seat,' the VC said.

'Thank you and good morning,' Alex replied while taking his seat. He barely had time to sit down before the VC was ready to start.

The VC wanted to get to the point as quickly as he could. 'I received a disturbing phone call early this morning.'

Alex thought it must be the day for receiving early morning phone calls, first it was for Gail about Matt and now it was the VC's turn.

'I see.' Alex was trying to sound sympathetic.

'It was concerning the anonymous letter. I've never received a phone call of this nature before,' the VC informed Alex.

'What about it?' Alex wanted to know.

'The caller reminded me that nothing had been done thus far, to resolve the issue of charging foreign students for places on the nursing course,' the VC said nervously. His hands were shaking and he looked very worried.

'What exactly did the caller say?'

'It was a male voice. He said to stop this scam or he'll contact the press. I must say he didn't sound as if he was kidding, he was very serious.'

'How long did the call last?'

'A couple of minutes at the most.'

'How would you describe the voice in terms of nationality?'

'He was not British. I would say someone with a Chinese accent.'

'Do you think he could be a student at this University?'

'It is possible. Since I don't deal with the students on a daily basis, it's difficult for me to confirm that. Unless one knows the student very well, it's virtually impossible to recognise the identity of the student.'

'How would you describe the tone of his voice?' Alex continued with his line of questioning.

'He sounded calm with a pretty strong and deep voice.'

'Think carefully, did he say anything else?' Alex kept on pressing.

'No. Nothing more was said,' the VC was adamant.

The thought that crossed Alex's mind was clearly the caller had been keeping a close eye on whether any action had been taken to put a stop to the illegal charge imposed on students to gain a place at the University. The phone call confirmed that the caller was either a student or a member of staff. The likely scenario would be someone from inside the institution.

Alex reassured the VC. 'I believe the anonymous letter was sent by the caller who is familiar with the practice of this place. This narrows my field of investigation and the need to focus internally and hope we get a breakthrough shortly. I'll continue digging to get to the bottom of this.'

'How would we know who that person is in this institution?'

'Impossible to know. Don't worry too much about it. You will need to keep this phone call confidential,' Alex advised.

Ironically, the VC asked Alex to keep the anonymous letter confidential and now the role was reversed in the case of the phone call.

'Can we contact the Police to put a trace on this?' the VC asked.

'The caller is astute and probably called your office from a public phone box. Tracing would be of no consequence in this instance. If the Police get involved, then the whole matter will become public which I believe you don't want,' Alex explained.

'I'm not thinking clearly at present. I totally agree with you about not involving the Police. I'll have to let the Chairman know about this,' the VC informed him.

'That's understandable,' Alex replied. 'Leave it with me, I'll follow this up closely.'

'You know Alex, I've complete confidence in your endeavours to solve the current problems of this institution,' the VC reiterated his faith in him.

'To be honest, I was hoping to have a chat with Matt this evening, but unfortunately he's gone off sick. I believe he could have, inadvertently, shed some light on the investigation regarding the anonymous letter,' Alex said. He was looking forward to the meeting because Matt was prepared to tell him about the 'list'.

'Yes, I heard from Gail that Matt wasn't well,' the VC replied.

'To bring you up to date, I'm probably a lot closer to the truth about the computer theft case.'

'Have you figured out what happened and who did it?' the VC asked, looking joyfully in anticipation at his reply.

'Well not quite yet, but I'm getting warmer and increasingly more optimistic,' Alex reassured him.

'Let's keep our fingers crossed,' the VC replied.

'We continue to make progress on the murder case as well. I keep in close contact with Sgt Cooper and we share information constantly,' Alex reassured the VC.

'I would like to thank you for keeping me up to date with the developments,' the VC said.

'You're very welcome,' Alex replied, and appreciated his comments.

'Well I'll let you know if there is any further contact from the caller. I do have a pressing engagement and I'm already late. Please keep me informed,' the VC asked.

'Will do. See you,' Alex replied, and left.

Chapter 19

After leaving the VC's office, Alex walked to the high street to get his lunch. He could do with a dose of fresh air as well. On his way, he could not help thinking about the threatening phone call the VC had received. Not surprisingly, the VC appeared a little shaken. The call was significant and conveyed an important message. The caller meant business and that he should be taken very seriously.

A few minutes later, Alex arrived in the town centre. McDonald's beckoned. Fortunately for him, the restaurant was half full and did not have a queue at the counter. He walked straight to one of the tills, ordered and paid for his favourite cheeseburger, French fries and a large diet coke. Once he was served, he went to sit at a table near the window to take in the hustle and bustle of the high street.

As there was an empty seat opposite him, it was soon claimed by another customer. Alex was hoping to enjoy his meal in peace and quiet, by himself. His new and unexpected companion had interfered with his tranquillity. Alex noticed the guy did not have any food in front of him, which was rather odd. He was of Chinese origin, young and casually dressed with a satchel which he placed on the table. He looked very much like a student, smiling at Alex and then he said, 'Excuse me Sir, sorry to disturb you, can I ask you something?'

Alex stared at him for a few seconds trying to figure him out.

'Yes, go ahead,' Alex replied, looking puzzled.

'Is your name Alex DuPont?' the guy checked.

'Yes it is. Why?' Alex was intrigued.

'You own the Mayfair Investigative Agency. Is that right?' the guy asked.

'That's correct. What can I do for you?' Alex replied, thinking of him as a new client.

Clearly, the guy knew who Alex was and that was the reason he was being approached.

'How come you know so much about me?'

'I know of you because you are investigating the computer theft case and a student's murder at the University. I was passing the restaurant and recognised you, so I decided to come in and talk to you,' the guy explained.

Alex quickly noticed that this guy had a strong deep voice. He wondered if this was the same person who sent the anonymous letter and made the anonymous phone call to the VC.

'Alright. What do you want to talk to me about?' Alex asked.

'I want to talk to you about how some of the foreign students obtained a place on the nursing course at the University,' the guy replied.

On hearing that statement, Alex tried to finish his food quickly. 'Who are you?' It was Alex's turn to ask questions.

'That's not important. All you need to do is listen to me carefully and take appropriate action quickly on behalf of the University,' the guy replied emphatically.

There was a pause. Alex was contemplating his next move. In the circumstances, he chose to listen.

'I'm listening,' Alex informed him.

'A senior academic has been charging foreign students illegally in exchange for a place on the nursing course. This has been taking place for over a year,' the guy said.

'Hold on a minute, you're accusing someone senior at the University of being involved in a scam. How do you know that and have you got any proof to support your allegation?' Alex was fishing.

'Because I know one of the students who paid a large sum of money,' the guy replied.

'What's the name of this senior academic?' Alex continued to establish the facts.

'I don't know his name.'

'That's great, you don't know the name of this academic and yet you are making a very serious allegation,' Alex pressed him.

'That's right.'

'Anything else you wish to tell me?'

'Each student was charged £2,000.'

'Did the student pay the senior academic directly?'

'No, he paid an agent in England, whom I understand, worked closely with this senior academic. Payment for an agreed number of students is made to the senior academic. The agent pays £1, 500 for each student. Then, the senior academic offers places to these students,' the guy explained the process of the scam.

'It's an amazing story,' Alex remarked.

'I believe it's a disgrace to charge students like this. This is illegal,' the guy said angrily.

'What's your country of birth?'

'I'm from the Philippines.'

Alex thought it was time to go on the attack. 'Did you send an anonymous letter regarding this matter to the Vice Chancellor of the University?' An eerie silence followed.

'OK. Did you ring the Vice Chancellor this morning threatening to go to the press if he did not take action to stop the illegal payments for a place on the nursing course?' Alex kept on pressing.

The silence continued.

'Are you a student nurse at the University?' Alex asked.

Again no response.

'How did you find out about the illegal activities of the agent and the senior academic?'

'After meeting some nursing students from other Universities, I was told every offer of a place on the nursing course is free,' the guy explained.

'Right. Do you know the name and address of the agent in England?' Alex asked.

'Yes I do. It's called, The Friendly Employment Bureau at 120, Bridge Street, EC1,' the guy was pleased to hand over this vital information.

'How did you know about the name and address of this Employment Bureau?' Alex probed.

'What matters most is that I've given you the relevant information for you to investigate this. Anyway, I know someone who used to work there,' the guy said.

'OK. So your information is accurate,' Alex checked.

'Of course. May I suggest, the only way to deal with this is to check out this Bureau and find the senior academic. This matter of charging students must stop immediately or else I'll go to the press and I mean it. These people are dishonest and are involved in criminal activities and you should bring them to justice,' the guy said sternly.

Making the link with Margaret's murder was his next move. 'Do you think the student's death has any connection to this scam?' Alex asked.

'I really don't know,' the guy replied.

Alex was assessing the strength of this guy's allegation. He did not agree or deny outright his involvement in the anonymous letter and the anonymous phone call to the VC. He was willing to provide information about the shady Employment Bureau. No doubt, the guy had put across a very convincing case regarding the scam.

The next move to pursue for Alex at least, was to reassure his informant-cum-threat maker, that positive steps were being taken to find the senior academic in question. Alex felt that the fact that the guy had made an attempt to approach him in the first place, indicated that he was prepared to give the University some time to address this issue.

'The Vice Chancellor was appalled by the content of the anonymous letter and is taking action to resolve this,' Alex informed him.

'It has to be done quickly,' the guy replied.

'Progress has been made and we are close to identifying the extortionist,' Alex reassured him.

'I want this meeting to remain confidential,' the guy insisted.

'No problem. How can I get in touch with you?' Alex asked.

'Don't worry, I'll find you,' the guy replied, and then walked away slowly.

***

When he got back to his office, Alex found a note that had been pushed under his door from Gail, asking him to see her urgently. He turned round and headed to Gail's office which was one floor below. He knocked on her office door.

'Come on in, Alex,' Gail shouted out loud.

'Hi, I came as soon as I got your note,' Alex replied.

'Thanks. I received an anonymous muffled phone call in the last hour. I've informed the VC who advised me to contact you.'

Alex was wondering about a second anonymous phone call in a day, the whole business was getting very cagey.

'What did the caller say?'

'Referring to a laptop in Matt's apartment.'

'Did you recognise the voice at all?'

'No. As I said it was a muffled voice.'

Alex tried to be practical. 'It could be Matt's own laptop which doesn't mean anything.'

'Why would he keep a laptop in his apartment when he didn't like using computers?' Gail explained.

'How do you know that he doesn't like using a computer?' Alex asked.

'This morning, Pam, his PA told me that Matt is not keen on computers,' Gail informed him.

Alex remembered when he had met Matt in the recruitment office, Matt said he did not like using computers. 'We need to contact Matt to obtain his permission to search his apartment.'

'If I can explain, Wayne and Pam went to his apartment this morning to pick up an interview file for today's interviews. They didn't notice any laptop. Probably they weren't looking for one. We had permission from Matt to have access to his apartment. I have just secured his permission again to return to his apartment but I didn't say anything about the anonymous caller,' Gail explained.

'Good. Can I go with a security officer to find out about the laptop?'

'Actually, Wayne and his fellow security officer, Ahmed are probably on their way back after checking his apartment.'

'Oh I see.'

At that very moment, Wayne and Ahmed brought a black holdall containing a laptop, to Gail's office. Having seen the black holdall and the laptop, suddenly, alarm bells started to ring in Alex's mind. While Gail was enquiring about access to the apartment with Ahmed, Alex turned to his colleague and asked, 'Wayne, do you recognise this holdall?'

'I do indeed, Alex,' Wayne replied.

'Is this the same one that you saw on your way to the car park on the evening of 12 May?' Alex asked.

'That's absolutely correct,' Wayne gave an emphatic reply.

'By the way, where in the apartment did you find the laptop?' Alex asked.

'The black holdall was under the bed among other stored away items,' Wayne replied.

'Thank you, Wayne. Please keep it confidential,' Alex expressed his gratitude and obtained his reassurance.

'Any time. You're very welcome,' Wayne answered.

Gail thanked both security officers and then they left.

'What was that all about?' Gail asked Alex because she could hear the conversation between Alex and Wayne.

'Oh just checking something, that's all,' Alex replied.

Obviously Gail sensed that the laptop was probably of great interest to Alex for him to engage in a serious conversation with the security officer and she wisely chose not to pursue the matter further. Alex became wide-eyed when he saw the laptop and was puzzled. 'How did it get into Matt's apartment?'

'That's your job to find out, Alex,' Gail commented cheekily.

'I know. Thanks for reminding me. This could be the break I've been looking for. Unfortunately Matt is not here to provide an explanation,' Alex remarked.

'I understand. If only he was here, we would have cleared this whole business up,' Gail said.

'I wonder whether I can talk to him, somehow,' Alex asked.

'I can't keep getting in touch with Matt because he is off sick. Therefore, according to our policy, we should wait to question him on his return. I know you wish to get on with it straightaway. Perhaps, he'll be here on Monday,' Gail put him in the picture.

'There is nothing we can do right now. We'll wait until Monday and see,' Alex was being realistic.

Both looked at each other for a few seconds searching for answers, but none was forthcoming.

'It's hard to believe that Matt would take a laptop to his apartment when he didn't even use this gadget.'

Alex was intrigued.

'I agree,' Gail replied.

'Do you think this is one of the stolen laptops?' Alex asked.

Gail stood there with her mouth open, in total amazement.

Alex picked up the laptop, pretended to examine it and then discreetly jotted the serial number on his business card. He positioned himself in such a manner, so as not to raise any suspicion in Gail's mind. Luckily, she did not notice. As he was meeting Tom on Monday, he would be able to check the serial numbers of both laptops. 'Could you lock the laptop away safely in your office till Monday?'

'Sure I can. I'll put it in my filing cabinet which will be kept locked,' Gail promised. 'Will this help your investigation?'

'I'm not sure but it's worth trying to find out,' Alex said.

'Don't worry, the laptop is safe in my filing cabinet and my office door will be locked as well,' Gail reassured Alex. She had her own office with only one door.

'Please could you keep our conversation and what has just happened confidential from everyone, except the VC?' Alex sought her co-operation.

'Of course I'll keep this confidential,' Gail promised.

'Well Gail, thank you for contacting me about the phone call, arranging the picking up of the laptop and keeping it safe. We haven't been able to do anything concrete today but at least we've the laptop to pursue in our investigation,' Alex said, and praised Gail for her contribution. 'You've helped a great deal.'

'Thank you for responding to my note so quickly. I'm sorry if I interrupted your work. Have a very nice weekend.'

Gail expressed her gratitude as she was getting ready to go home.

'It's a real pleasure to assist you. Enjoy your weekend,' Alex replied.

Alex left Gail's office and went to his office as he had a couple of tasks to perform before leaving for the weekend.

Chapter 20

Monday morning and Friday afternoon had presented Alex with dilemmas that most people of his disposition and motivation endured. Just as he was not keen to go to work early on Monday mornings, he found it equally difficult to leave work on Friday afternoons. There was never enough time for him to finish what he would have liked to do by late Friday afternoons. Still, he had to contact Melanie and Scott to catch up with the latest developments.

Alex rang Melanie from his office, 'Hi Melanie, how are you?'

'I'm fine. I've been trying to get hold of you for most of the day,' Melanie did not sound happy at all.

'I've been very busy, I'm sorry,' Alex replied.

'I did tell you I would be phoning you today,' Melanie went on.

'Yes you did but you didn't say what time. Anyway, you have me on the phone now. What do you want to talk about?' Alex pointed out.

He heard a big sigh from the other end of the phone, seemingly Melanie was mad with him.

'First of all, I want to thank you for taking me out to dinner last night. I really had a wonderful time. There, I said it now,' Melanie said it softly and probably felt a bit shy as well.

'It's very nice of you to say that. As it happens, I also had a wonderful time. We need to do that again sometime,' Alex returned the compliment.

'Now, now, don't get any ideas. I do have a steady relationship with Martin. Our dinner was a one-off.' Melanie put him in his place.

'Believe me, I fully understand.' Following Melanie's expression of her annoyance with Alex, they decided to talk business. 'Any development in the murder case?' Alex asked to set the ball rolling.

'Not really. My team hasn't come up with anything that's worth following up. As expected, my boss Inspector Richard Jenkins is restless for results. I think the Detective Chief Inspector (DCI) is putting pressure on him, and in turn, him on me. Understandable, I guess.'

Melanie sounded rather desperate.

'I see. Your department will have to be patient because progress has been made and there is more to come,' Alex reassured her.

'As you are aware, no arrest has been made. That speaks for itself. It doesn't look good for us.'

'I'm sure your boss realises that you can't just arrest anyone. You've got to be absolutely certain about a suspect with watertight evidence before making an arrest.'

Alex was trying to sympathise with her.

'You know what it's like. Results matter every time. Incidentally, I was persuaded by your arguments that the information you have acquired, probably points towards John being the potential killer,' Melanie was hedging her bets.

'You aren't suggesting that John should be arrested for Margaret's murder?' Alex was just checking.

'Not at all. As we both agree, not enough concrete evidence is available to make a positive arrest.' Melanie dispelled any possible Police action.

'I agree. If I can mention something else. I was supposed to meet with Matt, the Recruitment Officer, at 5.30pm at the Agency. He chose the venue but he reported sick this morning,' Alex said.

'That's a shame. Has he not been well lately?' Melanie asked.

'Apparently, he has been in good health since he joined the University 18 months ago,' Alex explained.

'Do you think there are other factors at play here?' Melanie asked.

'It's kind of suspicious for Matt to go off sick all of a sudden, especially on a recruitment day,' Alex replied.

'I think you're reading too much into it. Maybe he's genuinely taken ill,' Melanie offered another perspective.

'That remains to be seen. We'll soon find out,' Alex said.

'Do you think Matt is connected to our investigation in any way?' Melanie put Alex on the spot.

'Actually, I really believe that if our meeting went ahead, he would have given me a useful lead to follow.'

'What makes you think that?' Melanie was curious.

'When Matt phoned me to make the appointment, he mentioned he wished to talk to me about a "list",' Alex explained.

'What list?' Melanie jumped in quickly.

'I'm not sure. But I remember on one occasion, John told Matt not to forget about the "list",' Alex enlightened her.

'Do you think the "list" is linked to our investigation?'

'It's possible but I don't know how, until I talk to Matt. And another thing, why would Matt insist on meeting me at the Agency when it was easier for him to come to my office at the University?'

'Perhaps he would have felt more comfortable at the Agency.'

'Well, that's exactly my point. I believe Matt didn't want anyone to see him talking to me, that's why he chose the Agency.'

'But why?'

'I think he was frightened of someone or something. Who and what exactly, I don't know,' Alex went further with his theory.

'It sounds very intriguing,' Melanie remarked.

'It's all conjecture and nothing concrete.'

However, Alex made a strong point.

'I totally agree,' Melanie concurred.

Then Alex informed her of the VC's anonymous phone call and his chance meeting with "the guy" in the McDonald's.

'Another development occurred today. Gail Weston, Deputy Dean received an anonymous muffled phone call about a laptop in Matt's apartment,' Alex mentioned.

'A laptop!!' Melanie interjected.

Alex then gave her a detailed account.

'It could be one of the two laptops that were stolen. That's good news for you,' Melanie was getting excited.

'Not quite. It has to be confirmed first, whether it is the one that was stolen. I'll be checking the serial numbers of both laptops with Tom, the AVA technician, on Monday. I'm not convinced that Matt stole the laptop. Again, I've to discuss it with him first before reaching any conclusions,' Alex explained.

'Do you think there is a link between the stolen laptop found in Matt's apartment and him going off sick today?'

Melanie always asked searching questions.

'I honestly don't know. It's getting late for a Friday afternoon. I think you had better go home now and enjoy your weekend. The work will still be here for us on Monday morning,' Alex suggested.

'You're right. It's been a very busy week for both of us. Have a good weekend, Alex,' Melanie said.

'Thank you and you have a very good weekend too. We'll speak again on Monday,' Alex replied warmly.

Their conversation ended. Alex still had to talk to Scott before he set off home. He phoned Scott and his line was engaged. Alex left him a message to meet early on Monday morning at the Agency to discuss new developments and wished him a good weekend.

***

Being a party animal and having a good time when not working, Alex complained to friends and colleagues that one only had to blink and the weekend was gone. Alex had been known to burn the candle at both ends. Even on weekdays, he would go to the theatre, restaurants and clubs in the evenings. One of the main advantages of owning the Investigative Agency was that he could have the evenings off which was rarely the case in his previous occupation. Undoubtedly, he was enjoying his life. But after his pleasant weekend, he still had to get back to work on Monday morning.

'Have you had a good weekend?' Jenny asked.

'Yes. As usual I did and you?' Alex replied.

'I had a very nice one. I hear you went home last weekend.'

'We had a family gathering which we do occasionally. Everyone is expected to be there. Anyway, I always enjoy going home to relax with the family and close friends.'

'What were your parents' views about you still having the Agency?' Jenny asked.

Alex replied, 'Well I'm not going to change their mind about the Agency. Needless to say, they reminded me I am wasting my time and life. They spent so much money on my education from primary school to University and I ended up owning an Agency. They still can't believe that I gave up a great solicitor's job with a big city law firm. My dad is exasperated with my decision because, apparently, he is finding it embarrassing to show his face at the Club. Little does he know that one of the members from his club has been a client of the Agency.' A pause followed.

Then he said, 'He's finding it very hard to accept the way I are running my life. My mum is more philosophical about my choice of career now. She is not entirely happy but, at present, she's giving me the benefit of the doubt. Still, she would prefer me to work as a solicitor.'

'You've got to understand their point of view. As parents, they are very proud of your success, and I think you know that,' Jenny remarked.

'Of course I appreciate that. They have always treated me very well. I've been very fortunate to have my parents' complete love, continuous care and total support. I love them dearly. But going forward, I've to shape my own future,' Alex explained.

By that time, Scott had arrived and exchanged greetings with everyone. Shortly afterwards, all three went to Alex's office for a meeting which they tended to have as situations arose and time allowed. Being a small team, a close working relationship was pivotal to the Agency's success.

They preferred to touch base with each other on a regular basis.

Alex had a lot of constructive information to share with his team and developed a strategy to deal with this. He gave a detailed account of his meeting with Alison. Then he told them about coming across Gail who informed him of Matt going off sick, the anonymous phone call the VC received, his own encounter with the "guy" in McDonald's, the anonymous phone call Gail had received, the discovery of a laptop in Matt's apartment, the confirmation from Wayne, the security officer, of the black holdall which John carried with him on 12 May and his conversation with Melanie. That was quite a lot of ground to cover for Alex. Both Jenny and Scott listened attentively.

'You had quite a day,' Jenny was quick to observe.

'Oh yes, it was a day packed with incidents and all relevant to all three investigations,' Alex said.

'That's an awful lot of issues to address in one day,' Scott added.

'I guess you could have found out a lot about the "list" if your meeting with Matt had gone ahead,' Jenny commented.

'That's true. I feel the "list" will reveal a great deal about Margaret's suspicious death,' Alex added.

'I wonder whether Matt is back on duty today.' Jenny asked.

'I'll find out later,' Alex replied.

'This "guy" in McDonald's sounds very interesting,' Scott observed.

'I'll say. If he's right, we would probably be able to crack the issue of the anonymous letter which increasingly seems like a scam. We need to take this "guy" very seriously and check out the information he has provided.'

'Where do I begin with my enquiries?' Scott asked.

'First of all, Scott, I want you to check on this Friendly Employment Bureau and find out as much as you possibly can.'

Alex gave him the name and address of the Bureau.

Scott looked at the address and replied, 'I know the area well and I'll get on with it.'

Jenny was always eager to assist. 'Anything you want me to do?'

'Thanks for the offer Jenny, but not at the moment,' Alex said to her nicely.

'Don't forget about your meeting with Tom at 1pm today,' Jenny reminded him.

'I know. I've also got the two serial numbers of the laptops to check, one from the computer shop and the second from the laptop found in Matt's apartment. Let's hope we get lucky with Tom's equipment purchasing file,' Alex said.

***

It was noon when Alex left the Agency to meet Tom at the University. As usual, whenever he arrived at the University, he checked with Julie for any messages and then headed to his office. At 1pm he was knocking on Tom's door.

'Come on in Alex,' Tom said.

'Thank you,' Alex replied, and walked in.

'Let me get the lever arch file in which the invoice and details of each item of equipment that has been purchased, are kept,' Tom explained.

He went to the shelf and picked up the file and placed it on his desk and searched through it for the recently bought laptops. He looked stunned and his face went a purple colour.

'The invoice containing the serial numbers of the two laptops is missing. I don't believe it,' Tom exclaimed.

'What do you mean?' Alex asked.

'It's not here.' Tom was sweating rather profusely.

'Maybe it has been put somewhere else in your office,' Alex was trying to be sympathetic.

'No. This is where the invoices, leaflets and manuals for equipment are kept,' Tom explained.

'Who else has access to the file?' Alex asked.

'My deputy does but she was away last week. In reality, I'm the only one who uses the file. When I spoke to you last Thursday, I checked the invoice was in the file,' Tom replied.

'How about the Dean or Deputy Dean, could they have taken the invoice for budgeting reasons?' Alex continued to press.

'It hasn't happened before. Very rarely, if they require an invoice, they ask me to take it to them,' Tom replied.

'But are they allowed to do so?' Alex asked.

'Well I guess they are,' Tom said.

Then he phoned both the Dean and Deputy Dean to check whether either of them had taken the invoice in question. Both replied in the negative.

'They haven't taken it. I would have been very surprised if they had. I don't really know what to say?' Tom said.

That implied the invoice had disappeared from the time Tom checked the file last Thursday to Alex's arrival today for his meeting. There were two possibilities; one that the invoice had been misplaced or secondly, that someone had removed the invoice deliberately. He also concluded that Tom had not compromised himself by removing and hiding the invoice because he was genuinely upset.

'What will happen next?' Alex asked.

'I'll have to inform David about the missing invoice. I'm sorry you couldn't check the serial numbers,' Tom said.

'Oh, don't worry. Let's hope you find the invoice soon. If you do, could you please contact me immediately, I'll be very grateful,' Alex said.

What a setback? Understandably, Alex was feeling very disappointed. He had waited patiently for a few days to check the serial numbers and wrap up the computer theft case. When given the opportunity to do so, he could not perform that task for obvious reasons. Obtaining confirmation of the serial numbers would have solved the computer theft case and caught the thief as well. Consequently, he would have to come up with other possible solutions soon.

***

Alex went to see Gail. He knocked on her office door, she answered and he walked in.

'Hello Gail, did you have a nice weekend?' Alex asked.

'Very nice, thank you. And you?' Gail checked.

'Good, thanks. Can I ask you about Matt?' Alex said.

'Of course you can. Matt has sent a self-certificate for the first week and has informed me that a doctor's certificate will follow,' Gail replied.

'Would you mind giving me the laptop that was found in Matt's apartment which you locked away in your filing cabinet last Friday?' Alex asked.

'Of course you can have it.'

Gail unlocked her filing cabinet, removed the laptop and handed it over to him.

'Thank you,' Alex said with a smile.

'Do let the VC know you've got the laptop. Hope it will help with your investigation.'

Gail ensured the VC was kept informed.

'I'll let him know. I'm taking the laptop for examination,' Alex said.

Quickly, he cross checked the serial number he had written down with the serial number on the laptop, to ensure these were the same. Just in case Gail had swapped it for another laptop. He wanted to know more about Matt.

'What's wrong with Matt?' Alex enquired.

'Apparently gastric problems,' Gail confirmed.

'An ulcer?' Alex asked.

'That's right. This remains confidential.' Gail was very economical with personal information about her staff.

'That means he'll be off sick for a good while,' Alex remarked.

'I rather suspect so,' Gail confirmed.

'Surprising, given the fact that he has been in good health, and that now he's suddenly got this problem. It's kind of strange,' Alex observed.

'I'm inclined to agree but people can be taken ill at any time,' Gail explained.

That sounded like another big blow in Alex's solar plexus. He had just experienced the disappointment of the missing invoice and now he wouldn't be able to speak with Matt. Things just could not get any worse for him. A double whammy!! He decided to press on with his own agenda to explore more about Matt.

'I read somewhere that an ulcer could be brought on by pressure of work or stress. Is that possible?' Alex asked.

'You are absolutely right,' Gail replied.

'Do you think he's been under too much pressure lately?' Alex asked.

'I don't think so. The Faculty has always been able to recruit students successfully for a number of years,' Gail explained.

'I understand Matt has been working here for 18 months,' Alex asked.

'What are you driving at?' Gail was curious.

'Is it possible to know more about his background? For example, what was he doing before coming here?' Alex asked.

Gail was puzzled with Alex's line of questioning, especially his expressive concern about Matt. 'May I ask why you need to know so much about Matt and does this relate to any of your investigations?' Gail put him on the spot.

Obviously Alex had to be careful with his explanation as he did not want to tell her that the VC suspected Matt as the person responsible for charging the students.

'Gail, if I may say so, I feel you are the only senior staff member I can trust because of your high professional standards and transparency. I was supposed to have a confidential meeting with Matt at 5.30pm last Friday at his request, and then he went off sick that day. That's why I want to know more about the man himself,' Alex put his cards on the table.

Having listened to Alex, and after a brief pause, she replied, 'How can I help?'

'As I said, I need to know about his background. Did you appoint him?' Alex asked.

'No. I wasn't on the interviewing panel because no one asked me to be,' Gail replied.

'Who was on that panel?' Alex asked.

'I remember that one very well. David and John interviewed Matt,' Gail confirmed.

'That's strange. John was on the interviewing panel and not you,' Alex expressed his surprise.

'As you may recall, I mentioned to you at our first meeting, David prefers to work closely with John and that irritates me,' Gail said angrily.

'Thank you for your invaluable support. I'll get in touch with David.'

Alex expressed his gratitude and acting like a gentleman, stood up and bowed slightly to her.

Chapter 21

The mind of the legal eagle was buzzing with the speed at which events were evolving. A few of these were progressing well and others had turned into disappointment. As usual, the unexpected had an upper hand over the expected. If only events turned out as expected, life would be marvellous. The pursuit of achieving the most challenging, complicated and complex goals is in itself worthwhile. But, the successful achievement of these could be priceless. These were the thoughts occupying Alex's mind.

He would have to find a solution to the issues he had encountered. From his perspective, he could visualise the connection between the three cases but had not been able to impart that knowledge to Melanie. Assembling the components of the three cases, producing a comprehensive picture and identifying credible outcomes would be very challenging and exacting. His self-belief, self-confidence and good work ethics had been put to the test in a grand manner. Finding the solutions to these cases could propel him onto further successes. Getting there had also proved very difficult. However, some crumbs had been thrown in his direction which could yet turn out to be extremely productive.

It would appear that he had impressed one very senior staff member of the Faculty, Gail. She was prepared to keep matters confidential and willing to assist whenever asked to do so. With the exception of the VC, she probably saw Alex was not getting enough practical support from top management. Also, she could have been genuinely taken in by his charisma and sheer determination to get to his destination, and for that alone, he deserved her full support. Being a true professional who wanted to do her job correctly, Gail could see that same quality in Alex.

Increasingly, Alex began to think that he was getting closer to solving the three cases and yet he was coming up against some obstacles, but he believed they were surmountable being ever the optimist.

Walking past the offices of the lecturers before he left the tenth floor, Alex saw John coming towards him.

'Hello John, how are you?' Alex asked.

'I'm fine, thank you. I've just finished teaching and I am exhausted,' John said with a smile, as if he felt relieved.

Alex had waited for the opportunity to chat to him, but could not get the time. As the evidence against him regarding Margaret' murder was tangible and he had now probably heard about the missing invoice, Alex was looking for a reaction from him.

'Shame about Matt going off sick last Friday, I hope he's getting better,' John remarked.

'I hope so too,' Alex concurred with him.

'I tried to get him on his mobile phone to find out about his condition, but he didn't reply so I sent him a text, again no reply. I don't understand it,' John expressed his disappointment.

Very quickly however his mood changed and he was back to his usual self.

'How are your two investigations progressing?' John asked with a smirk on his face.

'Not bad, actually. We've made significant strides towards solving both cases. There is still more work to do, though.'

Alex was expecting some clever remarks because John had the tendency to show off. He was fully aware they could not stick anything on John regarding Margaret's murder. That would make him cockier than he usually was.

John was astute and sharp, and he chose not to pursue the path Alex expected him to follow. Instead he decided to do some probing of his own.

'What sort of results have you obtained thus far?' John tried to get Alex to divulge some confidential information. Alex was too smart to fall for it.

'As you know, I can't go into detail about our work, suffice to say that it won't be long before we resolve both cases,' Alex responded tactfully and yet provided John with a puzzle.

'Do you mean to say that the two cases could be solved soon?' John was very curious.

'There is a strong likelihood that will happen.'

Alex pursued his strategy of unsettling John. He seemed to be gaining ground when a bombshell was dropped.

'Incidentally, I heard a laptop was found in Matt's apartment last Friday,' John was keen to make that point.

'Laptop. How do you know that?' Alex was taken aback by John's declaration.

'I must have heard it somewhere, otherwise how else would I know?' John explained.

'When did you hear about it?' Alex kept pressing.

'I'm not sure exactly, either on Friday or today. Don't be surprised Alex. News travels fast in this institution,' John said laughing.

Alex did not have any choice but to concede. 'That's right. A laptop was found in Matt's apartment.' However he did not disclose the anonymous telephone call to Gail that led to its discovery.

'Is that one of the stolen laptops?' John asked.

'Rather too early to tell. We're looking into it but I'm curious to know how you found out?' Alex gave him something to think about.

'As I mentioned, someone told me,' John shrugged his shoulders.

'What's the name of that person?' Alex was persistent.

'To be honest, I don't think that is really important. You seem to be very interested in finding out about my informer, I wonder why?' John was also on the ball.

'The reason is very simple. This matter was supposed to remain confidential and yet, you're rather well informed,' Alex put him on the spot.

'Nothing remains confidential in this place for long,' John replied haughtily.

'If that's the case, how do you explain two laptops being stolen and no one seemingly knows anything about their disappearance?' Alex did not let John off the hook.

'Now for that one, I don't know. Anyway I have got to go now,' John avoided providing a reasonable answer.

Their conversation came to end in the corridor. Alex had given John something to think about. More importantly, he had made John fully aware that he was on his trail.

But John was clever, experienced, devious and tough. It would not be easy for Alex to instil fear in him and expect him to crack up.

What immediately crossed Alex's mind, which always worked at tremendous speed, was could it have been possible that John was the anonymous caller to Gail? Could he have heard it from his office which was next door to Gail's? The way his investigation had gone, he believed the former.

But how else would John know the whereabouts of the laptop? Had he seen it in Matt's apartment? Had Matt told John he had the laptop in his apartment? Then why the anonymous call? Why would the anonymous caller like to get Matt into trouble? Alex could not square the circle as to how John, Matt and the laptop fitted together. Some hard thinking was undertaken by Alex in the privacy of his office.

One mental activity he thoroughly enjoyed was to be fully engaged in critically analysing a complex problem and finding relevant solutions. And thus, he was to make maximum use of his legal knowledge and experience. As it was late afternoon, it was time for Alex to catch up with Scott about the Friendly Employment Bureau and to establish the voracity of the claim made by the mysterious "guy" in McDonald's. He managed to get Scott on the phone.

'Hi Scott, how are you?' Alex asked.

'I'm ok. How are you getting on with the checking of the serial numbers with Tom?' Scott had been waiting to hear if the checking would confirm John as the thief, meaning one case was solved.

'Not good at all. Would you believe it if I told you that the actual invoice on which the serial numbers are stated, has mysteriously disappeared?' Alex said angrily.

'Really! That's incredible. What will you do next?' Scott sounded despondent.

'To be honest, nothing. We're back to square one,' Alex said.

'I'm sorry, especially as you were doing so well,' Scott said sympathetically.

Alex brought Scott up to date with the various incidents he had encountered during the day.

'Again I'm sorry about your disappointments. I'm sure something will turn up soon for us to work on,' Scott tried to cheer up his boss.

'Thanks. I've thought about one or two plans of action to implement but I want to hear from you about the Friendly Employment Bureau first, before proceeding.'

Scott was delighted to hear the boss was in an optimistic mood as usual.

'I went to the address you gave me. It's an empty room in an office block which is sited on the corner between the high street and a side road. The door was locked with chains and a thick padlock. I peered through the glass window to see inside and there was no office furniture in this large room, and in fact, only a telephone on the floor. The company name has been removed,' Scott gave an account of his visit.

'Very interesting. There goes another lead,' Alex exclaimed.

'Don't despair Alex. Fortunately, all is not lost,' Scott tried to reassure him.

'You mean, you've something positive to tell me,' Alex interjected quickly.

'I have, actually. I went around the shops nearby, introduced myself and explained the purpose of my enquiry. I asked them whether they knew anything about the Bureau in question. Only two managers were willing to speak. They confirmed the Friendly Employment Bureau was operating from the cited address. The office was manned by three black people who were well dressed and polite. The secretary was female and the other two were male, possibly managers, and all in their thirties. The Bureau had been in business for a few years, usually enjoying a reasonable flow of clients daily,' Scott described thoroughly.

'Good. When did it close, then?' Alex was curious.

'Apparently, believe it or not, it was yesterday afternoon,' Scott replied.

'On a Sunday!!' Alex asked.

'That's right,' Scott confirmed.

'That's interesting. I saw the "guy" at lunch time on Friday and the Friendly Employment Bureau closed down on Sunday,' Alex remarked.

'What are you getting at?' Now it was Scott's turn to become curious.

'It would appear that someone from this Bureau has been watching the "guy" I met in McDonald's and most likely they know of my involvement as well. They put two and two together and decided to cease operating as a company,' Alex explained.

'My God, you're lightening quick in your analysis and conclusion. I can see your point,' Scott observed.

'It has also confirmed that the "guy" was right about the Bureau and, possibly everything else he told me. We were given a lead but the trail has gone cold,' Alex sighed loudly.

'What do you want me to do?' Scott was ready for the next move.

'Right now, I think you should continue with our usual workload. Leave this one to me for the moment. Thank you for your meticulous work. Tomorrow, I'll need to see both the VC and the Dean. It's getting late. See you in the morning, Scott.' Alex concluded his effective conversation with his Associate.

***

The momentum of the investigation into all three cases had to be maintained regardless of recent setbacks. The fact remained that the efforts invested, had started to produce some results and the right path was definitely being followed. Alex had decided to raise his game to reach the finishing line by challenging the top man in the Faculty, the Dean. It was pretty obvious to him that the Dean did not appreciate his presence in the institution. Alex's strategy, therefore, was to get the VC to put pressure on the Dean to co-operate fully and honestly with the investigations.

Hence, he wanted to meet the VC first and then the Dean.

To be fair to the VC, he was a staunch supporter of Alex, whom he had employed in the first instance, to find the two stolen laptops and the thief. He had also instructed the Faculty staff to offer their total support to Alex. As David was neither friendly nor receptive of his appointment as an investigator during their first meeting together, Alex devised a plan that would make him more co- operative in their following encounters.

'Good morning Peter,' Alex said after knocking on the door, which was open.

'Come on in Alex. Good morning,' the VC replied.

'I asked to see you to give you an update.'

'Sure. Go ahead,' The VC was very interested. Both sat down and had coffee.

'Let me start with the issue of the anonymous letter and telephone call,' Alex set the scene.

'That's good. What did you find out?'

'After I left your office last Friday, I went to McDonald's in the high street and was approached by a Chinese looking young man who was very keen to tell me about the illegal charging of students for places on the nursing course by a senior academic at this University.'

'He must have been the same person who sent the letter and made the phone call.'

'He wouldn't admit to it directly but I think he was…'

Then, he gave a detailed account of his conversation with the "guy" to the VC. Alex also told him that following an investigation, he had discovered that the Friendly Employment Bureau no longer existed.

'Oh dear. What will happen next?'

'My Associate and I will continue with our investigation and I'm sure we'll get it resolved soon,' Alex reassured him.

Next, Alex briefed the VC about the discovery of a laptop in Matt's apartment which Gail had already mentioned to him. He then told him about the missing invoice for the stolen laptops which, apparently, David had already informed him of.

'That was quite a progress report of your work,' the VC remarked.

Alex did not disclose his strong suspicion that John was involved in all three cases because the VC had been a fan of his. After all, John had saved the faculty substantial funds by extending the contracts of students who had failed their assignment three times, on compassionate grounds.

Each student brought in several thousand pounds a year to the Faculty. Even if Alex were to inform the VC of John's misdemeanours, it was very unlikely that the VC would believe him entirely.

'If my meeting with Matt had gone ahead last Friday, possibly, I would have received some useful information from him.'

'I see. You know, I still hold the view that Matt had something to do with the charging of students for a place and that Tom stole the laptops. Now a laptop is found in Matt's apartment and conveniently, the invoice has gone missing which means no check can be made to confirm whether the laptop belongs to the Faculty,' The VC expressed his suspicions and dissatisfaction.

'I know how you feel, Peter. With thorough investigation, more witnesses coming forward and a bit of luck, I believe, we'll be in a powerful position to solve all three cases. I need your help to make my next move,' Alex put him on the spot.

'Well Alex, you only have to name it,' the VC replied.

'I would like to talk to David about the background of Matt and how he was employed as the Recruitment Officer. I understand David interviewed him. Could you ask David to meet me to discuss the appointment?' Alex made his request succinctly.

'Why are you targeting Matt like this?' the VC was getting suspicious.

'You've just mentioned that you suspect Matt for the charging of the students. I'm on to something and would like to follow it through. I can't say anymore to you at this stage. Possibly, some crucial questions could be answered when I meet David.' Alex did not give too much away, must be his legal background.

'I'll have a chat with David immediately.'

The VC rang David and made an appointment for Alex to meet him later that morning at 11.30 am.

'Thanks Peter,' Alex was pleased.

'What about the killer?' the VC continued to press.

'Again, I must say our investigation is heading in the right direction. I must ask Peter, that you keep this conversation confidential,' Alex needed to get his commitment.

'As always, I give you my word,' the VC promised implicitly.

Chapter 22

Depending on the attitude of David Mallory towards Alex, it would be safe to assume that sparks could fly. No doubt a battle of wits would be on show. David did not rate Alex highly as an investigator in terms of solving the computer theft case. On the other hand, Alex was cautious of David's devious character. He was hoping the VC's intervention would have an impact and expected David to rise to the occasion and do some straight talking.

'Good morning, Mr DuPont, have a seat. The Dean is on the phone, he won't be long,' the Dean's Personal Assistant, Vicky said.

'Thank you,' Alex replied. He could hear some mumblings coming from David's conversation on the phone.

After fifteen minutes, Vicky offered, 'Would you like some coffee, Mr DuPont?'

'No thank you,' Alex replied.

Another fifteen minutes passed by before Alex was able to see David.

'Good morning, Alex,' David said.

By then, it was gone noon. Alex replied, 'Good afternoon.'

That shook David up a bit. Alex felt he had to press his advantage, basically to disarm David.

'If I knew you were busy and couldn't meet me at the agreed time, I would have used my time more productively and come to see you at another time,' Alex expressed his discontent as that was the second time he had had to wait for David.

'I do apologise for keeping you waiting,' David said gingerly.

'OK. I'm here to discuss a very important matter. Shall we do that?' Alex did not acknowledge his apology and preferred to get on. Alex always believed in punctuality and did not like being kept waiting for an appointment.

'Alright, what do you want to ask me?' David was ready to tangle with him.

'As you'll probably be aware I'm here to discuss your appointment of Matt as the Recruitment Officer to the Faculty,' Alex informed his host.

'May I ask the importance of this to your investigations?' David wanted to know before answering any questions.

'For the simple reason, I believe he is very much a part of our investigations. He could be a vital witness,' Alex emphasised his point.

'Could you tell me in what way?' David was persistent.

'I'm not at liberty to say at this moment. Can we talk about his appointment?' Alex wanted to get the discussion started.

'Where do you want me to start?' David was still trying to avoid any engagement.

'Who were the members of the interviewing panel?' Alex went for the jugular.

'Actually only John and I,' David replied.

'Is that your normal interviewing process?' Alex asked seriously.

'No. But on this occasion, I decided it would be better to have John helping me with the interviewing,' David explained.

'Could you enlarge on this approach?' Alex kept the pressure on, although he could sense David was still reluctant to provide detailed information about the interview.

'We'll be going into the realm of confidential issues regarding a member of staff. You're asking me to divulge personal information to you,' David stated the policy regarding personnel.

'If this was not important, I wouldn't have asked. There is a good chance that the information you provide will help to resolve both these cases or at least, Margaret's murder case which is a major criminal investigation. Your co-operation in this matter will be greatly appreciated,' Alex emphasised his point.

A pause followed. David got up and stretched his legs, probably playing for time to think how to reply to Alex. David let out a big sigh and then continued.

'Alright, prior to the interview John came to see me about Matt. He told me that Matt was going through a difficult time, his marriage was falling apart and he needed help. Apparently, Matt was working as a Senior Lecturer, in a University not too far from here, and had to give up his job because of drink problems. Both Matt and John were on a teachers' training course together and had been friends for a long time,' David recounted the scenario regarding Matt.

'Oh I see. Do go on,' Alex interjected.

'It's a kind of unwritten rule that exists in the field of nurse education; one helps another fellow lecturer to get on if that person is genuinely going through a difficult phase.'

'I understand that.'

'The recruitment post had been vacant for a number of months. Pam did a fantastic job, with the assistance of John, in keeping that department operational. With Matt's long experience in nurse education, and having been fully involved in recruiting students, he seemed the perfect person for the job. In the past, someone with office administration experience would have been appointed to this post. In this instance, Matt was better qualified and more suitable than the other candidates, therefore, he was given the job 18 months ago. Incidentally, Matt performed very well at the interview and fully deserved to be appointed,' David explained.

'How is Matt's drinking problem now?' Alex continued with his exploration.

'Funnily enough, he's been sober ever since he joined us. We have never had any problems with him. He's a good professional and a decent fellow,' David added.

'Do John and Matt still get on very well?' Alex was fishing.

'As far as I know, John has been very supportive of Matt and helped a great deal with the recruitment activities. Their working relationship has been very productive for the Faculty in terms of meeting our quota for student numbers, thus keeping us economically viable,' David was proud to express his appreciation.

'It has turned out well for both parties then,' Alex remarked.

'I'll say so. A good appointment all round,' David confirmed and then decided to do his own fishing. 'By the way, talking of Matt, I hear a laptop was found in his apartment.'

'That's correct,' Alex replied.

'I hope it isn't one of the stolen laptops,' David tried to find out more.

Alex was equally astute and more than a match for David. 'Until we get hold of the invoice and carry out a check of the serial numbers, it'll be hard to tell.'

'That's a shame, the invoice going missing like that,' David remarked with a smirk on his face.

'I do have a feeling this invoice will turn up pretty soon,' Alex predicted.

'I hope so,' David said.

'Well thank you very much for your time and providing me with this confidential information. I appreciate it,' Alex expressed his gratitude.

'You're welcome. I hope this will help your investigations.'

David got up and offered his right hand and Alex shook it in return, then left.

The information he had received from David was pretty much what he was expecting. He found David helpful for a change. Finding out that Matt was an alcoholic came as a big surprise to him. Alex never claimed to be an expert in spotting someone with a drink problem. The question that was occupying his mind was if Matt benefited by his appointment, did anyone else capitalise on this deal? He believed that Matt would have disclosed this at their scheduled meeting which unfortunately did not take place. Hopefully, the identity of the main beneficiary of his appointment, if any, would be revealed in due course.

***

Alex got back to his office on the eleventh floor. Shortly afterwards, the phone was ringing.

He answered, 'Hi can I help you?'

'Hello Alex, it's Jane here, Jane Fergusson, the Senior Lecturer; when you came to talk to the lecturers about the stolen laptops, I asked you a few questions. I wonder whether you still remember me,' Jane said in a soft voice.

'Of course I remember you.'

Alex was a bit puzzled about the tone of her voice. At the meeting, she had a loud and powerful voice.

'I hope you don't mind me ringing you.'

'No problem. What can I do for you?'

'Please keep this phone call and our conversation to yourself,' Jane tried to establish whether she could trust Alex first.

'Sure I will,' Alex promised.

'I wanted to know about Matt. How is he?' Jane asked.

'I've been told he's off sick and is not expected back for some time,' Alex explained.

'And where is he now?' Jane asked.

'To be honest, I believe he's at home but I can't be certain about that. May I suggest you ask Gail who will probably be able to tell you more?'

Alex was getting a bit confused about her interest in Matt.

'I would rather speak to you. Thanks anyway. You've answered my query,' Jane replied and then rang off.

Surprises never seemed to cease in this institution. Alex was aware that John and Jane had been together for a few months. And then Jane was enquiring about Matt. What was going on? Why would she be so interested in him? Did John put her up to it to find out about Matt on his behalf? If only he could get in touch with Matt. To achieve that objective, he decided to contact Gail about arranging a meeting in his office. As John's office was next to Gail's, he would have an opportunity to hear their conversation. Alex suspected John could have been listening to his conversation with Gail about finding the laptop in Matt's apartment. Therefore, it would be wise to meet with Gail on the eleventh floor.

***

Gail did not take a lot of persuading to go to Alex's office that afternoon. Both Alex and Gail felt that they were engaged in a good cause in the best interest of the institution and were prepared to pool their resources together to obtain positive results.

'Very good of you to come at such short notice, Gail,' Alex said and offered her a chair.

'It sounded a bit serious, so here I am,' Gail was pleased to help.

'Let me explain the reason why the meeting is being held in my office. This is to prevent John eavesdropping on our conversation.'

'Because his office is next to mine?'

'That's right. I hope you don't mind.'

'Do you suspect him of anything?'

'He gave me the impression that he knew what we were talking about last Friday, regarding the laptop in Matt's apartment.'

'Well, you can't be too careful, can you?'

'Exactly. I'm glad you're here.'

'Well it gives me a chance to get to the eleventh floor. Your office is very nice.'

'Thank you.'

'What would you like to discuss?' Gail made herself comfortable and was ready to go.

Alex informed Gail that he had just met with David regarding the interviewing of Matt for the post of Recruitment Officer. He told her about the details of his conversation with David.

'That indicates to me that the interview was fixed,' Gail observed.

'To some extent I agree with you, but Matt was a suitable candidate for the post,' Alex pointed out.

'Well, he's done a great job since his appointment,' Gail acknowledged Matt's performance.

'The reason I asked you here is to do with Matt's role as a Recruitment Officer. What is the procedure for selecting candidates for the nursing course, from the beginning to the end of the process when the offer of a place is made?'

Gail said, 'I'll be happy to go through it with you. Candidates send in their applications to the Recruitment Office. After a vetting process, the checking of their academic qualifications, personal details, work experience, additional relevant courses and personal interests is carried out. Assuming the Faculty requirements are met, Matt would call the candidates for interview. Matt is responsible for the interviewing days to be well organized so that the selection of candidates is conducted efficiently.'

After a brief pause, Gail continued, 'On the day of the interview, a senior lecturer takes over. Candidates are expected to write an essay, participate in a group discussion on a current health topic and undergo a face to face interview by a panel consisting of a member of the teaching staff and a clinical nurse manager. Due to the large number of candidates, three or four panels of interviewers operate at the same time and decide whether to offer or reject. If the candidates achieve an overall pass mark, they will be offered a place on the nursing course, if not they will be rejected. A verbal outcome of the interview is not given on the day. Matt will write to the candidates and inform them of the panel's final decision.'

Gail described the process well.

'Matt has a big responsibility ensuring that the Faculty recruits the right calibre of students,' Alex observed.

'That's correct. The quota for student numbers must be met. We recruit 300 students for March and another 300 for September each year. Many interviewing days are organised to go through the selection methodically,' Gail added.

'Normally how many candidates will be called for interviews at a time?' Alex asked.

'Between 20 and 25,' Gail replied.

'On each interview day, how many offers are made?' Alex asked.

'There is no specific number as such. On the whole, 5 offers are made, occasionally more,' Gail explained.

'Would all the offers be taken up?' Alex asked.

'Mostly,' Gail added.

'Really,' Alex was surprised.

'Generally, candidates are interviewed by other Universities as well. They could have more than one offer and therefore have a choice to make and undoubtedly, accept their preferred one,' Gail explained.

'What happens to the candidates who are rejected?' Alex asked.

'They are offered the opportunity to receive counselling over the phone,' Gail explained.

'I presume a record is kept,' Alex asked.

'Of course. Matt keeps all the interviewing files in his office,' Gail confirmed.

'Would an interviewer remember a candidate who was rejected?' Alex asked.

'It's possible but only the very bad ones. With the volume of candidates being interviewed, it makes it difficult for the interviewers to recognise them individually,' Gail explained.

'Thank you for explaining the whole selection and interviewing procedure of the Faculty,' Alex expressed his gratitude.

'You're very welcome. Can I ask why you need to know about this particular procedure?' Gail sought for a rationale.

'I wanted to establish Matt's role clearly in my mind. In fact, Matt gave me a brief resume of his responsibility when I first met him, but to get the details from you is very helpful,' Alex explained.

'Do you think there is a problem with the recruitment process or something?' Gail was very astute and sensed an underlying reason which Alex was not sharing with her.

'I know what you're getting at. Matt wanted to see me urgently, on the day he went off sick, and he mentioned something about a "list".' Alex decided to play ball.

'What about the "list"?' Gail asked.

'Within the sphere of Matt's duty, the "list" could relate to a list of candidates' names,' Alex pointed out.

'It's possible, but what does it mean?' Gail was puzzled. Although Alex felt he could trust Gail with the sensitive issues, he was not yet ready to share with her the real reason of his investigation regarding the charging of students for a place on the nursing course. He would have to circumvent around this particular topic.

'Until I talk to Matt or come across this "list", I wouldn't know,' Alex replied.

Gail seemed to buy Alex's explanation. 'Unfortunately, you'll have to wait for Matt to return to work and that could take a long time.'

'Can I ask you for his phone number so that I can contact him?' Alex asked.

'That's confidential information, Alex,' Gail reminded him.

'I appreciate that. But I need to talk to him urgently,' Alex emphasised his point.

A pause followed. Gail was trying to think through Alex's request before giving her final answer. 'I'm willing to assist you because I believe you're a good professional, doing your very best to resolve these outstanding issues for the Faculty. Both your heart and mind are in the right place and you deserve our support.'

She wrote Matt's contact number on a note pad and gave it to Alex.

'Thank you,' Alex said. 'I need to check something else with you, if I may.'

'Sure. What is it?'

'Can you tell me about Jane Fergusson?'

'What do you want to know?' Gail pinned him down.

'I understand she is in a relationship with John and yet she was asking me about Matt.'

Gail informed him. 'Yesterday I met Jane. She looked sad and worried. She decided to take two weeks' annual leave starting immediately as she did not have any teaching commitments. Due to family matters, she had to be away.'

'I'm sorry to hear that.'

'To answer your question, Jane has a crush on Matt and on others at different times, I wouldn't take it seriously.

She was probably curious to know about his illness. Jane and John have been in a steady relationship for a few months,' Gail explained.

'Thanks again Gail. You've been most helpful,' Alex complimented her.

He was very pleased with Gail's attitude which was positive and supportive. Getting hold of Matt would be a real bonus, though. As he was on sick leave, he probably would not feel obliged to take any calls from Alex. However, it should not deter Alex from trying his best to contact him. Pursuing his objective of talking to Matt, was his only option. His preferred method of working was to explore and exhaust every possible avenue before giving up on a particular idea. He passionately believed that Matt would provide him with the most crucial piece of evidence which could prove invaluable. Both Matt and John had mentioned the word 'list' in a very determined and decisive way. John impressed on Matt, 'don't forget the list' and Matt told Alex he wanted to talk to him about the 'list'. Looking at the views expressed, the 'list' could have a significant impact on certain processes regarding the investigations. Hence, the reason in finding out about it, had become much more pressing.

Chapter 23

Much to his surprise, as he was driving to his flat, Alex received a text message on his mobile. At the time, he was caught up in a traffic jam and was not in the best of moods. Initially, he checked the caller's name, Deborah, and number on his handset and did not recognise either.

He decided to deal with the message later.

When he got into his flat, he read the message which requested Alex to respond upon receipt of the message. Still, he did not think that it required an immediate reply. It had been a long and heavy day for him. After making himself a cup of tea, he settled down on the settee and watched the news. He was tired and was drifting slowly into a relaxing and well deserved quick nap when there was another message on his mobile. The sound of his mobile woke him up.

Again it was the same message as before, from Deborah. Receiving two messages from the same person in such a short period of time fully deserved a response.

Having phoned Deborah on the given number, Alex was not expecting any significant issue to deal with.

'Yes, Deborah here, who is speaking?' Deborah asked in a very soft voice which could hardly be heard.

'You sent me two text messages to contact you, I'm Alex DuPont,' Alex replied.

'Just a minute,' Deborah said.

Then, there was a brief silence. Could it be, Deborah was consulting with someone…. quick as a flash, it came to him, Deborah was the name of Matt's wife as well. He began to wonder whether she was the same Deborah. He should not jump to that conclusion, yet.

'I know who you are, Mr DuPont. Let me introduce myself. I'm Deborah Styles, wife of Matt who arranged to meet you last Friday.'

'OK. I've heard of you from Gail, the Deputy Dean. Thank you for introducing yourself to me. Can I ask why you've requested me to call you back?'

'Actually, I was acting on behalf of Matt to maintain an element of secrecy.'

'Where is Matt right now?'

'He's standing next to me.'

'Can I speak to him?'

'Of course.'

'Hello Alex. I'm sorry about last Friday, something unusual came up. Can we meet tomorrow somewhere secret, as I have some useful information to give you?' Matt said.

'Sure. I'd like that very much. May I suggest we meet at the first motorway service on the M4 leaving London, at 10 am? We could meet at the back of the Henry Walker cafeteria. Have you got a car?' Alex had found a quiet and discrete place for their meeting.

'That suits me fine. I do have a car and can meet you at the time and place you've suggested. Please come alone or else the meeting is off,' Matt set out his conditions.

'I'll be there on my own. See you tomorrow, Matt,' Alex confirmed and then Matt rang off.

At last, something positive and decisive had happened which put a wry smile on Alex's face.

He had been waiting for this break which arrived in a strange but pleasant manner. The phone number which he had extrapolated from Gail had become redundant but he intended to keep it for future possible use. The mobile number of Deborah had also been saved in case he needed to contact Matt urgently. He phoned Jenny and Scott to tell them he would be going directly to the motorway services on the M4 to meet Matt in the morning.

The plan was to have an early night to catch up on his beauty sleep. The previous night had been hectic and he didn't go to bed until 1 am. Having eaten his dinner alone and after a couple of glasses of Haut-Médoc, he watched television for an hour or so and then turned in. Quickly, he was in a deep sleep.

The following morning, Alex drove to the agreed destination and could not wait to talk to Matt, who in his mind, was a very important witness. He hoped to obtain some crucial information from Matt so that he could bring the culprit or culprits to justice.

When he arrived at the motorway services, he parked his car and headed to the Henry Walker cafeteria. The place was quite empty with only a few people having coffee. He had not met Deborah so it would be impossible to identify her, if she was there. It was 10 am and having looked around the whole cafeteria thoroughly twice, he could not see Matt anywhere.

Could it be that Matt had been held up in the traffic or he had changed his mind, perhaps?

Should he decide not to turn up, Alex would be very disappointed. But he was not giving up the opportunity of meeting Matt, quite yet. He bought a latte made with semi-skimmed milk and a croissant, and went to sit at a table at the back, near the window. He was there on his own as all the tables close-by were empty. One of the female assistants, wearing white plastic gloves, was hovering around, giving him a curious look. Probably wondering why Alex was sitting so far away from everyone else.

After finishing his croissant, he started drinking his latte. A few minutes later a woman approached his table, didn't say anything and sat opposite him. He did not know the woman, but he quickly noticed she looked gorgeous. She removed her sunglasses and introduced herself as Deborah Styles, wife of Matt Hughes. Alex introduced himself and shook hands with her. She asked for proof of his identity. Alex produced his business card with his photograph on it. Having carried out the check, she signalled to Matt to join them. As it happened, Matt was also wearing sunglasses but Alex recognised him pretty easily by his hair style. He had a full head of long straight light brown hair with a parting on the right. Matt also sat opposite him and Deborah went to get some coffee.

'Good morning Matt, how are you?' Alex asked.

'I'm fine, thank you,' Matt replied.

'That was quite a carry-on with your disguise.'

'You can't be too careful. I had to make sure that you've come alone.'

'You haven't been well, I hear.'

'I was never ill in the first place. I had to leave the place as quick as I could.'

'Why was that?'

'I strongly believed my life was in danger, that's why I went on sick leave because I didn't want anyone to know the truth and also to protect myself,' Matt explained.

'Why would your life be in danger so that you needed to take cover?' Alex continued to press.

'That's the main reason I agreed to meet with you,' Matt said.

'You could have gone to the Police and reported it. I'm sure you would have received the right protection,' Alex advised.

'I thought about it but I didn't have much time. I decided to go into hiding,' Matt confirmed.

'Alright, why don't you start from the beginning?' Alex suggested. Deborah re-joined them with the coffee.

Matt settled himself down and removed some papers from his inside jacket pocket, from which he described to Alex how the events and incidents unfolded from the very beginning until he went off sick. After a big sigh, he looked at Alex with a face which indicated he was very angry. He talked about his friendship with John which had been established on their teachers' training course in London. John was very familiar with life in the capital and took Matt around. Matt was from the West Country and knew little about life in the largest city. They became very good friends and spent most of their time together. Matt enjoyed John's company a great deal.

On completion of their course, they went their separate ways, working as lecturers in the Adult Branch of the nursing course in different Universities around London. Matt got married to Deborah, who was also a lecturer at the same institution. After a couple of years, he became a senior lecturer. For some unknown reason, he started drinking heavily. His marriage was badly affected. Deborah decided to move out of their home. His employer told him to sort himself out, stop the drinking or he would have to leave. He felt ashamed of himself and resigned from his job.

John heard of his problems and contacted him immediately. They had kept in touch over the years. Matt confirmed he had stopped drinking. John offered to help.

There was a vacancy for a Recruitment Officer position at his institution, which had not been filled for nearly six months.

Apparently, John had to help the personal assistant to look after the recruitment activities. John told Matt that he could swing it for him as he was on good terms with the Dean. John also convinced him that he had the skills to do the job on offer. Furthermore, John made a very attractive promise to get him back to a teaching post, which he loved dearly, within two years.

John, even, dropped a hint that he was in line for a senior post himself.

Having listened to John outlining the possible opportunities for him, he felt proud of his good friend and his generosity. Undoubtedly Matt was very impressed, relieved and delighted. As he was in a desperate situation, he trusted John and chose to go along with his suggestion.

Matt applied for the post of Recruitment Officer. He was interviewed by the Dean and John and offered the job. Matt started his new post in January 2004. A few days after he started work, John approached him to discuss a sensitive issue. Apparently, John had a friend who worked in the South African Embassy had asked for his help to get two young South African girls, with appropriate academic qualifications, onto the nursing course. When these girls finished their course, in three years' time, they would go back to their home country to make an invaluable contribution to the health care system there. It sounded like a very noble cause to assist with.

Being a Christian, he agreed to do what he could. The two girls were called for interview and offered a place on the course starting in March 2004.

After a few months, John gave Matt a list of 15 names of candidates to be called for interview. He thought South Africa was a big country and required a lot of nurses to meet the health care needs. These candidates were offered places for the September 2004 intake.

John continued to maintain his close relationship with Matt. Often they would spend time together, like they used to do when they were on their teachers' training course. Matt was living alone and John was a divorcee so that suited their needs to behave like single men again.

John regularly praised Matt for his continued efforts to help the South African candidates. Matt never doubted John's motivation and sincerity over the South African candidates' entry to the course.

Life in the recruitment office was great for Matt and he was enjoying every minute of being in the nurse education environment again. The recruitment of the South African candidates continued apace. Matt totally believed he was doing these candidates a great favour.

John then approached Matt with another list of 25 candidates, for the following intake in March 2005. Again, the established procedure was adhered to. All candidates were called for interview and were offered places. After a few months, John gave Matt another list of 25 candidates for the September 2005 intake. Matt claimed he just carried on in a normal manner and there was no reason to question anything until a major development raised its ugly head and created a serious doubt in his mind.

For no apparent reason, he decided to look through the three lists of candidates and noticed the name of Margaret Johnson, the student nurse, who had been murdered. He thought carefully through the sequence of events concerning his relationship with John since he had joined the organisation. It was then that he reached the conclusion that something sinister had been going on, but could not put his finger on what it could be.

Last Wednesday Matt went to see John in his office to discuss this matter. Much to his surprise, John made an outrageous announcement. He was bragging about taking an exotic holiday and buying a sports car. Suddenly, Matt felt a shiver travel down his spine. Initially, he was concerned about John's arrogant attitude. To his knowledge, John had always pleaded of a shortage of funds. He was amazed by his extravagance. In fact, John boasted that his enterprise had paid off handsomely and he was about to enjoy the fruits of his labour. Matt was fully aware that John was not involved in any outside business venture and wondered how he could acquire such large sums of money. That played on his mind and he began to question his own involvement in John's recruitment activities.

Two significant incidents stood out. One was Margaret's name on the list which meant that she was treated as a special case. The second incident was to do with John's announcement of his holiday and the purchase of a sports car. He could not make a credible connection between the two incidents.

He wondered whether John had been lying to him about being a Good Samaritan and helping the South African candidates. Did John's diplomatic friend really exist? Was John charging these candidates for a place on the course and using Matt to achieve his cynical objectives? For John to come into such large funds without any clear rationale, had raised serious doubts in Matt's mind. As Margaret's name was on the list of candidates for the September 2004 intake and she had been killed, it frightened him. These worrying thoughts prompted him to see John urgently.

That's when he told John of his decision not to be involved anymore in providing places for the South African candidates. He was very worried about his job in case the institution or the Police were to find out that Margaret was one of the students who had been helped, illegally, to get on the course. It would not be long before the Police investigation would lead to him and have serious consequences. He might even be a suspect in the murder case. The VC would take disciplinary action against him, and, he could be sacked. That outcome could ruin his life forever. Matt felt it would be better if he went to see the VC and owned up, then his punishment might not be so severe and he could keep his job.

John was not having any of it. He told Matt to keep calm and not utter a word to anyone.

Should he tell the VC, he would definitely get the sack for breaking the recruitment rules and regulations of the Faculty? In addition, if the Police were involved, then anything could happen.

Both of them could end up in jail. John reminded Matt about the arrangement for his appointment. He owed John a lot and should never forget it. Matt was not happy with John's response and became very scared of the potential consequences.

The next day, around 8pm, John went to pay Matt a visit in his apartment. He tried to talk Matt out of his decision, but to no avail. Matt was frightened of John because he was shouting loudly and was getting increasingly more angry. He had not seen John in that disturbing mood before. Half an hour later there was a knock on the door. Matt was relieved to see Deborah.

Unknown to John, they had planned to meet in his apartment that evening. John was very surprised that Deborah was there because he thought Matt and Deborah had separated. John was forced to leave because Deborah didn't like him. She used to tell Matt that John was too slimy and couldn't be trusted. Alas, Matt did not follow her advice and consequently he ended up in a mess.

Later Matt told Deborah the reason for John's visit and the events that had taken place since he left his previous job. He had been sober for nearly 2 years. She was annoyed with him because he didn't contact her for assistance. Once she heard the full story, including his appointment as Recruitment Officer with John's help, assisting the South African candidates, Margaret's death and John's newfound wealth, she took control of the situation by taking Matt to her place later that night. The following morning, she reported him sick.

Chapter 24

'That was quite a narrative, Matt,' Alex remarked. It would appear that Matt had given a comprehensive and detailed account of his unpleasant and painful experience since he left his previous job until last Thursday evening. He recounted the events and incidents that affected his life with passion and disappointment. With the benefit of hindsight, he most certainly had enormous regrets accepting John's offer of help. More importantly, he was worried about his job and even his life. Clearly, he had a conscience and could not go along with John's strategy for deception and law-breaking anymore. Both Matt and Deborah looked sad and helpless.

Alex decided to get the ball rolling again.

'Let me ask you a few questions, if you don't mind,' Alex wanted to obtain more details.

'Of course, that's the reason we are here,' Matt replied, ready to divulge information.

'Has John tried to make contact with you?'

'He's phoned my mobile and sent text messages several times but I refused to answer.'

'About the "lists" of candidates' names, have you got them on you?'

'Yes I have. I kept these in my apartment for safety reasons because I did not want anyone to see these in my office.'

Matt produced 4 lists which included the candidates' names: 2 for the March 2004 intake; 15 for the September 2004 intake; 25 for the March 2005 intake and 25 for the September 2005 intake.

'Have the candidates for September 2005 been given places?' Alex asked.

'I'm afraid so,' Matt replied.

'Does John know you've got the "lists" on you and did he ask for these?'

'No on both counts. I guess John would expect these "lists" to be kept in the recruitment office.'

'Do you remember when we first met in your office, John arrived and said to you, don't forget the "list"; is it the same "list" you are referring to now?' Alex checked.

'That's right. You've got a good memory and very observant too. John was referring to the 25 candidates for the September 2005 Intake,' Matt confirmed.

'How did he respond to your statement that Margaret's name was on the "list" for the September 2004 Intake?'

'He didn't seem to care.'

'Did he ever indicate to you that he was charging candidates for a place on the course?'

'No, he never said anything about that topic.'

'Do you believe now that he was charging these candidates?' Alex continued to probe.

'I don't know because I haven't seen any money changing hands, but his claim of having a lot of funds to pay for his holiday and buy the new sports car, triggered a strong suspicion in my mind,' Matt explained.

'Would you know, by any chance, the bank John uses for his personal affairs?'

'Yes. It's the National Bank. I've been there with him a few times.'

'Do you believe John killed Margaret?'

'My gut reaction is I don't think he did.'

Alex continued pressing with his line of questioning.

'Do you think John was responsible for Margaret's death?'

'That's hard to tell. It's possible but I've no evidence to support it.'

'When he came to see you on Thursday evening, did he bring any item with him?'

After a brief pause, 'I really don't remember, probably I was too pre-occupied with my own problems. I wasn't paying any attention to anything else.'

'I'm sorry to break this unpleasant news to you. Following an anonymous phone call to Gail last Friday, a black holdall was found under your bed and it contained a laptop. It could be one of the stolen laptops. I believe it was put there to frame you,' Alex got straight to the point.

Matt was speechless. Both of them looked at each other without uttering a word for a few minutes. Matt and Deborah were in a state of shock and horror.

'I didn't expect John to stoop so low. How could he do this to me? I have never been keen on using a desktop computer, let alone a laptop.'

'When people are desperate, they take desperate action. I believe John was trying to frame you to divert attention from his illegal recruitment activities.'

'I can see that now. But, what would the VC think of me?'

'I wouldn't worry about the institution finding the laptop in your apartment. On that score, I promise you, no action will be taken against you.'

'Thank God for that. Are you sure?' Matt sought confirmation.

'Absolutely. You've my word on it,' Alex reassured him.

'Thank you, I feel I can trust you,' Matt was grateful.

'Can you recall what John told you about getting you a lecturer's post and his own promotion in due course?' Alex prompted him further.

'Yes. He told me after two years or so I would revert back to a lecturer's post. He was expecting to get a very senior post very soon.'

'Did he say which post he would get exactly?'

'He didn't. According to the structure in the Faculty, from a Principal Lecturer's post, he could only become a Deputy Dean or Dean?'

'He could become a Dean!!!!' Alex expressed his surprise, emphatically.

Matt shook his head in agreement with a disappointed smile.

During the whole process of Matt's briefing of his employment history to Alex and the question and answer session that took place between them, Deborah was silent and kept her eyes pretty much fixed on Alex. Then she broke her silence.

'What will happen next?' Deborah asked.

'With Matt's permission, I'll need to give a feedback to Detective Sgt Cooper who is responsible for Margaret's murder case. As for the laptop, I'll follow it up, tie up the loose ends and finalise that particular case. Regarding the "lists" of candidates to be given places, more work has to be done. I agree with Matt, the Diplomatic person from the Embassy does not exist. I'll have to investigate further,' Alex explained.

'I'm happy for you to talk about this to Detective Sgt Cooper,' Matt said.

'What will happen to Matt?' Deborah asked.

'Well, I trust Matt will remain on sick leave. Apparently, Gail is not expecting him back for a while. I won't be disclosing the real reason for his absence from work to anyone in the Faculty. Hold tight for the moment. Unfortunately, there is no easy solution to these issues. He will have to wait and see.'

Alex did not want to give away a lot.

'Will any action be taken against John?' Deborah asked.

'I couldn't give you an answer right now. The University has to decide on that. Once the investigation into the charging of foreign students is completed, it could be a different matter altogether,' Alex explained.

'Can we get in touch with you, if needs be?' Deborah asked.

'Of course you can. Anytime. I'll be pleased to help,' Alex replied.

'Thank you. That's reassuring to hear,' Deborah said.

'Will it be possible for you to give me a copy of your written statement?' Alex requested.

'By all means. I've a signed original copy for you.' Matt handed over the copy and the 4 lists of names to him.

'We thank you very much for coming over to meet us and listening to our predicament. We wish you lots of luck in resolving these highly sensitive issues,' Matt said.

'I'm very pleased you decided to talk to me and provide me with some very important information regarding my investigations. I wish both of you well.'

Alex got up, shook hands with both of them and walked to his car. It was early afternoon when the meeting finished.

Alex could not hide his satisfaction with the way the interview had gone. He was full of smiles while driving back to his office. A very important signed piece of evidence had been received. Having heard Matt's description of events, there was a possibility for him to put the various pieces of evidence together and come up with some credible solutions. He still wanted to check more avenues before reaching his conclusions.

***

The first thing Alex had to do, was to give Melanie the signed copy of the written evidence received from Matt. He phoned her on her mobile but it was engaged. He left her a message to join him at the University at 3pm. In addition, he also contacted Jenny and put her in the picture.

Progress was slow, a bit too slow for his liking. In his mind, the three cases were interlinked but obtaining the right evidence to support his theory was proving a tad difficult.

The meeting with Matt had spurred him into speedier action. He recognised that Matt had risked his life to provide him with a signed statement. Although, Matt could not tie John to the charging of students and Margaret's murder, he had a distinct inkling that John could be involved.

As John was fully aware that he could no longer rely on Matt's co-operation with his scam, he would be looking for an opportunity to settle the score with Matt. Hence, it was imperative to get Melanie involved to ensure that Matt was duly protected.

No time to have lunch. Plenty to do. It was not the first time in his previous or current career that he had missed lunch. Work had often taken precedence over his various daily meals. He had the tendency to submerge himself totally in his attempt to get the job done. Invariably, his commitment had produced great results. On this occasion, he was working in partnership with Melanie and needed to utilise her resources and was hoping that she had got his message.

Melanie had got the message and duly obliged by turning up on time to see Alex. They exchanged greetings. He was delighted she could make it and made coffee. Both sat down. They drank their coffee with their eyes fixed on each other. The time was right for Alex to give Melanie an account of his encounter with Matt. He went through the various aspects of his morning meeting with Matt and his wife, Deborah, and the signed statement which he gave to Melanie.

'I think you had better have Matt's signed statement of what he told me at our meeting in the Henry Walker Motorway Services on the M4.'

Melanie took the statement, read it and digested it.

'Matt has outlined his personal and professional experience with John in a chronological order,' Alex pointed out.

'I can see that,' Melanie concurred.

'Matt has taken quite a big risk meeting me, giving me this signed statement and going over every single detail. I believe he needs our help and protection,' Alex put his case to her strongly.

'What type of protection do you have in mind?' Melanie asked.

'If you could arrange for someone from your department to keep an eye on him, discreetly, just in case John might try something sinister against him. John has tried to get in touch with him on numerous occasions but he had not responded,' Alex replied.

'I'll do that, no problem.'

'Thanks. That's great.'

'I fully appreciate his co-operation in providing the evidence against John. The fact that Margaret's name was on the "list" of candidates that John gave to Matt is a serious matter and we need to question him urgently,' Melanie said.

'I agree. It doesn't however indicate that John killed Margaret. No doubt, John would get worried that the net was closing in on him. He might panic, admit to killing Margaret or lead us to the real killer. Still, no definitive evidence is available to arrest him on the potential charge of murder,' Alex pointed out.

'From the Police point of view, we need to question John about Margaret's name being on the "list" as part of our investigation to cover all eventualities and even eliminate him from our list of suspects. I'll pay him a visit at 10 am tomorrow morning, would you like to come with me?' Melanie asked him.

'Of course I will. Would it be possible for you to ask him about the alleged framing of Matt by putting the stolen laptop under his bed?'

'Good suggestion. It'll help to turn the heat on him a bit more,' Melanie agreed.

'Thank you. I sincerely hope your visit will make an impact on John which might force him to drop his guard, then we'll get him.'

'Don't get your hopes up. He'll be a hard nut to crack. We'll do our best to get a kind of confession from him. You and I know, John is far too smart for that,' Melanie warned.

'Be positive, Melanie, be positive,' Alex responded.

'I'll be off now, I'll keep in touch,' Melanie said.

'Thank you for coming and for your support,' Alex expressed his gratitude.

'You're more than welcome. See you tomorrow at 10 am,' Melanie replied smiling and left.

As far as the information regarding the number of South African candidates given a place on the nursing course was concerned, Alex thought it would probably help to clear up the issue of the anonymous letter. The fact remained that the senior academic who was responsible for charging the candidates, had not been identified. Again an arrest on the grounds of extortion could only be made after the University's request for Police intervention.

Both Alex and Melanie were fully aware of that aspect of law and were not prepared to venture in that particular direction without crucial evidence. But they had a firm base to proceed with their plan to catch the perpetrator of this appalling crime; students who were not good enough to be on the nursing course, could buy themselves a place with the help of a crooked lecturer.

The consequences of this action could be catastrophic. If these students were not able to pass their examinations to qualify as registered nurses to practice legally, they would almost certainly fall by the wayside. A lot of public money would be wasted. Secondly, if inappropriate students were recruited, they might pass and join the profession as qualified nurses, only to provide sub-standard nursing care to patients. In the long run, this could prove disastrous both to patients and the nursing profession. The patients would not receive the high standard of care they deserved and the profession would be held back from making progress. The public would lose trust in the profession.

The only way to find out whether John was charging these students was via the Friendly Employment Bureau verifying its link with him. That opportunity had evaporated by its own disappearance. Getting additional information from the 'guy' in Macdonald's was also difficult because he did not leave a contact number. It was very annoying to have come so close and yet Alex felt helpless in catching the senior academic.

Alex's instinct in getting things done, regardless of the obstacles, was in itself very persuasive and relentless. His mind and body worked tirelessly and his desire to complete a job successfully was infectious. His team would readily testify to that outstanding quality, by which they had raised their own performance.

He was contemplating a possible strategy which he would deliberately keep away from Melanie and would let her know only when the time was right. Needless to say, she would not be pleased with him but his action could produce the desired result, and then all would be forgiven. He was banking on that notion. If his new scheme were to yield no fruit, then she would not be any the wiser anyway. Any scheme that could be a game changer was worth pursuing in earnest.

It was time for him to go home as he had a date with Claire, his girlfriend, whom he had not seen for a couple of days. After a heavy and very productive day, he needed to recharge his batteries. Spending the evening with his girlfriend was the right tonic for him.

But first he had some unfinished business to attend to. The only person, he knew could shed some light on his concerns, was Scott. He got Scott on his mobile.

'Hi Scott, how are things?'

'Fine. What's up?'

'It may be something or nothing at all.'

'Why don't you tell me first, then we'll decide whether it means anything at all.'

'I believe I've been followed by two goons in a black 4x4, X5, I wonder whether it has a bearing on our investigations.'

'How long have this been going on?'

'Twice during the last week, I noticed the car following me from the University to the Agency. It's probably nothing.'

'You need to take this seriously, Alex. These goons do not fool around. They could hurt you badly and can be very dangerous. I'm going to find out through my contacts who these two are. Take care and watch your back.'

'Don't worry about me, I can look after myself.'

'Alex, these are not your University chums, they are probably hardened criminals who could cause you a great deal of physical harm. So, be careful.'

'By the way, don't mention this to Jenny. As you know, she tends to worry too much.'

'I won't tell her anything. Take care.'

'OK I will. See you in the morning.'

Chapter 25

The following morning, Alex arrived at his office earlier than usual and noticed Jenny was already there. Jenny usually got on duty early and before everyone else. Once she settled herself, she would put the kettle on and ensured that Alex and Scott's desks were neat and tidy. Usually, she would make a cup of tea for everyone.

After a few minutes, Jenny brought Alex up to date with the progress of their other cases and any queries he was expected to deal with. Alex was pleased to hear that the investigation into the four cases was progressing well. He was able to assist Scott a little bit during the last two weeks.

Scott had been coping almost entirely on his own and had managed to make reasonable progress.

'You had quite an interesting time with Matt yesterday,' Jenny was curious.

'I think so. As I mentioned to you on my mobile, both Matt and Deborah, his wife, were very keen to tell me everything they knew,' Alex explained.

Scott reported on duty, exchanged greetings and joined the discussion. Jenny had already shared with him Alex's meeting with Matt. Scott was familiar with recent developments.

'I guess you've got all the information you need now,' Jenny observed.

'Not quite. I still have to find the crooked senior academic. Anyway Melanie agreed to question John about his involvement with the "list" of the South African candidates and the alleged planting of the stolen laptop in Matt's apartment,' Alex informed them.

Scott chipped in. 'Sounds promising.'

'At least, John will realise we're getting close to him,' Alex said.

'Do you still believe he's our man?' Scott checked.

'I do. More evidence is required to nail him down though,' Alex explained. He wanted to move on and gave Jenny a copy of Matt's statement.

'Jenny, could you put this copy of the signed statement from Matt into the University file?'

'Will do,' Jenny replied.

Alex spelt out his next strategy to his team. 'I've an idea which I believe we need to follow up quickly.'

'Let's hear it,' Scott was curious to find out.

'It really concerns you, Scott. I need to get a copy of John's bank statements for the last 2 years. That's where you come in Scott. You need to get in touch with your contact at the National Bank,' Alex stated his plan.

'That's no problem. I'll get onto it straightaway. If my contact can't provide me with a copy, is there anything specific I need to look for?' Scott asked.

'A good point and spoken like a true ex-Detective Sgt. You must establish whether large amounts of money have been paid into his account also, if a large amount has left his account to someone else's account,' Alex explained.

'What sort of amount are you referring to?' Scott sought clarification.

'Around £20,000 going in immediately followed by around £7,000 going out. I want to know where the money come from, and into whose account he subsequently paid the money,' Alex explained.

'Right, I understand,' Scott replied.

'I'm lost. How will this plan of yours help?' Jenny asked.

'If John had been taking money from the Friendly Employment Bureau for getting the South African students onto the course, then the payments would show on his bank statements. If he has an accomplice helping him, which I strongly believe he has, then payment from his account to theirs, will also show,' Alex explained.

'Well, that's clever,' Jenny said, and nodded in agreement.

'Jenny, could you make an appointment for me to have an urgent meeting with the VC today, preferably early afternoon and then text me to confirm.

Their meeting ended. Everyone got on with their individual tasks. Scott popped into Alex's office.

'Have you seen those goons again?'

'No. Nothing happened this morning. I didn't notice any black 4x4. Maybe it was just a coincidence that I was followed by the same car.'

'Let's hope it was. Be vigilant and ring me immediately when you see that 4x4.'

'Alright.'

Then Alex left for the University.

***

Alex arrived at 9.50 am to accompany Melanie to see John in his office. As usual, Alex was very impressed with Melanie. He could never stop noticing how beautiful she was and always immaculately dressed.

Up until then, Melanie had believed that John was a decent person and a good professional. He had always made an impression on her; he was polite, friendly and helpful especially when she was conducting the initial investigation regarding the two stolen laptops.

She had already interviewed him, to check Karen's statement about the threat he made to deport Margaret. John, seemingly, sailed through that line of questioning and provided an alibi in Jane Fergusson to vouch that he was with her on the fatal Tuesday evening from 7pm onwards. John was an astute man and it would not take him long to figure out where Melanie was coming from. For Melanie, it would not be easy to revisit issues relating to the same incident.

After the usual formalities, they sat down to start the enquiry. Melanie explained that some more evidence had come into the Police's possession and she needed to follow this through as part of their investigation. To his credit, John offered to assist in any shape or form to catch Margaret's killer.

Melanie explained about the 'lists' of candidates he gave to Matt and how he was expecting him to facilitate these to be given a place on the nursing course at the University. The 'lists' were in his handwriting.

John listened carefully. A short pause followed. His silence bought him some valuable time to formulate his answers. He confirmed that he wrote the 'lists' of names and gave these to Matt.

The purpose of that exercise was to assist the candidates to do the nursing course and return to their own country to help their own health care system in providing high quality patient care. He was doing a friend at the South African Embassy a favour. Places were only offered to those who met the entry requirements of the Faculty. He could not see anything wrong with what he had done.

Melanie could see his point of view and continued to probe. 'Did you at any time charge these students for the offer of a place? If you did, how much did you charge them? How was the money paid to you?'

'I've never done anything like that. It was a humanitarian gesture to help these students, not to take money from them. I resent that allegation,' John said angrily

'Take it easy John. No one is accusing you of anything. I have to ask these unpleasant questions to eliminate you from our list of enquiries,' Melanie calmed him down.

'I take it Matt had told you all these lies which he has manufactured against me. Do you know, I saved his life and his career, look how he has repaid me? I shouldn't have done anything for him and should have let him rot slowly in his personal and professional life,' John was expressing his venom towards Matt.

Melanie could see that John was very upset and also that she was unlikely to get him to admit to any wrongdoing. John was very adamant and strong in his own defence. He would not be intimidated by anyone. She decided to move to her next point.

'Last Thursday night, you went to visit Matt in his apartment. Is that correct?' Melanie asked.

'Yes I did,' John replied sternly.

'What did you discuss with Matt?' Melanie asked.

'That's personal,' John replied.

'Did Matt say to you that he did not want to be part of your plan to help the South African candidates?' Melanie asked.

'Among other things that we usually talked about as friends, he did mention something like that and I said to him that was fine,' John said.

'Did you make any threat towards Matt?' Melanie asked.

'Don't be absurd, Matt was my best friend, of course, not. I respected and accepted his decision in good spirit,' John made his point strongly.

'Did you leave anything in his apartment before you left?' Melanie kept the pressure on.

'I don't remember leaving anything there,' John confirmed.

'Are you sure that you did not leave your laptop there?' Melanie asked.

'I'm sure. I didn't take a laptop there,' John replied.

'OK John, thank you for your time, I appreciate it,' Melanie said and stood up. She nodded to Alex about leaving.

'This is the second time I've been interviewed regarding Margaret's death. I'm beginning to feel harassed by the Police,' John got his message across.

Melanie was waiting for an attack from John and was ready to respond. 'I'm sorry you feel that way. Given the fact that you had made threats to deport Margaret and that her name is on the "list" you gave to Matt for recruitment and Margaret has been killed, the Police have every reason to pursue their enquiry to establish the truth. Do you understand what I'm getting at, John?' Melanie expressed herself explicitly.

It would appear that John had eventually met his match. 'Yes, yes I do understand,' John said.

'May I also remind you that you had offered to help find Margaret's killer and we do appreciate your co-operation and support in this matter. Good bye, John,' Melanie said.

By the time Melanie had finished with John, and on hearing the reason for her visit, he was taken aback; he was almost speechless momentarily. Then he went on another attack. 'Have you spoken to Jack regarding the foreign students and whether he charged them for a place on the course? He is very friendly and supportive towards them. I seriously question his motive for doing so.'

'We're talking to everyone who can help our investigation,' Melanie replied. Undoubtedly, Melanie was not pulling any punches in her interaction with John. She dealt with his cunningness and threat competently. She could be very tough if needs be. The aim of her visit was to raise awareness in his mind, with the message, that the Police know that he was somehow involved in Margaret's murder.

That's exactly what Alex wanted to happen and Melanie had helped him to achieve his objective. As previously agreed with Melanie, Alex did not ask any questions. That approach was used to give John the impression that it was entirely Police business. It would be interesting to observe John's next move.

Both of them went to Alex's office.

'How did it go?' Melanie asked.

'It went pretty much as I expected and it has made a significant impression on him. You were very good,' Alex said.

'Only very good,' Melanie replied with a smile.

'Actually, you're excellent,' Alex changed his evaluation to give her the well deserved credit.

Melanie summarised the content of her discussion with John and highlighted her main observations. 'Firstly, John was already referring to Matt in the past tense. Secondly, he was tetchy but defended himself robustly, thirdly he was shocked to hear the rationale for seeing him again, namely that Margaret's name was on the "list", fourthly he did not take any laptop with him to Matt's apartment and lastly he accused the Police of harassment. The latter indicated that John was getting worried.'

Agreeing with her assessment, Alex gave an account of his own observation which was exactly as that of Melanie. He pointed out that when someone started to make allegations of harassment against the Police for no apparent reason that could indicate a sign of losing control.

He felt that John was a skilful performer, manipulating the variables in his favour, especially when he explained he was on a mission to solve some of the health problems of South Africa by facilitating the candidates onto the nursing course. Naturally, he was all heart in his transaction with Matt and the South African candidates.

His shortcomings had not been exposed adequately because he was clever but he was given plenty to think about. Pressure needed to be kept on him. Melanie mentioned to Alex that she would allocate someone to watch him closely.

'I'll keep Matt's signed statement in our file. I'm sure you have taken copies,' Melanie said.

'You guessed right. I do have copies which may be required for our file and potentially used to obtain further evidence. I'll have to show the VC a copy as he should know about developments regarding his own staff,' Alex explained.

'What do you want me to do next?' Melanie asked.

'Do you really want me to answer that? Alex replied with tongue in cheek.

'If you're going to talk like that, I may as well go back to base and engage in some useful work.'

'God, you're sensitive, aren't you? I was only joking,' Alex defended himself but to no avail.

'Time and place for everything.'

'I'll hold you to that statement.'

'Seriously, what's next?' Melanie asked.

'I've a meeting with the VC in a few minutes, I'll speak to you soon and thank you again.'

Melanie went back to her department and Alex went to the twelfth floor for his meeting.

To be fair, Alex would rather spend some valuable time taking his desires for Melanie to the next level, but he had more pressing matters to handle first. On this occasion, much to his personal cost, his attempt to woo Melanie would have to wait. He could sense that if he tried harder, she would give in to his charm. He did not rate Martin, her boyfriend, very highly in the department of good-looking. He often wondered however, how have Martin managed to catch a truly beautiful woman like Melanie.

***

By that time he had walked the one flight of stairs to the VC's office.

'Good afternoon Alex, good to see you,' the VC said.

'Good to see you too Peter,' Alex returned the compliment.

'I hear you have something for me,' the VC said.

Alex gave him a comprehensive report of his meeting with Matt and showed him the 4 Lists.

The VC could not believe what had been happening in the Faculty.

'That distasteful and criminal transaction has been taking place long before I got this job,' the VC observed.

'It all started after the appointment of Matt as the Recruitment officer in January 2004,' Alex informed him.

'I always suspected him to be responsible for underhand dealings like these,' the VC said angrily.

'Peter, it is important to consider the whole business carefully. Matt is not responsible for any wrongdoing. He has been manipulated by John. If anything, Matt was of the opinion that he was doing a good deed to those South African candidates. You could say he was naïve. John was supposed to be his friend and Matt trusted him. I would go easy on him when he returns to work. Matt will probably remain on sick leave for the foreseeable future, as he is suffering from a high level of stress. I would also emphasise that in his case, a written warning would suffice,' Alex advised caution.

'I can see your point,' the VC agreed.

Then Alex decided to put a copy of Matt's signed statement in front of the VC who read it with diligence.

'This statement makes it clear that John is responsible for the extortion,' the VC said out loud.

'Hold on a minute Peter. There is no suggestion that John is the senior academic who is responsible for charging the foreign students,' Alex was quick to explain.

Alex also pointed out that although the 'guy' he met in McDonald's made the allegation that a senior academic was involved, there was no evidence to tie John in with the charging of these candidates. Alex mentioned that Melanie and himself went to question John about Margaret's name being on the 'list' for the September 2004 intake and that John was too smart and gave credible answers to all the questions.

The VC expressed his regret. 'I always believed John was the good guy in this institution. My trust was misplaced. It's unbelievable. I've always thought that John had the potential of becoming either the Deputy Dean or the Dean one day. How wrong can you be?' He went on, 'Can we say that we are close to put an end to this awful business of charging the candidates for entry onto the course?'

'No we cannot yet. We are only in possession of the "lists" but we do not know who has been charging these students. We are on the verge of resolving this matter. I'll advise for more patience at present. We'll crack not only this particular case but all three cases very shortly,' Alex reassured the VC.

The VC was deep in thought, wondering if he had not brought Alex in, whether this extortion would have carried on under his stewardship. What else had been going on in the institution? It was quite amazing that on these very unsavoury issues, the man at the helm seemed to be the last person to know. It was not surprising for the VC to feel let down badly by one of his senior members of staff. The very idea of offering a place on any course via the suggested route had never crossed his mind. Recruitment had always been carried out according to the recruitment policy of the Faculty, ensuring that places were only offered on merit.

Alex understood the VC's frustration and sadness but requested that he remained calm and to pretend to be unaware of the recruitment fracas for the time being. He told him that as the Friendly Employment Bureau had disappeared, it would be very difficult to verify the transaction between that company and the senior academic. Other means would be required to obtain the confirmation of payment which he was exploring.

'Do I mention it to the Chairman?' the VC asked.

'I believe you've to use your discretion on this occasion,' Alex suggested.

'You mean to keep quiet for now and tell him later. Hopefully you will have caught the blighter by then.'

'That's pretty much it, really,' Alex was being very diplomatic and chose his words carefully.

The VC would have to cope with the problem of not informing the Chairman. That would not be easy. He was a man of high integrity and professionalism. He had prided himself on being open and honest in his dealings with everyone at the University. Being a very astute person, he understood fully what was at stake and how to respond accordingly?

'Well, it'll have to be done as you suggested,' the VC said.

'Thanks for your time Peter. I wish I had better news for you,' Alex said and departed.

-Chapter 26

Melanie was summoned by Richard, her boss, to his office. She had kept him in the loop with regard to Margaret's murder. She was also fully aware that he wanted a quick resolution. Who wouldn't? Knowing her boss, who was very keen to get results to enhance his own promotion prospects, he would not be pleased to hear that progress had been slow.

The idea that Alex also seemed to be more instrumental in leading the investigation than the Police, would almost certainly make him unhappy. He was not a fan of Private Investigators.

According to him, Private Investigators were only interested in at best making money or at worst, interfering with Police work. He reluctantly agreed for Alex to be involved, to placate the VC and to compensate for not solving the computer theft case.

'Have you got any firm suspect for the murder case yet?' Richard asked.

'Not really, we believe John Fairbanks, the Principal Lecturer is a strong suspect but there is not enough concrete evidence to make an arrest,' Melanie explained.

'Are you getting closer to the truth?'

'I believe we are.'

'How is Alex's contribution?'

'He has been very helpful. As he has been given an office at the University, he has easy access to staff and students who prefer to talk to him. He is in an ideal position to obtain information and passes it on to me. We discuss possible leads and together decide on taking any action.'

'You need to keep an eye on him. Don't give him too much leeway and you need to impress on him that we are leading the investigation and not him. You know my views on Private Investigators.'

'That point has been made very clearly to him. To be fair to him, he hasn't tried to take over the investigation or keep any information away from me. He has been very supportive and professional.'

'Still, be careful. Melanie, we need to get a result and quickly. A lot of pressure is being put on me right now from above. You understand.'

'I understand. We'll continue to work hard and find the killer soon.'

'Alright, off you go then,' Richard said.

Melanie's meeting with her boss was not too painful. He obviously emphasised the urgency that was required and the importance of achieving results quickly.

Melanie had got on well with him. She would be, forever, in his debt as he took the risk of promoting her very early on in her career. Clearly, he had spotted her leadership potential, sound knowledge and refined skills that would be invaluable to the Department. She had not let him down as she had been progressing well and was respected by her team members whom she referred to as colleagues.

The next course of action for Melanie was to talk to Alex about reassessing their murder investigation. She was conscious of the fact that Alex was dealing with three investigations concurrently; pressurising him was not her intention because he had a lot on his plate. She knew she felt relaxed in his presence and was able to discuss almost any development with him easily.

Furthermore, she would receive a genuine response from him and saw his legal experience as a bonus as well.

She called him on her mobile.

'Hello Melanie, how are you and what can I do for you?' Alex was delighted she had called.

'I'm fine, thank you. I'm no better or worse since I left you.'

Alex was wondering about the call. 'What's up?'

'I've just finished a meeting with Richard who wants the murder case resolved quickly. I'm suggesting that we meet to re-evaluate the case and develop a new strategy to deal with it,' Melanie was hoping he would agree.

'We're already doing everything we can. What other plan of action do you have in mind?'

'It's worth trying to think through what else can we do?'

'Alright, your place or mine?'

'Nothing like that, if you don't mind,' Melanie was not best pleased.

'My office or yours then?'

'How about meeting for dinner at your favourite Excelsior restaurant this evening at 7.30 pm?' Melanie proposed.

How could he possibly refuse to have dinner with Melanie? A courteous pause followed.

'That's a wonderful idea. It will be my pleasure to join you for dinner.'

'It's settled then.'

'I'm looking forward to it.'

'See you later. I must go now,' Melanie said.

Alex could not believe that Melanie had just invited him to dinner. Naturally, it was work related. His mind always switched on to the overdrive mode. She could have met him in his office at the Agency or the University. Why did she choose the Excelsior restaurant? It was kind of puzzling to him. Of course he would really find out for himself in the evening. Amazingly, he also felt comfortable in her company as it was easy to talk to her about personal, social and professional issues. To him, she was a delight to be with and he enjoyed every moment in her presence.

***

Following his meeting with the VC and his fruitful conversation with Melanie, he received a message on his mobile from Jenny to contact Gail as soon as he was free. He went straight to Gail's office. She welcomed him and signalled to him not to say a word by putting her index finger on her lips. They quietly left for Alex's office. Alex was bemused by Gail's demeanour but went along with her. Gail appeared as if she was seriously enjoying her newfound role of being a self-appointed detective. It was all very hush-hush. Clearly, it was necessary to be so careful to prevent John from hearing their conversation. His office was next to Gail's.

In Alex's office, Gail quickly sat down on the edge of her chair and showed him the missing invoice from the AVA department. Alex was very surprised to see the invoice.

'How did you obtain this?' Alex was curious.

'A few minutes ago, I received another anonymous phone call which said, 'the invoice is in Jack's office.' I went to have a look and saw the invoice in his in-tray. It was on the top, I could not miss it,' Gail explained.

'Where is Jack, right now?'

'He is at a conference today and tomorrow.'

Alex was also concerned about the anonymous call.

'Did you recognise the voice of the caller?'

'I can't be sure but it sounded a bit like the first anonymous call I received.'

'Have you informed the VC about this phone call?'

'Yes I have and he is very angry. Apparently, you had just left his office and he asked me to mention it to you.'

'Do you recognise the invoice?'

'Well it states clearly that we bought two laptops. But there is something more important.'

Alex noticed Gail was a bit fidgety, clearly something was worrying her; usually she was a calm and self-assured individual. On this occasion, her body language suggested that she was a bit scared. She looked serious with her eyes focused on him and sat on the edge of the chair.

'What is the matter?' Alex was being considerate.

'I've seen this invoice before,' Gail said with a certain confidence.

'When and where?'

Alex could sense his suspicion was about to be confirmed.

'Yesterday I was acting for David as he was away. In the morning, I was in his office searching for some papers, and I swear I saw this invoice in the top drawer of his desk. I did not pay any attention to the invoice at the time. What is puzzling me is how did the invoice get into Jack's in-tray, if it is the same one?'

'Are you sure it is the same invoice?'

'To be honest, I cannot be absolutely sure, but it looks similar.'

'I think the invoice was put in Jack's in-tray deliberately for you to believe that Jack had stolen it.'

'That's a horrible thing to do to one's colleague,' Gail expressed her disappointment strongly.

'I believe Jack has been framed in the same way as Matt,' Alex explained.

'It's getting worse. Who is doing this?' Gail felt exasperated and shook her head in despair.

'I wish I could be certain but I do have a theory circling in my mind,' Alex said.

'Would you care to share it?' Gail put him on the spot.

'When I am ready, at present I'm more concerned with the invoice.'

'Is there a way of checking whether the invoice is the correct one?'

'Of course, I can go and see Tom. It would be better if you wait in my office. I won't be long,' Alex suggested.

***

He went to the fourth floor to the AVA office and saw Tom sitting at his desk.

Tom was surprised to see Alex as no appointment had been made for them to meet. Tom tried to get up and Alex signalled to him to remain in his chair. Alex approached his desk and placed the invoice on his desk. Tom became wide-eyed and his mouth opened as if he had seen a ghost.

'Where did you get that?' Tom shouted.

'I wouldn't worry where I've got it from. By your reaction, am I to believe this is the same invoice that was stolen from your office recently?' Alex asked.

'Of course it is. The invoice has got the Faculty stamp and date of February 2005 on it. That's when I took delivery,' Tom replied.

'Is this the invoice for the two stolen laptops?'

'That's correct.'

'I have got the serial numbers of the two stolen laptops, and if these numbers match the numbers on the invoice, that means I've got a pretty good idea who nicked these laptops. I can assure you, it wasn't you.'

Alex was pleased to confirm the serial numbers he had, matched the serial numbers on the invoice.

'That's a massive relief. You've no idea what I've been through. I know I've been under suspicion for stealing the two laptops from the very beginning. Thank you for proving that I did not do it. I'm very grateful to you.'

Tom was in tears with relief.

Alex gave him time to regain his composure. He never doubted Tom at all but he had to keep his options open. Tom was a good guy trying to do a good job. He was decent, caring and professional. He was a conformist, did what was expected of him and discharged his responsibility efficiently. He managed his department well and helped both teaching staff and students to use the teaching and learning aids respectively.

The VC had suspected Tom all along. It was understandable for the VC to take that particular stance because Tom was the only person who had complete access to all the computer equipment.

Alex could not tell the VC that Tom was innocent until he was able to produce clear evidence.

After a couple of minutes, Tom was fine and smiling. Alex tapped him on the shoulder and said, 'You were never a suspect in my book.'

'That's nice to know.'

'I want you to keep quiet about the invoice, don't tell anyone that it has been found. Can you do that?' Alex asked.

'Yes, I can do that,' Tom promised.

'I'm taking the invoice with me for safekeeping. If I leave the invoice with you and it gets stolen again, then we may lose it forever. I will return it to you in due course,' Alex said.

'Will it help with your investigation?' Tom asked.

'It will certainly do that,' Alex confirmed.

Alex and Tom smiled at each other and shook hands.

Alex went back to his office where Gail was waiting for him. He apologised to her for taking more time than anticipated but it was important for him to be thorough in his fact-finding exercise.

He told her that Tom had checked and confirmed that the invoice was the right one. Furthermore, Alex informed her that the serial numbers of the stolen laptops matched the serial numbers on the invoice. That rendered her speechless.

'Does this mean that you know who the thief is?' Gail asked.

'I have a pretty good idea,' Alex replied.

'Would you like to share it with me?' Gail was determined to know.

'Not yet. I still have to tie up loose ends before announcing who is the thief and what happened to both laptops,' Alex said diplomatically.

During Alex's absence, Gail had been doing some thinking of her own.

'Tell me, why would David have the invoice in his office in the first instance?' Gail was curious.

'Difficult to know exactly. I would hazard a guess that someone has found the invoice and handed it to David as he is the Dean,' Alex explained.

'You said earlier that Jack was framed, but by who? How did the invoice get from David's office to Jack's office?' Gail was puzzled.

Alex could sense Gail had a very enquiring mind which she had used often in her role as Deputy Dean. He could not disclose what he knew to her as the time was not appropriate. Gail's confirmation of finding the invoice in David's office, but not being certain of its authenticity had given Alex another line of enquiry to follow.

'Now, I need to investigate further about the planting of the invoice in Jack's in-tray,' Alex said.

'Anything you would like me to do?' Gail was ready to get further involved.

'Can I ask you to keep quiet about everything? Don't mention to anyone, including Jack, that you could have first seen the invoice in David's office,' Alex insisted.

'Don't worry, I do not intend to jeopardise your investigation,' Gail promised.

After Gail left, Alex allowed himself the luxury of reflecting on the latest development. It had been quite an eventful day; finding the invoice, albeit in the wrong place, confirmation of the laptops' serial numbers and more importantly, an invitation to have dinner with Melanie had been a very productive day for him. The anonymous phone call was still very puzzling however.

***

It was late afternoon. Alex had to go home and get ready for his dinner date with Melanie.

He phoned Jenny and told her as much as he could of his eventful day. Jenny informed him that a couple of customers wanted to see him. She had heard from Scott who confirmed that he had made progress with his contact at the National Bank.

'Who could possibly want to frame Jack?' Jenny asked.

'The obvious answer would be John, who is Jack's biggest rival, but there is no clear evidence to support this notion,' Alex replied.

'It's beginning to look like John has been very lucky, no evidence is linked to him directly. Therefore, no clear case can be formulated against him.'

'I'm not entirely sure. Adrian has identified John as the guy who sold him the laptop and the serial number he gave me matched the serial number on the invoice. That is the one and only useful crumb of evidence we've got against him.'

'So you're meeting Melanie again for dinner. I hope you treat her well. She is very nice. You never know what might happen if you play your cards right.'

Jenny always got ahead of herself.

'Calm down, Jenny. This is a business dinner. In any case, she has got a boyfriend who is a friend of mine from our days at Oxford,' Alex was happy to explain to her.

'Well, enjoy your time with Melanie this evening.'

'Will do. Thank you and see you tomorrow.' Alex rang off.

Chapter 27

Time was flying and the evening was rapidly becoming a reality. Both Melanie and Alex had their own expectations for their scheduled encounter. Alex was looking forward to chatting her up and getting much closer to her. Whilst Melanie always enjoyed being with him as a co-professional, she could not help but experience some personal feelings towards him. A very important matter, of a sensitive nature, had been bothering her lately. She had recently come across a piece of evidence that needed Alex's advice. Equally, Alex would be seeking her support with regard to obtaining a particular piece of evidence.

Melanie was at the Excelsior restaurant a bit early and went to the bar for a drink. She chose a table from where she could keep an eye on the doorway through which Alex would come. The bar was not busy, only a few people drinking and chatting.

At 7.15pm Alex walked into the bar and spotted Melanie sitting at the same table as they had before. She had a radiating smile on her beautiful face as if she had just seen someone very special walking towards her. When he got near the table, Melanie stood up and offered her warm and soft hand. Alex held her hand for a few seconds and then let it go.

Both sat down. One of the bar assistants arrived, 'Hello Mr DuPont, what can I get you this evening?'

'I'll have an orange juice, the same as Melanie, please,' Alex replied.

They were both smartly dressed as usual. She wore a pale blue dress with a small floral design and a plain matching coloured jacket. With her blonde hair, she looked ravishing. He wore his grey pinstriped suit, blue shirt and a pink tie, looking very dashing.

They made a beautiful couple.

Having exchanged greetings and complimenting each other on their choice of outfit, they settled down with their drinks in their hand. After a few minutes, their table was ready and they walked into the restaurant. The waiter welcomed them and guided them to their table for two by the window. They chatted away about their day in general terms.

The waiter took their order. Roast chicken with roast and mashed potatoes and three vegetables for both of them. They chose not to have starters and were looking forward to their bread and butter pudding for dessert. As before, Alex ordered a bottle of French Merlot which they started drinking whilst waiting for their meal to be served.

'I've been wondering why you invited me to dinner tonight.' Alex asked.

'No particular reason. You invited me to dinner last time, now it's my turn to invite you,' Melanie replied.

'Really. I think there must be another reason.'

'Such as!!' Melanie was being cautious.

'Do you know this is the first time a woman has asked me to dinner in a restaurant?' Alex expressed his surprise.

'There's always a first time for everything,' Melanie was happy to put him at ease.

'OK let's get down to the real reason why we are here.'

'Alright. I wanted to talk to you and possibly, to get your advice on an important matter,' Melanie owned up.

The waiter brought their meal and they tucked in. They were eyeing each other continuously.

It looked as if they shared the same taste in food and drink or maybe one was trying to please the other.

'Where is Martin tonight?'

'Why are you so concerned about him?' Melanie did not like his question.

'Just wondering. After all he's your boyfriend.'

'As I mentioned to you before, he doesn't own me. I'm free to do what I like. He is still abroad on business. Shall we change the subject and talk about our investigation.'

'I don't mind,' Alex said, and filled her in regarding the invoice for the laptops and that the serial numbers had been confirmed. Someone had tried to frame Jack and that Gail had been extremely helpful.

'If the serial numbers of the laptops match, then you've got your thief.'

'That's correct, but there is one flaw in that theory. I believe someone else is working with John,' Alex raised the bar higher.

'Who might that be?' Melanie was curious. She had not considered that when she was investigating the computer theft case initially.

'I don't know. It's only a gut feeling.'

'How are you going to prove it then?'

'I'll get there eventually.'

'What about the charging of candidates? Have you thought any more about it?'

'All the time.'

He was in two minds whether he should tell her about Scott checking on John's bank statements. He concluded it would be best to inform her and test the water for her reaction. He knew a warrant would be required to seek such confidential and personal information. As far as he was concerned, desperate problems required desperate measures to be taken. He had never ducked his responsibilities; he liked to face his challenges head on.

'I do have a confession to make,' Alex owned up.

'Another one, what's it?' Melanie asked.

'I've asked Scott to try and gain access to John's bank statements. Just to check whether payments have been made into his bank account by the Friendly Employment Bureau.'

'That's illegal. You need proper legal authorisation to carry out this action,' Melanie warned.

'I do understand the law. One is allowed to bend the law a bit, but not to break it. I'm only asking for a copy of his bank statements, the National Bank has every right to refuse.'

'You're not allowed to do anything with the law, only conform to it,' Melanie appeared a bit disappointed.

'I'm hoping John's bank statements will prove he was receiving money from the Friendly Employment Bureau for charging the South African candidates to get onto the course.'

'I hope you're correct.'

'It could also tie him to Margaret's death. When you consider Margaret's name is on the infamous "list" and the threats John made to deport her, there would be enough evidence to arrest him.'

'To arrest him now would be very difficult. My boss would not allow it because of any backlash which could affect the Department's reputation. Also, he would not like to have that record on his CV,' Melanie put that notion on the back burner.

'To be honest, I do agree with you. I thought that if he was arrested and leant on, then he might admit to the crime or tell us who did it?' Alex explained his take on getting to the killer.

'You think someone else could have been involved as well?'

'As you are aware, we cannot rule anything out.'

'Anyway, we still need someone to testify that John was at the crime scene at the time of Margaret's murder.'

'I know. I've to work on that.'

It was Melanie's turn to seek his advice and support regarding something which had been bugging her. To some extent, she would also be telling Alex that she had not conducted herself in the best of ways. Then again, the fault was not entirely hers.

'I also have a confession to make.' It was Melanie's turn to be humble.

'Yes you said earlier you wanted some advice on an important matter. Go on,' Alex encouraged her to speak.

'Actually a member of my team collected a piece of evidence from Margaret's flat, put it in an envelope, locked it away in the top drawer of his desk and unfortunately forgot about it. To be fair to him, he has been on annual leave and only came back to work yesterday. He has just joined our team and is inexperienced in this line of work. This morning, he gave it to me. I decided not to tell anyone about it until a proper investigation was carried out to establish its validity,' Melanie gave her account gingerly and expected Alex to get annoyed.

'What is it?'

'It's a button.'

Alex was more concerned in getting to the new evidence than the oversight of her team member which could have affected the whole investigation. He put on a brave face and demonstrated his understanding rather than his anger.

'God, an easy mistake to make, I guess. A bit clumsy though. At least we've something to go on with our investigation. Have you got it with you?'

'I've got it here,' she pointed to her handbag.

She was very surprised at his attitude. He took it calmly. She put on a pair of gloves and removed the item which was sealed in a small plastic bag from her handbag. There was no one in the vicinity as the nearby tables were empty. She gave him a pair of gloves to put on. After Alex had put on his gloves, she showed the evidence to him. Alex's eyes widened. 'That's a Harry button which is found on trench coats. It's got Harry written on it,' Alex said after a quick assessment.

'You're familiar with this item. Have you got a similar coat?' Melanie asked.

'Yes I have a beige Harry trench coat and I know the buttons very well,' Alex replied.

'You're posh,' Melanie remarked.

'No I'm not. I just happen to have such a coat. Where, exactly, did your colleague pick this up?' Alex wanted more information.

'He found it under the cushion of Margaret's settee, wedged in the corner.'

'Right. There must have been a physical struggle between Margaret and her killer. She probably grabbed the coat of her killer and accidentally pulled a button off while they wrestled with each other. The button flung onto the settee and rolled into a corner,' Alex tried to visualise a possible scenario.

Melanie put the evidence away safely in her handbag and they both removed their gloves to continue with their dessert. There was a short pause. Both were eating their bread and butter pudding quietly. It gave them time to collect their bearings.

'What are you thinking?' Melanie asked.

'We need to come across someone who has got a Harry trench coat,' Alex replied.

'Do you think John has one?'

'That's exactly what I've been thinking. Who knows?' Alex tried to figure out a few possible scenarios and ran a couple past Melanie.

'The button could have been there before Margaret's death and it was only found after she was murdered. The conclusion, then, would be that the button did not come from the murderer's coat. Another possible explanation could be that she was messing about with a guy on her settee, as part of her escort duties, and the button fell off his coat. More substantive evidence would be required to link the button to Margaret's killer.'

'I agree. I hope we can use it.'

'Undoubtedly, we should be able to do that. I believe it could turn out to be very useful,' Alex pointed out.

'That would be great, and my colleague would not feel so guilty about forgetting about it,' Melanie felt relieved.

'So that's the real reason you've brought me here,' Alex teased her.

'Well I didn't know how to break it to you, especially as it's been a big mistake on our part. Thanks for being so understanding,' Melanie said.

'Everyone makes mistakes. This evidence could still play a big part in catching the killer,' Alex reassured her.

'I would still have liked to come to dinner with you though,' Melanie said with a smile.

'That's nice to know. I'll have dinner with you any time. You're great company,' Alex complimented her.

'Steady on. Martin will be here tomorrow,' Melanie was blushing which Alex clearly noticed.

'I want to have dinner with you, not Martin,' Alex rebutted.

'Alex, both of us are in separate relationships and we must honour our commitments accordingly,' Melanie reminded him.

'What a pity.'

'Well that's life, but many thanks for your time, support and your honesty. I thoroughly enjoyed myself with you this evening,' Melanie said.

'It's been a real pleasure. We should do this more often,' Alex said with a twinkle in his eyes.

Melanie wanted to share with him the contents of her meeting with Richard. Diplomacy had to be used as her boss was not a fan of Private Investigators whom he saw as interfering amateurs and had painted Alex with the same brush. She took a different view of Alex as a Private Investigator and had a lot of respect for him. She decided to move on to her next point.

'As I mentioned to you earlier in the day, it's something to do with my boss. I saw him before I spoke to you and he wants the murder case to be solved quickly or I'll be moved on to another case. Do you have any suggestions? Melanie asked.

'I'm sure he understands the complexity of the case which would normally take time to solve. I take it you shared with him the evidence we've received so far and which is not robust enough to make an arrest,' Alex sympathised with her predicament.

'I usually give him feedback on developments on a regular basis,' Melanie confirmed.

'Then he knows the score and has to trust you to deliver the killer soon. If it'll help, I can assure you I'm doing everything possible to find the killer,' Alex reassured her.

'I believe you, Alex. May I suggest we step up our efforts to get the job done,' Melanie requested.

'I've already done so with the input from my team,' Alex said.

'My team has been working very hard as well, to establish if anyone has seen or heard anything that could help with our investigation but no luck,' Melanie informed him.

'The search goes on and I'm sure we'll get there sooner than many people think. Incidentally, the Harry button could still prove to be extremely valuable evidence in the case,' Alex was being very positive.

'I wish I could share your optimism but you're right, we need to carry on,' Melanie said with caution.

She was aware that in her Department there were many unsolved murder cases. She feared that due to a lack of evidence, Margaret's case could end up on that pile of unsolved cases. That would be a disaster because both Alex and Melanie, and their respective teams, had worked very hard to find Margaret's killer.

They finished their meal, the bottle of wine was empty. Their conversation had been electric.

A few personal remarks were expressed towards each other, and they had shared crucial information about the investigations. Both had fully enjoyed each other's company and now it was time to leave. Melanie insisted on paying the bill but Alex would not have any of it. Both stood up and left the restaurant. They were on the pavement, no one was around, they embraced each other and, both felt the passion that ran in their veins and the raised body temperature when one's lips connected with the other's cheek and vice versa. They nearly went further and engaged in a proper kiss, but they exercised self-control and held back.

'It's a bit late, shall I walk you to the underground station?' Alex asked.

'Don't worry, I'll be alright. I do this quite often. There are plenty of people around. It's quite safe to travel,' Melanie said.

'It's no problem for me to come with you to the underground station,' Alex re-emphasised his point.

'No thanks. I'll be fine. I might see you tomorrow. Good night,' Melanie replied.

'Good night. Take care,' Alex said.

Chapter 28

Alex was familiar with a variety of tactics used by the other agencies to get results in the field of investigations. As a lawyer he had to utilise different approaches to find solutions. He had used that experience in his new career to great effect with the assistance of his trusted Associate. The creative use of the investigative strategy was justified as long as the means led to a desirable, acceptable and successful end. As long as the method used to obtain evidence was legal and practical.

Having Scott in his team was a real bonus. His previous knowledge and experience as a Detective had been instrumental in achieving results. He immediately made contact with his source at the National Bank to obtain a copy John's bank statements. Clearly, he would have to explain the rationale for such a request which, supposedly, his contact would weigh up before relinquishing any personal details about a client.

As Alex had explained to Melanie the night before, he was only asking for John's bank statements because a crime had been committed and the information was crucial to the investigation. It was up to someone at the bank to decide whether or not to release the information. Somehow, he failed to mention to her that Scott had a contact working at the bank.

At the Agency, Alex met up with Scott and Jenny to discuss the outcome of Scott's attempt to prise out such delicate information from the National Bank. All three sat down in Alex's office with their mug of coffee and were ready to engage in their deliberations. Jenny chose to start with her own personal question.

'Did you enjoy your dinner with Melanie last night?' Jenny was being nosy.

'Yes I did, thank you,' Alex replied.

They had not told Scott anything about the dinner meeting with Melanie.

Looking bemused, Scott wanted to find out more. 'What's been going on between Melanie and you?' he asked.

'Not much. According to Jenny we are having an affair,' Alex said while staring at Jenny.

'Well, are you?' Scott went on the attack.

'Of course not, I've a girlfriend and she has a boyfriend. If you must know, we've met on three occasions for business reasons. That's all,' Alex was pleased to explain.

'You have met her on numerous occasions,' Jenny was quick to add.

'It's called working together on the murder case,' Alex rebutted.

'Oh I see,' Scott said.

'That's enough about me. Let's talk about John's bank statements.'

Alex decided to get down to business.

'Happy to report that I saw my contact, explained the reason for the request and the information required for the investigation. She was disgusted with the devious tactics used to make money and horrified to learn of Margaret's death. She was willing to assist,' Scott said.

'Good to hear but did she give you the information?' Alex asked.

'Not in the manner you would prefer,' Scott replied.

'Alright, go on,' Alex suggested.

'She couldn't provide me with a copy of John's bank statements for the past two years,' Scott informed them.

'Why not?' Alex asked.

'I believe they are having some security problems at the bank. As a result, they have tightened up their procedure for the release of clients' bank details,' Scott explained.

'Another dead end for us, then,' Alex said disappointingly.

'Not quite. She has given me written details of large payments made to John by the Friendly Employment Bureau and details of large payments from John's account which were paid immediately into someone's account at the First Bank in Chelsea,' Scott said.

'That's great news. I've been waiting for this confirmation. Well done, Scott,' Alex expressed his excitement.

'You're welcome,' Scott said with a wide grin.

Although a copy of the bank statements was not available, it should not prevent Alex from challenging John on his extra-curricular activities in the arena of recruitment. Handwritten details could suffice if John did not ask for concrete evidence to be produced. Alex felt he could utilise the information received from John's bank to demonstrate that John had received money from the Friendly Employment Bureau and together with the other evidence, John would be in an indefensible position.

'What exactly have you got, Scott?' Alex asked.

'My contact has written down the amounts of money, the date it was paid into John's account and the large amount leaving John's account.'

Scott gave him the hand-written statement.

'Thank you. That's very useful information. Your contact has used her firm's headed paper to outline the details of his account which gives credibility to the statements,' Alex remarked.

He noticed the chronological order which linked the payment to the three 'lists': In March 2004 - £3,000; In September 2004 - £22,500; In March 2005 - £37,500.

Around the same time, large sums had been paid into an account at the First Bank which were as follows: In March 2004 - £1,000; In September 2004 - £7,500; In March 2005- £12,500.

Alex remembered the 'guy' in McDonald's telling him that each candidate paid £2,000 to the Bureau which then paid £1,500 to the senior academic for each candidate. After a quick calculation and having considered the number of students on the 'lists' Matt had given him, he concluded that the following had taken place. The Friendly Employment Bureau had paid John: In March 2004 - £3,000. This was for two students at the rate of £1,500 for each student. In September 2004 - £22,500. This was for 15 students at the rate of £1,500 for each student. In March 2005 - £37,500. This was for 25 students at the rate of £1,500 for each student.

He then worked out the outgoings from John's account to the one in the First Bank.

In March 2004 - he paid out £1,000. In September 2004 - he paid out £7,500 and in March 2005 - he paid out £12,500. These amounts equated to £500 per student.

It was essential to note that the dates of payment to John corresponded with the dates mentioned in Matt's signed statement. The evidence regarding the number of names on the three 'lists', supplied by Matt, had been confirmed through the payments made to John. The payment for September 2005 for 25 students on the fourth 'list', had not yet been made by the Friendly Employment Bureau. Alex had never doubted Matt, but this was clear proof that he had told the truth.

At the bottom of the bank statement, he noticed that the Bureau had made a payment in September 2003 for £22,500 to John, but there was no mention of John paying out to anyone soon afterwards. Obviously, he had been charging students prior to Matt's appointment as the Recruitment Officer in January 2004.

As he had not made any payment to anyone at that time, it was possible that he was conducting the act of extortion on his own. From March 2004, he had recruited a partner in crime as testified by his action of paying someone following the receipt of his own payment from the Bureau. The next conundrum was why did John recruit a partner in crime when he was doing well by himself.

In summary, the students paid £2,000 to the Friendly Employment Bureau which, in turn, paid John £1,500 per student. Then John paid someone £500 per student.

As Alex suspected, John was not working alone on this despicable venture, he had an accomplice. It would appear that his partner in crime was an employee of the University.

But who? It could be anyone.

Alex explained his analysis to Scott and Jenny and his suspicion of another crook operating in cahoots with John. They were blown away at the thought of the amount of money which was changing hands. If this were to continue then the sums would get bigger and bigger, the poor candidates would have to scrimp, borrow and pay for a place that was free in the first instance. It was impossible to imagine that those who were training nurses to look after sick and vulnerable patients would embark on this deplorable and criminal scheme.

'I'm speechless. Having listened to the way John is making money from these South African candidates, I feel very angry. Why don't you get him arrested?' Jenny was very annoyed.

'What can be done to stop this going on?' Scott put more pressure on Alex.

'He should go to jail for stealing computers and illegally charging these candidates,' Jenny continued.

'I believe there is now enough evidence for the Police to arrest and charge him with extortion,' Alex said, and agreed with their sentiments.

'John is a conniving, devious and corrupt academic and has been getting away with it,' Jenny expressed her disgust.

'This is what you call a real scam. It has been well structured and implemented without any care of being caught. The cynicism with which John went about it, is quite breath-taking. I'll hazard a guess that someone, in a powerful position, has been supporting him. That's the reason he feels empowered to carry out his distasteful money-making activities without fear of being caught. A web of deceit and extortion has been in covert operation at this institution,' Alex outlined his feelings strongly.

'What's your next course of action?' Scott asked.

'I'll have to contact Melanie. I'll ask her to use her influence to find out exactly who John has been paying large sums to, at the First Bank in Chelsea,' Alex said.

'Do you have any idea who John's partner in crime might be?' Scott asked.

'I think it could be either the VC, the Dean or the Deputy Dean,' Alex replied.

'You aren't suspecting the VC, are you?' Scott expressed his surprise.

Alex was prompted to think about the rationale of his own appointment by the VC. To cover the dirty tracks of his criminal activities, the VC could have appointed Alex to demonstrate that he cared about solving the computer thefts. In reality he did not. It was purely a diversionary tactic, to get the staff focusing on the computer thefts and most probably not suspect him of illegally charging the candidates.

As a lawyer and now as a Private Investigator, Alex was always careful to know enough about someone before trusting them. There had to be an element of trust between his Agency and the clients so that they could confide in him and he would solve their problems. Alex had trusted the VC through his old boss, Robert. He felt that it was possible for the VC to confide in him up to a point and yet keep useful information from him.

'It has happened before, you know. The person in charge could be at the heart of it all, pulling the strings and getting others to carry out his criminal activities,' Alex replied.

'How are you going to identify the accomplice?' Scott pressed him further.

'Once the identity of the person holding the account that John payed into, has been established, the circle can be closed on that particular issue,' Alex enlarged.

'I remember asking my contact about John's payment to another bank account. She told me it was someone at the First Bank which I mentioned in my report earlier,' Scott said.

'Yes, you did. But, how could she tell?' Jenny asked.

'Apparently through the bank sort code system and the account number which I've got here for you,' Scott replied and gave him the information regarding the First Bank.

'Thanks, but paid into whose account?' Alex asked.

'I think you should ask Melanie to help you on this one,' Jenny said with a big smile.

'As it happens, that's a very good suggestion. Let's hope she will be able to help,' Alex replied.

'Do you want me to carry on checking?' Scott asked.

'You've done very well supplying me with John's bank details. I think you should continue with our existing clients' cases. I'll check further on John's covert activities. I'm sure something will turn up,' Alex reassured him.

'Ever the optimist. You always believe in getting a positive result. Anyway, are you staying here today?' Jenny asked.

'I'll probably go to the University, you never know what else might come to light. I need to follow up on this statement from the bank and discuss it with Melanie. I'll be leaving shortly,' Alex replied.

On his way out, he told Scott that there were no new developments regarding the goons.

Alex reflected on the whole sordid affair and thought, if Matt had not had a conscience and not been willing to share his experience, then it would not have been possible to close in on John. The details of payments from the Bureau to John's account were very revealing on many fronts.

It had proved to be a lucrative stream of business which no one would have ever found out about.

Greed was at the heart of this scam. John had every intention of carrying on with his stinking plan. Worst of all, John is a well-paid Principal Lecturer and still decided to make money out of young people who wanted to train as nurses to provide care to patients. Sickening thought.

Chapter 29

The weather was nice, pleasant and warm. The sun shone brightly and there was hardly a breeze to contend with. Alex walked to the centre of town to buy a card for his parents' wedding anniversary. Then, he popped into an upmarket men's shop to peruse the latest shirts and ties.

Not very impressed with what was on offer, he decided to go for a cheeseburger at McDonald's.

As usual, he picked up his order and went to sit by the window. Looking out through the window, he ate his cheeseburger and admired a couple of beautiful women standing just outside. Suddenly, he felt someone had taken the seat opposite. He turned round and saw the 'guy' he had met the last time. He had been sitting at the same table a few days previously.

'Hello, nice to see you again,' Alex said rather surprisingly.

'Hi. I was passing by and I saw you here so I came in to see you. I did say the other day to leave it to me to make contact with you,' the guy replied.

'That's very kind of you. I must say the only place you seem to see me is here. What a coincidence?' Alex remarked.

'I'm pleased to see you and want to ask you about your investigation regarding the charging of foreign candidates?' the guy said.

'We're making progress,' Alex replied.

'Did you check on the Friendly Employment Bureau?' the guy asked.

'Yes, we did and guess what? That business has closed down completely, so we cannot check anything,' Alex said.

'What do you think happened to it?' the guy asked coyly.

'I'm sure you know the answer to that,' Alex was fishing.

'You are a good man, I can't lie to you. My friend left the business before it folded hurriedly. She doesn't know anything about it anymore,' the guy said.

'I think the last time you and I were here, someone saw us and reported it to the Friendly Employment Bureau. They got very nervous and decided to close their office and perhaps move somewhere else under another name,' Alex said.

'As this company doesn't exist, you can't make the link between the company and the senior academic. That means you won't be able to catch him and take action to stop him charging candidates,' the guy expressed his grave concern.

Alex was listening to him attentively, eating his cheeseburger and pondering at the same time. He was thinking and formulating a response to give to the 'guy'. The information the 'guy' had provided to Alex about the Bureau was accurate. He had mentioned the amount paid by the Bureau to the senior academic was £1,500 for each candidate, which turned out to be right and had kept his word by giving Alex enough time to resolve the extortion issue.

To be fair, the 'guy' did not own up to sending the anonymous letter to the VC, making an anonymous phone call to the VC, admitting he was a student at the University and providing his name. That could be acknowledged as his insurance policy to protect himself in case his attempts to rectify the extortion issue failed. Alex recognised his brave approach to eliminating an appalling and illegal matter at a well-known University. He owed the 'guy' a decent response.

Alex chose to share carefully selected information with him. 'I promise you, the senior academic will not get away with it. Through other means, I've been able to establish the real culprit. In fact, I'm on the verge of challenging this person directly about the extortion and the VC will then institute the University disciplinary action against this person.'

'I'm very pleased to hear that. I'll still wait for definitive action to be taken first. I hope you will be able to bring this matter to a quick and successful end. Thank you,' the guy said humbly.

'By the way, do you know whether the Bureau asked these candidates to pay more money to them once they started their course?' Alex asked.

'I haven't come across that sort of request from my contact at the Bureau. Why do you ask?' The guy wanted to know.

'It's something that was said to me, which I just thought I would check with you,' Alex replied.

'As I said, no one has said anything about paying the Bureau any additional sum. The candidates were expected to pay £2,000 and that's all,' the guy explained.

'Thank you for clearing that up for me.'

Alex got the confirmation he sought.

'How long will it take to stop this awful mess so that foreign candidates can compete on merit with the home candidates?' the guy made a very pertinent point.

'It won't take long for this matter to be resolved and for all candidates to be recruited fairly according to the recruitment policy of the University,' Alex reassured him.

'I'm sure you'll appreciate that I want to keep my threat to go to the press alive until the whole mess comes to an end. Just in case, it gets pushed under the carpet and ignored,' the guy kept the pressure on.

'I can assure you that the VC and I find it reprehensible to charge candidates for a place on a nursing course which is free to all applicants. We've worked relentlessly to find the person responsible and for correct action to be taken. This will happen shortly,' Alex promised him.

'I hear you loud and clear but I'll reserve my judgement till it happens,' the guy said.

'That's reasonable,' Alex nodded in agreement.

'Remember Alex, you haven't got a lot of time,' the guy warned.

'I'm fully aware of that,' Alex replied.

The 'guy' left and Alex finished his drink. He could not help but admire the sincerity with which the 'guy' conducted himself, a young man who only wanted to do good for his fellow prospective students, a decent man who cared about others. If, as suspected, he was a student nurse at the University and assuming he would complete his course successfully, he would make a very competent, confident and caring professional nurse.

Following his lunch and a pleasant and surprising encounter with his reliable informant, he walked back to his office at the University. He found it rather difficult to maintain any sort of rapport with the 'guy' because he remained very self-protective. He did not want to share any of his personal details for example, his name and status as a student nurse. Referring to him as 'the guy' was as if he were part of a mysterious thriller movie.

The 'guy', however, was serious and provided Alex with accurate leads to explore with regard to finding the crooked senior academic. Alex would have liked to contact him whenever he needed but could not do so because the 'guy' refused to give his contact details. As long as he could obtain information from the 'guy' that he could use, Alex did not mind putting up with his self-preservation tactics. It was productive to have him as someone who could help but protecting his identity, instead of disclosing too much about himself and was not being helpful at all.

He liked the 'guy'.

***

When he got back to his office at the University, the place was much quieter than usual, as it was a Friday afternoon. A very large proportion of the students and lecturers had already left. He decided to contact his favourite Sergeant.

After all, Melanie had promised to get in touch with him and he hadn't heard from her all day. Like all the detectives in her department, she was probably held up dealing with many cases at the same time. According to Melanie, hers was a very busy department with a high volume of work constantly filtering through. Alex rang her.

'Hi Melanie, how are you today?' Alex asked.

'I'm fine. I'm sorry I've got a lot to do and that's the reason I haven't been in touch with you,' Melanie explained.

Melanie informed him that she could spare some time to speak to him. Although she was very busy, she would always make time for him, clearly she was very fond of him. Hearing his voice was like music to her ears. Alex also fully enjoyed talking to and being with her.

'Oh, don't worry about it. I've been busy as well,' Alex reassured her.

'You're not mad at me for not phoning you?' Melanie asked.

'Of course not, busy people always have plenty to do,' Alex replied.

'Thank you for last night. I really enjoyed myself,' Melanie remarked.

'No, thank you for inviting me to dinner, that was very generous of you. I enjoyed myself as well,' Alex said.

'It's funny, isn't it?' Melanie observed.

'What's funny?' Alex was curious to find out.

'I invited you to dinner and you would not let me pay the bill,' Melanie said.

'It was my pleasure to pick up the bill,' Alex confirmed.

'Thank you, anyway. We need to do it again and next time I'm paying,' Melanie warned him.

'We'll see. The reason for me ringing you is to do with the murder case,' Alex changed the subject.

'Yes, go on,' Melanie said.

Alex went through the detailed information he received from Scott. He gave her a breakdown of the dates and amounts of the payments from the Friendly Employment Bureau to John and, the payments John made to someone at the First Bank. He also gave an analysis of the various payments. Candidates paid £2,000 to the Bureau which in turn paid £1,500 for each accepted candidate to John. According to John's account, on the same day he would pay £500 for each accepted candidate into this unknown person's account at the First Bank in Chelsea.

'That's extortion. This is Fraud. How long has this been going on?' Melanie asked with the air of authority of a Detective Sgt.

'It's a real scam. The record demonstrates that this has probably been going on since the year 2003 because John received his first payment in September 2003 for 15 candidates,' Alex explained.

'By the way, how did you get hold of this personal and sensitive information?' Melanie asked.

'From John's bank account. Remember me telling you about it,' Alex confirmed.

'This information has been received illegally and it will not stand up in a court of law,' Melanie stated her point strongly.

'I wouldn't worry too much about the method as long as the content is credible and correct. This will, undoubtedly, help us to catch the person responsible for the extortion and possibly Margaret's murder,' Alex reassured her.

'It is still against the law,' Melanie continued to express her disapproval.

'I'm aware you're concerned about my methods. Trust me, this is the only way to obtain information about John's shady dealings. I'll handle the legal side of my approach if required,' Alex tried to placate her.

'Alright, I'll hold you to that,' Melanie warned him.

'That's fine with me,' Alex was pleased to reach some kind of agreement with her.

Melanie could see Alex's point of view but in her role, she could not openly condone his approach. At the same time, deep down she trusted Alex's impeccable legal skills and that he would deal competently with any challenge raised. She felt she could not win on this particular matter, therefore she decided to move on with their discussion.

'So this has been going on before the days of Matt's appointment as the Recruitment Officer?'

'That's correct. The post for Recruitment Officer was vacant for over 6 months. John was overseeing the recruitment activities and most likely could see an opening for making money,' Alex added.

'Who do you think is the third party?' Melanie asked.

'I would guess John has been working with a senior person at the University and has been paying this person £500 per student,' Alex explained his assumption.

'Do you have a person in mind?' Melanie pressed him.

'Not really. Investigations continue until we uncover this elusive individual,' Alex replied.

'If we can connect this person as receiving payment from John for charging candidates, how do we connect either John or this person to Margaret's murder?' Melanie got down to the core issue.

'I believe the issue of extortion and Margaret's murder is inextricably linked,' Alex made his case.

'You still cannot produce watertight evidence against John,' Melanie reminded him.

'I know. We're very close, I can sense it,' Alex replied.

Given the fact that Melanie was a stickler for implementing the rules and regulations properly and did not believe in bending the law, let alone breaking it, Alex's next request could upset her calm composure. Nevertheless, she was his only means of obtaining another piece of personal and sensitive information. She might just make an exception for him.

'May I ask for a favour?' Alex said gingerly, half expecting her to refuse.

'In the circumstances, Alex, I'm not sure,' Melanie was not all that pleased.

'Don't you want to hear my request before you refuse to help?' Alex pointed out.

'Well, go on, let's hear it,' Melanie said.

'OK. Would you be able to find out the name of the account holder at the First Bank into which John has been making payments?' Alex asked, expecting an outburst from her.

'I don't believe it. You don't give up, do you?' Melanie said.

'I need to find out about the third party in his sordid affair and it could lead us to Margaret's killer. I would like to explore every possible avenue to get to the truth. I thought perhaps you have a contact who could help us establish this person,' Alex put his point robustly.

'I'm sorry Alex I don't get involved in illegal matters. We need to obtain proper legal authorisation before embarking on this expedition,' Melanie put her point across.

'I don't think there is a lot of time left for that. Thanks anyway. I'll find another way,' Alex was somewhat disappointed.

Clearly, Melanie was not pleased with Alex's request. She felt bad for not helping him but she had to stick to her values and beliefs of doing her job professionally. In any case, she did not know anyone that could provide her with the information required. Alex respected her for sticking to her high standards. It was an opportune moment for him to be light-hearted with his comments.

'Anyway, I would like to thank you for your views and comments. May I ask what are you doing this weekend?' Alex asked gently.

'Why do you need to know?' Melanie asked a question of her own.

'Do you always answer a question with another question?' Alex pressed her.

'No, not usually,' Melanie replied.

'Well, whatever you're doing, have a wonderful weekend,' Alex said warmly.

'And you,' Melanie said curtly.

***

Alex expected her to be a bit annoyed with him about his request. She would get over it in a couple of days. It was Friday afternoon and he always believed in going home early but rarely succeeded in achieving it. But first, he decided to go back to the Agency.

When he was leaving the campus, he had to stop at the give way sign before turning to the right to head to Mayfair. He spotted the black 4x4, X5 parked outside the University building.

Immediately, the other vehicle followed his car all the way.

When he reached the Agency, he parked his car on the road and the black 4x4 sped passed him. There were two guys in the car. The driver was a large white fellow with a bald head. The other person was also white of medium build.

Difficult to draw any conclusions, so again he thought it could be a complete coincidence. The other car was just going the same way as him. Nevertheless, he felt a tingling sensation running down his back.

Both Jenny and Scott were there.

'Any urgent matters for me to deal with?' Alex enquired.

'Not really,' Jenny replied.

'Well both of you get ready to go home then,' Alex advised them.

As usual, Jenny enjoyed finding out about Melanie.

'Did you see Melanie?' Jenny was curious to find out to satisfy her gossiping instincts.

'No Jenny, I didn't see her, I spoke to her on the phone,' Alex said.

'What did she say, then?' Jenny continued.

'About what?' Alex was teasing her.

'Getting in touch with the First Bank for the name of the person who has been receiving money from John,' Jenny said. As usual she was right on the button.

'Apparently, she doesn't believe in using underhand tactics to obtain confidential information and prefers to use the formal channels instead,' Alex explained.

'Good girl. I told you she is not only a very beautiful woman but also a very decent and honest person. You should really ask her for a date. You two will make a nice couple,' Jenny expressed her personal view.

'We've a professional working relationship, not a personal one,' Alex put her in her place. His uncle had asked Jenny to keep an eye on him and she never missed the opportunity to get him hooked on any beautiful woman. Then marriage could follow and he could settle down. That was her wish for Alex. On this occasion, Alex conceded Melanie was everything that Jenny had observed her to be.

'What do we do now?' Scott asked seriously.

'Well I'll have to think this one through carefully and I will probably deal with it myself. It's time for both of you to go home, have a good weekend,' Alex said.

Both wished him a nice weekend as well.

'See you both on Monday,' Alex said.

He was going straight to his flat from the Agency. As soon as he got into his car, he received a message on his mobile from Melanie wishing him a fantastic weekend. He returned the compliment to her from his mobile. So, she still cares about him.

Chapter 30

On Saturday evening, Alex was walking to his flat from the underground station when he experienced an eerie feeling that he was being followed. He turned round, had a look but could not see anyone close to him; there were a few people on the other side of the road. He carried on walking towards his flat. As soon as he turned left into the side street of his domicile, a black 4x4, X5, pulled in and a white guy of medium build opened the front passenger door and jumped in front of him with his arms spread wide. Alex stopped. It was the same car that had been following him recently. He was stunned by the sudden action, and practically froze for a few seconds.

By that time the car had stopped. The driver was white, tall and large male with a sarcastic grin walked towards him. Both were the same guys who had been following him in the black 4x4.

Understandably, he was worried for his own safety and decided to break the ice.

'Can I help you guys?' The big guy did the talking, 'It's more what we can do for you.'

'What will that be?' Alex decided to maintain full eye contact with him and showed no sign of being scared.

Both guys got closer to him. 'Just a piece of friendly advice, stop your investigations at the University immediately, otherwise next time, we might not be so nice. Remember, give it up now if you know what's good for you.'

Alex stood still and did not utter a word, looked serious, listened carefully and was watching for any move from either guy. Luckily, they did not lay a finger on him. They left hurriedly. Alex breathed a sigh of relief and went into his flat. He headed straight to the drinks cabinet, poured himself a large, single malt whisky and added a few ice cubes into it. He had a good slug and slumped down onto his sofa, thinking that he could have been hurt badly by these goons.

Their stern request for him to stop the investigations immediately was both puzzling and worrying. It would appear that he had ruffled the feathers of someone at the University very badly for that person to employ the services of two goons to threaten him with violence.

He was determined to carry on relentlessly with the tasks he had been brought in to perform and was not going to be frightened by anyone. Throughout his life, he had always risen to the challenges thrown at him. In fact, he had been at his best when his resolve was put to the test, be it in sporting activities, jealous boyfriends, bullies during his student days, he had prevailed over all of these.

It also convinced him that he was on the right track and was very close to exposing the criminals.

He believed he was within touching distance of catching the perpetrators of the three criminal acts. Therefore, no amount of intimidation or threats were going to deter him from finding Margaret's killer and solving the issue of extortion and the computer thefts. He decided not to tell anyone at the University or give any inclination of his encounter with the goons, he would act as if nothing had happened. But at some stage, he would have to inform his team.

At 9 am on Monday morning, Alex arrived at the Agency looking bright and cheerful.

In addition to his usual five mile runs in Hyde Park on Saturday and Sunday mornings, Alex had enjoyed a great weekend playing football and lawn tennis with his friends and clubbing in the evenings. Claire, his girlfriend, had gone home to spend some time with her parents.

Alex had every reason to be positive; his client list was improving gradually. He was expected to return a few phone calls from people enquiring about his services. Two of his current cases were all but finished and both clients wanted to have their last meeting with Alex and, of course, to give him a hefty cheque for the Agency's successful efforts.

As far as the three cases for the University were concerned, some more investigative work had to be done to reach a successful conclusion. The computer theft case was almost solved. The charging of candidates was also in the final stage, just the identity of the third party had to be confirmed which he felt was achievable. In fact, he was quite sure that Margaret's murder was connected with the extortion. Increasingly, an element of doubt was developing in his mind though, with regard to John being the killer. As a serious point for consideration, if John did not murder Margaret, then who did?

'There's a call for you. It's someone called Jane Fergusson from the University,' Jenny said.

'Hi Jane, how are you?' Alex asked.

'I'm fine, thank you,' Jane replied.

'What can I do for you?' Alex got to the point. He could hear her breathing was quite fast.

'I need to see you urgently.'

'Alright, what's it about?'

'It's to do with your investigations. I've some useful information to share with you. Can I see you this afternoon?' Jane enquired.

'Which investigation?' Alex wanted to know.

'Well, I'll tell you when I see you.'

'I'll be able to see you anytime this afternoon in my office at the University,' Alex replied.

'I don't want to come to the University right now as I don't want anyone to see me there,' Jane said.

'OK. Where do you want to meet?' Alex was being accommodating as he could sense Jane's willingness to talk. He also had to tread carefully because Jane was John's girlfriend and had been supporting him throughout.

'I can come to your office at the Agency at 1pm today, if that will help,' Jane suggested.

'That'll be fine. Do you know how to get here?' Alex asked.

'Don't worry, I'll be there,' Jane confirmed.

'OK then, I'll see you here at 1pm,' Alex said.

Having put the phone back, he was temporarily speechless and tried to make sense of the request to see him in a somewhat covert manner. The first time someone asked him for such a meeting was Matt and this time it was Jane. Matt had ended up spilling the beans on John's manipulation of his good nature. He wondered if Jane would have a similar story.

What a surprise to hear from Jane again! He never expected her to contact him as she was reputedly on annual leave. He began to wonder what type of information she had to share with him and why the meeting had to take place at the Agency and not the University. His suspicious mind was in overdrive. Who was she afraid of at the University? Could it be John or someone else?

'Who is Jane Fergusson?' Jenny asked.

'Jane Fergusson is a Senior Lecturer at the University and she is John's girlfriend,' Alex explained.

'What did she want with you?' Jenny continued to probe.

'You can rest easy Jenny, she isn't after me,' Alex replied.

'She sounded very young and sophisticated,' Jenny remarked.

'I agree with that description of her. She wants to meet me here at the Agency to talk about my investigations,' Alex explained.

'Which investigation?' Jenny asked curtly.

'That's exactly what I said to her and her answer was she would tell me when she sees me,' Alex explained.

As Jenny was getting too inquisitive, Alex gave her and Scott an account of his brief phone conversation with Jane. They seemed to share his suspicion of her request to see him at the Agency instead of meeting him at the University.

'It could result in the breakthrough you've been looking for,' Scott observed.

'I hope you're right,' Alex replied.

'As you're good at analysis, I'm sure you've already worked this one out. She is John's girlfriend and wants to see you here and not the University. That in itself would raise a strong suspicion. Another key point, she provided an alibi for John on the fatal Tuesday night when Margaret was murdered,' Scott provided an analysis of his own.

'You're right in your assumption. I've thought about it and I must say I'm hoping our meeting this afternoon will be very revealing and useful,' Alex was being positive.

'Are you staying at the Agency for the day?' Jenny wanted to know so that she could plan her work, in case he would require her assistance.

'I'll probably go to the University and return later to meet Jane,' Alex confirmed his intentions.

There was no doubt that his team had always wanted to play a full part in the work of the Agency, whether it concerned the University or not. Both Jenny and Scott were totally committed to the cause of the Agency and continued to work as hard as Alex, to ensure the long term success of their business. They worked together as an effective team, pushing each other to the very limit to get the best results and above all, they cared for their colleagues. In the case of Jenny, perhaps she cared too much about Alex's personal life.

***

Alex went to the University, calling first at the reception desk to pick up any messages.

Invariably, Julie took care of him because she had told Mary to leave her to deal with Alex. As usual, if she was on duty, she welcomed him with a big smile and a shy look. She informed him that he had a message from Sgt Cooper to contact her as soon as he could.

'Thank you Julie,' Alex said, and headed to his office to ring Melanie.

As a real professional, he thought Melanie probably had information concerning the murder investigation but on a personal level, he wished she would ask him to dinner again. He also knew that she was a bit cross with him on Friday so an invitation for dinner would more than likely be out of question. He phoned Melanie and they exchanged greetings before Melanie went on the attack.

'Where have you been all morning?' Melanie asked.

She was conscious that on Friday they had not left on friendly terms following Alex's method of obtaining confidential information regarding John's bank details. In addition, his request for her to obtain information about the third party from the First bank did not please her.

Over the weekend she had thought about it and reached the conclusion that he was only acting like most Private Investigators did, getting evidence by hook or by crook. And, as long as he could defend his actions and assist her in solving the murder case quickly, then everyone would be happy. She had been waiting all morning to discuss a couple of very serious matters with him.

'I've been very busy, I've just come to the University,' Alex explained.

'I thought you were avoiding me,' Melanie got straight to the point.

'Why?' Alex asked. He would never ignore or avoid her because he wanted to be with her.

'Because I didn't approve of your underhand tactics to obtain details of John's bank statement and I refused to help with getting information from the First Bank,' Melanie provided a rationale.

'That's water under the bridge stuff, I've moved on. No time for anger or bitterness, I've got to get on with the job in hand, finding solutions to the three cases,' Alex was happy to explain.

'That's good to hear,' Melanie said, and felt relieved.

'By the way, did you have a nice weekend? Is Martin back from his overseas business trip? Alex decided to throw that one in to test her temperament.

'I did have a very nice weekend and yes, Martin was back on Friday evening and we had a fantastic time. I hope you had a good weekend with Claire,' Melanie replied.

'As it happens, she went home. I spent my time with friends and had a great time,' Alex enlightened her.

'Good for you,' Melanie replied.

Alex went quiet for a few seconds and then changed the personal conversation to a more pertinent one. 'Any particular reason why you're looking for me?'

'It's to do with the Harry button, actually. It was drizzling with rain last Friday late afternoon, and one of my officers was passing by the Faculty site in his car when he noticed a man, could be a member of the University staff, wearing a Harry trench coat. He was walking towards the front door but unfortunately the officer couldn't see his face. Would you know anything about this?' Melanie asked.

'Not really. I'm not surprised to hear that. A few of the University staff appear quite affluent and could possibly afford such a coat,' Alex replied.

'I wonder if you could look into this and check discreetly who owns a Harry coat, if possible with a button missing, on your travels around the building,' Melanie suggested.

'For your information, I've already been watching out for it. Even if I find someone with a Harry trench coat, it doesn't mean that person is the killer. This is going to be very tough. If Margaret's killer realised one of the buttons on his coat was missing, he could just replace it with a new one and we wouldn't know any different. Whoever the murderer is, it seems to me that person is very smart and would take the necessary steps to cover his tracks. We also have to prove that the killer was at the scene of the crime at the time of the murder and we don't have any leads at all on this one,' Alex reassured her that he was on the case.

'That thought had crossed my mind too. The killer is clever enough not to leave any evidence which could be used against him or her. What do you suggest we do next?'

'We'll need to keep searching for that elusive evidence.'

Melanie was getting desperate as pressure from her boss was mounting. 'I was reminded again this morning, by Richard, to get the murder case solved quickly,' Melanie impressed on him.

'I fully understand your predicament but we can only make progress as far as circumstances allow us,' Alex sympathised with her.

'You and I know that, but for some reason, Richard is getting difficult. Then again that's his role.'

Melanie was being philosophical or perhaps feeling sorry for herself.

Alex knew she was a tough girl and could cope with the pressure and he was going to ensure that she succeeded. It was in both their interests to find the killer. For her, it would look good on her CV and could help with her promotion. For him, it would be a feather in his cap to have gained the experience of solving a murder case. They would have to stick together as unknowingly, they had a mutual interest in advancing each other's careers.

'Richard has to be more practical. We're doing everything we can. Listen, don't worry about it too much. I'm going to send Scott on a spending spree, to explore a possible avenue I've just thought of,' Alex informed her.

'Would you care to share it with me?' Melanie was curious.

'I'll let you know in due course. Incidentally, I've a meeting with Jane Fergusson at 1 pm this afternoon at the Agency. I think it'll be a very interesting one,' Alex said.

'You mean the girlfriend of John. Why does she want to see you at the Agency and not the University?' Melanie asked.

'That's a mystery. Remember Matt wanted to do the same,' Alex pointed out.

'Oh yes, that's right. I wonder whether she'll reveal anything sinister about John,' Melanie remarked.

'In the same way that Matt did?' Alex asked.

'Of course, you never know. Matt has provided us with a signed statement regarding John's recruitment activities. Let's hope, Jane will be just as helpful. Anyway, good luck and keep me posted,' Melanie said.

'OK Melanie, I must get ready to go back to the Agency for my meeting,' Alex said.

After quickly grabbing a ham sandwich and a cup of tea in the Faculty canteen, he set out to meet Jane at the Agency. Alex was ready to leave the site in his car when Alison appeared.

'Hi Alison, how are you?' Alex asked.

'Fine thanks. Can I see you sometime later today?' Alison asked.

'Of course you can. What is it all about?' Alex wanted to get an idea.

'It's to do with someone, I believe, could be useful to your investigation,' Alison explained.

'As you know, I'm always interested in listening to what you have to say,' Alex showed his willingness to meet with her.

'I know. I'll see you later,' Alison said.

'Sure. I'll be back here between 3.30 and 4pm, come to my office,' Alex replied.

'That's fine. My lesson finishes at 3.30pm and then I'll come to see you,' Alison confirmed.

'Good. See you later,' Alex said and drove away.

On his way to the Agency, Alex could not help wondering about the reason why Alison wanted to see him and who that particular person could be? And why didn't she tell him about that person at one of their earlier meetings? But then possibly she had been in an acute state of shock and had subconsciously blotted it out of her mind. And, as she was gradually coming to terms with Margaret's death, her state of mind was improving and she had regained clarity about the tragic event.

Chapter 31

On arrival at the Agency the first matter Alex had to deal was to placate a client whose case was progressing rather slowly by her reckoning. As usual, clients always expected a quick solution to their problems. Most cases were normally resolved within a two to four-week period. Alex had a chat with the client on the phone and reassured her that he would be able to provide the information she required by the end of the week.

'Have you had your lunch?' Jenny asked.

'Yes I have, thanks,' Alex replied.

'Are you ready for your meeting with Jane Fergusson?' Jenny asked.

'Of course. Is she here?' Alex replied.

'She has just arrived,' Jenny confirmed.

'I'll see her in my office,' Alex said.

Alex had been looking forward to this meeting. Jane had been outspoken at times, at his meeting with the lecturers, and had gone on annual leave without, especially, giving adequate notice to her employer. Jane looked elegant, she wore a peach coloured floral dress with a pink jacket and carried a beige leather handbag.

'Hi Jane, come on in and have a seat. How are you?' Alex greeted her.

'I'm fine, thank you,' Jane said, and sat down with her eyes fixed on her host.

'Good to see you again, I hope you don't mind if we get down to business straightaway as I'm sure both of us have many other things to do,' Alex sought her co-operation.

'That's why I'm here,' Jane replied.

'OK. Can you tell me what this is all about, and then we'll explore it further?' Alex suggested.

'Well, as you probably gather it's to do with your investigations. I have given John an alibi for the Tuesday night when Margaret was murdered, saying that he was with me, but he wasn't there the whole evening. He came in at 7.30 pm, so I told a lie to cover up for him. I had to wrestle with my conscience to do that for him. He swore to me, on his mother's grave, that he was telling the truth. He said he had been to Margaret's flat to persuade her not to report him to the VC regarding his financial activities but she would not budge. They ended up in an argument and heated words were exchanged but he did not lay a hand on her. When he left her flat at 6.30 pm, she was alive,' Jane said, and paused for a few seconds, her eyes were teary.

Alex was listening attentively and allowed her to express herself freely without any interruption.

She continued, 'I guess I've committed perjury but I'm willing to take the risk to talk about it instead of keeping quiet. In addition, on the Thursday when John went to pay Matt a visit at his apartment, I was driving past around 8 pm and I saw John entering the building with a bulging black holdall. Matt went off sick the following day. I believe you would like to have this information so that you can make use of it.'

Jane gave her account of the two incidents concerning John.

'That's very interesting indeed. Thank you for coming forward and putting the record straight,' Alex acknowledged her effort.

'After telling you what happened, I must say, I feel a bit relieved now,' Jane said, and sat back in her chair.

'I would like to ask you to clarify a few things, is that alright with you?' Alex asked.

'Of course, go ahead,' Jane replied.

'Why did you choose to meet here?'

'First, I'm on annual leave and it might look strange for me meeting you at the University. It could make people suspicious. Second, and more importantly, I couldn't meet you at the University where there is every possibility of me bumping into John or for him to see me with you. Knowing John as I do, he can become very jealous and could have barged into our meeting, creating a scene. He could also think that I was grassing on him. That's the reason I thought it would be safer to come here.'

'Did you tell him that you were in conflict with your conscience and you couldn't go on without letting the truth come out into the open?'

'No I did not say that to him. I advised him to come and see you about his visit to Margaret's flat but he totally refused. He said he would be incriminating himself.'

'Did he say why Margaret wanted to report him to the VC?'

'No, he didn't. And I didn't ask either.'

'What prompted you to see me now?' Alex continued to press.

'John and I have been together for quite a while and we have had a few disagreements which have not affected our relationship. For the past two months he has spent most of his time at my flat. Recently, I found a note, on my kitchen table, on which he had written sports car and Caribbean holiday. I asked him what it meant. He told me that he had been paid a sizeable sum of money for his hard work and he was going to treat himself to a car and a holiday. I was surprised to hear that. To my knowledge, he has always been short of money because he has to pay maintenance to his ex-wife and children from his failed marriage, and he had not done any additional work in the academic field to earn any extra money. He has a gambling habit, losing mostly.'

'Were you suspicious of the rationale for his new found wealth?'

'Of course I was, for the reasons I have given.'

'Did you ask him to explain about the new car and the holiday?'

'Yes I did.'

'How did he react when you challenged him?'

'After I asked him about the note, his mood changed and he became abusive and aggressive. He was swearing and banging his fist on the table. I felt I had to get away.'

'Let me get this right, you became scared of John's aggressive behaviour. Is this the main reason for you to volunteer information about his visit to Margaret and Matt?'

'I was scared to be alone with him.'

'Why do you think you felt that way towards him?'

'The more I thought about Margaret, the more I was convinced that John had something to do with her murder.'

'Do you think John is capable of murdering Margaret?'

'I don't really know.'

'Have you been in touch with John since you started your annual leave?'

'No but he has tried to contact me on my mobile and I have refused to respond to him.'

Then Alex changed the conversation and focused on her connection with Matt, if there was any.

'By the way, I know you're concerned about Matt's situation, have you contacted him at all?'

'No, I haven't because I don't have his number.'

'Did you confront John about his visit to Matt's apartment?'

'I did actually. He said he went to see him about something personal.'

'Did he take the holdall back with him to your flat?'

'Not that I noticed.'

'Has John made any comment about Matt to you?'

'John said he was very disappointed with Matt, especially after all that he had done for him by getting him the recruitment job. John said he had to talk to Matt again and make him see sense.'

'Did he say what he was disappointed about in Matt?'

'He didn't say but he was very angry with Matt.'

'Did John say what he wanted to talk to Matt about?'

'No, he didn't specify.'

'You have been very brave to come and talk to me about these sensitive issues,' Alex expressed his gratitude and respected her wish to put things right. 'Would you be willing to make a statement to this effect?'

'I've already got it here for you,' Jane replied, and gave Alex a signed copy of her statement.

'Thank you very much for this. I'll have to share the statement with Detective Sgt Cooper who is in charge of the murder enquiry. The section regarding Matt will be of great help in my other investigation,' Alex explained.

'I fully understand. What will happen to me for providing a false alibi for John?' Jane sought clarification.

'Well, I'll have a chat with Sgt Cooper about that. In the circumstances, I can assure you that by telling us the truth, undoubtedly, it will help your situation. From my experience, you will probably be cautioned and asked not to repeat this behaviour in the future. That should be the end of the matter.'

'Thank you, Alex. That's a big weight off my mind.'

'Don't speak to John about our meeting?'

'I don't intend to see him again, let alone talk to him. As far as I am concerned, my relationship with him has already come to an end.'

'Are you going home now?'

'Yes, I'm on annual leave. In fact, I went on leave to get away from John as I could not bear to be in the same place as him. I sincerely hope you can use the information I've given you.'

'You have been most helpful. Will you be alright to go back on your own?'

'Don't worry, I'll be fine. Good bye now.'

Jane stood up, shook hands with him and left with a smile on her face.

***

There was another important meeting on Alex's agenda and he had to rush to get back to his office at the University. Traffic was rather generous towards him and he managed to get to his destination in good time. He parked his car, and whilst entering the building he signalled to Julie, checking if there were any messages before taking the lift to the eleventh floor. No messages.

Alison's lesson had finished a bit early, at 3pm. So, she waited patiently outside Alex's office. She could have gone back to the residence but as she had an appointment with Alex which she had requested between 3.30pm to 4pm, she had no choice but to wait.

Shortly afterwards, Alex made his appearance which put a smile on Alison's face. They had met twice before and got to know each other quite well, albeit only on matters regarding Margaret's death. They seemed to have developed a warm rapport and mutual respect.

'Hi Alison, sorry to keep you waiting, how are you?' Alex said whilst opening his office door and ushering her in, he offered her a chair.

'I'm ok. I've just arrived myself. No apologies needed,' Alison replied and took her seat opposite Alex.

After putting his file on the table and hanging his jacket around the back of his chair, he was ready to give her all the attention she needed. They looked intriguingly at each other.

'Alright, would you like to start, Alison?' Alex said.

'I asked to see you because I came across someone who, I believe, may have something to do with Margaret's death,' Alison said quite confidently.

'Really. Have you seen that individual before?'

'Yes. I saw him going into the building where Margaret used to reside.'

'Where did you see this man again? What was it that triggered your memory to recall him?'

'This morning around 10 am when I was having my coffee break, I noticed this man walking towards me. He had a full head of grey hair, he was rather short, well built, wore a grey suit and was probably in his fifties,' Alison gave an accurate description of her suspect.

'You're very good at describing. How did you know he was the same person?' Alex asked.

'I could never forget that man because he had a slight limp on his right leg. His face was square and he had piercing blue eyes with bushy grey eyebrows. He wore a grey chequered double breasted jacket which he had on again today. He also wore a Harry trench coat with the front open,' Alison said.

'How do you know it was a Harry trench coat?' Alex's curiosity was gripping.

'I know because my boyfriend has one.'

'Tell me, how did you see him at the residence?' Alex pressed her further to ensure he got an accurate account.

'When I was standing just outside the residence finishing my cigarette that Tuesday evening around 7.30 pm, I saw this short, stocky middle-aged man walking past me. Our eyes did not meet as he was focusing straight ahead. He looked serious. I finished my cigarette quickly and stepped hard on the stub and decided to go into the building. I was only a few metres behind him. He walked up the steps to the front door, unperturbed. He entered the building without using the digital lock because someone left in a hurry and he sneaked in before the door self-locked. Margaret's flat was the first one next to the entrance door. He knocked on Margaret's door and was waiting for it to open. I saw him clearly through the glass door. I stopped outside, thinking, as she had a visitor, it would be better to leave her alone and see her the following day. I only wanted to see her for a social chat anyway.

Within seconds Margaret, I assumed, opened the door and he entered her flat, so I left,' Alison said.

'I did not know you smoked. Anything else you would like to add?'

'I only have a few cigarettes a day and I don't inhale, so I think I'm pretty safe. I can't think of anything else right now.'

'You are absolutely certain the man you saw this morning was the same man you had seen going into Margaret's room around 7.30 pm on that fatal Tuesday night.'

'Yes I am. As I said, I could not forget that face.'

'How can you be sure of the time you saw him there?'

'Because before I left the residence site, I automatically checked my watch and it was 7.35 pm.'

'Why have you decided to tell me about this man now and not at our previous meetings?'

'To be honest, I really don't know. Maybe it didn't click with me that the man I saw, could have anything to do with her death. Margaret was my best friend and I've been badly affected by her death.'

'Do you think this man murdered Margaret?'

'I can't answer that because I don't know but, he may be aware of something that could help find the killer.'

'Do you think this man recognised you today?'

'I don't believe he did. He wasn't looking in my direction. To be fair there were other people around the reception area as well.'

'Do you think this man works in the University?'

'I think so because he had a Faculty ID card hanging round his neck.'

'Did you check his name?'

'No. Everything happened so fast and I didn't have a clear view of his name.'

'Have you got anything else to tell me?'

'That's pretty much it really.'

It was an intensive line of questioning by Alex to encourage Alison to express herself freely and purposefully. It was typical of a lawyer to probe clinically for the precise details.

Alison did remarkably well in the way she described what she knew. She dealt competently with the questions that were thrown at her by Alex hence he felt the need to praise her for her efforts.

'You're a very observant, astute and caring young lady. What you've just told me about this man, in great detail, could yet prove to be the most crucial piece of evidence in finding Margaret's killer. You should feel proud of yourself for helping in such a constructive manner. I'm very grateful to you.'

'Thank you for your kind words. I sincerely hope you find this information useful.'

'I'm positive the information you've provided today will be very useful indeed. We're getting a lot closer to solving Margaret's murder. I'm sorry our meeting has taken so much of your time. Thank you again and keep in touch.'

The meeting had lasted for about an hour and understandably, Alison wanted to leave after her long day in the classroom. Both stood up, shook hands with a smile and then Alex walked her to the door. He has always been impressed by her initiative to come forward without any prompting from him. Seemingly, Alison was a very good friend to Margaret, and cared a lot about her. Such friendship was rarely seen.

Invaluable, relevant and pertinent information had been obtained regarding the crime scene, especially Jane's statement about John, and Alison's statement relating to the odious man she saw going into Margaret's flat. Alex felt there were still a few loose ends to tie up before he would declare his hand. However, Alison's description of the man she saw, had to a large extent confirmed the man he had been suspecting all along.

Chapter 32

Alex knew Scott was a resourceful and experienced person. He had a lot of contacts from a long career as a Detective, which had already proved invaluable in his current job. He wanted to have a particular matter checked out hence Scott's skills would be of great use. As soon as Scott arrived on duty, Alex went to see him in his office.

'Hello Alex, how are you?' Scott said while Alex found a chair to sit on.

'I'm fine, thanks. How are you? Alex asked.

'Alright. Is there anything on your mind?' Scott replied.

As things were moving fast and there was no time to waste, Alex got straight to the point.

'I've come to see you about something that needs to be tackled as quickly as possible.'

'What do you want me to do?'

'I want you to find a shop that sells replacement buttons for Harry trench coats.'

'I'll do my best.'

'Good, there is more. These buttons are a high quality brand and expensive. Is it possible to find out from the shop, if anyone has bought a button in the last few weeks? Alex spelt out his request.

Scott was always positive. 'I can do that.'

At that stage, Jenny was able to join them after finishing a phone call.

'You need to get some confidential information about the buyer such as his name or at least get his description,' Alex said.

'Why do you need to know this?' Scott asked.

'There are two reasons actually. First, Melanie told me that a member of her team had found a Harry button from a male trench coat on Margaret's settee. My guess is that this person was at the crime scene and is devious enough to buy another button and sew it back on,' Alex explained.

'And the second,' Scott asked.

'The second, Alison told me she had spotted an individual at the crime scene, who was wearing a Harry trench coat. Now you can appreciate the urgency,' Alex said.

'This is getting very interesting. Once you get the information about the replacement button, you've solved the murder case, that's fantastic,' Jenny commented, and was excited.

'Not so fast. We still have further checks to carry out to make our case watertight,' Alex said cautiously.

'If you can place this person at the crime scene, then you've pretty much got your killer,' Jenny said confidently.

'I still have to establish the motive for committing the crime. In other words, the reason for murdering Margaret,' Alex explained.

'Have you identified the motive, then?' Scott asked.

'I believe I have. When I receive all the information, I'll be in a more confident position,' Alex said, and did not want to raise their hopes prematurely.

***

Scott set off to conduct his enquiry into the button and Jenny went back to her office. Alex wanted to explore two additional issues that needed careful attention so that he could close the circle of his three investigations, at least that was the plan.

As he had received a signed copy of Jane's statement, he had sent Melanie a text to meet him at his office in the University around 11 am.

He made it just in time. Melanie was waiting outside his office with her handbag on her left shoulder and a notepad in her right hand. She looked very elegant and beautiful in her grey striped jacket and skirt and a white blouse.

Alex offered his apology, 'Sorry to keep you waiting.'

'Not at all. You're on time as usual,' Melanie replied with a smile.

'Please do come in and have a seat,' Alex said.

'Your text message sounded urgent,' Melanie remarked.

'It's kind of urgent, given the nature of the issues,' Alex said.

Melanie could not wait. 'Alright, let's hear it then.'

Alex briefed Melanie on what Jane had told him and gave her a copy of Jane's signed statement about John. Melanie took a few minutes to assimilate its contents and then let out a big sigh of relief. She looked pleased.

'This is the second signed statement against John, and is more damning. It places him at the crime scene and confirms he had an argument with Margaret. It also establishes that he had a bulging black holdall when entering the apartment building where Matt lives.

Furthermore, he was buying a sports car and going on a Caribbean holiday which seems to corroborate with Matt's statement,' Melanie said.

'That's correct,' Alex said.

'Are you sure that Jane and Matt did not have a discussion of their own before writing their statements. Aspects of their statements are strikingly similar,' Melanie said with a worrying look.

'The thought had crossed my mind. I asked Jane whether she had seen Matt, she responded negatively as she does not even have his contact number. I believe each has written his and her own statement separately and genuinely.'

'Although in the beginning I had my doubts about John being the killer, the evidence in the form of the two statements is overwhelming. We do now have a strong case against John. Do you want me to arrest him?' Melanie expressed her point more decisively.

'Again that had crossed my mind but I would ask you to wait for a brief period, may be a couple of days at the most, to allow me to get more definitive evidence,' Alex said, and sought her support.

'We've got everything we need to make our move,' Melanie stressed her case for John's arrest.

'I do see your point but I only need a little more time to make absolutely certain of solving all three cases in one fell swoop. By all means, you could keep an eye on John, in case he decides to run away.'

Alex was hedging his bets.

Melanie felt he was hiding something from her. 'You're not telling me everything, Alex.'

'Don't worry, all will be revealed in good time,' Alex promised her.

'I'll get one of my team to maintain surveillance on John. If Richard knew that I was doing you a favour, he would hit the roof and discipline me heavily.'

Melanie co-operated with him because she knew he had another two important cases to solve as well.

'Thank you. Very kind of you,' Alex said.

Melanie left and Alex headed to the First Bank in Chelsea to pursue his enquiry regarding the account into which John was paying a share of the money received from the Bureau. Having checked his list of old clients, he recalled one who was the manager of this particular branch and was hoping to call in a favour from her. He arrived at the bank and had a meeting with the manager, Carol Parker. He thought he had a 50:50 chance of getting the information he would like to have.

The secretary opened the door to the manager's office and, announced Alex was there for his appointment at 2.30pm. 'Mr DuPont is here.'

'Good to see you again, Alex. How are you?' the manager said offering him a chair and asking her secretary to bring in some tea.

'Hi Carol, you still remember me,' Alex said with a grin.

'How are you and nice to see you?'

Carol could not hide her pleasure at meeting him again.

'You do remember me, then,' Alex was also delighted.

'How could I possibly forget the large amount of money I paid you,' Carol said.

'For excellent service rendered, I might add,' Alex was quick to retort.

'Naturally. You are very good at what you do, I must say, and have a charming personality to go with it.

Anyway, what can I do for you?' Carol got straight to the point.

'I wonder if I can ask a favour from you.' Alex said gingerly.

The secretary served the tea, Alex taking his with milk and one sugar.

'I've told you before that if you ever need anything, just let me know. Through your impeccable efforts, I've got my life back and for that I'll always be grateful to you. So, go on and ask,' Carol said encouragingly.

'To put you in the picture, I'm dealing with a rather complex case of extortion and deceit at the University, and the murder of one of its students. I need some confidential information about someone's bank account,' Alex put his cards on the table and openly spelt out his dilemma.

'I see. I didn't know that you took on criminal cases as well,' Carol remarked.

'It's a long story. I'm doing a favour for a friend of my ex-mentor,' Alex explained.

'The case you're dealing with sounds very bad and dangerous,' Carol expressed her concern.

'Criminal cases always include an element of challenge and danger which is part of the job,' Alex explained.

'I would stick to your usual line of work, if I were you,' Carol advised.

'I can assure you, this is a one-off. As I said, it's a special favour. Can you help me?' Alex got back to the point.

'Well, giving confidential details about the account of one of our clients is not our usual policy, but on this occasion I'll make an exception because you're a rather special person dealing with a special case. I trust you when you say this person has been involved in criminal activities and that the information I provide will help catch this criminal, so I'm happy to assist,' Carol said.

Alex gave her the dates when money was transferred in, the sort code and account number of the person at the First Bank and the branch name of the National Bank from where the money was sent. He also gave her the sort code and number of John's account. Carol checked on her computer. It took her a few minutes. Alex waited patiently.

'I've found the transactions,' Carol said with a wide smile. She wrote the name of the person who had the account at the First Bank on a note pad for Alex and confirmed the dates when the transfers were made from John's account at the National Bank. Once Alex had looked at the pad and wrote on his business card the person's name and transfer details. Then, Carol destroyed it.

'Thank you very much,' Alex said.

'You're very welcome,' Carol replied.

'This will help us to nail that person down,' Alex said happily.

'Glad to be able to help you, Alex. The least I could do for you,' Carol said humbly.

'Thank you again,' Alex said and stood up. He shook hands with her and left.

***

Alex went back to the University hoping that Gail was still there. Usually she left early because she started early. Alex seemed to be in luck, she was still in her office and was working hard.

Alex knocked on the door and she asked him in.

'Hello Alex, you're still here, come on in,' Gail said.

'I can say the same about you. I thought you would have gone home already,' Alex replied.

'Anyway are you after something?' Gail wanted to know.

'I am indeed. As I'm lucky enough to find you here, I thought I would seek your invaluable support and the benefit of your wisdom,' Alex expressed his intentions.

'Flattery is one of your successful ploys and you use it effectively to your advantage. To be honest, you don't need luck to succeed. You've the ingenuity to create opportunities that yield positive results. Go on ask me,' Gail said whilst identifying one of his strengths.

'I've one outstanding issue to resolve and that's to do with the disappearance of the invoice for the two stolen laptops,' Alex said.

'I see what you mean. But you've already got the invoice which verified the serial numbers. What else do you wish to know?' Gail asked.

'I need to establish who removed the invoice from the AVA office,' Alex stated the real reason.

'Why?' Gail insisted on knowing.

'Because it will help with my other investigation as well,' Alex explained.

'Alright what do you want me to do?' Gail asked.

'I'm lurching in the dark here. I recognise it's difficult to find out who the person is...tell me who could have gone to the AVA office and remove the invoice unnoticed?' Alex said.

Gail looked straight into Alex's eyes and pondered hard at the same time.

'Those who are authorised to have access to the invoices are only the most senior people in the institution,' Gail explained.

'Well, if someone wants to go into the AVA office unnoticed to get hold of the invoice, how can that person do it?' Alex asked.

'I guess that person would have to go there when Tom has gone off duty,' Gail replied.

'Presumably, Tom locked the office on his way out and took the keys home with him,' Alex outlined his thoughts.

'Yes. That's right,' Gail replied.

'So how would a person get into the AVA office, then,' Alex asked to maintain his line of questioning.

'I don't really know. Fortunately, I haven't had to do anything like that,' Gail said.

'Of course you haven't. Please, this is very important. Can you think of any possible way to get into that office?' Alex asked.

After a big sigh, Gail looked absolutely lost and bemused.

'I wish I could help you. I've no idea at all,' Gail gave an honest reply.

'Thank you for listening and trying to help,' Alex said.

***

He made his way to his office, still thinking about the possible scenario he had just discussed with Gail. When he arrived on the eleventh floor, he saw the cleaner coming out of his office.

Suddenly it struck him; that could have happened at the AVA office. A cleaner had the keys to the offices and/or a master key to gain entry to any office for cleaning purposes. He stopped the cleaner in the corridor to establish his theory. She was of Asian origin, in her twenties and looking very attractive in her green uniform.

'Hi, how are you?' Alex asked while approaching her.

'Very well, thank you,' the cleaner replied.

'I'm Alex DuPont, you've just come out of my office. What's your name?' Alex asked politely.

'I know who you are. I always clean your office and hope it meets with your approval. My name is Sheena,' the cleaner replied.

'Can I ask you a favour?' Alex said.

'Of course, what is it?' Sheena asked.

'Do you clean any office on the fourth floor?' Alex asked.

'Yes I do,' Sheena replied.

'Can you tell me if you have ever seen any one going into the AVA office in the evening after Tom, the technician, has gone home?' Alex asked.

'No I haven't,' Sheena replied.

'Has anyone asked you for your key to open that office door?' Alex asked.

'No. No one has asked me for the key,' Sheena said.

Alex was not getting anywhere with his questioning. He stood there swallowing the saliva in his mouth and staring at Sheena who was waiting for his next question. Then the penny dropped.

'Has anyone asked you to unlock the AVA office door recently?' Alex asked.

Now Sheena was in deep thought and tried to remember, then it came to her.

'Yes, I do remember someone asking me to do just that,' Sheena said.

'Can you identify that person?' Alex asked.

'Sure I can. That person is obnoxious and looks down on people like me because I'm a cleaner,' Sheena explained.

Alex noticed the elegance with which she expressed herself and that she was very articulate.

'Are you a student?' Alex asked.

'Actually I'm a graduate and I am doing this job to save money until I'll start my Masters in September,' Sheena replied with a smile.

'Very good. Your Masters is in what subject and where are you doing it?' Alex asked.

'Law at London University,' Sheena informed him.

'Good luck with your studies,' Alex said.

'Thank you,' Sheena said.

Having digressed slightly from his original conversation albeit for a worthwhile matter, Alex resumed his line of questioning. 'Do you know the person's name?

'Yes I do, but I wouldn't like to utter that name,' Sheena said.

Sheena's disgust and contempt for this person was clear to see.

'Can you write the name on this note pad?' Alex asked.

'I suppose so,' Sheena replied and wrote the name on a note pad.

'Tell me, please, did you see what that person was doing in the AVA office so late?' Alex asked.

'Yes, I had a peep. That person removed a sheet of paper from a lever arch file,' Sheena explained.

'Are you sure about that?' Alex asked.

'Of course I'm sure because I never took my eyes off that horrible person,' Sheena said.

'Can you remember which day that took place?' Alex asked.

'It was a week last Friday. The whole place was very quiet. It was around 6.30 pm, I unlocked the door of the AVA office at the request of that despicable person,' Sheena said.

'Thank you very much,' Alex expressed his gratitude.

'Will I get into trouble?' Sheena asked.

'You can rest easy. Nothing will happen to you,' Alex reassured her.

'I hope I've been able to help,' Sheena said.

'Your help has been invaluable and I wish you every success in the future,' Alex acknowledged her contribution.

'Thank you for the good wishes,' Sheena said.

Quite a day for Alex, two issues had almost been resolved and he was waiting for Scott's feedback about the person who purchased the Harry button. Scott was usually very efficient in letting him know quickly about the outcome of an enquiry. He had probably come across some obstacle which had caused a delay in obtaining the correct information. He decided to talk to Scott in the morning.

Chapter 33

The next day Alex was in his office at 8.30 and was looking forward to talking to Scott about the issue of the Harry button. He had hoped to receive good news so that he could wrap up his investigations and inform Melanie and the VC of his solutions. He genuinely felt the time had come to unravel the three cases and expose the real criminal.

He had to wait for Scott to arrive. No message had been received from Scott with regard to him being late that morning. When he was on surveillance duty, inevitably, he would come to work when it was convenient to do so. That morning there was no such task and Scott was expected to start at 9 am. Alex was restless and rather impatient, as he wanted to have a discussion regarding the Harry button with Scott.

Alex thought it was rather unusual for Scott not to keep him updated on such an important issue. He had deliberately not got in touch with Scott yesterday because it was quite late when he left the University. As a rule, if it was not urgent, Alex preferred not to contact his Associate on the mobile when he was out on a job. He would give Scott plenty of time and space to do his job without any interference. He trusted Scott implicitly.

'You look serious and pensive this morning. Did you have a nice time last night?' Jenny asked.

'Yes I had a very enjoyable time, thank you,' Alex replied.

'I think you're wasting your time with Claire, that girlfriend of yours. Melanie is more your type,' Jenny suggested. Clearly, Jenny was not fond of his latest companion.

'Claire, surprisingly, is a very nice girl and I like her very much. Over the last few weeks our relationship has developed well. Melanie is only a colleague,' Alex explained.

'I know you have had a tough time since your affair with Emma ended two years ago, so do be careful with your new-found relationship,' Jenny warned.

'Don't worry about me, Jenny. I know what I'm doing,' Alex reassured her.

'I hope so Alex,' Jenny said.

Client issues and queries still had to be dealt with. Alex went through them with Jenny.

He made a few phone calls to reassure restless clients that results were imminent. Keeping the clients happy was his first priority and he always dealt with them personally. When clients paid handsomely for his services, they expected immediate result for their money.

Getting results as quickly as they would like, had not always been possible. The work required immense patience and diligence and Alex felt it was incumbent on him to keep in regular contact with his clients, to massage their egos and keep their expectations and demands to a realistic level. Hence, they should be handled with care and Alex was excellent at good client-practitioner relationship management.

Two hours later, Scott arrived with a big smile across his face and his eyes beaming. He went to his office and

Jenny followed him and asked, 'Where have you been? He's been waiting for you.'

'I've been very busy finishing the task he allocated to me,' Scott replied.

Jenny made him a cup of coffee.

Alex was on the phone again talking to a potential client. When he had put the phone down, Scott knocked on his door and walked into his office.

'Good morning Alex, I've some excellent news for you,' Scott said, and gave him a copy of the sales record for the purchase of a Harry button, upon which was written the full name of the buyer.

'Great. That's exactly what I've been waiting for,' Alex replied.

'Is that your man?' Scott asked.

'Pretty much, I'll say,' Alex replied.

'Are you ready to hear how I got this?' Scott sat down.

'Of course I am,' Alex replied.

'First of all, it took longer than I expected. I contacted a few shops on the phone and visited a few more, but to no avail. Then I bumped into a friend who suggested I tried a particular medium sized shop in Oxford Street which would sell the button in question. Whilst there, I experienced a few problems. The senior shop assistant said it was against company policy to give out confidential information regarding clients' names and their purchases. I explained the reason for the request and that I was from the Agency. We were investigating a murder case and the button was very important evidence. He wasn't having it. He was determined to stick to the rules. He wasn't a very pleasant chap, he hardly smiled,' Scott said, and then paused for a moment.

'Then what happened?' Alex asked.

'To be honest, I didn't know what else to do. I went back in the early afternoon and pleaded with him but he wouldn't budge. I could sense he had the information I was looking for but he wasn't willing to share it with me. Maybe he didn't like my face or something,' Scott said, and paused again.

'Scott, why do you always take your time to get to the point?' Alex's impatience was growing.

'Alright, I'm coming to it. I decided to go on the attack. I told him I was an ex-Detective Sgt and gave your name as the owner of the Agency. I said as he had been most unhelpful, I would like to see the manager. That shook him up. He started to stutter and asked me to wait. Half an hour later, the assistant manager appeared. Initially she towed the company line like her senior shop assistant. I said that you wouldn't be happy by their lack of co-operation on this vital case, especially as a student nurse had been murdered. The assistant manager asked me to wait. After a few minutes, she returned and said to come back in the morning when the manager would be on duty.'

Scott stopped to drink his coffee.

'This morning I went back at 9 am. I was led to the manager's office. The manager was very sympathetic and said she was very sorry to hear about what had happened to the student as her own daughter was a student nurse, at another University. She gave me a copy of their sales record for the item in question and hoped the murderer would be caught. She also asked me to give you her regards,' Scott said, and ended his report.

'Thank you. What's the manager's name?' Alex asked.

'Sandra Winters,' Scott replied.

'Oh I remember her. She was one of my earlier clients before you joined the Agency,' Alex confirmed.

Then Scott changed the subject as he was keen to know about the goons following Alex.

'Any more news about the black 4x4?' Scott asked.

'Not lately. As I said it was probably a coincidence, that's all. I've forgotten about it.'

'Well my sources haven't come back to me yet. Maybe you're right and it was a coincidence that the black 4x4 happened to be around at the same time as you.'

Alex decided not to tell his team about his encounter with the goons yet, as it would interfere with their concentration and work. No doubt, they would get very worried as well.

Finding the shop where the button was bought in a massive area such as London was in itself an achievement. All credit to Scott, he eventually managed to locate the right shop and obtain a positive result. For Alex, admittedly, it was a shot in the dark to try and find this crucial piece of evidence and it paid off. The next challenge was whether Alex could make efficient use of this?

***

Equipped with all the evidence that he could possibly amass to solve the cases, Alex was ready to consult with both Melanie and the VC with regard to calling a meeting to hear his deliberations. He was feeling confident and satisfied, allowing himself a few moments to reflect on the process he had to go through to arrive at this auspicious juncture.

It was early afternoon when he arrived at the VC's office. The VC was in a good mood following his very brief conversation with Alex, a few minutes earlier on the phone. 'Come on in Alex and have a seat,' the VC said.

'Thank you,' Alex replied.

'It sounded like wonderful news. You said you've got all the information needed to crack the three cases. You're very good. It's only been just over 3 weeks and you've already found the answers for not one but all three cases. I can't tell you how pleased I am. What shall we do now?' the VC asked with a big smile on his face.

'That's the reason I've come to see you. I haven't told Detective Sgt Cooper anything yet. Just between you and me, may I request you call an emergency meeting for tomorrow morning at 10 in the Boardroom here, and instruct David Mallory and John Fairbanks to attend. You should also ask the Chairman to be available for the whole day and you should cancel all your engagements as well. Present at this private meeting will be you, David, John, Sgt Cooper and me. You should let the Head of Security know that there will be Police officers arriving just after 10 am and they will be staying on site for the day and he should provide car parking facilities for them. All this should be given top priority,' Alex outlined his plan systematically.

'That's a bit dramatic, wouldn't you say?' the VC was taken aback by Alex's request.

'It has to be done this way. We've reached a pivotal stage in the enquiries and the outcomes must be discussed with the relevant parties,' Alex stipulated his conditions.

'I know you believe John had something to do with the computer theft case but why does David have to be present?' the VC asked.

'For the simple reason, that David is John's line manager. Could you also ask Gail to attend?' Alex explained.

'What has she got to do with the meeting?' the VC was very surprised.

'She has, in fact, been involved with some aspects of the investigations,' Alex said.

'I must say you do act like a lawyer by getting to the point in an uncompromising manner. I shall put your demands into operation, contact the people you've identified and ensure the venue is ready,' the VC acquiesced.

'Thank you for your co-operation Peter. I'll ask Sgt Cooper to attend the meeting,' Alex said.

'Can you give me an inkling about the outcomes?' the VC asked.

'All will be revealed tomorrow. I need to ask you to keep our conversation confidential,' Alex informed him. The VC nodded in agreement.

At that stage, it was right for Alex, not to have any further discussion with the VC who might choose to put pressure on him into disclosing sensitive information prior to the meeting.

Alex did not relish being in a position of having to lie to him or blatantly refusing to answer any of his searching questions on this matter. Difficult path to walk on, after all, the VC had employed him in the first place and he was always loyal to him. He told the VC that he had to go as he needed to get in touch with Sgt Cooper.

Whether it was wise for Alex to ask Jenny to make an appointment for him to meet Melanie at the Excelsior for a working dinner at 7 pm, would remain to be seen. He felt it would keep her entertained for a while, at the thought of him spending time with Melanie. As far as he was concerned, she seemed oblivious to the fact that he and Melanie were not having an affair.

Although he cherished the thought of being with Melanie and having an intimate relationship with her, he knew that was not possible, at least for the time being.

Jenny was delighted to text him and let him know that Melanie would be at the Excelsior in the evening.

***

Feeling very pleased with himself mostly, as it was time to get ready to meet Melanie, he was walking briskly in the direction of his flat and was totally immersed in his own world of fantasy.

Suddenly, he had a shock to see the two goons waiting for him. The shorter guy with spiky hair called out, 'Hey you. Don't you hear well? Why are you still conducting the investigations, especially after we told you to stop immediately?'

Alex thought carefully before giving his reply. Two against one was always going to be a tough challenge indeed. Assessing his options to deal with the desperate task facing him, he could choose to use humour as his main weapon, to take the sting out of the unpleasant situation. He had also taken some self-defence lessons when he was a University student. But looking at the sizes of the two goons, if he tangled with them, he could well end up in hospital. He decided to use humour.

'I thought you're joking. That's why I didn't take you seriously.'

'Do you think we're playing games here?' the large fellow said in an angry voice.

'Of course not,' Alex replied.

The shorter guy moved closer to him. Alex thought he was about to be attacked and he was right. The shorter guy took a powerful swing at him. If caught, Alex would have been badly injured and ended up on the pavement. Instinctively, Alex ducked and launched an attack of his own. He kicked the short guy in his right knee so hard that he could hear the joint snap, and next the guy was holding his knee in agony and slumped to the ground.

Not expecting what had just happened to his mate, the large guy looked stunned with his mouth open and eyeballs bulging out. Clearly, he was not aware that Alex would react with such a determined, measured and effective response. He was furious about what happened to his mate and wanted immediate revenge. Alex could see the large guy was ready to make his move. He threw himself at Alex who quickly moved out of the way. When he missed Alex, he lost his balance and hit the bonnet of his own 4x4. Alex was slightly taller than his assailant and following a razor sharp movement, he put him in a double arm lock with the side of his face against the car. The large guy could not move and gradually, was weakening. The shorter guy was still holding his knee and could not get up to assist his friend.

Whilst keeping an eye on the shorter guy, Alex asked, 'Why are you two chasing me and who put you up to it?

'Go to hell,' the shorter guy replied.

'I'm going to ask you again, who employed you to threaten me off the investigations?'

'As I said, go to hell.'

'Wrong answer. If I don't get the name of the person who hired you in ten seconds, then I'll have no choice but to bust the shoulder of your friend or even break his neck.'

After a few seconds, Alex tightened the arm lock which prompted the desired response from the large guy as he ran out of options to defend himself.

'OK, let go of my shoulder.'

'Not until I get the name.'

'A senior manager at the University,' the large guy replied.

'What's his name?'

'We don't know his name and have never seen him either. He is in charge of some health faculty or something. We only work through a contact and aren't given that sort of information. You are investigating a murder case and a computer theft case and we were told to scare you enough so that you'd give up and go back to your Agency. That's the truth.'

Alex felt the large guy's arms were getting flabby and could not offer much resistance. At that point Alex was also getting rather tired. He decided it was time to let go of his hold, but remained on alert, in case there was an unexpected physical response from either of them. None was forthcoming.

'Don't ever follow me again if you know what's good for you?' Alex warned them and then left.

Alex went to his flat. He had a shower and changed into fresh clothes. Drinking a quick cup of tea, he phoned his mum before setting off for the Excelsior. Conveniently Claire was enjoying a night out with her workmates from her accountancy firm, therefore Alex was free to have his own night out with his favourite Sergeant.

Technically, he could have discussed the emergency meeting with Melanie on the phone but he wanted to take her out to dinner one more time. Once the murder case was solved, the likelihood of seeing Melanie again was virtually nil, let alone having dinner with her.

What a coincidence? Alex and Melanie arrived at the Excelsior at the same time.

They noticed each other walking towards the entrance with only about five metres to go. They smiled at each other and exchanged warm embraces before entering the restaurant.

Melanie was looking as ravishing as ever in her lemon coloured dress and Alex was not far behind in the style department. He wore a thin striped navy suit and a pink shirt with no tie.

Without a doubt, they were the beautiful couple. Those present, were looking at them adoringly.

'Both of you look very smart this evening. Nice to see you. What would you like to drink?' asked their favourite waiter.

They sat down at a table and ordered a diet coke with ice for Alex and a seven-up for Melanie.

The waiter went to fetch their drinks.

'Well I understand from Jenny that it was crucial for us to meet for dinner this evening as we have to attend an emergency meeting tomorrow. I had to cancel a dinner date with a friend to be here. You had better have a very good explanation for this,' Melanie said.

'I have actually. But first about the dinner you did not attend. I do apologise for that but I believe this working dinner is necessary. By the way, who is your friend?' Alex asked.

Their drinks arrived and as their table was booked for 7.30 pm, they only had ten minutes to wait.

'Why do you need to know about my friend?' Melanie remarked.

'Just curious, that's all,' Alex said.

'I don't know why I'm telling you this. Martin, remember him, has gone to the cinema with his work friends, so I was meeting one of my female friends from Oxford,' Melanie explained.

'I was wondering…… never mind,' Alex mumbled.

'Wondering about what? Let me see, you're wondering if I was meeting another chap,' Melanie got to the point.

'Oh no. That's your business,' Alex was embarrassed he had been caught out.

'Really. I believe you,' Melanie said smiling.

The waiter advised them their table was ready and they went into the restaurant to sit at their usual table by the window. They looked at the menu and the wine list. They chose not to have starters. Both ordered sirloin steak, chips and green vegetables. Alex asked for a bottle of French Margaux.

'Now let's get down to business, if you don't mind,' Alex suggested.

'Yes by all means, that's the reason we're here, isn't it?'

'That's correct.'

He gave her a breakdown of his recent conversation with the VC about calling an emergency meeting tomorrow morning at 10 in the Boardroom, on the Faculty site to discuss his findings on all three cases. The VC would ensure that David, John and Gail would be there. As the Officer in charge of the murder case, it was essential that she should attend.

'So you've got all the necessary evidence to solve the three cases?' Melanie asked.

'I believe I have. I've received the final piece of evidence this morning,' Alex replied.

'I appreciate you've got a strong case against John, supported by watertight evidence, but why David?'

'Because David is John's line manager and should be present to hear the evidence against John and, if needs be, take appropriate disciplinary action against him,' Alex was pleased to enlighten her. He refrained from giving her other details in advance.

Both their food and drinks were served.

'Did you find out about the account holder at the First Bank who was receiving payments from John?'

'I know you don't agree with my method but I got the name of the account holder and dates of the payments from the manager, Carol Parker.'

'Did you know the manager?'

'Yes she is an old client of mine.'

'How old is she?' Melanie looked worried in case Alex had had a relationship with that client.

'Actually she is in her forties and not my type,' Alex explained.

Melanie let out a sigh of relief and looked at him directly. 'What do you want from me?'

'Is that a personal request?'

'No, a professional one.'

'I would like you to bring the Harry button with you tomorrow and organise for your officers to be around after 10 am. Parking facilities will be available on the Faculty site.'

'Consider it done.'

They finished the main course and ordered strawberry cheesecake for dessert.

At every dinner in the Excelsior restaurant, both had ordered exactly the same dish which demonstrated similarity in their culinary tastes. One would have thought they were behaving like a long established married couple or, simply trying to please each other.

'Do you know this is, probably, our last dinner and evening out together?' Alex expressed his concern.

Melanie looked at him for a few seconds and said, 'Do you think so? It doesn't have to be.'

'Can you think of any circumstance when we will get together again?' Alex asked.

'I don't know,' Melanie replied.

'I fully understand both of us have got a significant other which could make it difficult for us to meet,' Alex pointed out.

The dessert arrived and both smiled at the sight of their cheesecake, it was a mouth-watering prospect.

'But we aren't married to them yet and who knows, we could be working on another case together,' Melanie said.

'That's my view as well. You know, I would very much like to see you again in the future.'

Alex took the brave step to state his case.

'We'll see,' Melanie replied.

They finished eating and drinking. Alex paid the bill and they walked out of the restaurant.

They stood on the pavement outside, looked at each other with warm eyes and held back from getting up close and personal.

'I'll hold you to that,' Alex said.

Melanie just smiled. 'Thanks for a memorable evening, I thoroughly enjoyed everything about it.' Melanie looked really happy.

'Shall I come with you to the underground station?' Alex asked, expecting her to turn him down as usual.

'No thanks. I'll be fine and I'll see you tomorrow,' Melanie said.

'Alright, thank you for the company and be careful how you go,' Alex replied.

They embraced each other gently on the cheek. Alex could feel the warmth of her emotionally charged face, but again, resisted the temptation to go further. Undoubtedly,

Melanie experienced a similar reaction from her highly excited host and equally exercised self-control.

Then they went their separate ways.

Chapter 34

There was a flurry of activities taking place at the Agency as Alex prepared himself for the emergency meeting at the University. He arrived at the Agency early before Jenny and Scott got in. He had already checked the papers which he had asked Jenny to assemble over the last few days. She had also typed three summary sheets for him to use in his presentation. Each sheet covered a case.

'When did you get here?' Jenny asked.

'Not too early,' Alex replied.

'Have you got the papers you need for your meeting?' Jenny checked.

'Yes, everything is here in my file,' Alex reassured her.

Jenny went to make tea for him and was chatting at the same time. Needless to say, she wanted to know about Alex having dinner with Melanie.

'So did you enjoy yourself with Melanie last night then,' Jenny asked.

'Yes I did,' Alex's mind was on other important matters. He drank his tea.

Jenny could sense that he was pre-occupied with his preparation for the meeting, it would be better to leave him alone. Alex asked Jenny and Scott to come to his office.

'Both of you have been incredibly helpful to me in finding solutions to the three cases. You're always willing to assist, offer your advice and act as a sounding board for me. Without your thorough inputs, I wouldn't have been able to solve these cases and you've kept the other work of the Agency ticking over nicely as well. Thank you very much for your diligent efforts,' Alex said appreciatively and passionately.

'You're very welcome. Finding the killer of the student has made it all worthwhile,' Jenny said.

'It's part of our job to assist you on any project you undertake. It has been a real pleasure,' Scott added.

Both of them wished him good luck and he headed for the University.

***

On arrival at the University, he parked his car. He walked to the reception desk and checked with Julie for any messages. There were none. So, he took the lift to the eleventh floor.

Leaving his briefcase in his office, he took his file and went to the Boardroom.

At 9.45 am he entered this very impressive room with traditional mahogany furniture. Everyone was present as planned. Greetings were exchanged. Alex was given a seat at the top table. The VC and Gail were on his right, David and John on his left with Melanie sitting a couple of seats away from John. The VC's PA sat by the door to have a clear view of everyone and hear every word in order for her to make a record of what transpired and compile the minutes. Coffee was available on a separate table for people to help themselves.

Ten o'clock sharp, the VC opened the meeting, he explained that Alex would be reporting on the findings of his investigations and handed over to Alex who looked very serious and business-like. He removed the papers from his file and placed these in front of him. He stood up and had a wry grin on his face. He was rather apprehensive as this was a new experience for him.

'Thank you Peter,' Alex said. 'I'm very grateful to all of you for making the effort to be here.'

At that moment, there was an interruption. 'I can understand the senior people being present but what am I doing here?' John asked.

'Be patient John, all will be revealed in a few minutes,' Alex reassured him.

'I had to cancel everything in my diary to be here, it had better be good Alex,' David warned.

'I sincerely hope so,' Alex replied.

Both David and John settled down to listen to him.

'I was asked by Peter to investigate the theft of two laptops that took place last May. It was a tough assignment, especially when the Police had not been able to resolve that matter. Co-operation from some senior members of staff was not forthcoming at the best of times. But against the odds, through conscientious detective work, my team and I started to make progress. Then, I found out that Wayne, the security officer, had seen John taking a heavy black holdall home with him on the evening of the 12 May. Apparently, John had told Wayne that he was taking scripts home to do some emergency marking. I checked with the Assessment Officer who informed me that he had not asked John to do any such marking. Shortly afterwards, Scott, my Associate and I went to a computer shop in Hammersmith where Adrian, the shop assistant confirmed that someone had sold him a relatively new laptop on Friday 13 May for £200,' Alex said, and paused deliberately to wait for any reaction.

His strategy was to give those present the opportunity to make comments, challenge his statements, express their surprises and disagreements.

'What has that got to do with the stolen laptops?' John asked.

'Well everything, actually. You did not have the scripts in the black holdall on 12 May because you had the stolen laptops in it,' Alex was pleased to stress.

'That's utter nonsense,' John replied.

'Not at all. Adrian, the shop assistant, identified you as the person who sold a laptop to them when he saw your picture in the Faculty Magazine, and he provided us with the serial number for the laptop.'

John got up and said he was not listening to that outrageous allegation against him which was not true, and that he was leaving as he had better things to do.

'John, you aren't going anywhere. Please sit down and let Alex continue,' the VC said in an officious tone. John did not have any choice but to sit down.

Alex said, 'Surprisingly, the invoice for the two laptops went missing from the lever arch file in the AVA office and the checking of the serial number could not take place. Then, out of the blue, luck struck. Gail received an anonymous phone call informing her that the invoice was to be found in the in-tray on Jack's desk. Gail checked and it was there, alright. I immediately went to see Tom who confirmed that it was the real invoice and the serial number on the invoice matched the serial number received from the computer shop.' Alex paused again.

'What does it prove? I didn't steal the laptops,' John said.

'Thus far, it proves that you stole the laptops and sold one laptop to the computer shop in Hammersmith on Friday 13 May, not your lucky day John,' Alex explained. He was beginning to enjoy himself.

John waived his right arm in disgust, dismissing the accusation. 'I have nothing to do the stolen laptops.'

Alex said, 'It took a bit longer to check the serial numbers because the invoice initially disappeared from the lever arch file in AVA office as I just mentioned.'

'I didn't remove the invoice,' John said loudly.

'As it happens, I agree that you did not take the invoice from the AVA office. But you are the person who made the anonymous phone call to Gail, and you did put the invoice in Jack's in-tray,' Alex said.

'Rubbish. Why would I do that?' John asked.

'To frame Jack,' Alex said.

'Where would I get the invoice from?' John asked.

'That's a very good question. Gail remembered seeing the invoice in David's office in his desk drawer when she was acting for him,' Alex explained.

'Don't be stupid. Where would I get the invoice from?' David asked.

'Well, you asked the cleaner, Sheena, to unlock the door of the AVA office for you a week last Friday around 6.30 pm after Tom had left and she saw you removing a sheet of paper from the lever arch file, the one in which the invoice was filed. You gave the invoice to John in order to frame Jack,' Alex said.

'Utter rubbish,' David remarked.

'You, David, worked closely with John to implement your sinister plan,' Alex was trying to explain, when the VC intervened, 'What sinister plan?'

'David has been trying to undermine your authority and set you up to fail. He knew that your cherished strategy has been to implement the IT programme from next September, which needed funding to be approved by the Board. In agreement with John, he devised a cunning plan for John to steal and hide the two laptops which could not be easily recovered. No one would suspect John as he was the blue eyed boy for saving the Faculty several thousand of pounds by extending the unsuccessful students' contracts on compassionate grounds. Incidentally, that move was described as a lowering of standards by Jack, which was brushed aside by both John and David. For economic reasons, the Faculty sided with John who became a hero. He felt he had the authority to walk on water and no one could touch him. On hearing about the two stolen laptops, the Board would be unwilling to provide large funds for the IT programme,' Alex explained, and paused.

He then continued, 'Apparently, you had staked your reputation on making the IT programme available to students and staff alike. Therefore, David's assumption was that should you fail in your attempt to implement your brainchild project, you could not possibly continue as the VC and you would have to resign. Then, David who was overlooked for the VC job on the last occasion, would get his opportunity again. He was confident he would then get the VC job. To get John's involvement and commitment, he promised John that once he became VC, he would promote him to the Dean's post.' Alex paused for further reaction.

'Is that true David?' the VC asked.

'Don't listen to that drivel Peter,' David replied.

'David was very bitter at your appointment. He believes you're inexperienced and didn't deserve to get the job. He thought he was the right candidate for the VC post,' Alex said.

'The IT project was deemed by the Board as important for the institution's future. If the Board had decided not to fund it this academic year, I would have accepted their decision. In the line of progress, the Board will, inevitably, have to fund the IT project for the next academic year. There is no way I was going to resign over it,' the VC enlightened his audience.

Upon hearing the VC's statement clarifying his position, David looked disconcerted and went on the attack. 'What a load of nonsense,' David said and changed his position in the chair so that he would not face the VC directly. Suddenly, he looked very uncomfortable.

'I don't think so David. For your information, Wayne, Phil, Adrian, Gail and Sheena are all willing to testify against you and John on the stealing of the two laptops and the invoice, and selling the laptop and framing Jack,' Alex said.

'Why would I sell the laptop?' John asked.

'To pay for your gambling debts, perhaps,' Alex said.

'You've no idea what you're talking about. It's all speculation. These people will only add to your lies,' John fought back.

'Peter, is that why we've been asked to attend this emergency meeting, to be accused of so called wrongdoing by Alex?' David complained.

For a few seconds, the VC looked at Alex and decided it was time for him to take action.

The VC informed David and John. 'I've heard enough. I'm very disappointed with both of you. After this meeting, I want to see both of you in my office.'

'Don't be hasty now Peter and jump to the wrong conclusions,' David advised him.

'John, I sincerely hope that you have deleted all the sensitive data about the students before you sold the laptop,' the VC said in an authoritative voice.

'Don't worry about that, Peter. The shop assistant, Adrian has confirmed that all the data on the files had been deleted,' Alex said.

'I have nothing to do with the stolen laptops,' John replied.

Everyone was stunned. Melanie was watching Alex's performance with great interest. Gail was shocked when she heard that David had been the main man behind the whole sordid affair.

'If according to you, we stole the two laptops, John sold one laptop, then what happened to the second laptop?' David asked.

'I was hoping you'd ask for clarification. Well you see David, as you are aware, John planted the second laptop in Matt's apartment to frame him because he would not co-operate on the issue of providing places to the South African candidates. It was revenge time against Matt. Consequently, every one would believe Matt was the person who stole both laptops. Incidentally, Tom confirmed the serial number of the laptop found in Matt's apartment matched the serial number on the invoice,' Alex said, and paused for David's reaction.

'Why would John do that?' David did not disappoint.

'Just a moment. This takes us into another despicable arena, one of exploitation and extortion. Having listened to Gail, you and Matt on his appointment as the Recruitment Officer and more importantly, how the job was offered to him, it was nothing short of favouritism. John and Matt were friends. Matt had fallen on hard times due to his alcohol problems. John and David interviewed him and offered him the recruitment job. It was a cynical approach.

Matt believed his close friend John had come to his rescue only to find out later he was being exploited in a money-making enterprise. Following Margaret's death, Matt recognised her name from the "list" of South African candidates that was provided by John, to be given a place on the course. John had conned Matt into believing that he was doing a friend at the South African Embassy a favour by offering these candidates places on the nursing course. Incidentally, John, I checked your friend at the Embassy does not exist. Once these students qualified, they would go back to their own country and contribute to the health of their nation. In addition, John had boasted he would be buying a sports car and going on an exotic holiday. The number of candidates on the "list" was increasing and there was no sign of this coming to an end. Matt began to suspect John's motives to help these candidates and was frightened of being accused of Margaret's murder, so he told John that he would no longer be helping him,' Alex said, and paused again.

He then continued, 'He wanted to explain to you, Peter, his involvement so that he would not be sacked. John could not persuade him to do otherwise. That's when he framed Matt. Luckily, Matt's wife arrived at the apartment on time and John left immediately,' Alex said emphatically.

'David was aware of what John was up to because they discussed and decided their next move together. Matt was concerned for his safety and in fact his life, so he decided to go off sick as a preventative measure. He did not want to be murdered like the poor hapless student. Matt has given me a signed statement of his version of events involving John. This includes the four "lists" of names of candidates for the following intakes – 2 for March 2004, 15 for September 2004, 25 for March 2005 and 25 for September 2005, in total 67 candidates. These "lists" were given by John to Matt. John always reminded Matt of his responsibilities. On one occasion, in my presence, John even instructed Matt not to forget about the "list" in my presence. The overconfidence and arrogance, that John displayed, was breath-taking,' Alex said, and paused again for reactions.

The VC was livid at the thought of interviewing candidates against the University's policy. 'This practice is totally unacceptable; every candidate must be interviewed on merit.'

David and John sat motionless. Gail had her mouth open in amazement. Then Gail remembered Pam mentioning to her about John and Matt discussing the 'list' of candidates on the interviewing days.

'John was in an ideal position to oversee the recruitment for a period of six months before Matt was employed. He familiarised himself with the procedures as well as spotting the opportunity to use the recruitment policy to his own advantage. Matt happened to be the unfortunate guy to be slotted into John's scheme, and inadvertently, helping it to gain momentum until he suspected that John was benefiting financially,' Alex explained, and then paused.

'This is unbelievable,' the VC said loudly.

'It's an abuse of authority and power at the highest level,' Alex replied.

'I hope you've got all this in your notes,' the VC said to his PA.

'That's rubbish. How long are we going to have to listen to all these lies and unfounded allegations,' David said, while wriggling himself in his seat and leaning his elbows on the table. John copied his position.

In the meantime, Melanie smiled, nodded and winked at Alex, suggesting he was performing very well. He nodded back in acknowledgement. Having clarified the issues relating to the computer theft case, identifying John's pressure on Matt to participate in his sordid scheme, outlining the framing of Matt and Jack, Alex moved onto the next phase of his deliberations.

It was the appropriate time for Alex to go for the jugular and be as incisive as he could in his presentation. Naturally, David and John wanted to leave the meeting. The VC and Gail were very interested to hear what Alex had to say as his feedback, thus far, had been quite revealing.

'Peter, we need to have a courtesy break, if you don't mind,' David insisted.

'Alright, I expect everyone to return to this room within 15 minutes, is that understood?' the VC put his foot down. Everyone made full use of the break by going to the cloakroom or just stretching their legs in the corridor.

David and John went straight to the cloakroom. They were there alone. David had a stiff word with John about selling the laptop when he was only supposed to hide the laptops away. He told John not to admit to anything as their lawyers would have to deal with the allegations from Alex.

On her way out of the room, Melanie smiled, tapped Alex on his left shoulder and said, 'You're doing great. Keep it up. Good luck.' The time allocated for the break was observed and passed rather quickly.

'Everyone is here, so we can resume now,' the VC nodded to Alex.

Shuffling through his papers Alex looked at everyone and was ready to go.

'I would like to start with the concerns expressed by Peter, with regard to the matter of making money. Peter received an anonymous letter 4 weeks ago stating that a senior academic was charging foreign candidates for a place on the nursing course and that he should put a stop to it, otherwise a copy of the letter would be sent to the press. Peter showed me the letter and asked me to give the letter top priority over the computer theft case. The Chairman was informed. I set out to investigate the computer theft case and the letter case concurrently. The next day, sadly, Margaret was murdered. That became my third task, assisting Sgt Cooper who has been in charge of the murder case,' Alex said, and paused.

'So you've been working undercover on the so-called letter case whilst everyone believed you were investigating the computer thefts and assisting the Police with the murder enquiry,' John said, surprisingly.

'That's correct,' Alex said emphatically. Both David and Gail were speechless and totally bemused by Alex's revelation.

Chapter 35

Alex was in control of the whole process and growing in confidence. He moved on to the next phase of his presentation, systematically and incisively dealing with the issue of the scam.

'After a few days, Peter received an anonymous phone call making the same demand and threat as the earlier anonymous letter. It was a complex matter with no leads to follow. But fortunately, I was approached by a young man in McDonald's. He wouldn't give me his name, but I believe he was responsible for both the anonymous letter and the anonymous phone call, so I referred to him as the "guy". He told me that each candidate was charged £2,000 by the Friendly Employment Bureau which, in turn, paid a large sum of money to a senior academic, based in this Faculty, who ensured that these candidates from South Africa were offered a place on the nursing course,' Alex said. It was immediately followed by an interruption.

'No candidate, either local or foreign, should be charged money to obtain a place on the course. This is preposterous,' the VC expressed his outrage.

'Who is that senior academic?' Gail was curious.

'I'm coming to that. The next day we checked on the Friendly Employment Bureau and surprisingly, it had been closed down completely, so we couldn't secure any verification to the 'guy's allegation. We were none the wiser at that stage.' Alex paused to look at his papers on purpose.

John let out a big sigh of relief and turned to David and went, 'Phew!!'

'However, I managed to get hold of the details of the senior academic's bank account, a person I suspected for a while. The details are quite revealing and correspond with the number of candidates on 3 lists - 2 candidates for March 2004 intake, 15 for September 2004 intake and 25 for March 2005 intake. The Bureau paid the amount of money accordingly into the account of this senior academic at the National Bank,' Alex continued, but was again interrupted.

'You've no legal right to have access to anyone's personal bank account,' John said sternly, because he had an account with this Bank. Melanie listened with interest.

'Don't worry about that John. The nature of the bank details is of greater importance than gaining access to the account. It was also demonstrated that this particular senior academic, immediately paid a sizeable amount of money into the bank account of another senior academic of this Faculty, at the First Bank,' Alex said, and paused for reaction.

'That's incredible. How did you find out about the bank accounts of the two senior academics?' the VC asked.

'With careful and painstaking detective work. Matt told me about the bank account of the first senior academic and I worked out the bank account of the second senior academic,' Alex explained.

'How much money were these two senior academics paid for their despicable work?' the VC asked.

'Through a quick analysis of the amount paid each time, matched by the number of names on the 3 Lists provided by Matt, I was able to conclude that the Bureau charged each candidate £2,000 and paid the senior academic £1,500 for each candidate on the appropriate list. Then, I applied the same analysis to the amount paid into the bank account at the First Bank; I concluded that the first senior academic had paid £500 to the second senior academic for each candidate on the above-mentioned lists,' Alex went through his analyses and conclusions meticulously.

'In addition, according to Matt, the fourth list consists of another 25 candidates who have already been allocated places for the September 2005 intake. The Bureau has not made any payment for this to the senior academic yet,' Alex said, and paused.

He then continued, 'There is also another significant issue that requires careful consideration. On the bank details from the National Bank, it shows that the Bureau paid a large sum, for 15 candidates, into the senior academic's account at the National Bank in September 2003. Therefore this scam, of illegally charging the South African candidates, was in operation before Matt was appointed as Recruitment Officer,' Alex said, and deliberately paused for reactions.

'Alex, are you saying that this has been going on for a long time?' Gail asked.

'It would appear so, but it's rather difficult to be precise about when the illegal charging started,' Alex replied.

'Do you know the names of the two senior academics?' the VC asked.

'I do indeed,' Alex replied.

'Would you care to tell us?' the VC pressed him.

'I was going to do that now. The first senior academic is John and the second is David,' Alex responded loudly and emphatically.

David and John said at the same time. 'Absolute rubbish.' Both stood up and David was wagging his index finger and making threats.

'We'll sue you for slander Alex,' David added.

'Sit down, both of you,' the VC ordered.

The VC, Gail and Melanie were looking at each other in total amazement.

'I'm not listening to this anymore,' John said and got up to leave.

'Sit down John,' the VC shouted at him. John sat down grudgingly.

Alex could sense that both David and John's tempers were running high and they could get aggressive. He opened the door and asked Wayne who had agreed to stand outside, in case he was needed, to come inside and keep an eye on both David and John.

'Is that necessary?' the VC asked.

'Just go along with it for now Peter,' Alex advised.

Melanie was wondering why she had not been asked to help with keeping order in the meeting. Alex was using the institution's security staff to keep order because up until then it was University business and, not yet, a Police one.

'When John was overseeing the recruitment activities, before Matt was appointed, he was recruited by the Bureau to offer places to a certain group of candidates for which he would be well paid. It didn't take much to tempt him. Then another lucrative offer came along from David, regarding the promise of a promotion to become Dean in due course. John could not believe his luck and in return, wanted to reward David for trusting him. He offered David a slice of his gain from his extortion activities, and by having David on his side, he could do as he pleased. Thus, David became a partner-in-crime to John's scam,' Alex said and paused for reaction. He was not disappointed.

Both David and John stood up again and threatened to cause him some serious bodily harm.

David was going to bash his face in, and John would break his neck. Melanie was on her feet instinctively as well but refrained from taking action. Wayne moved closer to them and advised them to sit down. Wayne's physique was quite impressive and would put fear in most people.

Both of them settled down. Melanie also sat down.

'So far you've addressed two cases out of three. What about the third?' the VC asked.

'Glad you ask, Peter. The third one being Margaret's murder. The Chairman made it clear that finding Margaret's killer should be my main concern. As everyone is aware, I was assisting Sgt Cooper in her efforts to catch Margaret's killer. We have worked together very well. The Police have done everything possible to solve the case. We had a lucky break in Karen Fletcher, Lecturer, informing me that she had overheard John threatening Margaret in his office, saying that if she didn't accede to his demands, she would be discontinued from the course and deported back to South Africa. Margaret retorted by saying she would report him to the VC regarding his money-making activities,' Alex said.

'Alison, a student nurse, who was a very close friend of Margaret's, came forward of her own accord to assist us with the investigation. She told me that Margaret was being bullied by a senior academic into paying £500 to remain on the course, otherwise she would be deported. At the time, Margaret was not performing as well as expected on the course. The senior academic was aware that Margaret was working as an escort and making good money, so decided to blackmail her. That senior academic was you, John.' Alex said, and paused briefly.

'I have already clarified my position on that matter with Sgt Cooper and you, the other day,' John said.

'You certainly did,' Alex replied. 'But now I'm moving on to the actual death of Margaret.'

'I don't have anything to do with Margaret's murder. On that night, I was with Jane Fergusson. She has already told you that,' John declared.

'Just a moment, let me carry on, please. In fact, I have here a signed statement from Jane confirming that you went back to her flat at around 7.30 pm, after you had been to see Margaret and not at 7 pm as you had previously mentioned. You told Jane that you had been to persuade Margaret not to report you to the VC regarding your money-making activities, but she refused to listen to you. You also told Jane that Margaret was alive when you left her flat at 6.30 pm,' Alex said, and there was another interruption.

'I didn't kill Margaret, I swear on my mother's grave,' John said humbly, almost in tears.

'Actually, I do believe you on this one, John. Sgt Cooper informed me that a button was found at the scene of the crime. Upon inspection, I recognised the button as one from a male Harry trench coat. So, again with diligent investigation, it was established that someone from this Faculty had recently bought a button from a particular shop. I have a copy of the sales record here,' Alex said, and paused. 'And that individual is called David Mallory; his name is on the sales record.'

Everyone was looking at David in astonishment, wondering whether he could have murdered Margaret. What could he possibly gain by such an act? Even John was stunned by the announcement and started mumbling to himself. The VC and Gail were speechless and were staring at David. Melanie never suspected David because he was not involved in operational matters, and could not have known the victim personally. Alex was ready to reveal more.

David snatched the sales record from Alex and said, 'This button was bought on the 22 June, days after Margaret's death. She was murdered on Tuesday 7 June Assuming I had lost the button then, why would I wait for such a long time to buy a new one?'

'Funny you say that. It's been puzzling me as well. I believe you expected Sgt Cooper and her colleagues to check the shops, for any purchase of a Harry button, soon after Margaret's murder. You, deviously, decided to wait a bit longer, for the dust to settle, before you bought the button and no one would be any wiser,' Alex replied. 'Fortunately, we continued looking out for the purchase of this very important button.'

Alex caught Melanie's eye which were wide open with amazement. He nodded towards her and she responded with a nod and smile.

'Utter rubbish,' David shouted. 'Anyway, what has it got to do with Margaret's murder?'

'Plenty. Without this crucial piece of evidence, collected by the Police, it wouldn't have been possible to identify the killer. On that Tuesday night which turned out to be fatal for Margaret, John failed in his attempt to change Margaret's mind, and phoned you, to let you know before going to Jane's place. John is correct in saying that Margaret was alive when he left her flat around 6.30 pm. What happened after that was to cause the demise of a beautiful girl who only wanted to become a qualified nurse,' Alex said, and paused, a sombre mood spread across the room.

'I still cannot see where this is going?' David said.

'Be a little more patient, I'm getting there as quickly as I can. Following Alison's description of the man she saw going into Margaret's flat and at the University reception area along with the confirmation as purchaser of the Harry button, I was able to put the pieces together,' Alex explained.

'So what?' David said.

'Can you shut up, and let Alex continue?' the VC said angrily.

Alex asked Sgt Cooper for the button. She duly obliged. He then held the button up for everyone to see. To solidify his case against David, he went on to state Alison as his firm witness.

'You see, Alison told me that she saw someone going into Margaret's room on that fatal Tuesday night on 7 June at around 7.30pm, and last Monday morning she saw the same man again in the reception area of the Faculty building and that man was you, David. This confirms that you were at the crime scene at the time of Margaret's murder,' Alex said.

'Alison's description of the man fits you accurately, David. I have also seen you with a Harry trench coat and this button is from that coat.' Alex got to the point and paused.

There was a lot of murmuring in the room. Everyone was looking in a perplexed way at each other. The VC had his mouth and eyes wide open in disbelief. Sgt Cooper looked shocked at Alex's revelation. Gail was shaking with fear. John just stared at David.

'That's slanderous Alex and I'll get you for that,' David said whilst hitting the table hard with his right fist in anger.

'That Tuesday night, after John had contacted you and informed you that Margaret insisted on reporting him to the VC; you probably was sitting in your car close by, decided to pay Margaret a visit to do some persuading of your own. You couldn't succeed in your attempt. You knew everything would come out into the open if Margaret reported John to the VC and you would be exposed as well. You couldn't take that chance. Probably you struggled physically with her and she pulled a button off your Harry trench coat. Unfortunately, you didn't have your way and hit her with a heavy object on the back of her head, killing her. David, you murdered that beautiful girl to save your own skin,' Alex said angrily.

David stood up and was about to go for Alex when Wayne grabbed him and pushed him into his chair. No one said anything. Alex signalled to Sgt Cooper to call her officers. Within seconds, two Detectives surrounded David and John. Wayne moved aside.

Alex decided to declare his hand properly and why he had suspected David for a while.

He said, 'I had this gut feeling that it was you, but I couldn't prove it conclusively. You had objected to my presence from the start which kind of puzzled me. You should have been supporting the VC on my appointment but you derided it. I made notes of my encounters with the various staff. After checking the notes, I noticed that when Sgt Cooper gave us details of Margaret's murder on Wednesday, you mentioned that Margaret's flat was on the ground floor, next to the entrance of the residence, and that someone must have heard or seen something. Well, how did you know where Margaret's flat was, if you had not been there? Sgt Cooper did not mention it in her report.' Sgt Cooper shook her head in agreement.

'That prompted me to believe you were a very strong suspect. I had to secure confirmation that you were at the crime scene at the time of Margaret's murder and your reason for murdering her. It took a bit of time but we got there, eventually. Incidentally, as for the two goons you employed to scare me off, I am pleased to inform you that both of them have been receiving hospital treatment; one with a busted knee, and the other with a dislocated shoulder. Unfortunately, your goons did not expect me to be smarter than them. Also, they confirmed it was you, David, who had employed them, to use any means needed, to stop me,' Alex said sternly.

Everyone in the Boardroom was shocked at Alex's last statement. His life was in danger which could have resulted in serious consequences. Sgt Cooper was so concerned, she stood up.

Alex reassured them, 'It would have taken a lot more than those two goons to deter me from my determination to find Margaret's killer.' A brief pause followed. Melanie sat down and everyone breathed a sigh of relief that no harm had come to Alex. They stared at David with obvious disdain for his despicable action against Alex. Then Alex decided to continue.

'Somehow, I don't believe it was pre-meditated murder but your action led to the death of Margaret. You were very clever. You removed the murder weapon and wiped off any potential fingerprints so that you couldn't be connected to the crime. In your breath-taking arrogance, you didn't bank on anyone seeing you going into the residence building on that fatal Tuesday night, but Alison saw you. She remembered you, and later described you with meticulous accuracy. Alison is a very astute girl and clearly noticed your craggy face, your Harry trench coat and you're limp. David, you are the killer,' Alex said emphatically.

David was steaming with anger and looked at John, 'Your bungling incompetence has got us here.' Then he protested his innocence loudly. 'I did not kill anyone.' As expected, both John and David rejected all allegations and denied being involved in any crime.

Detective Sgt Cooper read them their rights. David was arrested for murder, extortion, theft and perverting the course of justice. John was arrested for extortion, theft, framing and perverting the course of justice. The officers cuffed them both, and walked them to an awaiting police car in the University car park.

Alex, finally, smiled and felt relieved that the whole thing was over. Melanie approached him and congratulated him with a gentle tap on his shoulder. The VC and Gail also walked towards Alex and congratulated him. Alex acknowledged each one with a nod and a smile.

Melanie was none too pleased that Alex had kept her in the dark about the threat to his life.

She launched her own personal attack on him and poking him in the chest with her finger said,

'Why didn't you tell me about those goons who had been threatening you? You could have been badly hurt. Don't you ever do that again?'

At least it was clear that she cared about him, not only professionally but personally as well.

Alex replied, 'I do appreciate your concern thanks, but, I had to handle it in my own way.'

'You can be very stubborn, Alex,' Melanie said.

By that time the others had joined in and expressed their concern and the VC said, 'I'm glad you are ok. I agree with Sgt Cooper, you should have mentioned it to us. At least, I should have known.' Gail nodded in agreement. 'Oh, forget about it, everything has ended well,' Alex reassured them.

The VC could not hide his satisfaction regarding the success of the three investigations. 'This has been a marathon of intense investigations into the three cases, and you've done a stellar job. At times, the Boardroom felt like a courtroom, you're simply magnificent. Thank you very much, Alex.'

'I knew you would come up trumps. I didn't know anything about the illegal charging of candidates. I was very surprised at John and David's involvement in these shady activities to undermine the VC, framing colleagues and extortion. Then, finding out that David murdered Margaret, was the final blow,' Gail said.

'You kept issues regarding David's involvement in all three cases secret from me, so much for working together,' Melanie knew she was outflanked. She did not care as long as the murder case was resolved, and she had got the killer. Her boss would be very satisfied.

'I'm sure you understand. It had to be done that way to ensure total confidentiality and besides, you've got your man,' Alex replied with a wide smile.

'Yes, I've got Margaret's killer. Many thanks and regarding the Harry button, I think you handled that very well,' Melanie said.

'Actually obtaining the button from your colleague rather late into the investigation proved to be very useful and I bet he'll be a relieved man now,' Alex added.

'I'm sure he will,' Melanie replied.

'All's well that ends well,' Alex concluded.

Melanie was ready to take her leave. 'I guess you're right. It has been quite an experience working with you and I've enjoyed every moment of being in your company. You're a very talented man. I hope to work with you again in the future and I wish you continued success with your Agency. Thank you for everything.'

'You have been great to work with, Melanie. You've been a fantastic companion and we had a great working relationship. I would like to work with you again soon, if convenient. Thank you for all your support. Maybe, we could meet sometime as well,' Alex said.

'Maybe. Take care,' Melanie replied, while placing her right hand on his left arm and with a twinkle in her eyes.

Conveniently, Alex's mobile was ringing and Jenny was on the line. 'How did you get on?'

'Very well, thank you. Both John and David were arrested, and we are all about to leave in a few minutes. The job at the University is done,' Alex was pleased to inform her.

'Scott and I send you our warmest congratulations. Time to celebrate. Make sure you get paid adequately and more on top,' Jenny said happily.

'Many thanks to both of you for your amazing help,' Alex expressed his appreciation.

'You're very welcome,' Jenny said with a loud and happy voice.

'It has been an absolute pleasure,' Scott added.

'Are you coming back to the office today?' Jenny asked.

'Probably. I'll see you later,' Alex replied.

By that time everyone had gone back to their individual offices. Melanie left for her department as she had to follow up on the arrests and report to her boss in person. She had pulled off a major coup for her section which would place her in good stead. No doubt, her boss would benefit as well.

Alex's work at the University was finished. He wanted to say goodbye to a few people before leaving and chose to call on Gail first.

'It has been a real pleasure having you around, I shall miss you and your wonderful smile. Best wishes for the future,' Gail said humbly.

'You have helped me immensely throughout. Thank you for your assistance, support and for making me feel welcome. Good luck,' Alex said. They shook hands and Alex left her office.

He headed to the VC's office.

'Come on in Alex. What a relief everything is over. I was wrong in suspecting Tom for the computer thefts and

Matt for charging the candidates. Well, the computer thefts, the issue about the anonymous letter and Margaret's murder, have now all been resolved, thanks to your superb efforts. In addition, the personal data of students has not been affected and the reputation of the University has remained untarnished. I know the Police helped with the murder case but you did most of the work to bring Margaret's killer to justice. Your Agency will be very well rewarded and the cheque is already in the post. I shall miss you. I owe a great debt of gratitude to you and my old friend Robert who recommended you. If I can be of any help to you in the future, please do not hesitate to contact me,' the VC said.

At that very moment, the Chairman walked in. He looked very pleased.

'Sorry to interrupt your conversation. I was hoping to catch you, Alex, before you leave. I would like to add my congratulations and warmest gratitude to you,' the Chairman said whilst holding Alex's hand.

'Thank you for your trust, hospitality and support. It has been my pleasure to help you,' Alex returned the compliment.

Both men shook hands with Alex and he went to pick up his briefcase and other personal items from his office. Then he took the lift for the last time. When he arrived on the ground floor, he went to the security office and, thanked Wayne. Then, he said a special thank you to Julie, his favourite receptionist, by kissing her on both cheeks. Soon, he was in his car heading towards the Agency.